# Dosha

### flight of the Russian Gypsies

# a novel by Sonia Meyer

Published in the United States by
Wilderness House Press
145 Foster Street
Littleton Massachusetts 01460

www.wildernesshousepress.com

ISBN 978-0-9827115-1-4

Library of Congress Control Number: 2010929986

Cover photo "Flying Mane"
© 2010 by Bob Langrish
Used with permission

1 2 3 4 5 6 7 8 9

# Dosha

## flight of the Russian Gypsies

*To*

*Dickie + Rolin*

*Sonia Meyer*

**Wilderness House Press**

To my husband Richard
and our children
Carl, Robert and Steven.

# Acknowledgments

During WWII they stood out like tiny islands of peace floating through a world of war. I wondered how the war must have looked when seen through the eyes of these peaceful nomads, who lost millions of their own to the Nazi genocide.

Fifteen years ago I embarked on a journey into the hearts and minds of the Roma people, mistakenly called Gypsies, to tell the story. During this journey, from the idea to the finished novel, I was helped by many extraordinary people without whom this undertaking would not have been possible.

**Mateo Maximoff**, prolific Russian Gypsy writer, evangelical pastor to his people, great humanitarian and bridge-builder to some of France's prominent politicians and artists. I found a copy of one of his novels in the stacks of Harvard's Widener library, complete with his Paris phone number. I made the call and entered a deep, generous friendship with several visits that lasted until his death in 1999.

**Judith Latham**, former 'Voice of America' International Broadcaster, who invited me to accompany her on a trip to Macedonia, Kosovo and Hungary where we were graciously hosted by Gypsy/Roma families.

**Dorothy Morkis**, U.S. Olympic Dressage Rider, whose beauty and harmony on a horse inspired me to capture it on paper. Anriejetto (A.J.), Dotty's magnificent dressage stallion whose movements and brilliance were the inspiration for Rus.

**Kathleen Spivack**, writer, poet, writing coach of great skill and know-how, who not only honed my craft, but knew how to navigate and sort out the different languages and cultures I grew up with.

**Steve Glines**, Wilderness House Press. I found in him the type of editor/publisher some of America's greatest writers had the fortune to work with in the past.

**Doug Holder**, poet and founder of Ibbetson Press, who generously arranged for me to give a public talk as well as interview me on TV.

**Zvi Sesling**, poet and PR specialist, who gave me valuable PR advice.

**Susie Davidson**, Boston journalist, writer and specialist on Holocaust survivors, who published a wonderful article about my project.

**Denise Cassino**, Internet Marketing Specialist, who helped a novice navigate the wondrous new world of internet publicity.

**Sandy MacDonald**, superb line-editor with an eagle's eye for inconsistencies.

# Contents

## Part One

## Part Two

# Part Three

# Dosha

## flight of the Russian Gypsies

# Part One

# 1

# Waiting For Nikita Khrushchev

FINLAND, Helsinki. . .

They call her "Daughter of the Baltic." White metropolis of the north, bleaching like a desert of stone in the biggest heat wave on record: June 6, 1957, a Thursday.

Beyond the white face of the city and her dark granite shores, a cloudless sky, deep and blue as outer space, fuses with the flat cobalt waters of the Gulf of Finland. These form a horizon so vast that, according to legend, seafaring Vikings in days long gone believed they were staring at the rim of the earth — where, should the Fates decide to send forth their poisonous black winds in pursuit of the sleek longships, the conquering seamen would be blasted across into nothingness to float in limbo for all eternity, never to reach Valhalla.

This is the land the Arctic Circle divides for nine months of the year into bitter cold and colder. But on this day it was 90 degrees in the shade. Fish were rising in record numbers to the surface of shallow lakes, dead.

The *Suomen Uutiset*, Helsinki's largest daily, went so far as to brandish at the top of its front page a gigantic headline:

"BLACK AFRICAN FAINTING FROM FINNISH HEAT."

The few lines running across the page underneath stated it was "amazing" that this visit of the first black man most Finns had ever set eyes on should coincide with this once-in-a-lifetime heat wave. The text left the French journalist Jean Leurquin staring in disbelief at his short, dark-haired Finnish translator/chauffeur. "Is this one of those inside arctic jokes — some northern type of gallows humor?" he wondered aloud.

He had flown in from Paris that morning to cover the arrival in Finland of Nikita Sergeyevich Khrushchev. He was curious to see the man who, after a four-year struggle for dominance, had emerged as Stalin's successor by holding out hope for the liberalization of the Communist regime. The satellite states had responded with the first rebellion of its kind - the Polish Stand, which climaxed in September 1956. Those leaders — intellectuals intent on loosening Soviet control — were lucky: the rebels were rebuked but left standing. Not so the Hungarians who, one month later, united in a heady popular uprising and demanded all-out, unconditional freedom. Their dreams of freedom quickly turned into a nightmare of blood and gore as Soviet tanks came rolling in, crushing rebels and anybody else in their paths. The free world — unbelieving, indignant, paralyzed — tuned in to their radio stations or remained glued to their TV sets. In the end, help from the outside turned into no more than a perceived promise, giving way to the brutal reality of military might.

Watching his Finnish translator, Jean Leurquin thoughtfully lit a cigarette, looked at the match, and blew it out. What would come next? Was this simply a state visit, as announced — though relegated to a lower column on the front page of that country's major daily newspaper? Or was Finland about to lose the freedom it had fought so hard to keep?

When the Finnish translator folded the paper and silently handed it back to him, Jean Leurquin shrugged. He would table all questions until a scheduled briefing at his embassy in Helsinki.

Meanwhile, behind the forbidding façade of the Soviet embassy, a gray stone palace on the Baltic Sea, senior intelligence officer Comrade Natalia Yemekov stood before General Alexander Raskov, who had the *Suomen Uutiset* spread out on his desk before him. Comrade Yemekov had been with the First Chief Directorate of the KGB for Baltic affairs as it worked through several trade and border conflicts as well as two major wars. She had never understood why tiny Finland had been allowed not only to remain free of Soviet rule, but to thrive right in Russia's backyard, the only country along the Eastern Baltic to do so. On the other hand, Comrade Yemekov, daughter of an illiterate peasant family, had not achieved her high rank by questioning her superiors. Nor did she expect to be briefed now as to what this alleged "state visit" would ultimately turn out to be.

Their own translator was a young girl in a flowing summer dress, who stood next to General Raskov. She barely got beyond translating that same headline, when General Alexander Raskov cut off further translation with an impatient gesture. "He's not even from Africa," he said in his thick Georgian accent. "He's *Amerikanski*. The Finns are merely trying to divert attention away from the anti-Soviet agitators out in their streets, which is precisely what happens when and if you allow radical ideas to openly escape the brain. On the other hand" — he heaved his fat body forward in his armchair — "they've been smart enough to haul most of their antisocial elements off their streets by now."

In Comrade Yemekov's view, this merely meant that the Finns had put free speech on hold for the duration of the Russian visit, which hardly came as a surprise to those who had dealt with Finland in the past. This nation of lumberjacks and farmers had always been masters at knowing when to retreat in order to regroup for an ambush later on.

"What matters" — the general raised his deep-set brown eyes straight to Yemekov's impassive face — "is for that motorcade to pass fast and safe. After that...." He lifted both hands.

And that, as far as Comrade Yemekov was concerned, was that. General Raskov had been in charge of the deportation of thousands of citizens from the Baltic Republics, as well as the settlement into the Soviet Union of thousands of previously annexed Finns. She presumed that if any Soviet official in this embassy had been briefed on the goal of this visit, it was he. Nobody knew this field of operation better than General Alexander Raskov.

Comrade Yemekov's specialty, by contrast, lay in noticing the details. Her primary role was first to detect, then interrogate any subversive elements in their own midst—or worse, to prevent potential defectors. She knew from experience that a tiny crack in the wall often led to major trouble spots. Always on the lookout for irregularities, she kept her senses alert, and what struck her right at that moment was the inadequacy and youth of the translator — her timid voice, how she struggled with the few words of the headline. Comrade Yemekov couldn't shake the feeling that even if the headline were printed in Cyrillic, this girl would have trouble with it. She could barely read. How had she fallen through the cracks of the Soviet educational system, and gotten away with it?

"Who is this girl?" she asked.

The general, taken aback at being questioned by someone of Comrade Yemekov's rank, leaned back in his chair.

"Why?" He stared her down. "Her name is Ana Alexandrevna

5

Dalova, and she is one of the street agents recruited for the visit today. I'm surprised you haven't received her file."

Natalia Yemekov, the only woman in her branch of Central Intelligence, was considered by her colleagues to be a robot of the Agency. There had never been a single slip-up in her assignments — no errors, no oversights. And, no, she had not come across a file on the girl — not here, and not in Moscow.

"Ana Dalova was chosen on account of her association with previously annexed Finns," the general said. "Not only does she speak Finnish like a local" — he turned to the girl who stood stock-still next to him — "she could pass for one."

"The question remains, is she in fact a Finn?" Comrade Yemekov's suspicions, once aroused, were not easily assuaged. "Could she be the daughter of a previously annexed Finn? Or ..."

"Her name," the General said, "as stated in her papers, and officially approved for travel abroad, is Ana Alexandrevna Dalova. Finns, annexed or otherwise, do not take on Russian names."

Undeterred, Comrade Yemekov stared at the girl opposite her. The girl had not raised her eyes once. Her long reddish-blond hair was pulled back and lay tamed in a twist on the nape of her neck. She gave an overall impression of subservience.

"Maybe she's only distantly related or, for that matter connected to some other ethnic minority. With all due respect, General," Comrade Yemekov hastened to add, "you know as well as I that members of many minorities change their names more often than their underwear, in which case it would not be in the interest of our Soviet State to have her serve out in those streets. Not today, not on a day like this. Not among a reluctant host population. Especially when," she said, "in this place there is always the added risk that some intoxicated lumberjack lurking in their midst could start remembering encounters during wartimes not that long ago, go berserk, and start shooting to kill."

Something else still puzzled her. She squinted at the translator, searching for the missing piece that would confirm her suspicions. Why had a girl of—what, seventeen, eighteen at most, been chosen by the general himself not only as translator of local news, but as a street agent whose duties would be to watch for saboteurs during a motorcade which, on direct orders from the Kremlin, had to pass swiftly and safely through the streets? Upon arriving at General Raskov's office, Comrade Yemekov had been handed a file listing Finnish Communist sympathizers. She was sure that most of them would be more than willing to serve as lookouts as a means to advance within party ranks.

Natalia Yemekov had been transferred to the Soviet embassy at the last minute in response to various irregularities, the foremost being that many street agents had been appointed without prior clearance from Intelligence in Moscow. She knew that the Ministry of Culture and Sports had dispatched Leningrad's and Moscow's best ballet and musical companies ten days ahead of the visit, to pave the way for positive press and to downplay the threat of military invasion. But Moscow had not intended for these dancers, singers, musicians, and even embassy waiters, to act as the eyes and ears of the Soviet Embassy out in the streets today. Some of these artists were well known in the West, a fact that for her raised the red flag of possible defections, the worst Soviet crime of all. It was precisely her responsibility to prevent any such potential defectors from slipping through the cracks, especially at a time like this, when — given the recent disturbances in the satellite states — the very foundations of the Red dogma were cracking underfoot like ice in spring.

However, never before had Natalie Yemekov been obliged to interrogate a general, significantly higher in rank than herself. She hesitated. With downcast eyes she watched Raskov meticulously fold the Finnish paper before sticking it into a wastepaper basket, leaving his desk as bare as the rest of the windowless office. No file, not a single piece of paper remained in sight. Like one of those rooms set aside in the Kremlin for interrogations or the occasional visit of an out-of-town official, this office consisted of a desk, a chair, and a phone. Behind the desk, two surveillance cameras, attached to the ceiling, blinked red. As she entered the room, Yemekov had noticed that, in addition to Raskov's wooden armchair, two side chairs had been placed in the two adjacent corners. Everything was impersonal and in full sight under stark floodlights recessed into the ceiling. Yet Natalia Yemekov detected an undercurrent, something she could not put her finger on.

With roughly two hours left before the scheduled arrival of Comrades Khrushchev and Bulganin and the accompanying Soviet delegation, an investigation into the girl's background and credentials would have to wait. First and foremost, Comrade Yemekov had to make sure that the motorcade reached the embassy compound without incident. Back in the motherland, the task of routing out the corrupt remnants of Stalin's government had left the new regime shaky at the top. The purging of government branches abroad, such as this embassy in Helsinki, had been put on hold — for the time being.

"I'll need her dossier by tonight!" she said, and with that Natalia Yemekov, squat and short, whose KGB uniform — blue skirt and jacket — stretched tight around her ample chest and hips, opened the leather-padded door behind them.

"Follow me," she beckoned the girl. "There is no more time to lose."

The girl in the summer dress followed Comrade Yemekov at a respectful distance. Quickly but noiselessly, they strode down the green corridor over rubber-padded floors, past rows of leather padded doors. The subbasement of the embassy housed the offices and conference rooms of the Soviet Union's Foreign Intelligence and State Security Services. The space had the coolness of a tunnel, admitting no hint of the heat or the brightness of the day outside.

Most striking was the silence, trapped like stale air within the maze of narrow corridors, as if the hidden offices and conference rooms were all deserted. No voice, no sound of any kind reached them from behind the brown stone walls and padded doors. Only the occasional ringing of a phone drilled through the silence as if from the other side of a rock.

Yet Comrade Yemekov knew for a fact that behind those doors the *residenty* — KGB employees assigned to residencies abroad— were frantically at work. After the bloody events in Hungary, the new leadership was careful and thorough. Much was at stake.

Stopping short of a rectangular entry where three corridors converged, just out of earshot of two armed soldiers guarding a wooden double door, Comrade Yemekov paused. This door was bigger and wider than the identical doors they had passed, some of which led to the upper levels. The checkpoint was brightly lit from the ceiling, and tiny red lights on both sides of the double door indicated active surveillance cameras. Comrade Yemekov turned to face the girl, who stood a head taller than herself but appeared demure, with downcast eyes.

They had done an excellent job with her appearance. Her slender body looked graceful and fluid in a white cotton dress covered with bold strokes of green, clearly of Finnish make. No Soviet file, Yemekov thought, would make mention of the extraordinary beauty of the girl — the flawless skin, the soft exotic eyes. Like the song, she thought: *"Ochi chornea"* — black eyes.

Under Stalin's regime innumerable young girls like her had disappeared after being sent to the offices and *dachas* of the higher-ups. Hidden nests of pedophiles had indulged in unspoken vices, their activities raising eyebrows but never questions. In those days it would have been the girl's youth, not her beauty that would have put her in danger. Many a flabby pedophilic *apparatchik* — especially those within the ranks of the Secret Police, including their former chief, Lavrentiy Pavlovich Beria — had been executed under the new regime, although on unrelated charges. Yemekov herself had been instrumental in digging up that kind of dirt. But even in today's climate, the girl's beauty endangered her. Yemekov took another look at her and thought of the general back in his office. Her suspicions grew.

"You're a dancer, of course." Natalia Yemekov's eyes focused on the girl's face. "A member of our Kirov Ballet, yes?"

The girl glanced at her with eyes as dark and empty as the windows of an abandoned house.

"Yes? No?" Natalia Yemekov grew impatient. Time was of the essence, but in response to Yemekov's raised voice, the girl withdrew further, dropping her eyes again.

"I have spent time at the Kirov," she answered at last. Her voice sounded husky, intimidated. "But only to study choreography. I am a rider, Comrade Yemekov," she added, looking up again, "a member of our Soviet dressage team."

"You're the rider of the stallion Rus," Comrade Yemekov said. "You're that girl." The reason she had never set eyes on the girl's file was because this dressage rider had been under the direct sponsorship and protection of the Chairwoman of the Ministry of Culture, Galina Gregorovna Popov, the highest-ranking woman in the USSR, now under investigation and recently suspended from her position.

Unlike Galina Popov, Comrade Yemekov was no horsewoman, but even she understood enough to know that Grand Prix dressage riders don't happen overnight, any more than ballet dancers turn into solo performers within a year, and it was exactly one year ago that the new regime had started to collectivize suitable horses off stud farms all over Russia, with the goal of putting Russian horsemanship back onto the international map in both jumping and dressage. Most riders had been recruited from within the military. This girl was an exception, and maybe in the rush of having to achieve the government mandated goal, proper scrutiny had been lax. Comrade Yemekov tapped her teeth, suspicious still. The girl was already talked about in the USSR. She was said to be brilliant. However, this rider had fallen through way too many cracks.

"He came from somewhere, didn't he?"

"Who?"

"The horse Rus. Some unregulated collective in the North, wasn't it? Didn't I read something about it?"

The girl said nothing.

"Where is the stallion at this moment?" Comrade Yemekov asked, her eyes never leaving the girl's face. She knew at once she had hit a nerve. The girl was holding her breath. A deep furrow appeared on her brow between her dark, dark eyes. Suddenly her whole person looked darker — un-Russian. Yemekov could smell her fear.

"Back at the barracks," the girl said. Her Russian sounded softer than before, as if instinctively reverting to an accent Yemekov could not place.

"And where are these barracks?"

The girl regained control, exhaled. Her eyes narrowed and she shot Yemekov a look of such stinging intelligence, it cut right to her soul.

"Out in the country, in the military barracks near the Finnish Olympic stadium."

Natalia Yemekov couldn't help but smile triumphantly. So the Embassy was holding the stallion hostage. And although Yemekov was convinced this girl was ready to bolt, her well-tuned instincts also told her this girl was connected to her stallion as a mother to her newborn. As long as guards were holding the stallion in a secure spot, this girl was collared and leashed. For the first time Natalie Yemekov relaxed.

She waved one of the two guards over. "Escort this girl out into the street," she said. "You," she nodded to the girl, "report back to me after your day's work. Meanwhile, keep your eyes open in the interest of this embassy."

It never occurred to senior Intelligence Officer Yemekov to check on the actual whereabouts of the stallion Rus.

It was half past ten when the girl known to Soviet officials as Ana Dalova exited the Soviet Embassy and stepped into the brilliant light of the interior courtyard. She stopped and drew a breath.

The street in front of the Embassy — in fact, the whole area consisting mostly of embassies and consulates and nearby Kaivopuisto Park — had been emptied of pedestrians and moving traffic to secure the area. Only a group of some fifty students wearing the white caps of Helsinki University stood loosely gathered on the sidewalk in front of the high forged-iron fence that enclosed the Soviet Embassy compound. The students were holding small Finnish and Soviet flags in their hands. They were Finnish communists, carefully screened by the Soviets, props in this staged street scene.

Two Soviet soldiers, fully armed, unlatched and swung the heavy double gate inward just as a group of Soviet dancers from the Kirov Ballet spilled forth from the embassy, laughing and jostling. Once in the street, they mingled with the Finnish students.

One of the dancers, a young man with blond hair and blue eyes but with the high cheek bones of a Tartar, raised his face to the brightness of the day, then spotted the girl standing in the courtyard. For a moment their eyes locked.

"Ana," he whispered

To Ana, who in reality was Dosha, granddaughter of the most hunted Gypsy in all of Russia, the intensity of his eyes brought home what she had just barely escaped and upon which she must not dwell — not on a day like this, a day of flight, and without hesitation or a further glance she walked past him and on down the coastal road toward the ocean. For a moment the young man stood looking after her, before turning back to his fellow dancers.

Nobody followed Dosha: neither the dancer, nor any of the cars she noticed parked along the road, nor any of the isolated men or women who stood idly at street corners or at designated bus stops, waiting for the unknown.

The girl known as Ana by the Soviets continued to walk on to where, in a little over an hour, the Finns would roll out the red carpet at Helsinki's Grand Central Station to welcome Nikita Khrushchev, known to the Gypsies as the Butcher of the Ukraine. Finnish security and military personnel in uniform had been posted on street corners and in front of government buildings and foreign embassies. Agents and double-agents in civilian clothes were randomly sprinkled all over town, like raisins in a cake.

They were prepared, she thought, those Finns. To them the

threat from the East was as old as the Russian flu. They weren't caught off-guard, like the unsuspecting Gypsies, among them her people, the Lovara, an aristocratic tribe of horse-dealers, who for centuries had crossed Russia's vastness mostly unchecked through wars and revolutions, until the year before. In 1956 — one year after Dosha's mother, Azra, daughter of the king of thousands of traveling Lovara, had died — the Red net began, without warning, to entrap nomadic Gypsies into the grinding mill of Soviet standardization. This turning point would enter Gypsy history as the "Great Halt."

Approaching the water, Dosha found the normally bustling marketplace in the South Harbor stripped of the usual vendors, their booths, and their buyers. Ahead of her the Baltic Sea stretched toward a distant horizon, a flat expanse of luminous blue, dotted with tiny islands of gray rock and tufts of trees. There was no wind. The air was still, as if nature were taking a deep breath while the Fates rolled the dice, and not one single ship, not even a boat could be spotted as far as the eye could reach.

She wondered with a shudder of fear whether the ship transporting her stallion to Sweden had managed to leave before the harbor had been blocked, or whether the magnificent horse had even gotten on the ship. Caught by a piercing cry, Dosha looked up to track a seagull soaring into the empty sky. If instead of a state visit, she thought, there was to be an attack, it would happen with bombers suddenly roaring in from the East and dropping bombs from that deep blue sky.

# 2
# Skies Of War

Dosha was a little girl when in 1941 she first listened to the roaring approach of bombers. From deep within the Polish forests she watched them fill the sky like giant birds flying in formation. They fanned out wide and rose up high before the bombs dropped with piercing whistles onto villages nearby. Flames and smoke shot back toward the killer sky.

"They're moving closer," her mother whispered. "The day will come when we won't be able to run anymore."

"*Dale!*" Dosha pulled her mother down until they lay pressed against the forest floor in tight embrace. "*Dale!* Mother! In a war zone when you stop running, you die" — a fact known by every child of war.

Week after week, year after year, the fighter planes kept coming, dropping bombs, lighting up the nighttime sky. Rarely was there a break of more than a few days. When on the move, the Gypsies ducked into roadside trenches, but mostly they huddled in dugout shelters in their camps hidden in the forest. Of those who were caught, most were never heard from again.

One hot afternoon a group of Lovari women and children were crossing a mostly harvested potato field looking for left-over potatoes they might eat, when they were spotted by twin Stukas, accompanying a bomber. By the time they heard the piercing whistle and raised their eyes, the Stukas had dropped their noses and were diving straight at them. Women grabbed their children and started to run across the parched dug-up earth of the field toward a set of nearby railroad tracks and the shelter of a railway tunnel cut through a rocky mountain range. They were within reach of the dark opening arch of the tunnel, when the Stukas began machine-gunning them down. Dosha and her mother had

13

barely squeezed into an oval niche cut into the rock along the railroad tracks, when a bomb blast picked up those still running on the tracks outside and flushed them through the tunnel like dead leaves in a storm.

Almost simultaneously they heard the Stukas lift and drone on across the low mountains, before petering out in the distance. All was still then, suffused by the stench of smoke. The acrid odor of wet coal and spilled oil exuded from the rock like sweat from skin.

"They're gone, *Dale*." Dosha whispered. The smoke started to subside. She stepped onto the railroad tracks. "We better leave," she said. "Now," she insisted. "We must leave now."

Yet her mother would not leave the protection of the oval niche, and when she did at last, she stood there, in the semidarkness of the tunnel, like a tree long dead, hollowed out and lifeless.

With growing alarm Dosha pulled her mother by a hand. One slow step at a time they walked back into the open. In front of them, like rag dolls dropped from a height, the dead lay scattered across the railroad tracks. Her mother's hand started to tremble. Soon her whole body began to shake. She let go of Dosha's hand and covered her eyes with both her hands as if not seeing would keep her safe.

"Once again" — she lowered her hands and stared at Dosha with eyes that had no focus — "I am the one who's left alive. Since birth," she cried, "I've brought death to those I love. My mother Sanija, beloved by all, died when I was born. And they only told me when I was almost grown, that death in childbed casts a curse of misfortune onto a whole Gypsy tribe, especially," she sobbed, "if that someone is the wife of a Gypsy who is king over thousands of traveling Lovara. Gypsies value children as their biggest treasure of all, yet most of my siblings, seven in all, do not have children. Since my birth we've gone from revolutions to now this war. I am the carrier of a curse of not only infertility but of death as well."

"*Dale! Dale!*" Dosha pleaded, grabbing her mother's hand again, "I did not die. You are the one who gave life to me."

"What kind of life? A life of war!" Azra's haunted eyes went from the railroad tracks back into the tunnel. "I often wonder, had my mother's death not driven my father into isolation, away from his tribe, if he would ever have let us enter this war?"

14

Dosha knew only that they must make it back to the protective cover of the forest, back to Dzumila, Azra's older sister. Only the forest could offer them shelter. Only *Dzumila*, a *drabarni*, herb healer and Gypsy sorceress, could soothe the sobbing Azra. They were still standing in middle of the railroad tracks, exposed, among the scattered dead.

"Dale," Dosha whispered, "the Stukas could return." This was not the first massacre she had witnessed, and they were hours away from their forest camp.

It took them almost till nightfall to reach their camp. Again and again Azra had to sit down and lean against a tree, her breathing shallow. When they reached the camp, Dzumila at once took the trembling Azra into her arms, whispering, "What happened, what happened?" She laid her distraught sister down just inside their make-shift tent, where Dzumila lit a small fire and started boiling water with herbs to calm her sister, but Azra could not stop talking, in the lowest of whispers, in sentences that were not connected. Nobody understood a word.

The widow Javorka, her three children by her side, took Dosha a short distance away and asked, "What happened, child?"

"They're all dead. They all died!" Dosha muttered, breaking down at last, softly sobbing. Javorka took her by the shoulders, before raising her chin. "Now look here," she said, "if these Lovara had died in normal times, we would now, every one of us, prepare for a proper Gypsy funeral, mourning them for three full days before lowering the lifeless shells of their bodies into an open grave dug next to the path we travel. And right after, we would walk away, leaving our grief buried along with our beloved in that grave. But this," she said, "is a war and you have to bury them in your mind and fast.

"Never forget," she said, letting go of Dosha's chin and stroking instead her sweat-soaked hair, "you are a Gypsy. and just as in the wild a foal has to get up and run with the herd right after birth, so the child of a Gypsy has to learn early on to leave the past behind and walk into the future to survive. The war must not change the life you were meant to live, our own life from before this war."

Dosha, hugging Javorka, tried hard to bring back the past — barely reaching the window of a rolling caravan on tiptoes, watching forests and meadows flowing by, listening to the clip clop of horses traveling across asphalt roads through villages and towns in the early morning hours, watching dogs run along, bark and scatter.

Dosha was the child of Russian Gypsies who in 1941 had answered Stalin's call to sabotage the German occupation of Poland and thereby slow the advance of Nazi troops into what even the Lovara considered the Russian motherland. Gypsies were not in the habit of taking part in *Gadje*, or non-Gypsy, wars — not by choice. But this was for Russia, a country that for centuries had offered the Gypsy people welcome and acceptance. That was why in the early months of that year a great number of Russian Gypsies from all the *natsias*, the tribes, had started moving toward the western front. Among them were many of Dosha's people, the Lovara, a tribe of horse-dealers and breeders, who left their wagons and most of their valuable horses in the care of elders at an encampment in Belarus, in an isolated valley where two brooks fork into a river. Then, mostly on foot, the Lovari partisans crossed the border into Poland to join Russian partisans already operating there.

Their mission, a Soviet officer in uniform told them, was "to cut off German advances and retreats, and kill anyone in the way." But Gypsies are not killers by nature, and while German and Russian planes kept chasing each other across the war-torn sky and mass killings shocked the population down below, the Gypsy contribution to the Soviet war would be mostly as spies.

To protect their women and children, the men mostly lived apart. Women tended to stay in hiding, providing food and healing herbs, though they also, like the men, spied on the movements of the occupying troops. All the Lovari partisans — men, women and children alike — dressed like Polish peasants to blend in, although their dark faces and sharp features clearly marked them as Gypsies on closer inspection. Even Dosha, light-skinned and with hair as bright as *galbi*, Gypsy gold, had the dark and melancholy eyes of her tribe. Like many of the children, Dosha acted as a runner, carrying food and information between partisan units.

Some of the Gypsies brought along their horses for the fight. Leading them was Patrina, tribal mother and Queen of the Lovara, who before the war had traveled from the Urals all the way into France. With the help of her adopted son, a *do-pash Rom* or half-Gypsy named Larkin, she led her own partisan group of Gypsies, fighting alongside Russian Tartars and some ethnic Russians against the common enemy. Tales of her courageous assaults against the Germans would be recounted and embellished around campfires deep into the night for years to come. Like Russian saboteurs, these Gypsies blew up bridges, ammunition depots and German army camps. In addition, Patrina recaptured many of her people who had fallen into German hands. One of these was her own great-niece, Dosha. At the age of six, returning from one of her runs to carry a message to her father Djemo and his group of partisans, Dosha had been spotted and captured by German soldiers. After hours of searching, Patrina, with the help of a dog, had tracked her down. The child lay unconscious and physically bruised in a pile of leaves alongside a road leading to a concentration camp. When the little girl came to, she only told them of German soldiers jumping off a truck and chasing after her as she tried to escape into the forest. She would say no more.

In 1945, in the spring following the fall massacre near the railway tunnel, bombs stopped falling. A week went by, then two. The snows had melted, barren fields were sprouting weeds, and the forests were recycling back to life. Dosha was now seven years old. In the early morning hours she stepped, hesitatingly at first, right into the middle of a wide-open clearing not far from their forest hide-out. When she raised her eyes, she saw, instead of planes, flocks of birds lift from the greening treetops into a blue and hollow sky. There they soared and dipped freely and fluidly like shifting water spray. In a sudden irrepressible explosion, life around her rose from within the forest as never before. She held her breath and was filled with a sudden feeling of lightness, as if she too could rise and fly. Her feet seemed to barely touch ground as she dashed along a deer path through the dense forest, back toward her camp and to her mother, only to find the women and children of her family gathered around a Lovari fighter who was leaning against a tree. His body was crisscrossed with rifles and ammunition.

"I come from Patrina," he said. Dosha watched him with dawning expectation and growing joy as he lit a cigarette and re-laxed against the tree. "Fighting has stopped, and I am here to mark a trail for all Lovara to follow me to a clearing at the edge of this great forest, half a day's walk from here."

"Why didn't my father come to tell us that?" Dosha asked.

"Shhh, child," Dzumila hushed her.

"Everybody will be at the meeting," the fighter said, turning to Dzumila. "All you have to do is follow the signs I'll leave for you along the lumber road and ...."

He didn't finish the sentence but gave a wave of his hand,

before silently slipping into the woods. They saw him lean down to pick up twigs and early flowers and tie them with grass or ferns. He was making *patrins*, Gypsy road signs, which he attached to trees or shrubs or placed on the ground along his path. His signs would lead all the way to the designated meeting place. He looked back once and then disappeared.

"No more bombs! No more fighting!" — The cries of joy were repeated over and over, as Lovari partisans of Dosha's *kumpania*, her traveling group, hastily packed their few belongings into back slings. In less than an hour they had broken camp and started to follow the marked path. Along the way more Gypsy partisans emerged from dugout shelters, from makeshift tents of sticks and army blankets, and from caves. Gypsies climbed down from platforms half-hidden by the branches of tall firs. There was much jostling and laughing, and anticipatory joy. Families were about to reunite.

It was almost nightfall. They had walked for hours without a break when they reached the designated clearing, and there Patrina stood, waiting for her people. Dark-skinned and tiny, she was almost hidden by her fighters, who stood gathered around her. Their horses were grazing free and close by, the Gypsy way.

Dosha saw her uncle Angar, Dzumila's *rom*, her husband. But neither her father nor his horse was present, although he and Anger had fought side by side all through the war.

"Mami," Dosha wanted to run toward Parina, the great-aunt who had taken the place of her grandmother since birth.

"Not now, child," her mother said, motioning Dosha to sit down beside her in a half-circle with other Lovara. They were joined by more and more Gypsy partisans who came trickling into the clearing. Their tribal mother and queen stood waiting in the center of the circle.

"Where is my father?" Dosha called out. "How come he's not with these other *rom*, these other men?"

At that moment Patrina lifted both hands and called out, "Hear me!" Even the children fell silent, paying tribute to their wise female leader.

"The war," Patrina said, "is over."

The statement that all had been waiting for, had prayed for, was greeted with hollow silence. Those present, even the older children, dropped their eyes to their hands resting in their laps or on their thighs. Until a woman's voice rose from the half circle of seated Gypsies, crying over and over again, "Thank you! Thank you, *o del!* Thank you God!" The voice was that of Javorka, the *romni* who had lost her *rom* but none of the three children in her care. More voices broke free. "Thank you, God! Thank you, *o del*, for giving us peace at least."

Patrina stood silent. She was of advanced age, yet her thick black hair, pulled back in a bun, showed only few strands of gray. Her dark and piercing eyes went from man to woman to child, until she had covered everyone sitting before her in that semicircle. She was taking note of all those who were no longer there— of the price they paid.

"Of us partisans," she said, "on average two out of ten have survived. Hundreds of thousands of our fellow Gypsies from all over Europe, we will never find on the romani trails again. Captured and processed by Nazi commandos and driven into concentration camps, they were devoured by a system of unimaginable evil."

There was a long and heavy pause of remembrance.

"The killers of Gypsies, Russians, Poles, and Jews alike," Patrina said, her eyes like glistening daggers, "are gone at last."

There was no hint of jubilation, no sense of victory in the old woman's voice. Once again Javorka's voice rang out: "It's over then, praise *o del*, it's over," and only then did the reality sink in that those present need no longer fear Nazi persecution. The circle of seated partisans visibly relaxed. A lively chatter ensued, the excited cries of ragged children piercing the hum of adult voices. Once again the *phuri dai*, their tribal mother, halted the commotion with outstretched hands.

"Hear me," she said. "The *Gadje* will now return to the plots of land they call their homes. We Gypsies must return to the open road. The road to take is first to Belarus, where we have left our elders and most of our horses, then on to Russia, because that country has shown us safety before. That, you must always remember, is why we fought for them."

"Russia is where we were safe before, right?" Dosha asked her aunt Dzumila.

"Shhh."

"Didn't you tell me that Russia has been kind to the Gypsies? Always welcoming?" Dosha persisted. Patrina's voice cut through her words, as this time her mother shushed Dosha again.

"But first," Patrina continued, "before you walk back into a life that is your own, before you take back the possessions you have left behind with our elders in Belarus, you must cleanse yourselves of the memories of this *Gadje* war. You must feed these clothes we wore for the sole purpose of blending in with *Gadje* to the purifying power of Gypsy fires, and in doing so leave this war behind."

The Lovara jumped to their feet. Shouts of *"Latcho drom!"* popped like firecrackers as they wished each other "Good road!"

"Not yet!" Patrina cried. "Hear me! That," she said, pointing to spirals of black smoke in the distance, "is not the work of Russian partisans, fighters for freedom like us. Nor is that the work of the Germans in defeat. That," she said, and Dosha could see that she was trembling, "is the continuing slaughter of animals and people by the victorious Red Army of our beloved Russia. They may be in rags like us, they're probably hungrier than us, but they got liquor in their veins as a reward for victory. So now, drunk and out of control, they're scorching and burning whatever is in their way. They're killing for whatever food is left. The officers are looking the other way, simply because the army has no food left to give them."

The Gypsy partisans needed no further warning. They had seen these Reds from up close. They were nothing like the Russians they had known in earlier years, before the Revolution. They were not like the poor peasants who had opened their hearts and homes to their Gypsies in the past, offering them shelter through the harshest part of winter and sharing their joys and sorrows. Nor were these new leaders like the former aristocrats who had shared the Gypsy's soul and loved what they believed to be the romance of the Gypsies' free way of life.

"As many of you know," said Patrina, reading their thoughts, "my younger brother Khantchi, elected by all traveling Lovara to be our leader and King, warned us, warned me not to enter this war. He said that our beloved Russia was in the hands of an evil man, a man called Stalin. Maybe I should have listened, because when it comes to understanding Gadje, Khantchi always had an edge. Our tribe allowed him to be adopted by the Countess Perzoff, to replace the son that she had lost. Seduced by the love and respect that the aristocracy offered us, the freedom and protection across their vast lands, we gave in—mostly because we Gypsies know that you can no more turn a Gypsy into a Gadje than you can turn a wolf into a dog. We knew that Khantchi would always return to his own people. However, he was the first among us to witness the killings of the former lords of all of Russia, and he felt torn. With those aristocrats, he told us later, died the only true protectors we Gypsies have ever known.

"As for me," Patrina continued, "I had to see with my own

eyes that these Reds are indeed a new breed of Russian, killers of their own people. I myself have witnessed how they shot their own soldiers in the back of the neck, whenever they showed signs of a will of their own. You must avoid these Bolsheviks at all cost. We'll go back to Russia, the beautiful land we love, but we must be careful. Till now these new rulers have ignored us. But in the end, with the aristocrats gone once and for all, they will hunt the Gypsy down. Sooner or later, mark my words! "

Then Patrina went from seated person to seated person and assigned each one to small *kumpaniyi* of no more than eight. "It's to avoid your getting pulled into the Soviet system," she explained. The newly formed *kumpaniyi* were to depart one by one, at intervals of at least a day. "No one travels in large groups anymore."

Only when Patrina stood in front of her did Dosha jump up and ask again, "Where is my father. *Mami?*"

The tiny queen of the Lovara took Dosha into her arms. The rifles that still crossed her wiry body dug into Dosha's cheeks, as she stroked Dosha's head with a hand as gentle as the feathers of a dove. "Your *dad* is alive and well," Patrina said. "And I will make sure you see him soon. Now sit down." With that she stepped once more in front of her people..

"You'll have to make your way to Russia's High North," Patrina addressed them once again. "Once there, you must vanish into the tundra of the Kola Peninsula or the taiga alongside the Finnish border. The land is empty up there, and there's plenty of it. At this point, it's still too hard for the Soviets to control. The only people you're likely to come across up there are Sami. They're nomads like us, only instead of horses they herd reindeer. But until you get there," the *phuri dai* finished by saying, "you'll have to make yourselves scarce. There will be refugees everywhere. They, too, you must avoid. Keep as much as possible to forests and back country. The rule again is *Gadje* with *Gadje, Rom* with *Rom,* as dictated by Romani law."

# 3
# 1945, The Aftermath

But the war was not like a forest that could be left behind. Once the Lovara left the Polish forests that had sheltered them, they came face to face with an endless plain of devastation. Nothing left standing but the heavy iron stoves that had once been the center of modest peasant homes and the iron bedsteads they had used to sleep in. Mixed in with the rubble of leveled village after leveled village were the dead bodies — mostly of women, children of all ages, and the aged. The few survivors moved about like ghosts among their dead.

And like a chaotic stream flowing through this wasteland, the survivors — the young, the old, the crippled, and those by some whim of fate left whole — were marching west. Most of the refugees were hollow-eyed women, some clutching listless babies to their chests, others were dragging unresisting toddlers by the hand. A few lucky women pushed baby carriages, obtained by miracle or theft, and piled with infants, small children, or whatever possessions they had left. Occasionally men on bicycles — presumed to be deserters on the run — came zigzagging past.

"We're the only ones with a horse," Dosha whispered to her uncle Angar.

"Just keep close and walk straight ahead," Angar said. "And do not talk." Dosha realized that the four adults of their *kumpania* were surrounding the Gypsy pony like a fruit its pit.

"Everybody keep calm," Dzumila added. "The worst is over."

But Dosha felt as if they were driftwood on a flooding river, their course at the mercy of the constantly shifting and regrouping masses of walking *Gadje*. The only ones being marched off in orderly rows were captured German soldiers, now under the vigilant guard of Soviet soldiers prodding them on with tommy guns.

It was in the wake of such a column of prisoners of war that Dosha suddenly spotted her father, Djemo. She gasped. She hardly recognized him. His dark brown hair was cut short, and he wore the uniform of an officer of the Red Army. He came toward them riding his horse at a walk, as visible as a lone tank crossing an open field.

"*Dad*!" Dosha rushed from her group into his path and touched his riding boot. "*Dad*, get down! Somebody will shoot you up there."

"It's not me at all you should fear for," he said, leaning down toward her, "it's the horse." Then he jumped off the horse's back and placed his hand gently on her hair. "Why do you think Angar is sticking so close to his own?" he asked. "It's because now that the war is over, it's all about food." And like Angar he drew the horse close to his body by grabbing the reins right below its face.

"Look!" Her father pointed with his head toward the distant skyline, where what had once been a city was now nothing but a graveyard of burnt-out houses. Jagged ruins surrounded a lone church spire that pointed sharply toward the empty sky. "Not only is there nothing left to go back to," he said, "most of all, there's nothing left to eat."

Dosha ran her hand along the horse's chest and shuddered. "You mean they'd eat...." To the Lovara the horse is sacred, and the eating of horseflesh a heinous crime.

By then the rest of their *kumpania*, still disguised in peasant garb, had gathered around them. Rising to his toes, Djemo scouted for a more private spot, while Angar, Dzumila, Javorka, and Azra all talked at once. They examined the two rifles slung across Djemo's chest. They opened one saddlebag still packed with ammunitions and hand grenades. In the other ... They held their breath: he had bread and cheese and sausage. They tightened their circle to block off this unexpected treasure from the *Gadje* masses passing by. Djemo gestured with his head to a trench that cut a line along the stream of refugees. He turned his horse and walked ahead of his group to the ditch where he started to divide his cache of food into equal parts. The Gypsies, still circled tight, ate fast, as Djemo looked on, not partaking.

"We must move on," Djemo said. Unlike the rest of them, he appeared neither hungry nor broken down like Dosha's mother, who stood right next to him, looking brooding and forlorn. Dosha was used to Gypsy men and women not showing affection in public, but she was struck by the silence that separated her parents like an impenetrable wall. Her father, instead of scrutinizing her frail mother, making sure she was unhurt, merely kept one arm around Dosha's shoulders. Dosha looked up into his handsome face. His eyes were restless, searching the distance. *More like those men on bicycles,* Dosha thought, *zigzagging through.*

Djemo was famous among the tribe for his bravery under Patrina, and also for his exploits with the Russian freedom fighters. During the war, Dosha had lived for the moments when her father would ride into one of their makeshift camps, always in the company of Angar. They never spent more than a few hours, a night at most, in whatever shelter their families had managed to build or find. Their arrival was always greeted with great fanfare, and for those short moments the women and their children gave themselves over to the joy of reunion. These were especially happy times, since the men always arrived with food and supplies that were not accessible to their wives, who, toward the end of the war, rarely left the protection of the woods. Djemo used to spend most of his visits with Dosha, his beloved only child. For as far back as she could remember, he used to lift her onto his horse, Rakli — the very mare she was stroking now, and who nuzzled her in recognition. It was Djemo who taught her how to ride.

During those years Dosha had dreamt of a future when she could be with her father forever. But now that peace had finally come, not only was Djemo among the last to rejoin the tribe, he didn't have the air of someone who had come to stay. Even so, it became clear at once that their small *kumpania* had a *rom baro* — a daring male leader — once again.

"We have to get away from this." Djemo's hand swept across the human march of survivors: masses of walking *Gadje,* who were leaving more dead and dying behind on their way to where nobody knew.

"Break up into pairs," he said "then fan out across those fields!" He pointed to a meadow where new growth was rising from the dead, matted weeds of the previous summer.

The fields appeared to have been left unplowed for years. The lumpy, rock-hard earth was difficult to cross, especially for the Lovara walking barefoot. However, Djemo's arrival had pumped renewed energy into the group. As Djemo led the way on his horse, even Azra, in the grip of feverish anxiety, managed to keep pace. As for Dosha, she felt again as if she had acquired wings, like the flocks of blackbirds that swept across the fields gone to seed. Exhilarated, she savored the freedom of walking across open land.

Hours of walking brought them to a hamlet that had escaped extinction: four peasant huts in all. The Lovara regrouped.

"Go in," Dzumila told Dosha. "Go ask for some water!" She turned to Djemo as he dismounted. "On account of her blond hair," she explained.

"Go on then," he agreed.

Dosha took the metal water mug that Dzumila handed her and ventured into the cottage closest to them, but immediately ran back out, screaming. *"Dad, Dad!* They're killing a *Gadje* in there."

Djemo threw the reins to Dzumila and rushed in, cursing. "It's a German soldier, of all people," he said, reemerging, "probably begging for civilian clothes in order to escape the Red Army, but getting beaten to death instead. I guess the Poles have had enough."

Fearing for their own safety, the Lovara slipped away.

"The truth is," Djemo explained to his daughter, "once the killer instinct is unleashed, it can't be simply turned off overnight. And you'll find that, although the killings are no longer sanctioned by the laws of war, they're continuing under cover."

From then on, as the Gypsies sought out dilapidated barns and burnt-out peasant homes in which to spend the night, they stumbled upon the rotting corpses of soldiers in all types of uniforms, but mostly civilians only recently slaughtered. Keeping a safe distance, they witnessed stray Russian soldiers entering peasant homes.

"Always be careful," Djemo told Dosha. "Those Russians are out to kill the farmers to get at their hidden storage of food, and," he added, "before leaving they'll do harm to the women."

Nor did the killer craze stop there. What horrified the Gypsy soul most of all was the slaughter of dumb and innocent animals — creatures, like the Lovara themselves, who had survived the years of slaughter and hunger through the mercy of *o del*: big animals with soulful eyes — cows, goats, even horses, reduced to skin and bones like their human counterparts. The *kumpania*, moving stealthily through the countryside, saw terror in these animals' eyes and heard their anguished cries as they were clobbered to death with the butts of empty rifles right out in their pastures by passing soldiers or escapees from civilian prisons or German prisoner camps.

"That's why Rakli is so valuable, isn't she?" Dosha said, patting her father's mount. "It breaks the heart."

The Gypsies averted their eyes when they came across such slaughter and covered their children's eyes with their hands. Only Dosha, always at her mother's side, tore her father's hand away from her face. "Closing my eyes would have killed my mother and me," she said, thinking of the times her mother had covered her own eyes during and after bomb attacks. "Why would it save me now?"

She realized that she barely knew her father. Although he never left the *kumpania* for more than a few hours, and once for one night and a day, he nonetheless still kept coming and going. It was always he who volunteered to head out, scouring for food. He did return with provisions: *manro* (freshly baked bread), cabbage and cucumber in aspic. These were some of the few foods handled by *Gadje* that a Gypsy would eat. But every time he returned, he seemed more distant, averting his eyes when his child searched them for answers.

"What are you bartering with?" Dosha asked him one day.

He looked up as if surprised at the inquisitive tone of her voice. "Ammunition and hand grenades, what else?" he announced. "The peasants need to defend themselves from hungry soldiers."

They had been walking for many days, hiking east toward Belarus and the life they had left behind. The adults started to recognize terrain. "Now you see our ancient trails," they told the children. "We traveled them as often as once a year." But the trails from Russia to Poland that once had crossed well-tended fields and meadows dotted with grazing livestock were now no more than dumping grounds for the ravages of war. Bomb craters riddled the whole expanse of open land, and, amid the destroyed or abandoned vehicles and tanks, the bodies of Russians, Germans, and Poles lay rotting side by side. The Gypsy women wrapped their faces and those of their children in headscarves, trying to block out the stench of human decay that engulfed them in the unrelenting heat of the summer of 1945.

Late one day the *kumpania* came upon a refugee camp: a

collection of Soviet military tents surrounded by barbed wire, where *Gadje* refugees lined up in front of an iron gate tended by two military guards.

"The Bolsheviks are regrouping." Djemo sat his mare grimly. "If we get into their processing system, we'll never be free again. First they'll take away our horses, then our souls. We have to get away from here."

At that moment the iron gate opened. As the refugees started to push and crowd their way in, Azra gave a cry. Turning toward her mother and grabbing her hand, Dosha felt her starting to tremble, despite the boiling heat, as if she were cold. Whatever strength Azra had briefly regained now trickled out like the last drops from a leaky bottle. Her trembling turned into shaking. All color drained from her face, she started gasping for air.

"*Dale!*" Dosha cried, "Dzumila, look at my mother!"

Dzumila reached them just as Azra slid to the ground. Letting out a sharp whistle Dzumila grabbed her sister under her arms just in time to prevent her head from hitting the ground. The rest of the *kumpania* rushed to their aid. Only Djemo, seated on his mare, seemed unmoved.

"What's wrong with you?" Dzumila yelled at him. "Look at my baby sister, your *romni*." Dzumila was a big woman, all skin and bones like the rest of them, but still heavy-bosomed despite the war.

"You don't seem to understand," Djemo said, with a brief glance at Azra. "There's typhoid everywhere. I've seen it with my own eyes. Those *Gadje* are dropping like flies. We have to make it to the woods and clean water, or we'll all...."

"It's not the typhoid my mother is frightened of!" cried Dosha, "It's those military tents. She must be afraid they'll send forth more of those diver planes."

"What your father is telling us" — Dzumila's black, unyielding eyes were nailed to Djemo's face — "is that in order to survive we too must leave our weak behind to die!"

Dosha could see anger flare up in her father's eyes. Then his face changed as thoughts crossed his restless mind. His mouth tightened, as he finally got off his horse. He was brave but not foolish. Dzumila was the unquestioned female leader of their jointly governed *kumpania*. She had the power of the curse, and Djemo, like most Gypsies, was superstitious. He slowly got his anger under control, but the look in his eyes had turned to ice.

Dosha shuddered. What was wrong? She had never felt more alone in her life.

Dzumila was helping Azra off the ground. With Djemo's help, they lifted her onto Angar's sturdy pony. The feel of the pony under her seemed to revive Azra somewhat. She hunched forward and grabbed its mane to steady her.

They turned and walked away from the camp. For the time being, harmony returned to the dual leadership of Djemo and Dzumila — except that now Dzumila's presence hovered over her delicate sister like the widespread wings of a hawk. She kept Azra close by her side, leading Angar's pony by its rope.

To avoid detection by the still-visible military camp, the Gypsies once again separated into ones and twos, the better to blend into a stripped landscape just starting to be overgrown with shrubs and saplings. Night was falling when they stepped into dense woodland. They followed the gurgling sound of running water to a brook, whose shallow, slow-moving water barely covered a bed of dark rock. Dzumila dropped down to her knees and scooped up handfuls of water. "It's clean," she said. The rest of the *kumpania* knelt by the water's edge and cupped their hands to drink, while Djemo took the two horses a distance downstream to drink their fill.

That night, while the Lovara lay sheltered in the underbrush, thunderstorms broke the brutal heat that had set the death-fields festering. Savoring the freshly washed air, Dosha bedded down next to her father; his horse was tied to a nearby tree. She immediately fell into a deep and dreamless sleep. When she awoke, she was alone. Still not fully conscious, she heard the *kumpania* breaking up camp. Their movements were unhurried, and their low voices were subsumed by raucous birdsong as the forest awakened. Dosha's mind lingered on the gentle gurgling of the woodland brook, the peaceful sound that had always been the pulse of Gypsy life. Heavy layers of mist stretched from the forest across the open space toward the camp in the distance. A red sun was rising like a body emerging from the waters of a lake, setting the mist to drift and sift into the forest. It had the smell and taste of smoke.

Dosha came to her feet and stretched luxuriantly. That's when she noticed a dark shape racing toward her across the meadow beyond the woods. Like a huge black bird, it dove in and out of the vaporizing mist. As it drew closer, she realized it was no bird at all, but a foal, jet black, its neck stretched out and forward like a goose in flight. More shapes arose — soldiers with the exploding sunlight bouncing off their helmets. First one and then a second emerged from the mists. A shot rang out, reverberating through the otherwise deserted space. The foal's speed accelerated, until it barely touched the ground. Another shot. The foal was racing for its life. It had almost reached the tree line, fleeing straight toward Dosha, who closed her eyes. Trained since childhood that any noise could give her *kumpania* away, she imitated the screech of the owl instead, the sound of imminent danger. She held her breath.

The killers, shadowy in the misty distance, stopped and clumped together. She heard their voices but could make out no words. The foal, which, though still young, was bigger than most full-grown Gypsy ponies, had disappeared among the trees. The soldiers turned back, first one and then the other. They were not going to follow.

Dosha spun around, listening for the horse thrashing through the underbrush. She could see it coming toward her. Suddenly it veered. It must have picked up the commotion ahead. With renewed panic it wheeled, jumped a shrub, and suddenly pulled up short as the rope hanging from its halter tangled in a branch.

The foal thrashed about, trying to break free. It wheeled and pulled, dipping its head, trying to bolt, only to become even more entangled. His rope was now wrapped around several branches. In a last desperate attempt to cut loose, the black foal reared, raking the air with his forefeet. Branches cracked and flew. The foal, clearly a stud colt, dropped squarely onto all fours, where he stood, exhausted and wild-eyed, nostrils flaring.

"Whoa there," said Dosha, holding out both hands and moving slowly toward the trapped animal. "Easy now! Don't be afraid."

She heard the Lovara approaching behind her. From the corner of her eye she noticed them linking their hands: they approached the young horse cautiously, like a solid fence. Only Djemo, moving along like a gate in their midst, kept his arms to his side. He started to whisper, softly, to calm the foal.

"He's wearing a Soviet cavalry halter," Djemo whispered. "But look at the size of him! Russia hasn't seen the likes of this foal since it fed its finest horses to their revolution. I think," he continued in a whisper, "that what we're looking at here is war booty. This looks like Germany's finest."

At no time did Djemo's eyes leave the foal, even when he bent down and grabbed some grass, which he held out, moving it gently toward the frightened creature's quivering lips. The colt hesitated, but his breathing slowed, and his eyes started to reflect the calm of the Gypsies, who by then had fenced him in. He began to relax, stretching his muzzle tentatively toward Djemo and the proffered grass. The foal looked well fed and was clearly used to being handled.

Minutes passed before Djemo, his hand stroking the foal's neck, freed the entangled rope (a heavy knob at the end had been caught in the shrub) and held it securely in his hand.

Dosha's gaze, like that of most of the little group, remained solely on Djemo, who continued to touch and stroke the foal. And the foal, though slowly calming, still trembled with fear. *The way my mother* does, Dosha thought, *ever since we were under attack.* Only, she realized, Djemo never stroked and soothed her mother as he stroked the foal.

*He doesn't love her anymore.* The thought sent shock waves into Dosha's heart. There had been times when she had seen her mother happy, had watched her dance around a blazing fire with more spirit than any other *romni*, when she had laughed brilliantly, and when Djemo had observed her every move with shining eyes. Now her mother's pretty face was permanently tight, branded with fear, and Djemo hardly looked at her.

Dosha felt she had entered an empty space, a moment frozen in time. The emptiness filled with an image at first too vague to discern, until suddenly the image crystallized, and she saw her father splitting apart from himself like a spirit stepping out of the dead body it leaves behind. The image wavered in her mind like a flag in the wind.

Dzumila shaking her by the shoulders snapped Dosha out of her trance. "What are you seeing, child?" she asked.

Dosha looked into the savage face of her aunt. "He doesn't mean to stay." Her voice broke in anguish and sadness.

Dzumila turned to watch Djemo approach with the foal. Her eyes went from his Soviet uniform to his hair, cropped short.

"*Gadjekano*," Dzumila cursed. "He has turned *Gadje*. Real Gypsies don't cut their hair."

Dosha knew that Dzumila loved only Azra, the sister who had lost their mother at birth. Now, for the first time, she extended her protection to Azra's child, when she boldly took the rope from Djemo's hand and handed it to Dosha.

"This foal was sent to Dosha from De Develeski, the divine

mother of the Roma," Dzumila announced, turning toward the *kumpania,* who stood oohing and aahing over the beauty of the foal.

Djemo's face was inscrutable. The muscle in his jaw jumped and his eyes narrowed, as he studied the powerful woman's face. Then, after a prolonged pause, he yielded. He would not cross the female head of their jointly governed *kumpania.*

"Yes," he agreed, "my daughter saw it first. The foal is hers by our laws of the road. Whoever sees it first is the one to whom it belongs. And it was toward her the foal was running."

That is how the horse that would become famous as the stallion Rus under the rule of Comrade Khrushchev entered the life of Dosha of the family of Khantchi, the Khantchisti.

Taller, stronger than the wiry, reddish-blond Gypsy girl, the foal obediently walked by his new-found partner's side. Dosha in turn stayed close to Dzumila, who led her *kumpania* deep into the virgin forests of Belarus along the banks of what the Gypsies called the black creek, a meandering forest brook with crystal water rippling across blackened stone and rock. It was shaded on both sides by ancient trees.

Sure-footed and silent, the Lovara followed the twists and turns of the creek in single file along its rocky water edge. But whereas the two Gypsy mares blended into the woodlands that surrounded them, the black foal whinnied and shied whenever anything moved or cried out from within the trees and undergrowth. The dense forest of pine, beech, and oak kept encroaching upon the shallow creek, until trees from both sides joined branches above its narrow path, and the water ran dark and straight between tight grids of trees.

"We'll spend the night," Dzumila said. Dosha gradually released the tight grip she had kept on the lead rope and let the foal graze alongside the Gypsy mares for the first time. She kept a close eye on the foal while the women gathered and then cooked their meager meal of ferns and nettles. While the *kumpania* sat down to eat, she let the foal graze free — the Gypsy way — until the fire was doused. Then she tied it to the tree next to where she would sleep, in case some prowling animal might spook her new friend during the night. Unlike the Gypsy mares, sleeping on their feet, the foal, exhausted from its first day of Gypsy life, bedded down and almost immediately fell into an uneasy sleep. By the nervous twitching of the foal's legs and lips, Dosha guessed that he was reliving the trauma of that day, until darkness and sleep blanketed all.

A light kick from the foal, as he struggled to get up, snapped Dosha back awake. It was a moment suspended between night and day. Slowly her eyes fastened on an empty, dawning sky. She jumped to her feet and was grabbing the foal's lead rope when her eyes fell upon her father mounted on his mare. He was in the middle of the brook, with his back turned to Dosha. He was riding his mare away from the still sleeping Gypsies, away from her.

Wrapped in eerie stillness, Dosha watched as the mare, with lowered head, carefully picked her way through the rocky bed of the brook. With limber movements, Djemo kept shifting his own weight along with the mare's, until he leaned forward and trusted his obedient mount with free reins. At the next bend in the river, Djemo bent his upper body parallel to the mare's, his arms embracing her neck as she climbed the rocky embankment onto a clearing where the grass stood high. There he sat up tall, and they fell into a smooth and fluid canter. He never looked back. He never said goodbye.

Later, she would wonder whether she should have run after him, asked him why. But at the time, she did not have the will to move. She felt as hollow as that early morning sky. She recognized the moment and the place, as if she had lived it once before. It was a knowledge she had carried and would always carry deep within.

Dawn broke fully with the pearly light that precedes the rising sun. Not a single cloud loomed; nothing stirred the foliage of the trees that had sheltered them for the night. Djemo was leaving the way he had arrived, his two rifles slung across his back and his saddlebags full. He had reverted to the quiet stealth of a partisan fighter.

"*Dale!*" Dosha called out to her mother who sat cross-legged on the forest floor. She hesitated, then continued, after what seemed a long, long time, "Where is he going, and why? He never turned to say goodbye!"

Her mother regarded her with eyes that were *mulikanes*, the eyes of the dead. "He is going to live with a *Gadji*," Azra said through gritted teeth. Her mouth twisted. "She's been fighting alongside him all through the war. She must have been following us closely all this time. He's leaving us for her."

The rest of the *kumpania* had started to stir. From among them Dzumila came rushing to Azra's side. One look and she

32

must have understood what had occurred. She pulled her younger sister to her, enfolding her for a moment in comforting arms, until the rest of the *kumpania* were on their feet and gathered around them. Amid much shouting and screaming, Dzumila flicked her Polish peasant shirt in the direction that Djemo had disappeared. All eyes were on Dzumila. "I expel you" — Dzumila's voice cut through the sudden silence — "from this tribe for life."

Dosha averted her eyes from Dzumila and her mother, from the whole *kumpania*, frozen in place. Dosha's vision of the day before had come true. She walked over to where the foal was calmly grazing on the sparse grass that grew between the trees. He had remained calm through all the shouts and angry cries. *He's getting used to Gypsy life*, she thought, as he lifted his head and nuzzled her outstretched hand.

# 4

# Return To The Red Empire

Where two brooks form a river, a four-day walk across the border from Poland into Belarus, the Lovari partisans found a remote valley dotted with ornate caravans and Gypsy bender tents of all sizes and shapes. Small individual fires were burning below kettles hanging from iron tripods as well as grilling spits with sizzling meat suspended between forged branches. Horses grazed nearby and in between. Geese and goats ran loose. As the returning Gypsies poured down from a steep embankment into the valley like water from a cliff, screaming and yelling for those they had left behind, a pack of dogs from the camp charged them with raised hackles, bared teeth, and the high-pitched yelping of dogs on a hunt. But when, at the bottom of the embankment, the Lovara partisans and their elders came together like linking hands, the dogs scattered, realizing they had been charging Gypsies, not *Gadje* peasants.

With much fanfare, the returning Lovara were led by their elders back into the traveling homes they had left behind. First to reemerge from their brightly painted caravans were the *rom*, dressed again in loose pants stuck into high leather boots. Despite the heat, they'd put on hats, and tied colorful scarves around their necks; some carried instruments. Then the *romni* stepped out, wearing voluminous Gypsy skirts, their braided hair covered once again with colorful kerchiefs. Most spectacular among the reunited clan were the elder women, who displayed the traditional tribal wealth: arrays of gold coins woven into their plaited hair and chains of gold coins that hung around their necks and dropped almost to their waists.

That night, stick-fires were burning wide and high for those

34

who had survived. United with their elders, the Lovari partisans stood with their faces to the fire as, one by one, they fed their *Gadje* clothes to the devouring flames, ritually cleansing themselves of the darkness of the war years.

They then linked hands and together stared into the purifying flames. One after the other, they picked their instruments off the ground — their violins, seven-stringed guitars and tambourines. They held them close, like children once lost and now recovered. No one had the heart to play a joyful tune, let alone dance. A lone violin rose like a wail above the rushing flames, in memory of those left behind.

The next morning eight wagons departed along the narrow river flowing east into Russia: three ornately carved caravans and five bow-top Gypsy wagons packed with tents and cooking utensils. Metal trays upheld by chains at the back of the caravans held hay for the horses. Geese that had been running free were now confined to cages attached to the undersides of the wagons. The *rom* walked to the left of their harnessed horses, holding long driving reins in their hands, while goats and dogs, women and children — Dosha and her foal among them — walked behind their own traveling homes. Only the delicate Azra traveled inside her caravan, her dark, cavernous eyes glued to the low waters of the river flowing by.

The Russia that the returning Lovara entered was as devastated and charred as the war zones they had left behind. The "Gypsy post" — a network of secret contacts that the Lovara had established along their yearly treks before the war — was no longer in place: the peasants who had once been friendly to the Lovara and willing to pass messages from one *kumpania* to the next had been either massacred by Germans or replaced by hostile Bolsheviks. Now when the Lovara sent a band of musicians into a village, the peasants, instead of rushing from their houses to the village square to welcome the entertainers, chased them away with pitchforks, shouting "*Tzigani!* Gypsies, go away!" And worse, in one village the Lovara were confronted by uniformed party officials and police who pointed loaded rifles into their direction, as if the Gypsies were not entertainers but invaders.

They came across no fellow Lovara traveling the country roads. At a deserted crossroad near Novgorod they spotted one lone Gypsy. He had no wagon and his horse was covered with pots and pans. He was a coppersmith of the *natsia,* or tribe, of

Kalderash. When asked, he said, "I haven't seen any Lovara in these parts." He knew nothing of their whereabouts. "But if I were you," he cautioned, "I would keep those gold coins out of sight."

So now Lovari elders wore their tribal gold tied in hiding around their waists and under their skirts. They traveled on to Leningrad, the city that the Gypsies still called "Saint Pete," and camped beyond city limits at the edge of a small river filtering into swampland, a site where Lovara used to meet before the war. There, under an enormous, pink-streaked sky, they turned their horses loose. They lifted a patch of damp sod and got a fire going. They had just settled around the fire when a covered wagon with harnessed horse stopped a hundred yards from where they sat. A Gypsy handed his long reins to his *romni* and approached.

"*Te trajis,*" he said in Lovaritska, "I wish you a long life." He was the first Lovara they encountered since returning to the land that had once been a safe haven to Gypsies of all tribes. Without a further word, the man sat down next to Dzumila by the fire and said, "I can't stay long."

"You've barely arrived," Dzumila said, looking him straight in the face. "What's the rush? And where is our leader? Where is Khantchi? We've had no word of him since we walked into the *Gadje* war. Nor have our elders here who stayed behind in Belarus."

"That's just it," the Lovara said. "I'm here to tell you what to do. Two earlier *kumpaniyi* of your elders told me that you'd be coming, so here I am. Khantchi wants all Lovara to stay away from the bigger villages and towns like Saint Pete. Gypsies are no longer allowed to travel in peace, especially us Lovara. Khantchi has been declared a traitor and a spy. They suspect him of smuggling valuables for some of the elite, the ones afraid to be purged, across the border into the West. They captured him right here near St.Pete. They loaded him on the back of a truck to throw him into jail, but he escaped in the middle of the night. He told me he bribed a guard during a stop in the evening with — get this — a promise of locating and returning with hidden Lovara treasure. They've been looking for him all over the place ever since. "

Dosha had crept close enough to hear. Khantchi was not only the elected King of the Lovara, he was her grandfather. Yet she had never set eyes on him. And whenever, as now, she asked Dzumila, "How come?" Dzumila answered, "Not now. Later, child, you've got to grow up some more."

"What's your name?" Dzumila turned back to the stranger. "What's your *tsera?*"

"Look," the stranger said, "the less you know, the better for the tribe."

Dzumila cast a warning sideward glance toward Dosha, who instead of moving away remained attentive, following their every word.

"Wait till you get up further north," the stranger continued. "It's the devil's climate up there, but you can spot a Bolshevik from far away. Winters, you've got to head back toward the forests along the Finnish border. You'll find plenty of contacts and Gypsies on the lookout over there. Lots of us are hugging that border now. Don't look for Khantchi unless you're in the greatest need. Meanwhile, wait for him to contact you — at least until the dust of this latest war has settled."

After that the stranger, without a further word, got up and walked back to his horse and wagon. The Lovara watched him depart. He waved back, shouting, *"Bachtalo drom! —* Lucky road!"

The next morning, the *kumpania* followed the far side of Lake Ladoga toward Russian Karelia. The great lake stretched ahead of them like an open sea. As much as possible, they pulled their painted caravans and bow-top wagons away from its open shore-line and into the back country along its eastern side, close to the cover of as much forest as they could find. From here, they made forays into small *Gadje* villages to barter. The *romni* traded healing herbs, lace made by women, and baskets made by men for freshly baked bread, as well as grain and hay for their horses. Dzumila, hoping to collect some rubles with which to buy fabric and thread for new clothes, went door to door peddling good fortunes and glimmers of hope to the peasant women. But where once the Russian women had wanted to know about their prospects for success in finding love and achieving wealth, they now asked, "Tell us who will live and who will die."

"Those peasants are living in terror," Dzumila told her *kumpania* upon her return.

They soon found out why. Observing from the edge of a nearby forest, they watched with horror as Soviet soldiers pulled men, women and children out of their houses, loaded them onto open trucks, and hauled them off like sheep.

"We're suddenly called enemies of the people," an old peasant told them. He was walking in the woods with his dog at his side and a rifle across his shoulder. He carried a dead rabbit by its feet.

"Anyone who owns a little something," he told them, "is called a *kulak,* a prosperous landowner now. They're leaving behind only the poorest of the poor."

When they followed the hunter into his village, they found it empty of people. "See?" he said. "They drain our villages of life like a body drained of blood. Russia is hunting down her very own."

The Lovara realized that they were crossing a world different from the one they had left behind. And wherever they wandered, the Red net appeared to be growing tighter, skimming off whatever freedom was still left. Soon they reached areas where life was as poor and meager as mountain grass - the woods and lakes and country lanes of sparsely populated Russian Karelia, its own taiga divided from that of Finland by only a clear-cut strip of no-man's-land, with border towers here and there. At a safe distance from that border, they found the first roadside *patrins,* telling them that other *kumpaniyi* of Lovara were traveling ahead of them and had passed by not long before.

They were back in territory they could trust. No matter that the different *kumpaniyi* still kept a distance from each other and that most of the *patrins,* made of available flowers and branches tied together with tall grasses, all contained white birch, a sign of danger. Often surveillance planes drew circles high up in the air. But the Gypsies knew how to hide. They felt safe, knowing that the Finnish border was only one day's walk away. All they'd have to do to escape to freedom would be to cross that tiny strip of no-man's-land and find one tiny crack in the wooded border that separated them from the West.

Once again, Gypsy life was enveloped by rushing winds and the barking of the half-wild Gypsy dogs, who serve as eyes and ears when Gypsies sleep in their tents or caravans. Spring turned to summer, then back to winter and another spring. Life resumed its accustomed pace, and the change of seasons once again dictated the directions of Lovari travel.

To keep the different *kumpaniyi* connected and informed, Lovari messengers kept moving from traveling camp to traveling camp, and when Javorka told one of them to let Khantchi know that her son Tohen was ready to marry, to her surprise her son left with the next messenger to arrive and returned with a bride. By the following spring he'd erected the first of many bender tents for birthing, away from the camp. The *kumpania* knew a baby had been safely born when one of the *romni* assisting in the birth lit a small fire at the mouth of the birthing tent to keep evil spirits at bay. The whole camp, exuberant, listened to the first cries of the newborn Lovara.

That same spring Dosha's foal started to carry its neck in a powerful arch. He had shed his black coat and was turning white. His ears now perked up when he heard the mating calls of the gentle Gypsy mares, and Dosha, scrawny but tall for her age, had a hard time restraining him with a rope. The foal was four years old now, and Dosha a girl of eleven.

"Look at him," Angar said to Dzumila. "Good breeding stock. Our next crop of horses will be big at last. Look at that neck. Look at him move."

The young stallion had torn loose from Dosha and was cantering circles around the stirred-up mares. Dosha ran after him, angrily waving her arms.

"We should make him into a circus horse," Dzumila said.

"He'd be the best circus horse Russia's High North has ever seen," Angar said. "And if she," he said pointing to the girl with the bright red hair, "is anything like her father, the two together will make magic. You mark my words."

"As long as you remember," Dzumila said, her dark eyes gazing past her *rom* into the distance, "that sticking out above the rest could get us trapped. "

# 5

# A City Gypsy Named Jano

Eight years after they left Poland, Dosha and her stallion were performing as a pair. Instead of returning to the State Circus in Moscow, Angar had put together a small traveling circus of his own, which performed in areas too remote for Soviet central planning to care about.

The group consisted of Tohen, Javorka's son, and two goats performing tricks on a platform placed on top of two folding ladders, a handler and his bear dancing to the sounds of a tambourine, three musicians, and Dosha and her now seventeen-hand rose-gray stallion. To start, Angar had taught the girl to lunge her magnificent stallion in a wide circle on a loose line. With powerful strides, lowered head, and arched neck, the limber stallion cantered with fluid movements to the wild beat of Gypsy music and much applause.

Day after day, Angar trained Dosha and her stallion in the art of circus riding under saddle. "For which," he added, "you also have to learn how to mount a horse as big as he is without a leg up." He showed her how to train the stallion to get down onto his knees by tapping his right front leg; then Dosha was to climb onto his back whispering soothing words, lean back, and, with a clicking of her tongue, signal to the stallion to get back up.

Suddenly — it seemed almost overnight — Angar noticed that the scrawny girl had turned into a dazzling beauty with dark almond eyes and masses of red hair tumbling to her waist. She and her high-stepping stallion danced a melancholy waltz to the soft sounds of Gypsy guitars and violins, pirouetting and seemingly floating above ground as if they were one. At the end of each performance the stallion again dropped onto one knee, and

40

together they bowed to the enthusiastic applause of small audiences of backward peasants and lumberjacks. Dosha had turned into their company's star.

"They think we stole you," Dzumila whispered in her ear. "Just because your skin is white, your hair is red, and you are tall, they think you can't possibly be a Gypsy."

What struck Dzumila above all was that Angar had been so intent on training Dosha that he had failed to notice that the eyes of Stervo the bear-leader, were glued to Dosha instead of to his dancing bear. Once Dzumila caught him looking straight into Dosha's eyes. For a man to look into the face of a Lovari virgin, one not promised him by her elders, was strictly against romani law. That law demanded that he now be chased from the *kumpania*.

"I warned you," Dzumila told her *rom*. "It's no good mixing the tribes."

Unlike the other circus members (including the musicians), who were all of the nomadic *natsia* of Lovara, the owner and trainer of the bear belonged to the *Ursary*, a well-known tribe of bear-handlers, considered by the Lovara to be a lesser *natsia*.

"You know yourself that we lost most of our young men in that war," Angar protested. "I couldn't find anybody else to perform in my circus."

To make things worse, the next day the bear-leader—leading his bear, on all fours, with a chain linked to a ring piercing its nose — walked straight up to the formidable Dzumila and boldly asked that he be granted Dosha as a bride.

"Why?" Dzumila asked. "It's because of her beauty, I bet. When every Lovara knows from early boyhood" — she was close to calling him a fool — "that you can't eat beauty with a spoon. Besides, Dosha and that stallion of hers would hardly fit in with your tribe and all your bears, now would she? How would your tribe feel about your bringing home such a bride, with such a frisky horse?"

The bear-leader said nothing in return. His eyes, deep-set in his swarthy face, kept shifting around like those of his bear. "I'll give you my bear for her," he stuttered in a last attempt.

Dzumila wanted to scream at him. How dare he think of marriage to the only granddaughter of a Lovari king, a girl who all believed was destined one day to be the next female leader of the Lovara? Instead, she demanded, "And what is a Lovara supposed to do with a bear — frighten away our horses? Not only that, but what are you without your bear? I'll tell you what: a man without a livelihood. Besides, Lovara don't sell their girls by asking for a bridal price."

With that Dzumila left the bear-leader standing there, holding his bear, and marched straight to where Angar was tending their horses.

"May the curse eat that bear-leader's liver," Dzumila said. "He has asked for Dosha as his bride. The time," she emphasized, "is overripe for that girl to get hitched before some young fool snatches her away and gets a blood feud going. The girl is strong-willed, too. Having taken care of her mother all these years, she has never been under anyone's control — so far, that is. But now she's fifteen years old. Most Lovari girls her age would have long since been married.

"With her father gone, her mother ailing," Dzumila continued, "I feel this one is for Khantchi to decide, and although he is harder to catch than a shadow, he's still the leader. My other siblings have been cut off from us, somewhere in the rest of Europe, through wars and revolutions. I believe that Dosha is, most likely, the only remaining descendant of a long line of Lovari leaders, both on my father's and my mother Sanija's side. Her marriage is of tribal importance. I bet my father will insist on an alliance with a Lovari *familiya* of high standing."

Angar, who himself was of a lesser Lovari family, knew better than to contradict, let alone advise, his fuming wife. He kept his eyes on the horses, offering no reply.

The next morning the Lovara set out for Russia's Kola Peninsula, where they believed their leader was hiding out among the reindeer herders. At a crossroad near Lake Umbozero, Angar took the now sullen bear-leader aside.

"Our *kumpania* has been called to attend a *kris* on the Northern shores of the Kola Peninsula," Angar informed Stervo, presuming that even a bear-leader had to know that no outsiders were ever allowed to be present at a tribal court of justice.

"I didn't want to tell him," Angar later explained to Dzumila, "that we're cutting him loose because he's making eyes at a Lovari virgin. I thought a lie would be better than a blood feud between our two *natsias*. After all, who knows, they may have different laws. He told me," Angar added wistfully, "that their women, unlike our own, walk three steps behind their men."

42

He waited for Dzumila to be out of earshot, before whispering to himself, "And with that girl's looks, it's lucky there's nobody else sneaking around." He was sure, in any case, that the girl was well aware that, as a Lovari virgin of royal lineage, she'd be within her tribal rights to choose her own mate, elope, and be welcomed back into the clan. Hadn't Dzumila done the same?

At the next major fork in the road leading north, without a word or threat of retribution, the bear-leader split off. He told Angar that he planned to rejoin his own tribe in the forests west of Imandra Lake. His bear, chained to the back of his wagon, ambled behind like a big shaggy dog.

With Dzumila's elaborate caravan in the lead, the Lovara continued on to the high cliffs of the Kola Peninsula's northern shore, then back along the Voronja River in search of Khantchi. Herds of reindeer spilled across the rocky hillsides and the grassy plains. But the Sami herders, their colorful hats and jackets visible atop rocky ledges, made no effort to meet the Gypsy caravan. The nomadic Sami who had in the past, both in the mountains and along the Voronja River, harbored and helped any fellow nomads now exhibited the same avoidance maneuvers that the Gypsies themselves had long employed to avoid feuds between different tribes.

Another arctic winter was about to deprive the harsh land of all means of travel, except by *pulkka*, the traditional reindeer sledge used by the reindeer herders once the plains were buried under masses of snow.

"It's no use," Dzumila said. "We must turn back before the winter buries us alive. Besides," she said to Angar, who was walking ahead of her alongside their harnessed horse, "if Khantchi's among these nomads, he's telling us he doesn't want to be found. Not here, not now. "

By then, although nobody said a word, the members of their *kumpania*, lacking direct contact and guidance from their ultimate leader and king, felt like a body without a head. The dust of war had long since settled, yet Khantchi remained more elusive than ever.

"He's deliberately avoiding us," Dosha said. "My grandfather is respected by all, yet he left my mother in your care since birth. I have never set eyes on him. The time has come for me to know the reason why."

They had just stopped for the night. The horses were unhitched and grazing free. Dzumila was building a fire. "Sit down," she said to Dosha. "Here, by the fire." When others approached, she waved them away, but she then sat silent, for quite some time.

"You'd have to understand the times," Dzumila said at last, the fire highlighting the darkness of her face. "Imagine us Gypsies beloved by the highest in the land! It had never happened before, as long as tribal memory recalls. Yet there they were, Russian counts marrying Gypsy women. One count asked our tribal members if he might adopt Khantchi as his son. It wasn't that unusual: it happened quite a bit, especially if the youngsters had beauty of looks or of voice. It was heartbreaking for the *romni*, their mothers, to leave their children behind as we moved on, and those children, adopted into a life of wealth, watching us from afar, tearless.

"Mind you," Dzumila explained, "We knew all along that the *chavo*"—Gypsy boys—"as soon as they grew a beard felt the call of the road, and were gone. They would want nothing more than return to their own.

"Khantchi happened to be camping with his *kumpania* on the land of the Count and Countess Perzoff — who had loved him as their own — when a messenger told him his adoptive parents were about to be slaughtered by their serfs. My father told me that he hesitated at first, weighing his responsibility toward the people who had loved and protected him against the need to lead his own people to safety. In the end, he ordered his people to disperse, to break up into small groups, but never to leave his very pregnant wife, my mother Sanija, alone until they reached the encampment of his sister Patrina.

"'If I don't help them,'" Khantchi told my mother, "'they'll be slaughtered like the ones before them.'"

Dzumila kept a long silence, staring into the fire. "You have to understand," she said, turning almost in anger toward Dosha, "that in her youth, my mother Sanija, your grandmother, had been famous at the court of the last Czar — first as a singer, later on as a fortune-teller. The courtiers felt that her deep throaty voice reached into the deepest, darkest corners of the Russian soul. Poets at the last czar's court celebrated her beauty, her flaming red hair and dark, dark eyes. Like yours —" Dosha saw tears run down Dzumila's face. "But to us Gypsies," Dzumila whispered, "she was as fierce as any full-grown Gypsy woman. Who could have known she would get separated from her clan? It happened amid all the fighting that was going on around us. We scattered in panic. She almost made it back to us. Almost, that is…. "

Dzumila covered her face with both her hands, "I'll never know what made me turn away from the path we were walking. I'll never know, for there was no noise when I first set eyes on Azra in that dark part of the forest. Our mother Sanija lay curved around her in death. Her face had not turned waxen yet. And your mother was the tiniest baby I had ever seen — so quiet that at first I thought the baby, too, was dead. But then I saw those little lips move, so tiny, so perfect. She must have been born early. It seems my mother's dying powers only lasted long enough to save the infant but not herself. She had severed and tied the baby's navel cord and placed her protectively in the crook of her arm.

"What I never understood and I can't explain to this day is...." — Dzumila once again kept her eyes on the blazing fire — "is whether, with all her psychic powers, her healing hands and flashes of insight, she knew all along that Fate demanded that she die alone in the forest giving birth to Azra. Did she imagine that her death in childbirth, if she did it all alone, would prevent the curse of misfortune that such an event brings down upon a tribe? Look at me — I never had children of my own, and isn't that the worst fate that can befall a *romni*? I don't know the fates of my brothers and sisters who married far away. Was Sanija trying to cheat Fate by stopping short of reaching us, and by not erecting a birthing tent? By giving birth all by herself, did she hope to take the curse onto herself alone?"

Dzumila got up and threw more sticks into the fire. "So now that you are old enough," she said, "do you understand why your grandfather still cannot bring himself to face you? He sacrificed the only woman he ever loved for the lives of two aristocrats whom he led across the border into Finland. They survived. Whereas . . ." Dzumila turned back to Dosha. "Your grandfather feels he is to blame. He went into hiding the minute they covered her grave. He has been leading us and guiding us, but always from afar, moving in and out of camps like a shadow, or simply sending his messengers instead.

"He keeps promising he will return. In the end he will return because of you." Without another word, Dzumila disappeared into her caravan.

As they traveled on the next day, Dzumila made one more gallant effort to track down her father, King of the Lovara. They were near the ancient village of Lovozero, where the Soviets had forcibly settled many Sami nomads years before. There Dzumila took Angar and Tohen aside.

45

"By now he must have gotten news that we're looking for him," she said. "Take this she-goat and barter her for food and pelts. If Khantchi is among the Sami, here or elsewhere, and wants to meet us or send a message, this is his last chance. Winter is too close: we have to leave where we cannot survive. So leave a message. You, Angar, you know some words of Sami — use them! Even if they pretend they don't understand. Let them know that it's about Dosha, Khantchi's last living grandchild, and that if he won't choose a *rom* for her now, he is courting disaster."

Dosha at once withdrew into herself, pondering the meaning of her aunt's message to her grandfather Khantchi. And when Angar and Tohen returned with generous amounts of dried reindeer meat and pelts, but neither news nor message, she felt relief. *If it's just about forcing me to marry,* she thought, *then I'd rather have him stay away.*

The *kumpania* spread out into a half-circle to spend the night. In the morning Angar divided up the reindeer meat and pelts and handed each family their rightful part. Ahead of them, the treeless tundra, dwarfed by an overpowering sky, was aflame with shades of red. Winter was on their heels. They harnessed their horses and lined up to leave. That's when Dosha first set eyes on the Gypsy stranger.

"Look!" She raised her voice for all to hear. A tall and slender young man, darkly clad, looking as ominous as a crow, came walking toward them across the windswept tundra. He wore a dark *Gadje* two-piece suit and black leather shoes to match. Only his long black hair under a wide-brimmed hat betrayed his Gypsy blood. He was holding the hat in place with one hand, his upper body bent over as he walked into the wind.

"What happened to his horse?" Dosha asked her aunt Dzumila, whose caravan was lined up in front of her own. "All he's got is a back-sling with that violin sticking out behind."

"Looks to me like some Gypsy from the city," Dzumila said. "They have no horses. They travel by train, and when there's no train, they walk. Before the *Gadje* war, many of them popped up just like that one, all the way from Moscow to wherever we *diviliyi* Roma — that's what they call us wild Gypsies — were still roaming free. They knew all about our 'Gypsy post.' Especially musicians like himself over there with that violin. They kept telling us that without returning to their roots, their music didn't sound Gypsy anymore."

The stranger had stopped at a distance from the last wagon of the line and respectfully remained there, waiting. Angar handed the long reins of their driving horse to Dzumila and walked up to the stranger. They spoke, gesticulating with their hands, long enough for the rest of the *kumpania* to grow impatient. The horses, each harnessed to a wagon and ready to go, were growing restless. Dosha's stallion pawed the ground.

"*Eh romale!* Heigh Gypsies!" Dzumila shouted at last, beckoning them with a wave.

Angar walked the city Gypsy to the middle of the lineup. "His name is Jano. He is of the *Shevelisti,*" he announced. "They're the ones who settled in Moscow all that time ago."

The stranger had swarthy but unmarred dark skin and sculpted features. His dark eyes were not stinging but soft as feathers. They went from *rom* to *romni,* noting every child and horse, and for a moment they lingered on Dosha's stallion, hitched to the outside of her harnessed horse as a sideliner.

"That looks like no Gypsy horse to me," the stranger said.

"Not born and bred." Dosha's voice was razor-sharp. "But mine nevertheless and therefore Gypsy."

"What news do you bring us?" Dzumila asked.

"The only news I bring you," Jano said, his Lovaritz sounding foreign to the ears of Lovari nomads, "is that the man whose call you followed into the *Gadje* war has died."

"Stalin?" Dzumila asked.

"He died two years ago."

"So?" Dzumila turned toward the others of her *kumpania.* Everybody knew that the Man of Steel was evil, a murderer of his own people.

"We city Gypsies think that Stalin was the last Russian dictator to let the *diviliyi* Gypsies travel with any freedom. The new Russians will hunt not only Khantchi, but all those not settled down. You should stand warned. They're picking up Gypsies, resettling them in far-away collectives, some in cities. They took. . . ." — and here he named whole lists of people and tribes they knew. "You should be careful."

Dzumila shrugged her shoulders and handed the driving reins back to her *rom.* "Where we travel," she said with a dismissive gesture of her hand, "*Gadje* matters, *o del* be thanked, are far away." The caravan started to move on.

Jano, the tall stranger who had blown into their midst like

tumbleweed, casually walked along with them. No one sent him away. Angar assigned him to Javorka's wagon, where he slept next to her one as-yet-unmarried son, Rajko.

Dzumila noted with annoyance that the newcomer cast covert glances at her beautiful niece and her horse. She was relieved, though, to observe that Dosha paid no attention in return.

Crossing the marshy terrain with horses and loaded wagons was difficult and slow. Again and again, the Lovara had to stop to dig out wheels. Rivulets of water veined the sparse bright red vegetation which clung tightly to the soil.

Both Dosha and Dzumila had their hands full taking care of Azra, who had taken a turn for the worse and rarely left the candle-lit semi-darkness of their caravan. Dosha had found blood on two pieces of lace.

"Did you cough this up?" She asked. In reply to her daughter's questioning look, Azra whispered, "I've got this lump in my throat. No matter how hard I swallow, it won't go away. Stay with me," she pleaded. "Don't go away. Whenever I'm alone, I'm afraid I'm going to choke to death on that lump, with nobody near to save me."

Much as she loved her mother, much as she worried about her, Dosha felt imprisoned by her mother's illness.

Winter darkness was closing in on them a little earlier every day. Each night, the Lovara drew their caravans and wagons into a tighter circle to create a barrier from the wind. They unhitched and herded their horses and goats to the inside of the circle to give them shelter and protect them from roaming wolves and arctic foxes. The sweeping winds prevented them from burning outdoor fires now, and the Gypsies stayed inside their traveling homes, where they burned peat to heat and cook, each family on its own little iron stove. The dogs, whimpering and yelping through the stormy night, were the only ones to keep guard outside of the protective circle.

Dosha believed the lump in her mother's throat came from her fear of life, and it was that fear that kept Dosha more and more chained to their caravan and her stallion tied as a sideliner to their driving horse. She felt trapped inside their dark caravan. Only during the early morning, as soon as the sun pierced its own glowing membrane and burst into the sky, did Dosha leave her mother's side. She stepped inside the circle of Gypsy caravans and led her stallion out to face the wind-swept tundra. Holding his mane, she had him bend one knee so that she could jump onto his bare back. As soon as he was up on all fours, the frisky stallion started stepping in place, sensing that this was their moment of freedom. As she lowered her upper body to his mane, the stallion — energized by the howling winds — playfully reared before exploding into the open distance. And Dosha, burying her face in his mane, her body glued to his, gave herself to the power of his flight.

Upon their return, each and every time, she came upon Jano, the *Gadjefied* Lovara, waiting for them. His eyes never seemed to leave her. Whenever she stepped out of the caravan and looked up, he seemed to be nearby. When she walked down to a brook or river to wash her clothing or bathe her horse, he followed her — though always at a respectful distance, with eyes cast down.

No one could have faulted Jano with breaking custom by looking directly into Dosha's face, or talking directly to a Lovari virgin. He seemed to know that such behavior would have been condemned by *romanija,* the Lovari code of morals, and that the men of her *kumpania* would have chased him away — just as they had forced the bear-leader to leave their tribe.

Yet every day Jano loitered outside Azra's wagon until darkness fell, only then retreating to the bow-top wagon of Javorka and her son. Even there, he'd linger, sitting on the steps of Javorka's wagon, his hooded eyes sweeping over Dosha's face and person. Most of the time, before climbing into Javorka's wagon for the night, he'd pick up his violin. His elongated fingers proceeded to pull one string at a time, it produced languishing sounds reaching out with the softness of feathers. However, as soon as he picked up the bow and started to play haunting melodies of eerie beauty, she felt him drift away, into a world she could not fathom.

By day, when the *kumpania* was in motion, Dosha sat at the front of their caravan to drive their two horses. With daylight falling through the side window, Dosha, by simply turning her head, could see her mother's face as she lay motionless on her *dunha,* her Gypsy featherbed, but her mother's eyes, which for so long had been dull and dark as the entrance to a cave now glittered with fever by early afternoon, then died out at night.

"It's the *tchixotka,*" Dzumila said one evening as she stood at the door of the caravan. She raised her dark sculptured face to the blackening sky. "Somewhere along the road she's managed to pick up the curse of the *Gadje.*"

"What does it mean?" Dosha asked, but she knew the answer. She had seen many *Gadje* in remote villages die slow and lingering deaths. No Gypsy herb had ever made a difference.

"They linger on for years," Dzumila murmured. "Year after year the same feverish eyes that die down at night."

Consumption was rare among the nomadic Lovara. But then Azra's frailness was an anomaly among the strong, fierce Lovari women. Azra was the weak link in their chain.

"What about medicine of the *Gadje*?" Dzumila asked Jano, the city Gypsy. After all, hadn't he lived, maybe even grown up, among *Gadje*? "Your hospitals?" she asked.

"We city Gypsies," he said, "go to their doctors and into their hospitals only when we're ready to die, in order not to pollute our city dwellings."

By then they were only one day's journey away from where the taiga rose like a wall, and Azra's life force was fading fast. Every chance she had, Dzumila climbed into their caravan to administer water and *drarnego* — special healing and calming herbs — as Azra hovered between dream and wakefulness. Her mind kept turning back to the war and the dead that lay spread across vast open fields.

"They're standing around my bed in a ghostly circle," she kept whispering. Dzumila took Azra's hand into her own and talked to her as if she were soothing a terrified child.

"She keeps dragging the killer fields behind her like a sheet," Dosha said. "Why can't my mother leave the past behind and walk into the future like all the other Gypsies?"

"They say," Dzumila softly answered, "that a child who loses its mother at birth will never see the full light of the sun. So the whole tribe became her mother. Those who had newborn babies at the time fed her as well. And me, I cuddled her but now I worry that I never allowed her to grow into who a Gypsy woman is meant to be."

# 6
# Call Of The Owl

Lengthening shadows trailed the slow-moving line of caravans and wagons as they climbed the steep rise to the outer edges of the taiga. By then the blood red of the late fall tundra had
bleached into lifelessness. Up on the plateau the ground had hardened. Birch trees stood starkly bare and white against the dense
conifers that created shelter from fast-sweeping winds and the
deepening cold. Winter was about to invade the desolate arctic
vastness with killer force. The soft ground was covered with an
icy crust that gave way under the weight of the passing wagons
and caravans.

To camp for the night, the Lovara chose a marshy clearing
encircled on three sides by dense forest and bordered on the north
by a swift river. Night was falling like a heavy curtain across the
fading glow of the early afternoon sun as the caravans positioned
themselves in the shape of a semi-circle open to the river.

A subtle but distinct physical separation from the rest of the
tribe had gradually evolved between Azra and the rest of the *kumpania*, like the distance that will develop between a dying horse
and its herd. Azra's caravan was securely positioned in the lineup,
but with empty space on both sides. The Lovara walked close to
one another. They spoke in whispers, careful to stay out of earshot of Azra's only child. "Her time has come," they said. "Azra
is dying."

Observing their suddenly secretive behavior, Dosha guessed
their thoughts and words. Eyes flashing belligerence, she walked
up to them and stated out loud: "My mother is not about to die."

Dzumila threw them damning glances, "Hush," she said,
stepping close to Dosha, "Azra could hear."

51

The *rom* and *romni* scattered to prepare for the night. The children fed and watered the goats and geese before walking to the edge of the forest to gather firewood. The *rom* fed and watered their horses, never losing sight of Dosha, who insisted on looking after her own two horses.

Suddenly the stallion snorted, spun around, and stood tense as a bow. Several voices shouted, "Watch out!"

Like a dark, spread-out sail, a silent shape came billowing from the gloomy height of a fir at the edge of the tree line. The stallion's head snapped up. With dilated nostrils, ears pointed forward, the white of its eyes showing in fear, he followed the steep drop of an owl. A few hands above ground, the silvery bird broke flight and hovered for a second or two in place. Eyes gleaming, it swiveled its head from side to side before it flew on with a powerful upswing of its widespread wings, skimming the marshy surface. Reaching the river, the arctic owl slowly, with deliberate control, descended as if to land, its dark claws briefly touching the rushing water. Instead it drew its legs back toward its body with the same slow control and headed downstream in soundless flight, searching for prey.

"*Mulesko chiriklo,*" Dosha whispered, "the bird of death!" She watched the last glimpses of the snow owl's flight reflected in the sudden stillness of her stallion's eye. All eyes were on her. "It's passing us by," she said, "this time." She defiantly looked up into the circle of eyes. In awkward silence, adults and children alike returned to their chores.

The *rom* now started to tie their haltered horses by their lead ropes in circles around some of the bigger nearby trees. This left their hind legs free to strike out should wolves get hungry and move in for an attack. It also prevented them from bolting, should sounds or movements frighten them. Dosha tied her own horses to a tree closer to her caravan.

In the middle of that night the owl returned. Its piercing call woke Dosha from a deep sleep. The haunting screech pressed down on her breath like a choking hand. Gasping for air, she sat upright and opened her eyes. The darkness around her was absolute, as was the absence of noise: not even the dogs were moving about the encampment. Only her mother's raspy breathing reached her from the other side of the caravan. Dosha wondered whether the owl's cry had been a dream. She moved from her own *dunha* over to where her mother lay. There, sitting cross-legged on the floor, awaiting dawn, she listened to Azra's fading life.

At daybreak Dosha left her mother's side to do chores. Closing the caravan door behind her, she fed her two horses and led them to the river to drink, but afterward, instead of harnessing them to the caravan, she tied them again to the tree. Having done that, she walked over to where Dzumila stood talking to the men. Some *rom* had trapped small forest creatures which lay by their feet. The *romni* had lit the fires and were preparing the first meal of the day.

They turned to look at her, Dzumila and the men, their dark eyes collectively focused upon her as if they had been expecting her. Dosha felt the ground beneath her feet start to shift like dunes on a stormy day. "My mother's time has come," she said. The circle of dark faces and questioning eyes fused and started to spin.

"You must," she ordered in a loud voice, "pitch a death tent by the path that has led us to this clearing." Her voice reverberated like an echo. "My mother must die and be buried along the road we've traveled, like any" - she lowered her tone - "true nomad."

Dosha felt her legs starting to give way. One of the *rom* held out an arm as if to catch her should she fall. She straightened up, turned, and walked alone back to her caravan. She sat down in front of the closed door.

Wrapped in eerie stillness, she closed her eyes and waited for the violent storm of her emotions to subside. When she reopened them, the world around her had moved solidly back into place. A short distance away, the *rom* were using stiletto Gypsy knives to cut birch saplings. The women emerged from their caravans and wagons bearing heavy blankets. Together they erected a tent without walls, a sheltering canopy close to the path that had led them here. Their movements were slow, their faces dark.

The tragedy of Azra's birth, when one life was exchanged for another, and the curse it had brought down upon the Khantchisti were about to come full circle. Never would the power of superstition that Azra exerted be greater than at these moments close to her end. For now, the Lovara believed, the spirit or *mulo* of Sanija, the one who in life had been a powerful sorceress, was about to return to reclaim the infant she had left behind. She would hold her people to account for the quality of Azra's life.

Angar, as the *rom baro*, the leader of their *kumpania*, at once sent messengers on horseback to alert as many of Azra's closest kin as were traveling close by. Dzumila and four *romni* entered Azra's caravan with a body-size washbasin filled with warm, salted water. They pulled back the dying Azra's *dunha*, undressed her, and

53

bathed her. She was barely breathing by the time they dressed her in a bright red blouse and five of her finest, most colorful skirts.

Then the somber-faced *romni* stood by her side and waited. They waited until the sun, high in the sky, passed from east to west, marking a dead moment in time, the mysterious hour of noon. The time had come for Dzumila to remove Azra's *dunhas,* the fine featherbeds she had always valued, and for the four *romni* to place the motionless Azra onto a stretcher made of birch and canvas. With slow steps they carried her to the center of the death tent, where candles were burning. Here they gently placed the dying Azra on top of her *dunhas.* This would be the last time Azra would feel the touch of her loved ones, for now that death was near, her dying body was turning *mahrime,* unclean to the touch.

Fires were lit, small ones inside, larger stick fires outside. The whole *kumpania* gathered around the death tent to eat and drink. The rom sat down in circles to play cards and talk about horses. The *romni* moved about as usual, serving their men and children food and drink, until they too sat down to eat and talk about their everyday concerns: the conserving and storing of food, the need to find brides first thing next spring, before the *kumpania* headed back north. All kept their voices low. They were careful not to show too much emotion, so as to keep panic at bay and ease Azra's slow transition into the other world. Those around her feared that one whose life force had been weak would return as a *mulo*—a spirit — of great strength and take revenge on her kin for a life not fully lived.

Azra's death throes proved long and agonizing. Attacks of coughing wracked her emaciated body, until there seemed to be not enough life force left in her either to keep the spirit from escaping her battered body or to expel it and end her agony. Forbidden to touch her dying mother, Dosha picked up Angar's *rom baro* chair, the one made of twisted branches, with both her hands. Hoping to use it as a conduit, she tried to transfer some of her own vitality into her mother in a last attempt to hold off, for just a few moments more, the impending loss.

To everyone's surprise, Azra grabbed on to the other leg of the chair with one hand and pulled herself up. Her eyes flew open and for a moment fastened on her daughter. But just as quickly she relaxed her hold on the chair, and her frail hand slid away as she fell back. Dosha lowered her eyes and rose to her feet. Still holding the chair, she turned and gently placed it onto the stick fire just outside. For a moment she remained standing there, her face bathed in the flickering reflections of fire, and watched the chair burn. *"Akana mukav tut le Devlesa,"* she whispered, lifting her face to the dimly moonlit sky. "I now leave you to the will of God.

"Diana," she prayed, half-walking, half-running away from the death tent, "goddess of the nomads, help my mother's spirit free itself from her tormented body.

"Forgive me, Diana" — she continued to flee, still praying — "for leaving my mother in the hands of my tribe for these last few moments." She knew that she had to leave with an image of her mother still alive in order to face a future without her. *Or else,* she thought, *her image will mingle with the masses of all the nameless dead spread across those killer fields that never let go of her.*

An arctic chill was in the air and the moon was shrouded in gray when she returned to their caravan. She doused the fire still burning within their pot-bellied stove, but lit a candle and placed it on a shelf by the open door. An unbearable fatigue hollowed out her mind and body, as she sat down, cross-legged facing the open door and the night outside. It was as if instead of transferring her own life force to her mother, she had absorbed the heavy burden her mother had dragged along all of her life.

Images of stories told by fellow Lovara arose in her mind - of thousands of German soldiers trapped in the drifting snows of the Russian plains. After days of marching they had lain down at last, she had been told, surrendering to the sleep forced upon them by snow and ice, never to wake up again. *If only,* she thought, *I could die like that, just bed down in snow and ice, never to awake again.*

That's when, for the first time Jano, the Gadjefied Lovara, walked up the steps and sat down, partially blocking the entrance to her caravan. In the flickering light of the lone candle, his face and dark curly hair were a contrast of black and light. *He has the face,* she thought, *of a Christ suffering on a Gadje cross. Only his is the face of one of us.*

"Why do they leave you alone like this?" The warmth in his voice penetrated her numbness.

"I am supposed to follow in my grandfather Khantchi's footsteps. Like him, I must be strong. They would not have told you, but my mother was the carrier of a curse," Dosha said, fighting back the tears that suddenly rose to her eyes. "Because of her, her own mother - my grandmother Sanija—had to die."

"They still talk about Sanija in Moscow," Jano said. "She is still famous among the singers and the dancers, both in Moscow and in Saint Pete. They remember her as the *romni* with the flaming hair."

"Here, if they hear you speak about the dead, they'll chase you away," she said. Only in rare circumstances, and then only to clarify mysteries, did nomadic Gypsies mention the lives of their dead.

Silence surrounded them, except for the *detlene* — the black wind of winter called forth by the spirits of dead Gypsy children — that howled and blew through the cracks of her caravan. She wondered whether the Gadjefied Gypsy knew about the origin of the *detlene*. It blew out the candle, leaving them in the dark.

Suddenly the loud lamentations and wails of the Lovara rose and mingled with the rushing of the winds. The Gypsy dogs started their nocturnal baying as the wailing of the mourners turned into rhythmic chants.

"My mother's spirit will soon pass into the world of the *mulo*," said Dosha standing up. "The curse has died."

Jano respectfully rose as she walked past. He watched her disappear behind the dark wall of the forest, toward the tree where her horses were tied. She must have untied them both, because he heard all of them walk off into the night.

But he would not leave her be alone. *Not tonight*, he thought as he followed her, *even if they end up chasing me away.*

Fires were kept burning through the night: their rising flames fingering the darkness. The Lovara believe that death does not fully enter a person's body for three days, and that during that time the spirit of the deceased lingers among its own. Although Azra's face was turning waxen, her dark hair still looked alive. The *romni* rushed to cover all mirrors in their caravans, lest her spirit would use it as a shelter and linger. The *rom* led all the horses, goats and dogs to a small clearing hidden from the death site, to prevent the departing spirit from possessing one of them and start haunting and taking revenge on the living left behind.

Once these tasks were done, the Lovara gathered close and cried out words of love and reassurance to this lingering spirit as it prepared to embark on its last trek across the river of shades to enter the land of the dead — a happier world. One after the other, one at a time, they asked for forgiveness for any harm done or offense given.

The night gave way to a gray winter's day, and caravans of kin and friends started to arrive into the marshy clearing that was

about to turn into a Lovari burial site. The newly arrived caravans positioned themselves in an arc within the arc of those already there. A killer frost the night before had turned the clearing
hard as stone. The newcomers unhitched their horses, fed and watered them, then followed Angar a short distance away from the
mourning site, where they too tied their horses in defensive circles
around several free-standing trees.

By the third day of the wake, more than thirty caravans were
bivouacked near the makeshift death tent. Among the last to arrive was an oversized caravan decorated with gilded images of
horses, twirling vines, and scenes of Gypsy life painted against
a background of lacquered red. Instead of the usual single harnessed horse, it was pulled by a magnificent pair of brown-and-
white paints. Dzumila hoped and prayed that it was Khantchi, arriving for the wake of his seventh daughter, but it was the caravan
of his sister Patrina instead, the *phuri dai*, their tribal mother and
queen of the Lovara. *I suppose,* Dosha consoled herself, *it's because
he was too far away.*

Angar had told Dzumila that one of the messengers he had
sent out when Azra lay dying had returned with news that her
father had been in contact with Djemo, his former son-in-law,
way up north, between the Kola Peninsula and the Finnish border. Djemo, the messenger had informed Angar, was running an
unofficial collective farm that also served as winter quarters for a
small traveling circus.

Patrina's caravan, as well as twenty others making up her
large *kumpania*, drew up on the other side of the path that bordered the death tent, away from the other mourners. The *rom* tied
their horses, however, among the other horses. Young unmarried
girls, with loose hair falling down their backs, kept small children in line and lit fires for cooking, setting up tripods for pots
and pans.

A group of young men now detached themselves from these
latest arrivals and slowly approached the mourners, who had not
touched food, nor washed, nor combed their hair since the closing
of Azra's eyes. Men with bloodshot eyes kept on drowning their
loudly proclaimed pain in home-brewed vodka. The children were
clamoring for food other than the dry bread and cold meat they'd
been fed. The woman's combined wailing rose and fell. Jovarka's
high-pitched voice rang out above the others'. "We've lost the one
we loved most in life. . . ." Jovarka, who had been part of Azra's
life since the days of war, improvised a song about the life and fate

of the Lovari *romni* whose sun had been eclipsed at birth. "Hers was the beautiful and tragic face of *romanija* . . ." Her haunting voice slithered though the relentless wailing and clamoring like a snake through high grass. "Azraaaaaa . . ."

The young men from Patrina's *kumpania*, their loose pants stuck into dusty but fine leather boots, carried a rolled-up rug and spread it across the frozen path toward the candle-lit death tent. The tent itself was packed with mourners, both men and women. Four *romni* had, without touching Azra, lifted her up by picking up the four corners of her *dunha*, and placed her into an open casket made of branches. They had covered her chest with a yellow shroud and remained standing on either side of the casket, shielding her body.

Dzumila stood up. All songs, all laments ceased. The mourners fell silent as she approached her departed sister. Protected from pollution by the dead through her powers as sorceress and *drabarni*, healer of the sick, she started her own prayer. Chanting ancient words, she lovingly closed her younger sister's eyes. For a moment she stood still, and then she pulled out one of Azra's hands from underneath the shroud. Her face a map of pain, Dzumila proceeded to break her sister's little finger. Tears were running down her cheeks as she tied a piece of gold with a red ribbon to the broken knuckle. "To pay your passage," she intoned, "across the river of shades into the happier world of the dead."

At once the *borja*, the young brides of Patrina's *kumpania*, who had stood waiting on the other side of the path, approached carrying an ornate armchair made of twisted and interwoven tree branches and placed it in front of the body, now fully prepared for burial. The young brides were dressed in the colorful skirts of their tribe, and their hair was tied back with scarves, indicating their married status. They in turn were followed by the tiny *phuri dai*, Patrina, who, with the help of a silver-headed cane, walked slowly but erect from her camped caravan toward the assembled mourners. Whatever hair was not covered by her head scarf had turned a steely gray, and her weathered skin clung to her sharp features like ancient papyrus. Long, gold earrings dropped past her shoulders down to her frail chest, which was wrapped in many layers of Orenburg shawls, woven of the finest angora wool, to keep her warm.

For a moment, as Patrina seated herself on the ornate chair, the wailing that had resumed, stopped. Once again the Lovara were paying tribute to their wise female leader, tribal mother and advisor to thousands of traveling families. Children were the first to gather around Patrina, albeit at a respectful distance. Adults stepped aside to keep open a view of the shrouded body.

The old woman sat still, as if the short walk had taxed her frail body and she had to catch her breath. Her dark eyes, by contrast, were intense and piercing. She took in every detail of her surroundings.

"Dosha!" she uttered. "Where is Azra's only child?"

At once Dzumila, who had been standing beside her dead sister's head, walked over to her aunt, took Patrina's tiny, bony hand into her own, and brought it to her lips.

"The girl," she said "left her mother's side shortly before she died. She has not come near since. She's out there," Dzumila said, pointing to the far edge of the woods. "She walked into the night to be with her stallion and that other horse of hers. I believe she doesn't want to see her mother's face in death, that she needs her mother's image kept alive. Nor does she want to leave her horses, especially her stallion, in anybody else's care, since they're all that is left to her now. So instead of joining the mourning, I'm told she's keeping an eye on all the other horses as well. She keeps adding oats to their feedbags and watering them, all day and into the night, with no fire nearby.

"The girl," Dzumila whispered, leaning toward the old woman's ear, "does not fear the *mulo*. Worse, she appears to feel safe within their midst. It is rumored that when times are perilous, it is the *mulo* she calls upon for help. There are no witnesses to these instances, but many within the tribe think she has the sight. They tell me she has the power of a sorceress, though she's only fifteen years of age."

Patrina pensively waved a hand in the direction of the *borja* who had brought her chair and now stood clumped together close by. One from among them hurried to their queen with a stubby little pipe, already lit, and placed it into Patrina's eager hand. The old woman closed her eyes, drew deeply from the smoldering pipe, and as she exhaled wispy white smoke, she let her body relax deep into the ornate chair. She released her grip on her shawls, exposing her array of heavy gold coin necklaces.

"And who," Patrina asked, "is watching over her? Who is watching over Dosha?"

Dzumila then told Patrina about Jano, the Gadjefied Lovara. "He says he used to be an actor and a musician at the Teatr Roman in Moscow — you know the one that's famous among the new rulers of Russia? He's the one keeping watch over the girl. Always at a respectful distance, of course," Dzumila assured the *phuri dai.* "For, although he comes from the city, he is Lovara, he knows the rules."

Patrina lifted her sharp eyes to the edge of the forest beyond the death tent, where she saw neither human nor horse. In her mind's eye she conjured up the image of Dosha when she was still a little girl, back in Poland behind enemy lines — the way they had dressed her to look like a little Polish peasant girl. They had braided her reddish-blond hair into two tresses with ribbons at the end. Larkin, the half-Gypsy and her adopted son, the one who could read and write, had told her the girl looked so *Gadje* that nobody would ever suspect her of working for Gypsy spies. He had given Azra rolled-up messages to braid into Dosha's hair, so that she could carry them out of the forest to where the partisan groups operated in populated areas.

Patrina herself had impressed upon the child that, if asked by *Gadje,* she should say her name was Ana. The name, like her looks and dress, could have been Polish or German and was meant to safeguard her little grand niece from capture and evil. "In reality," Patrina remembered telling the little girl, "Ana is the name of the beautiful queen of the Good Fairies, the *Kelshalyi.* They live in a secluded palace high in the mountains. Nobody can reach them there."

Of all the children, Gypsy or Russian, whom the partisans had trained to act as runners, Dosha had proven to be the best — except for one day when something went badly wrong and she did not return from her run. The *kumpania* had searched for her as extensively as they could, all through the forest. Their search efforts had been highly dangerous but had proven useless. At the end of the day it was one of the Gypsy dogs, zigzagging in and out of the forest, who caught their attention with his anxious barking. Patrina had followed the dog out of the forest, and found the child lying as if lifeless in a pile of leaves by the side of the road, only a mile from the towers of a concentration camp. Patrina had bent down and placed her cheek close to the little girl's mouth. Her breath was faint, but she was alive.

Back in their forest encampment, Azra examined her child's body carefully. She found no signs of sexual assault, although bruises covered Dosha's body. She had been kicked and beaten. Mercifully, the little girl had no memory of what happened, except for "that dream — a very strange dream," she kept whispering. Nobody insisted on further details, believing that the dream offered protection from the memory of the trauma she had lived through.

Dosha recovered from the ordeal, but the incident sent her mother even deeper into her world of inner darkness. More and more, Azra refused to allow the girl to leave her side. *Azra kept her only child buried alive,* Patrina thought. *And out of superstition we went along. We sacrificed the girl.*

"The dark sadness of Azra's life is lifted now," Patrina said, watching a pale winter sun start to emerge from beyond the taiga to the East. The time had come to place Azra onto a bier and carry her to a grave dug at some distance alongside the trail.

As violins, tambourines, and cymbals struck up the slow and deeply emotional funeral march, Dosha decided to return to her people. She tied her stallion and her other horse loosely to a tree and slowly walked toward the procession that had started to form. She could hear friends and kin, who had answered the call to attend, start up the chorus of funeral chants. Their voices rose in intuitive harmony, blending with the instruments, as if they shared the same soul, as if none of them had ever been apart.

The mourners walked in scattered groups, holding on to each other as they followed the band, some leading their children, others helping along crippled elders. Amid a distinct break in the procession, Dosha noticed a tiny old woman walking slowly, apart from the rest. That's when Dosha recognized her great-aunt and adoptive grandmother, Patrina. She had not seen her since the Gypsy partisans had broken into separate *kumpaniyi* eight years before in Poland, after the defeat of the German army.

In a sudden rush of joy she started to run toward the old woman, shouting, "*Mami, mami!*"

Patrina turned in the direction of the voice. With narrowed eyes she watched a breathtakingly beautiful girl, with masses of fiery red hair wildly waving about her light-skinned face, running toward her. The strong arctic wind pasted Dosha's skirts to her strong, young body, tall by Lovari standards. Patrina froze in place. It was as if a cold hand had plunged into her chest and grabbed her heart. For there stood the specter of her beloved sister-in-law Sanija, returned to life. The approaching girl was closely followed by a tall and slender young man dressed in the ill-fitting garment of a *Gadje*. He wore no hat and his dark, curly hair fell down to his shoulders; the wind blew it away from his dark Gypsy face.

*"Mami!"* Dosha swept the tiny elder up into her arms. "It's me, Dosha!" Looking lovingly into Patrina's eyes, she paused. "My mother never did find the promised happiness on the other side of the war," Dosha said as she gently placed the old woman back onto her feet.

Patrina's piercing gaze remained on the girl's face. "Azra was doomed from birth," she said. "There was to be no happiness for her in this life, except in her love for you. How she loved you! " And with that she took both of the girl's hands into her own.

The music had stopped as the Lovara of the Khantchisti clan watched the reunion between the *phuri dai* of all the Lovara and the orphaned girl. Soon the music struck up again, dragging like heavy footsteps, reflecting the somber occasion.

Dosha was swept up in the communal mood. As they approached the grave site, women came to hug and embrace her like someone just returned from exile. But unlike them, Dosha could not break the seal to her grief and cry — not even when the mourners started to drop earth and mementos they believed would soften the separation of Azra's spirit from the living. Not even when Dosha herself took a gold chain from her neck, kissed it, and dropped it into the grave.

Jano had joined the men and the drinking. Their hoarse voices, evoking the gods, cried out: "Why her? Why not us? Why not me?" They poured some of the vodka they had been drinking into the grave as it continued to fill up with earth and mementos for Azra's ultimate journey ahead. They sang and recited beautiful Gypsy poems, some of which were composed for just that day and would be forgotten by the end of it — forgotten like the name of the deceased and the location of the grave.

All along, the men and women of the Khantchisti kept talking to the spirit that they believed still lingered all through the *pomana*, the abundant funeral meal prepared by the *borja*, the young brides, back at the encampment. This was the first good food the Lovara had eaten in days, and it was plentiful - goose and chicken served in aspic and cooked nettles and cabbage and potatoes - the first signs of the return of joy into their lives.

Throughout the burial and the ensuing feast, Dosha held on to Patrina's tiny hand, breakable as a chicken bone, as if it alone had the power to pull her out of the cocoon of isolation that her mother's illness had so tightly woven around her. She held on to this link to safety until it was time to burn Azra's caravan, her *vurdon*, and feed all her belongings to the purifying flames. For only fire can destroy the last links to the living and prevent the return of the dreaded *mulo*, the ghost of the departed.

Night had fallen when the *rom* pulled Azra's caravan onto a knoll at the edge of the clearing. They circled the painted home with burning torches, and then they tossed them inside to set the caravan ablaze. Dosha let go of Patrina's hand and approached the fast-spreading fire that burned through the outer shell of the *vurdon*, until all that was left was its skeleton, glowing like the grid of a cage inhabited by flames. Dosha's past was engulfed in fire. The force of the blaze sent the roaring *vurdon* rolling down the knoll toward the swift river at the bottom of the clearing, where it slowly sank in the water, broke apart, and was swept away.

Dosha tried to conjure up her mother's face, without the deep lines that illness and suffering had left behind. But her mother's features had started to dissipate, as did the memory of her presence, growing as weak as her life force had been. Her mother's face was so unlike that other face — the mirror image of herself, the grandmother whom she knew only from the photograph that Dzumila always kept on a wooden ledge in her *vurdon* next to where she slept. Dosha shook her head. How strange to sense the face of her mother already starting to fade, yet to remember so clearly the face that had appeared to her only once, an image in a dream on that momentous day when the Germans had captured her.

That morning, she had just returned from a partisan hideout near a village. Once back in the forest, she walked along a lumber road instead of sticking to the dense underbrush as she'd been told to do. She heard the motor of a truck she could not yet see. The lumbering road was curvy, so, hoping to avoid detection, she dove into the forest toward thicker underbrush, but the truck had caught up with her. With a backward glance she saw three Nazi soldiers jump out of its cab and make straight for her. Cowering in fear behind a bush, she remembered hands grabbing her by her hair and pulling her to her feet. They shouted German words at her that she couldn't understand, except for "*Partisanen.*" With fuming expressions, they were slapping her face. A boot came up toward her . . .

When she woke she found herself flat on her back on a flatbed wagon. She tried to open her eyes, but her lids were caked shut with dried blood. Opening them a tiny crack, she realized that there were others, some sitting, huddled, some seemingly lifeless on the floor of the wagon. She crawled to the edge of the flatbed, stuck her head beyond the rim, and caught a glimpse of what she took to be a concentration camp, bounded by a high wire fence.

She was losing strength. She was barely able to pull her head back onto the wooden planks, where it fell onto the floor of the flatbed. Her mind struggled to remain in its state of semi-consciousness, only to sink back into the dark inertness she had just escaped, where her grandmother, Sanija, stepped into her vision, as clear as life.

"*You must not linger here.*" Dosha's floating mind tried hard to capture the words by trailing the movements of Sanija's lips. "*Return to your body lying there amidst the others. They are on their way to death.*" Sanija's voice grew strong and immediate: "*You must will your body to roll off the side of this wagon. Now!*" she commanded. "*And crawl silently into that forest by the side of this road!*" — Where Dosha woke once again with the dog sniffing her face and Patrina staring into her eyes.

For a moment Dosha remained atop the knoll as her mother's burning *vurdon* was engulfed by the river, mesmerized. Crests of smoke lingered where the burning caravan finally sank and disappeared. Within the curls of wispy smoke the diaphanous images of Azra and Sanija intertwined themselves, whirling together in a tender dance high and higher into the nightly sky.

For a moment Dosha felt a surge of joy and hope. Her mother's *mulo*, the spirit her people feared would return and take revenge for a life not lived, was pacified at last. It would not return. In death Azra was reunited with the mother she had missed all her life. But no fire would ever burn their ties to the one they had left behind. *They'll be by my side forever*, Dosha thought. *They will guide me on the road ahead.*

The other mourners had long since returned to their wagons and fires, leaving only Dosha and Jano standing by the river. The night felt hollow, a vast emptiness magnified by the rush of the river.

"What now?" Jano asked. "Who will you travel with now?"

"Patrina," Dosha said. "She's my great-aunt. If I were to travel with Dzumila, it would only keep reminding her of my mother's death. She has always thought of my mother as her child, her only child. I still have my father as well, although I haven't seen him since the end of the war."

"What happened?"

"He's living with a *Gadji*," she said, "way up North. One of our messengers just told us."

Dosha wondered whether Jano, a city Gypsy, knew of the seriousness of what was considered among nomadic Gypsies a betrayal of the tribe, taking a *Gadji* for wife or mate. She could barely make out his face in the falling darkness. Racing clouds chased each other across the sliver of a moon, so that the faint beams of moonlight came and went. Jano's eyes were lowered, and he remained silent. She was getting used to his quiet presence.

"Why are you really here?" she asked.

When he did not answer, Dosha shrugged in annoyance and started to walk toward the circle of fires, where adults and children alike could be seen moving about. The Lovara were getting ready to bed down for the night.

Jano turned and fell into step alongside her, his eyes shooting discreet glances. He knew that she was fifteen, an age when most Gypsy girls are already married and often with child. She was tall, a striking beauty with eyes that seemed too knowing for one so young. But even a city Gypsy knew that for a nomad, safety lies in knowing the dangers of life as early as possible.

"I'm like Khantchi," he said at last, "fleeing authorities. Worse, like your father, I have crossed the forbidden line and become involved with a *Gadji*. Only this one," he added, "happens to be the daughter of a high-ranking Soviet apparatchik.

"A big Russian woman," he continued after a pause. "She thinks of us *tzigani* as wild and romantic. She considers her Russian compatriots pigs, wallowing in abuse, of their women, of those in their service."

In the faint moonlight, Jano searched Dosha's eyes for a reaction, even though he knew that in looking a Lovari virgin straight in the face, he was crossing another forbidden line. She seemed not to care, although her expression remained inscrutable. How could he explain to this girl, whom the *Gadje* would still consider a child, that this Bolshevik woman had given herself to him without restraint, believing that she would share his romanticized stage version of Gypsy life forever?

"Worst of all, she started to divulge all sorts of official secrets concerning the future of us Gypsies," he said. "She described, in detail, their plans to throw the Red net right across the paths of those of us still roaming free — haul us into their Soviet cages just like everybody else. And when she felt me starting to withdraw, and it became clear I had no intention of staying with her, she turned against me. I was about to be denounced and shipped off to some *gulag*."

The circle of fires threw light and warmth their way. Dosha stopped on the path, reading Jano's face.

"Now that I have spent some time living the life of my ancestors," he continued, "I am ashamed of what I've done. Sooner or later they'll track me down, and I'd be putting your whole tribe in danger. The problem is, I have never learned to survive on the open road alone."

Living in close quarters, surrounded by a world hostile to most Roma, Dosha had not been spared either the realities of life between a man and a woman, or the lure of deceptive *Gadje* claims of offering Gypsies a better life. She had no choice but to grow up fast. And Dzumila had warned her, early on, that many *rom* fooled around with *Gadje* women. Some even married them, despite the threat of expulsion from the clans. What Dosha couldn't fathom was that Jano, who spoke like a Lovara and looked like one, would be afraid to travel the road alone.

She studied the Gadjefied Gypsy's face and demeanor with much care and decided that she, too, would confess her fears. "Now that my mother is dead," she said, "I don't think it will take my father long to come and claim me. I'm his only daughter and of marriageable age. To increase his own power in the tribe, he would insist on my marrying a Lovara of high standing in the tribe, whether I wanted to or not. Only Khantchi could prevent him from starting such marriage negotiations, which would be in his interest, not mine.

"But as usual," she added with bitter disappointment, "Khantchi is nowhere to be seen. I know our customs and our laws," she went on. "I know well the power struggle that will follow when either he or Patrina die. I'll become a trump card for anybody who wants to become the future leader of traveling Lovara, here in Russia and abroad."

Without a further word, she turned away from Jano and walked ahead to where the various *kumpaniyi* had stationed themselves. The Lovara were busy packing for the next day's journey: they were ready to leave this sight of mourning. Women and young girls were carrying *dunhas* that had been left out to air, back into the caravans. They placed the cooking tripods, pots, and pans, into wooden boxes which they attached to the underbellies of the wagons. Wash was being taken off lines strung between the caravans, before the lines themselves were brought down. Dogs scavenged for leftover food by the fires. The men were tending to the

horses that had been brought back into the vicinity of their owners. Dosha noticed her own stallion attached by a lead to Patrina's
gilded caravan. Sitting by a fire in front, Patrina beckoned Dosha
to come and join her.

Dosha turned once more to Jano, who still followed close behind. "If only I could take my horse and leave all this behind for a
while," she said, "just until I'm healed."

A shaggy black-and-white dog came toward them in a low
crouching walk. Dosha noticed Jano tense up. She looked at him,
surprised. "We don't have dogs in the city," he said, embarrassed.

"That particular dog is more attached to me than to the pack,"
Dosha said, "I found him in the woods when he was only a pup."
*He is stalking Janos as he would an outsider,* she thought, *not one of
us.*

"You could leave with me," that outsider said.

"As friends?" she asked, looking up.

Jano looked straight into her eyes. She noticed that his features contained none of the quick grasp, the restless impatience
and diffidence of a Lovari leader.

"However you would like it," he whispered. "Only," he added, "it'll have to look like an elopement. Otherwise, between the
Bolsheviks pursuing me because I know too much, and the Lovara
intent on punishing the abductor of a virgin of royal blood, I'd
have no place left to hide."

Dosha watched as Patrina talked to two men of her *kumpania;* she was pointing in Dosha's direction. Soon, Dosha realized, her conversation with the stranger would have to come to
an abrupt end. Eloping was an accepted way for Lovara to marry.
If they pretended to elope, they could actually kill two birds with
one stone.

"All right," she agreed, speaking softly. "An elopement will
avoid a marriage arranged by my father, and if we go north, it may
help take you out of Bolshevik reach.

Speaking more firmly, she added one proviso: "But the marriage has to remain a pretense."

To marry was every Gypsy girl's fondest dream. But for
Dosha, who had witnessed her parents' loveless marriage, that
dream had turned into a nightmare.

Patrina's men were almost upon them when Dosha whispered
in parting, "Watch the road we'll take tomorrow. Watch it carefully. At the first fork, the different *kumpaniyi* will separate back

to the trails they were traveling before. Take note of that fork in the road, get off right there, or else walk back to it after everyone's asleep. Then wait for me."

Dosha followed Patrina's men back to the *phuri dai*'s gilded caravan, where she was to spend the night.

Before the morning light had fully broken, the *rom* hitched their horses back onto their caravans, ready to leave their grief behind and return to the concerns of the living.

Soon the raging *detlene*, merging with the black wind of the High North, would sweep away all evidence that the Lovara had ever crossed that way. Only pieces of broken birch, a symbol of sorrow, tied with long grasses at eye level along the edge of the taiga would tell any *rom* who followed that a burial ceremony had taken place there, and which direction the mourners had then taken.

# 7

# Into The Arctic Night

The cold, alien light of a starlit arctic sky fell through the small window in front of the caravan, bouncing off the silver of the ancient tribal samovar and highlighting the fine china secured on low shelves along one wall. The crystal light framed the dark mass of a low table and extra bedding piled up along both sides of the room and dissolved into the small square of fire around the iron door of the pot-bellied stove, which dominated the long and narrow space.

Patrina's *kumpania* had put the greatest possible distance between the site of mourning and the life ahead. After a proper meal Dosha and Patrina bedded down. Dosha lay for a while watching with great tenderness the tiny shape of Patrina as she slept in close proximity to the stove. *In sleep,* she thought, *our powerful* phuri dai *looks like any other Lovari elder.* After a time Dosha rose. As noiselessly as possible she tied a few provisions and personal possessions into a scarf, and stood at the door, ready to leave but the sight of the sleeping Patrina held her back. She felt tied to her past like a horse to a tree. *Only,* she decided, *if I don't break free now, my life will be nipped in the bud like my mother's, never fully to bloom.*

The stallion's nickering reached her from outside, and she thought of Jano waiting back at the first fork in the road. Resolutely she reached for the latch of the door, when the sound of her name, "Dosha," took her hand off the iron lever. She swung around and saw the old woman emerge from her *dunhas.*

"I wondered how long it would take you to finally say good-by," Patrina said, rising to a sitting position. She picked up a stick next to her bedding on the floor, leaned over, and with it opened the latch to the door of the pot-bellied stove. As the flames leapt higher, she used the wooden stick to light her pipe. Then blowing out the feathery flame, she re-latched the door.

"From the way you kept watching me sleep, one would think you'd never see me again," she said, blowing a curl of smoke into the semi-darkness of the caravan. "Just because you don't see me stirring up much dust, doesn't mean I can't kick anymore. Besides . . ." Patrina looked lovingly at the girl who, both by heart and by tribal custom, she considered her own. Gypsy children belong to the tribe and the war had taken all but one of the children Patrina had given birth to.

"Besides," she continued, "has Patrina ever prevented anyone from leaving? Especially you, of whom I have known since birth that it is your destiny to fly alone, at least for part of your life. But, mark my words, a true Gypsy will always return in the end. As to the man, the one who is waiting for you somewhere back there? I trust him to protect you while you find your way, but he is not for one like you. Sooner or later you will have to leave him and lead your people. I know lots about him through his kin, the Shevelisti. His clan was lured to the city generations ago, musicians and singers all of them. They are who they are. Though in him I do pick up an additional weakness, that, were he to travel with us, could endanger us all. Above all, you must not carry his child. I will give you herbs to chew. They will prevent you from being tied to him at least for the time being."

"But," Dosha protested, "I am not getting hitched. It is not going to be a marriage in the true sense."

Patrina took several quick drags from her pipe, until it glowed like burning grass. "Youth talks with the body," she said. "Always has, always will. Yours is not different from the rest." She rummaged on a shelf. "Take this."

Dosha took and opened the little pouch and held it to her nose. The mixture of herbs smelled of mold and old hay. Used to the peremptory behavior of tribal elders, and just as equally used to ignoring what she did not want to hear or do, she was nevertheless surprised that Patrina would encourage her to carry these means to be without child. Their use, although a valuable means of barter with *Gadje*, was strictly forbidden by romani law for Gypsy women themselves.

"I talked to your man," Patrina said. "Did you know he reads books?"

Dosha was startled. "Books?"

"That's what he carries in those blankets he keeps so close,

*Gadje* books. Don't worry. Some Lovara believe the written word corrupts the purity of the Gypsy mind, but that's sheer superstition. In truth, it's just another way to stay up on news. He told me what, unbeknownst to him, I already knew. Times for us Roma are about to turn dangerous here in Russia. There will be no more protection for us as in the past, when the aristocrats pampered us like pets. They loved our dances, our music. They bought our finest horses. Even the first Bolsheviks let us be. But now, this newest chief—rumors run that he will grind us down like common wheat, trying to mix us with the Russians. I say it's nothing but an excuse to take away not only our gold, but our horses as well. He's trying to put a halt to our romani way of life.

"They, as always," she added, "will call it 'settling' us, 'furthering our rights.' Equal opportunities for all! Big words! Don't believe any of it," Patrina said. Then, in a softer tone of voice, she added, "they don't understand. It is us Roma who are God's most beloved children. We were brought into this world to spread cheer and happiness. Like birds we were meant to move in freedom and it is true, you take our freedom away, we look like birds trapped in dirty cages. I've seen it all over Europe. Tribes trapped in the *Gadje* way of life resort to stealing and begging just to survive and now it will happen here as well. You see Khantchi, your grandfather. . ."

"Who never came to hold my mother's hand, his own daughter's, not in all her suffering," Dosha interrupted bitterly.

"Come come," Patrina said, "you have to understand, you're grown up now, that to your grandfather facing your mother was reliving Sanija's death over and over again. They had loved each other since they were children. Sanija pined away the years he lived with the countess. He returned to his tribe as soon as he was old enough to claim her as his wife. But you — my brother told me himself — you will bring him back to where he — ... "

"Khantchi has never even set eyes on me."

"He has followed every step of your life though. He believes that, just as the birth of your mother brought a curse upon his tribe, you will bring luck and health, *baxt and sastimas,* back to us."

For a moment the old woman sat still and ancient, sucking on her pipe. Dosha impatiently bent over to kiss the frail elder good-bye.

"Not yet." Patrina once again stopped her in her track. "There is the matter of the Ursitory,"

"Another legend, *Mami*?" Dosha grew increasingly impatient, ready to tear open the front of the caravan, let in the pure night air and escape Gypsy life and fire caged inside their caravans for winter, with all the stifling superstitions and confining legends spinning around them like cocoons.

Patrina, however, was used to handling hot-headed Gypsies, especially when confined. "Hear me out," she continued without a pause. "As you know, it was Dzumilla who first found your mother in the forest as she lay crying next to her own mother, Sanija who lay dead on the forest floor. Dzumila was younger than you are now. She picked up the crying baby still wet with afterbirth like a foal. It was at that moment that Dzumila bonded with your mother like a mare and foal, from then on she loved your mother above all others. Just as Azra, from the moment you were born, loved you with every inch of her being, although what she felt uppermost, was fear, the fear of losing you.

"That's why she begged Dzumila to use her powers as a *drabarni* to call upon the *Ursitory*, decider of Romani fate, to reveal your destiny. For although your mother was afraid of what he might divulge, she felt she must be prepared, she had to know. So, on the third night after your birth Dzumila, to calm your mother down, called upon the Ursitory and his two companions to see into the future.

"First to speak was the Voice of Misfortune. She foretold the great Roma massacre that was about to occur. She pronounced that you would die along with the countless other Roma in those German concentration camps during what we now call *Porraimos*, the devouring of the Roma people, our own Holocaust.

"Next to pipe up was the Voice of Happiness, who said that here she had to contradict. "On the contrary," she stated, "this child, whenever in extreme danger will be saved last minute, always by someone, something unforeseen. She will fly above the misery and destruction that will surround her early years. Like a feathered seed she will always land and thrive on safe and solid ground. "

It was at that point that their master, the mighty Ursitory himself, inserted himself into their diatribes and stated once and for all, that your role would be that of *vadni ratsa*, the rebirth of the wild goose of Romani legend. Only instead of averting danger, as Khantchi has done all these years, you would enter the *Gadje* world and be separated from your people. Alone you were going to cross the *baro kalo pani*, the one the *Gadje* call the ocean, to find new paths enabling the Lovara to return to our free way of life.

For a moment they faced each other in pensive silence, until once again the whinnying of Dosha's stallion reached them from outside. The dogs began to bark.

"*Mami*," Dosha whispered. "I have to go. I promise, I will always keep your legends in my mind. But now," she went to the frail old woman, bent down and hugged her tight, "the time has come for you to empower me with luck."

"Where will you go?"

Dosha shrugged her shoulders. "I will follow some tribe by the *patrins* they left behind."

"Go to your father," Patrina said. "Angar informed his wife that Djemo is somewhere up North, between the Kola Peninsula and the Finnish border. Dzumila told me he's the *rom baro* of some settled camp that serves as winter quarters to a small traveling circus. You can follow Angar's *patrins* to get you there. They will be wilted, but still visible along the way. "

At the mention of Dzumila's name, Dosha dropped her head in sadness. "If I tell her I'm leaving, she'll stop me." She conjured up her aunt's face. Her stark impenetrable features were a testament of *romanija*, the Gypsy way of life, which had also been their survival. "She'll remind me of my responsibilities to my tribe."

Tears started to run down her face. "Forgive me," she whispered.

The old woman stroked Dosha's face with her bony fingers. "It is clear this time you must follow your inner calling." Wiping away her tears, "*Bachtalo drom*," she wished at last. "In my heart, still young like yours, I will travel with you on what I hope will be your lucky road."

So in the depth of that same night, when fear of the *mule* kept the Gypsies inside their caravans, Dosha left Patrina's side and stepped out into the night. Scintillating crystal stars were flickering like candles in a breeze. The half-wild Gypsy dogs howled like packs of roaming wolves, trying to keep the frenzied movements of the creatures of the wild away from the camp site of caravans and covered wagons. The horses were fidgeting and tearing at the ropes that secured their heads to nearby trees.

Dosha led her own jittery stallion out of the closed circle of caravans to the steps of Patrina's caravan. There she slipped the rope bridle across the horse's face and neck, cinched on a saddle blanket to hold her gear, and securing her scarf with provisions to one side of her improvised saddle, a rolled up blanket to the other, she was about to mount, when a black and white dog detached itself from the pack and ran up to her. She tried vainly to shoo it away, as the haltered horse pranced in circles while she climbed on bareback from the steps. The dog, its eyes never leaving the horse's hooves, ran circles just beyond where it could be struck. The stallion, held back by the girl's soft voice, for a short moment still pranced in place, before breaking away from the caravan in a few steps of springy trot. As soon as they stepped onto the path of travel, Dosha stretched her hands forward along the horse's neck and gave the silver stallion free reign. The stallion took off at break-neck speed galloping back along the trek that slithered like parallel snakes toward the North.

The dog, whom Dosha had named *Tsikooroo Zhookel*, Puppy, was old by Gypsy standards, but he kept up, following all the way back to the fork that Dosha had designated to meet with Jano. As they approached, a dark figure moved from the trees onto the open path and there he stood, Jano, the Gypsy who traveled without a horse. On his back he carried a bulging blanket. His violin was slung across his front. At the sight of the slow-moving lumpish shape, the horse shied and snorted, its ears pointing forward. The dog bared its teeth and, his body flattened to the ground, started to crawl with low, menacing growls toward the perceived threat.

"*Tsikooroo Zhookel!* It's all right," Dosha called off the dog.

"May your horse live long," Jano addressed Dosha with a grin. It was the traditional greeting of one Lovara to another that sounded strange coming from his lips. Especially since his eyes never left the wolf-like dog, which remained crouched and growling. Dosha jumped off her horse.

"*Tsikooroo Zhookel!*" She snapped her fingers at the dog.

She was surprised, and suddenly couldn't help but feel a little contemptuous of Jano, who clearly knew little about the old Lovari ways. It was not the *mule* in the midst of night he feared, but the animals who shared the nomads' living space. Suddenly Dosha felt uneasy about being all alone with this stranger. He was tall and slim, more handsome than ruggedly male, and the softness of his voice was more like the longing in a song, than the haughty, challenging tone of the men she was used to. She stared at the heavy blanket on his back.

"Are those books," she asked pointing to his back-sling.

"Why?" he asked.

But she turned away, suddenly shy. "We better find a place to wait out the night," she said and, walking ahead of him, she led the stallion off the path into the forest. Soon they came to a small clearing near a pond, where she let the stallion free to graze.

"We need to gather wood. Some kindling, some small branches and some bigger pieces to build a fire," she said.

That done, she showed Jano how to dig, with the end of a branch, a shallow pit and build the fire. She was about to make fire by rubbing two sticks together until they sparked, but it was late and she gratefully accepted the matches which he offered her.

"As soon as it's light," she said, "we'll head north."

"Why north?"

"I'm hoping to reach my father, Djemo. Maybe we'll find *patrins* left behind by Angar, when he went there on his way to notify my mother's closest kin. As soon as I'll find them, they'll lead us there safely."

"Is he expecting you?"

"No, but I'm hoping he'll protect us. With you a hunted man and winter settling in, we need a place where we can survive, before making plans for separate futures."

The next morning, at the break of a damp, cloudy day they started their travel into land already bleached and trees bare of leaves. With daylight hours shrinking, and the light never more than a dusky gray, their journey west of the Kola Peninsula took them almost twelve days through harsh and windswept wilderness, consisting mostly of marshy plains and straggling forest that seemed untouched by man. Early on they came across a few *kumpaniy*i of no more than three to four caravans, some Lovara, some Kalderash, left-over stragglers of the many nomadic tribes that had preceded them on their annual return to winter-quarters further south and denser forest to protect them from the elements.

In passing Dosha always stopped to exchange a few words of greetings with their fellow travelers, some questions of what lay ahead. Along the way, when camping at night, Dosha taught Jano the survival skills of the forest clans: how to trap small game, how to catch fish in the river, how to gather edible plants. She taught him how to build a shelter by weaving tree-branches together to form a roof and covering them with dead leaves or branches of fir. Most importantly, she showed him how to make a fire by rubbing sticks together, how to contain the fire, cook on it, and in the morning bury its remains so completely under previously lifted pieces of sod or bare earth, that no one would guess that Gypsies had passed that way.

She furthermore taught him how to look for and read the *patrins* left behind by different tribes guiding them through the trackless northern wilderness, and that in the winter months was crossed by Laplanders only. He in turn, despite her initial objections, started to teach her how to read and write, as they camped by a fire. First he scratched letters into the hardened earth and had her follow their loops with her fingers, and when she knew her letters, he scratched them into words. It was miraculous.

"They're *patrins* of another kind," she said with a brilliant smile.

Sometimes he read to her from one of his books, but during their nights in the open, he would not trust the dog to keep them safe, as a Gypsy nomad would. Instead he insisted Dosha take turns with him in safe-guarding each other's sleep. When she argued, he added with a timid smile that it was "mostly because of the stallion's safety, since the horse means so much to you."

In reality Jano had no feel for a horse, a fact that astonished Dosha. Yet his presence comforted Dosha like a warm shelter. His behavior remained respectful and unchanged, and Dosha's sleep was deep and quiet.

Then one day they reached their goal. They stood a moment in awe and surprise. "It's a town," whispered Dosha.

"It's a bunch of shacks," Jano laughed, pointing at the square log cabins that were built on stilts along both sides of a muddy road.

"Why are they on stilts?" she asked under her breath.

"The permafrost," he answered. "You couldn't dig a foundation in earth that remains frozen, and if they build the houses on the plain earth, they'll move with the frost." He now walked ahead of her, less frightened by the settlement than she. "Come along."

As they approached, Dosha noticed a distinct difference between the houses. On the left side of the road the log huts were neat and free of clutter. They stood like rocks that belonged. The houses to their right, although equally large, seemed smaller and ramshackle, with geese and chickens running loose. On this side added lean-tos and makeshift sheds clung to the houses, with horse-blankets laid out to dry. Fire-pits with tripods for cooking were dug in the open, wash hung from lines strung between the huts, and children of all ages stood watching the strangers, the dog, and the horse approach.

Most of all, Dosha had a keen sense of being watched from behind the windows by the inhabitants of the other side of the encampment, as she and Jano led her horse down the center of the road. Only a few children, some blond and blue eyed, some dark, stood stiff as sticks by the steps that led up to the closed doors of their homes.

Suddenly a great clatter arose. A stream of women and children poured from the huts to their right, running toward them, shouting and whooping. The stallion reared. The dog barked. Dosha stepped closer to Jano until she realized the women were bearing bread and salt.

"It's a wedding," Jano laughed, one arm around her shoulder.

"It's ours," she said, though she wasn't sure how she felt about it.

To all the different tribes of Roma, weddings are of utmost importance. Alliances are chosen and discussed long in advance, sometimes at the time of the birth of either bride or groom, and on the wedding day relatives from near and far will arrive for this great celebration. For a Lovari bride of Dosha's lineage, the festivities would last for weeks. No expense would be spared. All quarrels and enmities would be put aside in a sacred truce respected by all.

But this was an elopement. Dosha, groomed since birth to be the carrier of her tribe's culture, had made use of her right to choose her own mate. She also knew to expect the tribe's mock scolding of the groom who had dared to run away with a bride. What both elopement and planned weddings had in common was acceptance by an offering of the traditional bread and salt.

So now, a group of *romni* walked toward them, carrying bread and salt on a fine porcelain plate. A group of *rom* surrounded by dogs, Dosha's father, Djemo, in their midst, stood watching by the last hut of the encampment. There was minimal mock scolding at the elopement; some women pointed a finger at Jano who had turned beet red, and two or three men lifted fists into the air, cursing the *rom* who had dared seduce the girl. It soon came to an end, finishing with the women laughing, touching and hugging, and welcoming the young couple. Others, mostly men, by contrast oohed and aahed at the sight of her splendid horse. One *rom* ran his hands admiringly along the horse's flanks, calling him *Rup*, after the silver color of his coat. But the women still pressed their platter on Dosha and her handsome husband. Except for her father, Dosha did not recognize any of the Lovara present.

"Kneel down," Dosha whispered to Jano who stood next to her as if he'd swallowed a stick, kneeling down herself. "Kneel," she repeated. "We have to receive and exchange bread and salt, declaring us man and wife."

She was first to take a piece of bread, sprinkled it with salt and fed it to Jano. As he repeated the courteous gesture to her, Djemo strolled over, standing over the kneeling couple.

"Who told you?" Dosha looked up at Djemo, who, as father of the bride, had taken a place beside her.

"Dzumila," he answered close to her ear. "She sent a messenger to let me know that you went missing and would probably come here to stay with me. It was right to come to your father." His speech was slow and deliberate. It had none of the warm familiarity that exists even between the most powerful Lovari leader and his people.

Djemo now bent to embrace his daughter, but Dosha froze to his touch and came to her feet, subtly averting her face. Djemo was a tall, aristocratic looking man, 'white' by Gypsy standards with his dark brown hair, sharp features and facial expressions that were both aloof and commanding. But in his face she read a permanent fatigue, the first sign of aging. The hero of her early years, her beloved father, had turned into a stranger.

At the time of his own wedding, her father had been at least ten years older than Azra. Lovari virgins think of their parents' choice of an older husband as punishment for inappropriate behavior. In Azra's case, it was the curse placed upon her at birth that had limited her choice of a life partner. It had also allowed Djemo's ancestry to be of little importance. All Dosha knew was that Djemo's mother, her paternal grandmother, had been a famous Lovari dancer, and that Djemo was believed to have fallen in love with Azra precisely because of what kept the families of other *rom* at a suspicious distance, her delicate beauty.

But once Djemo left his wife and family, Dzumila had spoken solely with hatred of the brother-in-law she had once admired. "Looking back," she said, "it was only by marrying Azra that your father achieved the status of a Gypsy chief and the sworn loyalty of some followers. Not because of some bravery," she had hissed, "with the partisans in Poland. Furthermore, for him to step away from the center of Lovari life, just when life was supposed to go back to normal! Going off with his *Gadje romni!* I now, when it's too late, have to question his *romanipen,* his Gypsyhood."

"Won't you introduce me to your *rom?*" her father called her back to the present. "Djemo," he held out his hand to Jano.

"Jano of the Shevelisti," The younger man rose to his feet.

Dosha took a closer look at her father now. He was dressed like a local hunter in a heavy felt jacket trimmed with fur and loose woolen pants that were stuck into high felt boots.

"I came because I want to be a circus rider," Dosha injected herself; "I was told you have a real circus up here."

"Too dangerous," Djemo said. "I had to abandon that plan. It would get us pegged to the Central Planning Board of the Soviets in no time at all."

"How then do you survive?" she asked, unable to hide her disappointment.

Djemo's eyes lingered on her stallion. His expression softened as he motioned the newlyweds to follow him.

"Mostly by cross-breeding Siberian ponies with Gypsy pintos," he said. They were walking along the already frozen mud-track that divided the encampment in two. "They pull sleds and flatbed wagons," he said, "built by the Karelians over there." He pointed to the huts to their left. "Their sleds and wagons work much better than the *pulkkas* drawn by reindeer, which are of no use at all for pulling logs and other supplies used by locals other than Laplanders. In return," he said, "we get food, medicine, hay and other winter-feed."

"Who's we?" Dosha asked.

"These Finnish Karelians," he said. "Two truckloads full of them and us of course. The Karelians we found wandering about near death from cold and hunger when we got here. The Bolsheviks had dumped them here to die. Together we built these wooden cabins. It works," he shrugged, "for both of us. So far that is."

Dosha, looking closer at the almost identical square log cabins built on stilts on both sides of the muddy road, clearly saw the difference between Finns and Roma running like a border smack down the centerline: the one side neat and tidy, the other sprawling and friendly.

The Roma, now that the reception was over, were slowly

returning to their houses, chatting and laughing with one another. They waved at Dosha and Jano, smiling and gesticulating. Their children ran alongside the couple, swarming around the horse.

"Go on," Djemo shushed them away. "Get away from him, he's frisky."

To Dosha these settled Lovara looked like chicken in a barnyard, their wings clipped to keep their inborn restlessness contained to these two rows of houses on stilts. Gypsy dogs were slinking back to their sheds, to sleep no doubt, now that the excitement was over. One or two prowled around Dosha's wolfish dog, sniffing with curiosity.

"And where do you live?" Dosha asked her father.

"Over there," Djemo pointed to the Finnish side, "the house beyond the end of this row."

The structure her father pointed to was twice the size of the others and stood apart from the rest. It looked like a *dacha*, oblong in shape with many windows. Dosha wondered if her father lived there with the woman Dzumila called his *Gadje* whore. For a moment she was afraid Djemo would ask Jano and her to come live with him and the woman who had caused her mother so much heartache. Although Dosha was certain Dzumila's messenger had mentioned that Azra had died, he would never have mentioned her mother's name, since the names of the dead were to be forgotten.

To her relief, Djemo led them to "a place of your own," he said, a wooden hut on the Gypsy side. For the first time in her life Dosha walked into what the *Gadje* call a home. The hut consisted of one square room, bigger than the inside of a caravan, with an iron stove centered against the back wall and one square little window by the door. An unlit oil lamp hung from the ceiling by the stove. Dosha felt as if she'd walked into a trap. She turned to Jano.

"This is pitiful," he said in a dismissive tone. "You have to understand that I lived in great luxury in the Soviet capital, not in some box," he said with a sweeping gesture, "like this."

"To me," she whispered in reply, "it would still feel like a cage." *It's why in nature he walks around in fear,* she thought. She quickly returned to the outside, where Djemo stood holding the stallion. He was watching her openly.

"Come on then," he said, handing the stallion's lead rope back to her. Dosha followed him to a large wooden shed. She judged

80

it to be 25 wide by 50 *Gadje* meters long with a peaked roof. It squatted alone in the dusky light, its long side facing the settlement. Beyond, a herd of ten or fifteen Siberian ponies grazed in the open on frozen grass. At the sight of them the stallion lifted his head, ears pricked, and neighed. The ponies whirled and thundered off toward a stand of dwarfed trees in the distance.

Dosha had expected the shed to house the flatbed wagons her father had spoken of. However the inside of the structure, looking surprisingly big, housed no such vehicles, and was mostly empty. In the corners of the far short side there were two sets of narrow stalls, separated by an empty gap in between. The makeshift stalls were built with rough-cut boards, the doors consisted of shoulder-high iron gates. A horse occupied each of the two left-hand stalls, their heads thrust over the shoulder-high iron gates. The two horses, on full alert, watched them approach.

"Those are mine," Djemo said, "I don't ride in a circus anymore, but I keep in riding shape." He walked the stallion to the farthest stall on their right, leaving an empty box between him and the other two horses. "Just to be on the safe side," he pointed out.

"He's never been confined before," Dosha said in concern.

"I'll watch over him," her father promised. He placed his hand lovingly onto the stallion's neck, walking him resolutely into what was to be his stall. It was clear Djemo had been expecting the stallion as well, for the floor was deeply bedded with straw, and in the dim light from a kerosene lamp suspended from the ceiling in the empty space between the two sets of stalls, she noticed a heap of hay in one corner and a full water bucket suspended from a hook in the other.

"Go run on now, to your husband." Djemo commanded. "The stallion must get used to being here."

Dosha forced herself not to look back as she stepped back outside. Deepening darkness had snuffed out the last gray glimmers of the short winter's day but fires were burning high and bright along the path that separated Gypsy from Finn. She saw Jano in the midst of the men and realized that even without her, the bride, the Lovara were resuming celebrations in honor of the newly-weds. A young woman began to dance flicking her skirts and beating her feet in the old-fashioned way to the clapping of hands and the stamping of feet. Rough voices rose in ancient tunes. After a moment, Jano took his violin and after tuning it, he struck up his own languishing tune. He seemed slender and graceful in the glowing light of the fires, but it seemed to Dosha his tune was at odds with the voices of the celebrating Lovara. She saw one *romni* throw a sideward glance at this man who was known to have come from the city, and whose music sounded unusual even to her. Not one single Finn was out in the night.

Dosha threw a worried glance back toward the wooden shed that housed the stallion for the night. She heard no striking of hooves against the wooden box and no frantic whinnying from the stallion. Her father was guarding the stallion and keeping him calm. *At least,* she thought, *he's keeping his word to me this time,* and a pang of jealousy hit her that he tended her horse better than his child.

The music accelerated, other violins, accordions, tambourines joined in. The rhythm grew faster and faster, the *romni* drew Dosha into their midst, this was the bridal dance. It was late when Dosha and Jano left the celebrants and entered the closed-in hut that would be their home. The Lovara had left gifts of the traditional *dunhas,* and Dosha now placed these carefully at opposite sides of the room. She looked at the generous platters of food and tin goblets with water also left for the newlyweds.

Dosha watched Jano help himself to roasted goose and *manro,* Gypsy bread. She herself had eaten earlier and wanted nothing more. She threw herself on her *dunha* and turned her back to the room. At once the walls moved in on her, and she jumped back up. She wanted to run to where the stallion was stalled for the night. But Jano in his soothing voice murmured, "Please lie down. If you go out now, your father will be suspicious of our marital state." Then, like someone telling a fairytale to a child, he started to tell her more of his life of luxury as a Gypsy actor in the Soviet capital, of the cars, the theatre, of the rhythmic applause.

She lay down again, facing the center of the room, but all Dosha could think of were the tales told around Lovari fires, of Gypsies stuck in cities like Moscow and Leningrad, locked in cement cages where, according to Patrina, they were easy targets for persecution, bombs and famine. *Like crabs in a bucket, struggling to get out,* Patrina's voice echoed through her mind. *I couldn't bear it. I never will,* she promised herself. *For us forest clans, our only chance to survive lies in avoiding closed-in spaces.*

At last the familiar howling and baying, the constantly changing pitch of the chorus of Gypsy dogs, lured Dosha into an uneasy sleep.

# 8
# Father And Daughter

Djemo, leader of the voluntary collective of Roma and Karelian Finns, gave "the newlyweds" a day to rest and settle in. To the Roma, hospitality is a sacred obligation, especially in regard to a woman like Dosha, the descendant of a long line of elected *voivods* and *rajs,* Gypsy leaders and kings. With winter almost upon them, the Lovara offered Dosha extra shares of their smoked and pickled foods, as well as other necessary winter supplies, such as the grains that Dosha would need to bake *manro.*

On the second day, Djemo led Dosha and Jano back into what he called his equipment shed. "It was here when we first arrived," he said, "almost finished but abandoned—the first building, probably, of some future gulag. They gave up on account of the hellish climate in this godforsaken corner of nowhere, I bet, although it can't be any worse than Siberia. What matters is that nobody has returned since we've been here."

He walked ahead of them toward the horses. The stallion, his head sticking out above the iron stall guard, nickered as they approached, but kept munching away, with hay hanging from both corners of his mouth.

Djemo led them to the other set of stalls. In one stood a heavy-boned horse which, even in her stall, looked close to seventeen hands tall. "She's mine," he said. "Look at the size of her!" He nodded toward the stallion. "Booty of war, like him — Prussian, I bet, conquered by Russian partisans and myself while the Prussians were fleeing to save their most valuable stock. She was brought up here by a friend of mine."

Dosha wondered whether that friend was his *Gadje* woman, whom she had not yet met. She forced the thought out of her mind as, for the first time in her life, she smelled the pungent aroma of horses confined to a stall.

Walking over to her stallion, Dosha noticed Djemo introducing Jano to one of a group of young *rom* who had entered the building after them. Two of them at once started to muck out the stalls of Djemo's horses, while others brought in several haltered ponies on lunge lines. Having groomed the ponies, one at a time, the men proceeded to lunge them in as big a circle as the shed would allow. Then Djemo, stepping into the center of the riding circle, motioned one of the young *rom* to get onto the barebacked pony previously lunged; he instructed another young *rom* to teach Jano to do the same. Dosha — by now safe in her stallion's stall — was spared the look of utter amazement that the *rom* threw this fellow Lovara, when he discovered that Jano knew nothing about horses.

That morning Dosha and her stallion began their rigorous training under Djemo's strict and expert supervision. On the first day her father merely watched Dosha get on the stallion bareback from a mounting block and ride him — "the way you're used to," he said. The next day he introduced the stallion to his first bridle with a metal bit. On the third day he taught Dosha how to gently place a saddle on her stallion's back, climb on by placing her right foot onto a lowered stirrup and lift herself up by grabbing the pommel. It was their first saddle ever. It was heavy, with a deep seat, and the leather felt slick as ice from overuse. Dosha, securely seated, turned toward her father, standing as usual in the center of the riding circle, and wondered what made him so different from all the other Lovara.

Roma were not riders per se. They certainly did not ride with saddles. Their horses were venerated members of the tribe, to be respected as equals. If the Lovara rode them at all, they jumped on bareback and rode close to the withers, so that, should a horse rear, they could bring it back down by leaning over and embracing the horse's neck with both arms. Lovari children learned early on how to balance themselves easily on horseback and stay on no matter how fast the pace but when Djemo finally mounted the stallion himself at the end of the session, Dosha realized that she had never before seen such a combination of grace and movement.

At first the stallion tensed. Djemo responded by giving the horse total freedom, applying no force of any kind. Only after the stallion visibly relaxed did Djemo ever so gently pick up the reins, gently flexing the stallion softly to the right, then softly to the left.

After several minutes of this waving back and forth of the horse's neck and head, Djemo applied a slight pressure of his lower legs, and the horse started to move as if guided by thought.

"*Shookar* — beautiful!" Dosha exclaimed. The word caught Djemo in the quiet of the shed. He turned to her, pride glistening in his eyes.

From then on, Djemo and Dosha followed a strict daily routine — again, a process so unlike the ways of a Gypsy, who only accepts the order imposed by nature herself. Dosha had been forewarned of her father's *Gadje* ways. Each day Djemo started out teaching Dosha on his own horse, the tall, wide-chested Prussian mare. With Dosha riding the highly trained mare, he taught her how to move sideways, in circles, at a walk, at a trot, and lastly at a highly controlled canter. He taught her on his horse how to trot in place, which he called the *piaffe,* and how to *pirouette.* He showed Dosha how, by touching the mare lightly with a flexible whip just below the hock, she could get the mare to settle back onto her haunches and then go up in a highly controlled manner. This he called the *levade.* He told Dosha that these were only the beginnings of the "figures off the ground," all part of the teachings of Russia's High School of Riding, as applied to the art of circus riding.

Only after a full teaching session on his mare did Djemo allow Dosha to start working on those same movements with her own stallion. First he taught Dosha how to slow the pace of the stallion into what he called "collection," before lengthening his steps into a powerfully forward-flowing gait. Little by little, with love and patience, Djemo and Dosha taught the powerful stallion to perform willingly, on command and under saddle, the free-flowing movements bestowed on him by nature.

Halfway through their first winter on the collective, Djemo confirmed a fact which Dosha believed that any Gypsy would recognize immediately, at first sight: Her stallion was indeed a king among horses. Djemo further observed that Dosha and her stallion were a combination of talent he had never before witnessed.

"Come spring," he told her, "we will start working on the movements of the High School of Riding. Till then, we prepare. Your aim, however, should be far beyond the State Circus of Murmansk — beyond the Circus of Moscow as well!" He warned that her talents would be totally wasted among "small groups of Roma," however appealing they might seem — "just because they feel familiar to you."

Despite her father's ambitions for her, Dosha had begun to miss the circus Lovara she had left behind. They were her own people. And although she had distanced herself from those she loved in order to fulfill her need to heal the wounds of her past, their absence created a growing ache inside. She wanted to ask her father whether he didn't at least miss Angar — the man with whom he had fought side by side, and with whom he had worked in the circus of Moscow but the face she looked at for one brief moment, told her, more than words, that their communication had best remain limited to the horse.

Still, she persisted: "If we could just put together a small traveling circus right here, like the one I left behind, that would do fine for me," she said. That way, she argued, she could go on the road during the summer months and contribute to the tribe's livelihood. "During that time, my *rom* could travel with your horse dealers and learn bartering horses for supplies. He is more than willing to learn."

By then Dosha realized how little she knew about the man who was her father. During the war years, back in their hiding places in the Polish forests, when she had seen him only for a day here and there, it had not struck Dosha as unusual that during those short visits Djemo had kept mostly to himself, apart not only from her mother, but from the other *rom* as well. So, too, in this remote place, where — despite the cultural divide — families from both sides interacted freely with each other, he remained apart. *Like a man,* Dosha thought, *who has something to hide.* She still had not set eyes on the woman Dzumila had told her about, and she did not dare ask.

Yet despite — or maybe because of — his separateness, Djemo was the undisputed leader of both groups. It was he who had designed the pulling sleds as well as the flatbed wagons, it was he who oversaw and enforced the breeding program that had produced suitable animals for this harsh world of snow and darkness. The survival of this isolated community depended on his ingenuity and foresight.

Djemo was an exacting taskmaster. He made sure everyone contributed their utmost to the collective. To Jano he said, "Never mind the knowledge you arrived with — here you have to blend in with the rest. Your music has to follow theirs, the voices and seven-stringed guitars of the musicians who were here when you arrived." The musicians were hired to play at weddings and other festivities within traveling distance, in return for food supplies.

"And you better get used to what the peasants want" — he looked straight into Jano's eyes — "because there is no way you can elevate them to the level you are fortunate to have reached."

"Elevate" seemed a strange word to Dosha. *"That man,* she thought, *who happens to be my father, does not like the ways of us divliyi, us purely nomadic Roma.*

The long winter months clearly served as preparation for the short-lived summer. Dosha watched with interest as her father trained the young men from both sides of the collective in horse-care and barter. He singled Jano out and prepared the Gadjefied Gypsy for extended bartering trips to far, isolated villages, during which he would learn, from a group of seasoned Lovari dealers, the art of barter so as to realize the best possible rate of exchange for the community's homebred ponies. Jano would be leaving to join the other dealers as soon as the ground would allow.

To Dosha, Djemo entrusted the fine-tuning of the small, sturdy ponies. After they'd worked the two fancy horses, Djemo would pop Dosha onto the young ponies that they were breeding. Under his supervision she taught the rugged crossbreeds basic controls. They had to respond to aides, or signals, for walk, trot, canter, and, most important, halt — at first with the help of her legs and hands, then in response to her voice commands. This training prepared them for their job of pulling the sleds and the flatbed wagons, which in turn permitted the locals to use them for transportation and travel."The better the training, the greater their value," he impressed upon her.

Djemo kept his interactions with Dosha strictly limited to their work with horses, and she found herself feeling relieved that his haughty aloofness kept her at arm's length: she was not ready to reconcile with the man who had left his family behind. Yet, during those long hours together, Dosha slowly started to recognize parts of the father she had once loved and admired. As soon as he gave himself to the horses, his angular features softened and his voice lost its sharpness. In their company the Gypsy in him emerged. "Of all the animals that can be domesticated," he told her one day, "the horse is the hardest to train."

*Not for a true Gypsy,* she thought.

"Unlike the dog, the goat, the donkey, and the bear," he continued, "the horse will always keep a mind of its own. *Gadje* train horses in enclosed spaces to follow them and do their bidding, but when faced with an open space and no constraints, the horse, like a Gypsy, will take off."

87

*How come, then,* she wondered, *that with us nomadic Gypsies, the horse, even when loose, will stick around?*

"I am talking circus horses," Djemo said, as if reading her mind.

"Even the ponies we trained here," she said, "if they bolt, so far they've always returned. And that's because," she added defiantly, "it's Gypsies handling and training them." Even so, she had to concede that, when it came to the training of horses, nobody had a finer touch than her father. At times, while riding the magnificent stallion under her father's supervision, she briefly turned her eyes to his and caught them melting with pride and warmth.

They were deep into winter already. She and Jano had been with the collective for several months, and Dosha was grateful that Djemo still had not mentioned the woman Dzumila had labeled his *"Gadje* whore." Nor did he invite Dosha or Jano, who all believed was her true *rom* in every sense, into his house. Furthermore, if Djemo actually still lived with such a woman, nobody had ever pointed her out to Dosha out of respect for her recent loss.

Then one day during a training session with the stallion, Dosha felt somebody's eyes on her. When she turned her own eyes from the stallion's neck to the shadowy space under the sloping roof by an outside wall, she noticed a woman, clearly from the Finnish side, watching her from below an eave where the dull light of the oil lamps barely reached. Whereas most of the Karelians were scrawny and dark, this woman was buxom and blond, with calculating eyes.

"Kylliki Tervo," her father said by way of introduction following the direction of Dosha's eyes, "a Finnish rider. She used to help me with what you do now."

Dosha continued to ride without acknowledging the *Gadje* stranger. She understood at once that she had unknowingly usurped the woman's work with Djemo — just as she knew in an instant that this was the one whom Dzumila had called her father's *Gadje* whore. In the tense silence that followed the introduction, Dosha felt Azra's sadness well up within herself. Echoes of Azra's tales of deception and abandonment pulsated through her body, stronger than the sudden loud beating of her own heart.

The woman walked into the center of the shed, where Djemo handed her the big-boned mare. With the help of a mounting block, the woman placed one foot on a stirrup and one hand on the pommel of the saddle, and lifted herself onto the horse's back.

Without a word, she at once fell into step behind Dosha and followed her around the riding circle, making the mare piaffe and pirouette. Although they were on the same circle, each was engaged in a program of her own, without interference from the other. Djemo, addressing his two female riders by their first names from his usual spot in the center of the arena, hollered instructions and corrections as to the horses' gaits or the riders' positions and aids.

After that, Kylliki Tervo became part of the iron routine imposed on everyone by Djemo. The woman who had lured her father away from her mother had become part of Dosha's daily riding routine. And in truth, Dosha did not know what to make of the situation, or even how best to behave.

With the collective locked in by snow and darkness, their riding was restricted to a 20-meter circle under the flickering oil lamps in an atmosphere that was more frigid and silent than the great Arctic outside. *He couldn't have chosen a better moment,* Dosha later mused, remembering that forced introduction. *There was no place I could escape to.*

After riding the dressage horses, both riders would turn their attention to training the ponies to be offered for sale. With a self-control she never knew she possessed, Dosha watched the Gadji with her rigid back and punishing hands attempt day after day to impose her will on one young horse after another. Djemo made every attempt to talk Kylliki through the increasing resistance that the young horses displayed once they'd grown used to Dosha's ease and patience with them. In frosty silence, the *Gadji* ignored him, throwing furious looks at Dosha, as if this were all her fault. Ignoring Djemo's woman, Dosha calmly and with fluid ease continued to concentrate on her own riding.

One particularly cold day, a storm was howling and tearing at the shed's roof and the big double gates flew open. As Djemo rushed from the center of the shed to close and latch them tight, one of the young crossbreeds Kylliki was riding became so tense and frightened that it began to nervously step in place. In mounting panic, its eyes rolling, the horse suddenly lifted its head, shifted its weight to its hind quarters and was about to rear. Kylliki, furious at the resistance of a horse that she had been riding for weeks, started beating down furiously across its neck and then between its ears with her crop, until half-rearing, half-bucking, the horse bolted forward.

At that point Dosha, who had been several horse-lengths

behind, could stand it no more. She stopped her horse in front of Jano — who, ever since the woman's first appearance, seemed to always be hovering nearby — and jumped off her own pony, whispering, "Hold him for me."

She remained standing right next to Jano, forcing herself first to calm down by breathing deeply. She then closed her eyes, raised both her hands to her temples, and with great intensity focused all her mental powers on the *Gadje* woman, who was still racing around and around the shed, all the while continuing to beat down on the panicking horse. When Dosha had the other woman clearly in her mind's eye, and nothing else, she spoke, slowly and deliberately: "Fall!.... Fall!"

A great thud echoed through the shed as Kylliki was thrown against the wooden wall of the shed. Dosha opened her eyes just in time to catch Jano's expression of utter disbelief. Dosha next turned her eyes to Kylliki, who was lifting herself off the floor. The frantic young horse continued to race around the narrow circle of the shed, while Kylliki, spewing a string of Finnish curses, headed for the door.

Dosha decided to ignore the hysterical *Gadji* and instead calm the frantic horse, the way her father had taught her when she was still a child. She spread both arms out wide and, talking softly, walked straight into the path of the bolting horse. When it stopped, she stretched out a hand for the horse to sniff, grabbed its reins, and started scratching its neck.

It was at that moment that Djemo, who had remained in the center of the shed as if frozen in place, his black eyes flaring, came storming toward his daughter and the still trembling horse. He stopped, a hand raised, threateningly close.

For a moment he looked as if he were about to strike her. Dosha in turn focused in on his angry eyes. He lowered his hand.

A memory rose in Dosha's mind, a scene of the past as clear and real as the present. To the group of Lovari fighters who had gathered around him in the forests of Poland, Djemo had boasted that there wasn't an animal he could not train. Dzumila had openly laughed into his face. To prove his point, Djemo caught a wolf pup; the one animal all Gypsies believe can never be tamed. He told the unbelieving Lovara that — never mind their beliefs and superstitions — he himself would turn that wolf pup into a pet.

With that in mind, he kept the wolf pup in a little cage always by his side; as it grew, he tied it to a tree. In those days he came to

camp more frequently. There, he spent much time with the growing wolf pup, named *O ruv,* the Gypsy word for wolf. Wherever
he went, he took it along with him on a long leash. He played
with the wolf, fed it meat. He went out of his way to supply it with
milk stolen from cows and goats. He also asked Dosha to do the
same during those times when he had to leave to fight the war.

The day arrived when Djemo, once again in front of a gathering of Lovari fighters, men, women, and children, pronounced
the taming of the wolf complete. In front of everyone, he un-
chained his pet. The wolf, fully grown, was splendid. For a moment it stood there stock-still, its knowing yellow eyes gazing
with perfect calm at those assembled. Then without a moment's
hesitation it turned and with increasing speed made for the depth
of the forest that surrounded them, never to return.

Djemo was staring at his daughter as if she were that wolf.

# 9
# The Cult Of The Horse

Like most other Roma and nomads of central and western Asia, the Lovara followed the cult of the horse. A horse is a Gypsy's best friend — not a possession to be used for sport or pleasure, but an equal partner in his harsh and unpredictable life, a symbol of what is sacred and ritually clean. For a Gypsy, making a living with the care and trade of horses is the noblest profession one could have. The trading of horses is surrounded by ancient rituals that cannot be brooked. The exclusion of women in this noblest of trades is absolute, even for women—like Dosha—of the highest lineage.

What was not out of Dosha's reach, however, was helping with the sale of the sleds and flatbed wagons that went with the ponies they had bred. These were built to perfection by the Finns, out in the open, on the other side of the divided camp, and so it came about that Dosha drew closer to these strangers. She began by playing with their children, who had picked up some *Romani* from the Gypsy children. She also let them ride the gentler ponies. In the process she made an effort to learn their language. Pointing to herself, she exclaimed *"Minnae muskalainen* — I am Gypsy." The children of the Finns looked at her red-blond hair, the paleness of her skin, and laughed.

Whenever one of the children took ill, she would visit their cabin bringing them healing herbs and medicinal teas. She knew how to cool a fever or soften a cough. Soon word of Dosha's healing powers spread. It created respect among the Lovara, and aloofness among some of the Finns. "She is a sorceress," many whispered behind her back but when, again and again, her herbs and teas worked, their mistrust dissipated. Soon Dosha was proficient in their language. She told them she admired the fine craftsmanship of their carpentry. The Finns responded proudly, "It was us Finns, us Suomi, who built the fast boats of the mighty Vikings, the greatest warriors ever to roam the sea. With them, too, we lived in harmony."

Upon her request, the Finnish men now took Dosha along on their trips as they bartered with wagons and sleds. Dosha, who had been trading herbs and home-brewed vodka with Dzumila since she was a child, proved excellent at bartering with the locals. In fact, with her reddish-blond hair and fair skin, the local Russian hunters and loggers believed her to be "of the motherland." As a result, the exchanges were increasingly profitable, and Dosha, without asking, got a cut. The trips were so successful that the Finns asked her to come along again and again.

Through all of Dosha's dealings with the Finns, Kylikki, her father's woman, kept out of sight, like a dog expelled from a pack. Djemo never mentioned their confrontation in the riding shed. As before, his dealings with his daughter revolved solely around the training of horses — her white stallion and the ponies destined for barter.

Dosha never lost sight of the fact that a man with Djemo's discipline would never be content with ruling over a bunch of families who survived on the fringes of their populations, trapped for months on end in snow and ice. She believed he was focused on what lay beyond.

"I bet you," she told Jano when they were alone one night in their hut, "that you and I are part of whatever plans he has for the future." *And in that future,* she thought to herself, *he's planning to be in the world of Gadje. Why else, would he allow me such close contact with the Finns, and not object to my choice of a city Gypsy as my rom?*

Nobody could deny that Jano was a good-looking Gypsy. Messengers and members of her tribe had told Dosha that Jano had indeed been a famous actor and violinist at the Teatr Roman, the only all-Gypsy theatre in all of Russia. He was, however, of no importance to nomadic Lovari tribes, who themselves were regarded as noble and powerful in the world of Roma. It took Dosha a long while to understand what her father liked best about the arrangement with Jano, because everybody else in her tribe would have condemned it. Every evening, Jano taught Dosha how to read and write. He even taught her some French, telling her that his mother's clan had mostly traveled France. It was the French lessons that Djemo seemed to value above all.

As to the Finns, they taught her the ways of *Gadje*. "Do you think," she asked Jano, who by then she trusted implicitly, "that my father is trying to lead me away from the life of my people? To be like him?"

"And what way is that?" Jano asked. "He certainly does not confide in me. Other than for work, he even keeps me away from the other *rom* and the young Finns who work for him. He keeps me apart as much as he can."

Dosha looked at Jano long and hard. She was struck, not for the first time, at how he lacked the quick insight of a nomad. "You must feel lonely, away from your own people," she said, reflecting upon what he had just confessed.

"For right now," he said, "I guess I should be happy to be safe."

"Are your people, the city Roma, like Djemo?" she asked.

"City Gypsies don't have horses, unless they work in a circus."

"See," she said, "I believe he wants me to be like him. Somebody," she stressed, "who is a Gypsy to the Gypsies, *Gadje* to *Gadje* — one who plays both sides of the divide."

What Djemo did not realize was that the reverse was happening. Instead of alienating Dosha from her origins, her dealings with these outsiders made her appreciate her own even more. What the Finns (placed, she felt, like rocks on a plot of land) taught her most was how much she missed the ever-changing landscapes of life on the road. She longed for the joy and security of being surrounded by a *kumpania* that was her own. She suffered from a homesickness that even the semi-settled Lovara of the camp could not assuage.

As for Jano, instead of luring Dosha away from her origins with his knowledge of the written word, he himself was falling under the spell of the magic that the city Gypsies had forsaken. As soon as he learned to sit a pony, he rode out with Dosha and the other Roma of Djemo's collective into the wide-open spaces, far away from all semblance of enclosure. There, once a month, they celebrated the rebirth of the moon, the heavenly mascot of the wanderer — ever-changing, like the life of the Gypsy on the road. In great deference they jumped off their ponies and stood in a circle with linked hands and bowed heads, half-speaking, half-chanting a special prayer:

"*Shonuto nevo ankliste. Tal aminghe bachtalo. Alacl'ame bivolengo. Te mukel ame bachtasa Ai sastimaso Ai lovensa.*

"The new moon has come out. May she be lucky for us. She has found us penniless. May she leave us with good fortune. And with money. "

When alone in their cabin, Jano and Dosha acted increasingly like trusting friends. It made the physical distance that Dosha insisted on seem more and more artificial. Yet without fail, as if they were truly man and wife, Jano continued to contribute to their livelihood by his work with the ponies, and by leading the musicians from the collective to play at local weddings, from which they returned with valuable supplies and horse-feed.

He could no longer hide his weaknesses from her. He never drank in Dosha's presence, but he not only drank more than others at Lovari festivities, he willingly joined the Finns in their silent drinking habits. Out of respect for Dosha, the Finnish women let him sleep it off along with their men, out of her sight.

*It is of no concern to me,* Dosha told herself irritably. *As long as he sticks to our agreement, his life is his to live a*nd he had promised that upon Gypsy honor. Still, she often wondered, *what is the pain, the sadness he is drowning in vodka?* But she must not interfere, she told herself, especially since he never tried to hamper her freedom or rein in her decisions. Nor did he ever try to move physically close.

Yet sometimes, when she caught him unawares, Dosha noticed his eyes following her and whenever he sat in a corner playing his much finer version of a nomad's home-made violin, his tapered fingers stroking the strings, the music reached out to her like caressing hands. She had begun to sense Jano's maleness. His dark, brooding, heavy-lidded eyes could not hide the smoldering fire he barely kept under control within. Her own eyes were drawn to the maleness of his black body hair, curling from his arms down to his sensitive hands, and from his chest toward his finely muscled belly, visible when he opened his shirt by the stove in their cabin.

Soon she could single out his scent from among that of all the other men. Her whole body was on high alert. She could sense his physical presence with every fiber in her body. He seemed to call forth heat from her body, like healing hands suspended above a wound and always she felt his liquid eyes upon her, their warmth licking her soul.

It was after one of the moon rites of the Lovara, when they were back in their cabin alone, facing each other in the orange glow of the oil lamps, that he first touched her face. Her body caught on fire.

Without a word they started to undress, face to face. Traditionally, Lovari newlyweds undress back to back with bashful shame. They never look at each other in the nude. Yet Jano's eyes conquered every part of her body and for the first time Dosha saw his aroused maleness stand out against the glowing light like the tree of life.

Overcome, they held on to each other's eyes as he lowered her gently to the floor beside the burning stove. Outside, Tsikooroo Zkookel started to yelp by the entrance to the hut. Dosha looked up into Jano's face as his body descended onto her own. His lips on hers sealed all further thought. She felt a short pain, like the breaking of a seal, before — in a powerful upsurge of need — they delivered themselves to the flames that consumed them. For the first time since her mother's death, life rushed through Dosha like a flooding stream. Her physical awakening overtook her feverishly. Their bodies were a perfect fit, as her body exploded again and again, and the pain she had carried within herself for so long started to recede.

For weeks she walked on air. She now understood why nomads keep their newlyweds in caravans apart. She loved this first step into womanhood, loved the explosions of the body that shattered her mind. The hunger for more spread through her like a fever, and the same was true for Jano. She was more than willing to feed his ever-increasing hunger for her, until she realized that her body had become the altar upon which he worshipped. The intensity of his devotion frightened her. Opening her eyes right at the moment when ecstasy exploded, she saw in his face the expression of a Christ in death, and she knew, with a sharp unbearable pain in her heart, that he was a man destined to die young.

Every morning thereafter, it was Patrina's voice she heard as she stepped outside. In a lean-to out behind their hut, she dug up Patrina's little pouch. Without fail and in secret, she went against Romani law by chewing the herbs that would prevent her from being with child.

They lived as man and wife up until the first spring after their arrival, when, as planned, she joined a little circus group that Djemo assembled. With them, once again, she followed the call of the open road, while Jano took off with the horse dealers to barter with the locals. This had been her plan; it was what she had wanted. Yet her heart was heavy at parting from her *rom*.

# 10
# Khantchi, Elusive King Of The Lovara

Their summer apart had come and gone. As before, Dosha's dancing act with her stallion had been received by the backward peasants like an act straight from heaven. The group returned with bountiful supplies of food, horse feed, fabric for clothes, canvas and hardware for the sleds — enough goods to survive the winter.

"Your *rom*, on the other hand," Djemo informed his daughter upon her return, "will never be any good at selling horses. He is not able to convince any of those peasants that even a pony with flaws is worth a price. We're better off just letting him play at *Gadje* weddings."

Dosha, however, found Jano more at ease. His demeanor had lost the furtiveness of someone constantly looking over his shoulder.

"I think the Bolsheviks have called off the hunt," he told Dosha on their first night back together in their cabin. "Maybe I'm not going to be dragged off to some Siberian *gulag* like some wayward *tzigani* after all."

A thin layer of snow already covered the ground. Russia's slice of Europe's last true wilderness was about to turn once again into a desert of snow and ice. Djemo's collective was about to be cut off from the rest of the world, and Jano relaxed even more.

The severe conditions which Jano counted on to keep the Bolsheviks at a safe distance were what inspired Dosha's grandfather Khantchi to come out of hiding at long last. Traveling with a reindeer and a *pulkka*, he set out to meet the granddaughter he had never seen.

It was the middle of the night when he arrived. The waxing moon was almost full when Dosha awoke to two pitch-black eyes riveted on her face. At once fully alert, she stared at this

97

Laplander, this Sami in a long fur coat bordered by colorful red felt and a fur hat with ear-flaps that left only his face exposed. It was a dark, weathered face, partly covered with bushy and silver-gray eyebrows above a moustache that descended to a shaggy beard. It was a face that Dosha recognized by instinct, as his highly intelligent eyes absorbed every feature of her face. Dosha also knew that he was losing himself in the mirror image of the woman who had been his *romni,* the wife he had never replaced.

As tenderness and something close to relief entered his gaze, Kantchi's pudgy hand gently removed the strands of hair that had fallen across Dosha's face as she slept. The warmth of his touch erased all former resentments from Dosha's soul. She threw her arms around his neck, whispering *"Papo, Papo."*And for the first time since leaving Patrina, she felt the comfort of being close to one truly of her own.

"How come the dogs didn't alert the camp to your arrival in the middle of the night like this?" she asked, sitting up,

He laughed. "Time to take you back to your nomadic roots!" His eyes sparkled with mirth. "Have you forgotten already that a Gypsy will always be able to sneak up on his own — let alone their dogs? Besides, your father knew I was coming. I've been here before."

"He never mentioned a word," she said. "Not to me."

The next morning, word was out. The Gypsies of the encampment were abuzz with excitement. They hastened to pay homage to their raja, the King of the Lovara. Fires lit the daytime darkness. Children, laughing and giggling, untied the reindeer that had been tethered for the night and began leading it up and down the one street, back and forth. Their parents respectfully stepped up to the old man, who was seated on a chair in front of Dosha's house, and kissed his hand. He in turn handed them fistfuls of rubles.

"They might as well spend it," he whispered to Dosha, who was standing behind his chair. "They're worthless on the other side of the border. In fact, people laugh in your face when you try and pay with them. It's known as 'funny money,' anywhere but here."

"Are you planning to go across the border then?" Dosha asked. Khantchi took and squeezed her hand, without replying. Music resounded through the arctic stillness. For the semi-settled or still purely nomadic, any excuse will do when it comes to celebrating. So now, on top of a thin cover of snow and ice, young *romni* were dancing in circles, their natural movements hampered and slowed by their layers of heavy clothing.

The Finns from the other side and finally Djemo himself came to pay their respects as well. Djemo stood stiff and aloof in front of Khantchi's chair. While the two men talked, Khantchi never took his eyes off the fire. Moments later, he got up. "Let's have a look at my granddaughter's stallion," Khantchi said. "All my messengers came back talking about the horse Dosha found."

The two men walked to the shed, with Dosha in tow. Djemo opened a narrow side door and was the first to step into the oblong interior where his two horses had been turned loose and were cantering and bucking around.

"We're using it for turnout in the winter — just for our personal horses," Djemo said, holding out a handful of grain. The two horses at once stopped running and calmly approached him. He allowed first one, then the second to eat the grain out of his hand. Holding them by their halters, he led them back into their stalls. Dosha, leading Khantchi, walked toward the stallion's box, where she pulled a heavy felt blanket off his back. "He grows hair like a bear," she said. Khantchi, his eyes glistening with admiration, stroked the stallion's coat, which shone like silver silk in the semidarkness of the shed.

Dosha placed the blanket in a corner of the stall and led the powerful stallion out of his stall by his halter, over to a side wall of the shed where Djemo awaited them. There she let go of the halter, and they watched the stallion tear loose and buck off along the walls. He stopped next to the narrow exit door, spun around, and, eyeing them, started to snort and paw the already frozen dirt.

"Watch!" Djemo grabbed a bullwhip from a hook on the wall behind him and walked into the center of the circle. The cracking whip resounded through the frozen shed, and, as if on cue, the stallion, neck arching, tail lifted, started high-stepping in precise circles around Djemo and his whip.

Khantchi, his black eyes gleaming with pride, turned to Dosha. "He is more than I had hoped for." He then addressed Djemo: "I'm sure you've never had the fortune to train a finer horse."

But later that night, once the festivities were winding down and Khantchi and Dosha were alone, sitting cross-legged in front of the burning stove in her cabin, Khantchi's face turned grave. "You have to get yourself and that stallion out of here — the sooner, the better," he said.

"But — " Dosha stammered as she started to tell Khantchi about her plans to make her way toward Murmansk next summer, where Djemo had told her that official competitions were being held for an act in the State Circus there. "It would be highly profitable," she hastened to say. "It would also get me back to a life mostly spent on the road."

"Murmansk!" Khantchi said with a dismissive motion of his hand. "It's just more of the same — nothing but a prison of snow and darkness. No life for a Gypsy like you, or for your horse. Besides, what your father feels sets you free here—namely, being out of reach of the Bolsheviks — there would put you right into their grip and should the Soviet machine wish to pick you up, you'd be trapped like a rabbit in a one-exit hole.

"Besides," he leaned forward, "I believe the only reason Djemo has chosen this place is that he knows as well as I that in a two-day drive by *pulkka* you can actually slip across the border into Norway or Finland and that three-way corner is so godforsaken once under snow and ice, it opens up like an escape hatch during most of the winter months. Of course," Khantchi noted, "you have to know where you're going, and you couldn't take along the horses. They'd never make it."

Djemo had never mentioned the proximity of the border to his daughter. "It's all about sitting on the fence again," Dosha said out loud. "He's done it all his life."

"That's right," Khantchi said. "And I know," he added, taking Dosha's hand in his own, "we chose a bad father for you. He turned out to be a bad husband to your poor mother, too." At the mention of her mother, Dosha dropped her eyes. Shouldn't she hold her grandfather to account for also having abandoned her mother?

Khantchi bent over and held her close. "I know," he said, kissing her hair. "It's impossible for you to understand. There is much at stake for us Gypsies at all times and when it comes to Djemo, although he's not honorable in many ways, he has served the rest of the *natsia* of Lovara well — even in his choice of this place, which just happens to be within reach of one of the few cracks in the iron wall. The Soviets are convinced that only Laplanders can survive in this world of night and ice. For the time being, we are safe."

Dosha would have liked to ask her grandfather why, unlike Dzumila, he had not rejected Djemo. But before she could open her mouth, he continued: "For now," he said, "all feuds among us have to be put on hold. It's *baxt,* the tiniest fleck of luck, that we need, not strife among us. We're about to be hauled off our ancient treks, as I'm sure your *rom*" — this was the first time he'd identified Jano directly as her *rom* — "has told you."

"Jano is not my *rom* in the true sense, *Papo,*" Dosha replied, looking her grandfather straight in the eyes. "We had an agreement, he and I." She blushed. "Since then, our relationship has gone further than I'd intended, but Patrina gave me the forbidden herbs to chew." She waited for her grandfather to tell her that because of what had happened, whether she liked it or not, she was married now. Instead he merely patted her hand.

"I haven't changed my mind about not wanting to be married," Dosha said defiantly. "I mean, Jano and I ... It was only so that Djemo wouldn't marry me off with his own interests in mind. I lied to him. But I don't owe him the respect of the truth. I don't think he knows that Jano is in trouble with the Bolsheviks. Jano is on the run. Some Bolshevik *Gadji....*"

Just at that moment Jano, who had remained with the Roma still celebrating outside, entered their cabin. He must have caught her last words, for with downcast eyes he pulled a cigarette pack from his jacket and nervously lit one of the black cigarettes Khantchi had brought as gifts. He paced in back of them, clearly tense and unsure of himself in the old man's presence. The old man kept staring pensively at the stove, at the glow at the upper edge of its half-moon door, the way a Gypsy likes to watch an open fire leap and play, although here the fire could only be heard, not seen.

Khantchi displayed little of the trappings of a Russian Gypsy king — no showy silver buttons on his jacket, no heavy gold chain, only a Lovari leader's staff with an intricately carved silver horse head. And once he had removed his long Laplander fur coat, he could have passed for a Russian hunter or backwoodsman, or a worker on a collective. He was clearly dressed to slip easily across cultural and ethnic divides.

Sitting next to his granddaughter, Khantchi appeared at peace within himself. Yet even Dosha felt the invisible shield that kept him apart — that kept all those Gypsies who approached him to pay their respects at a respectful distance. Khantchi had chosen that which every Gypsy fears the most: isolation from his tribe. Yet whenever his hand touched her, Dosha felt his boundless love and warmth. She wondered how her life might have been different had her grandfather stayed around to head the *kumpania* of his motherless children. Instead, Khantchi, in his self-chosen exile, had turned into the ultimate father of all Lovara.

Patrina had told Dosha that Khantchi and Sanija, the children of two powerful families, had been promised to each other at birth. Their fathers had sworn a blood oath to unite the two families through marriage, thereby consolidating leadership of all the traveling Lovara. Ordinarily, a Lovari bride is chosen in her early teens—and not for her beauty, nor for love, but for her shrewdness and potential earning power, since Lovari women often are their families' prime breadwinners.

Khantchi and Sanija had been thrown together almost since birth, and not just through their families' design. Fate had made them love each other deeply, long before Sanija had turned into a beauty, and long before she had turned into a valuable asset to her tribe. It was Sanija's absence from his life that made Khantchi sneak from the Count's estate back to his tribe—just as later, when he learned of her death, he had abandoned the life of his tribe. Khantchi had disappeared for years. Rumors, spread by Kalderash, ran rampant that their leader had gone to live the life of a *Gadje*. Did he? Many wondered. But no Lovara ever doubted his loyalty to his people, for he channeled all knowledge and whatever wealth he acquired from the *Gadje* back into the lives of his own. Patrina had told Dosha that Khantchi was known to smuggle valuables of corrupt Soviet party bosses into the West for safe-keeping, for which he charged high fees.

For a long moment, the three of them sat in silence. Jano, stubbing out his cigarette on the top of the stove, had finally seated himself on the floor next to Dosha. Khantchi lifted his shrewd but melancholy eyes toward his granddaughter. "You know," he said, "it would be easy enough to slip Jano across this particular border into Finland. The only Soviets patrolling are young, miserable kids from the city. They have no choice but to walk out into the cold, regular as *Gadje* clockwork, twice a day. Twice a day, they have to march along the line where soon border posts and barbed wire will lie deeply buried under snow and ice. You never even see the guards. All you see are their footprints from the day before, and those only as long as they aren't buried under new layers of snow. That and ..." Khantchi turned to Jano, "Of course, there's no way you can do it with a horse. On the other hand, with a reindeer pulling a *pulkka*? No problem."

Jano gave no reply. Once again, Dosha realized that what felt like a cage to her, gave Jano a sense of safety. He would or could not leave that false safety net behind. So instead, when the moon was full and high, Khantchi invited Dosha along for what he described to Jano as "a little whiff of freedom."

Having swathed both himself and his granddaughter in fur from head to toe like Laplanders, the old man hitched the reindeer to his *pulkka* and, with Dosha settled behind him, flew into the eerie whiteness that cast no shadow and a silence that was absolute. The cold sliced away at the small parts of their faces that were left exposed with the sharpness of a knife. Away from the encampment, the only sign of life was the powerful rise and fall of the shovel-like feet of the reindeer, attached to its sled by a single leather strap. To guide the racing animal, Khantchi held a second strap in his fur-gloved hands. He never hesitated as to the direction they were taking, as if he knew by heart the way across the trackless moonlit wilderness.

They had traveled for hours and the moonlight was growing dim when they arrived at a lone hut. "My friend, a Russian Laplander," Khantchi told Dosha, as an older man dressed like Khantchi and two wolf-like dogs greeted them in front of the hut. The man had been expecting them. Without a word, he unhitched the reindeer and led it to an enclosure sheltered by a stand of fir, with plenty of feed spread out at the foot of the trees.

"It's his," Khantchi informed Dosha, indicating the reindeer with a tip of his head. Then he and the Laplander conversed in silence with their hands. Khantchi opened a fur pouch that had lain hidden among other fur-wrapped packs tied to the sled. He handed the Laplander a pack of cigarettes and a small bag of salt.

The old Laplander led them inside his windowless log hut, where a fire burned in a shallow pit surrounded by heavy rocks, its smoke vented through a hole in the roof. He offered them some meat that had been roasting on a spit. After they had eaten, Khantchi passed around a wineskin full of vodka so strong, it spread like fire down Dosha's throat.

As they bedded down by the fire, Khantchi told Dosha, "A Bolshevik raid took his whole family while he was away at a reindeer roundup last spring. They were suspected of having harbored some of those Karelians in your camp, 'enemies of the people.' That's what will happen to you, if they track down Jano, your man. Besides, I have met some of his tribe, the ones settled in Moscow. I met with them after he'd gone. They love him, of course, yet they told me he is rash, and that he drinks. He is not for one like you."

"I know," Dosha whispered in return. "From the start, I told Jano that eventually we would have to go our separate ways, no matter what."

Yet how could she explain to her grandfather that Jano's love had for the first time in her life soothed the pain of her past? That whenever she thought of the inevitable separation, she felt hollow — like a body suffering from lack of food?

Already, though, Jano was starting to fade in her mind like a picture on a wall. In Khantchi's presence, she knew that her fate was taking shape. Soon that fate would take her away.

As soon as day's darkness was lit by the stark light of the moon once again, they continued their race across the rolling terrain of the moonstruck land. The speed of the forceful reindeer sent the flat sled at times high into the air, only to hit the ground again twisting and turning like flat stones skipping over water. Dosha kept her arms tightly wrapped around Khantchi. As they approached a straggly forest of low-growing trees, he turned to face her, his eyes glistening like burning charcoal in the silent night.

"You're in the land of the free." His voice was muffled behind a heavy scarf that covered the lower part of his face.

They were skirting silver-limbed trees. Loose reindeer scattered at their approach. An hour at most later, a group of houses of various sizes lay sprinkled in a dip between rolling hills. Small square windows emitted cones of light, and smoke curled and hovered in the wind still night above sod-covered roofs. With barks and yelps, a pack of dogs came racing toward their approaching sled. At once doors flew open, and three heavily dressed men— Laplanders — stepped out. They silently unhitched the reindeer and tied it between two houses, tossing it some dried lichen. They then helped Khantchi unload saddlebags stuffed with gifts of coffee and cigarettes and other carefully wrapped-up items from the pulkka. They carried everything into what looked like the biggest house in the village.

Again a fire burned in a pit surrounded by heavy rocks, the smoke venting through the roof above. There, Khantchi took off his Laplander coat and fur cap and replaced it with his Gypsy hat. For around the open fire sat not only six moonfaced Laplanders, who greeted them with a nod of the head and vacant eyes, but, seated across from them were five Lovara with heavy gold amulets hanging around their necks. The Lovara greeted Khantchi and

Dosha with excited wishes for long lives for their horses, many children, much health, and a lucky road.

"These," Khantchi informed Dosha, "are chiefs of important *kumpaniyi*, who crossed the Russian border months ago and traveled back all the way from the southern tip of Finland to see me." They had come to pay homage to their king.

Again, Khantchi offered gifts of cigarettes and wineskins of Gypsy vodka to his friends the Laplanders. They and Khantchi now greeted each other in sign language. Cigarettes were lit and wineskins passed around. No other women were present. It would have been proper for Dosha to sit in the rear, behind the men. She knew nothing of the customs of the Sami, as the Laplanders called themselves, but to the other Roma she was a girl of menstruating age, and therefore considered *mahrime*, possibly unclean. Yet to her surprise, Khantchi motioned her to sit by his side, although not close enough to touch.

"This is Dosha," Khantchi said, "my granddaughter. My sister Patrina, the *phuri dai* of our tribe, believes she is to be the next pathfinder for our tribes."

Dosha's realized with surprise that this had been no impulsive excursion into open space, as Khantchi had made Jano believe, but a prearranged journey to meet with Lovari chiefs, part of a carefully laid-out plan that would allow many Russian Lovara to start crossing the border into Finland, as early as next spring.

"This can be accomplished," he told the respectfully silent *voivods* — Lovari leaders — already on Finnish soil, "by searching for unguarded border spots all the way from the High North down to the Finnish town of Ivalo on the Russian border. It has to happen," he emphasized "during a short, very specific moment of the new year, smack in the middle of mud season and the start of new growth."

"That would make sense," agreed one of the Lovari chiefs.

"Again," Khantchi said, "our people will have to split up into small groups. They'll have to leave their wagons and their caravans on the Russian side. You," he pointed to the Lovara from the Finnish side, "will have to help them find new wagons to purchase on this side of the border." Toward this end, Khantchi now handed into their safe-keeping *galbi*, Gypsy gold belonging to the tribe. He also pulled out from one of his fur-wrapped packs Russian icons of the finest quality. "To raise local money," he said, "once our people from the Russian side are safely across."

Together, with much back-and-forth discussion, they started to prepare for the impending "great escape"—imperative because, Khantchi told them, it was only a matter of time before the
Bolsheviks would take away all their gold, their wagons and their
horses. "They're also in hot pursuit of me," he added. "They know
I carry knowledge that would fetch lots of money in the West.

The five *voivods* in turn talked about the Kaale, a Gypsy *natsia* who lived in Finland. Like the Lovara, they traveled with and
traded horses, and their women read fortunes, but their language
was hard to understand. The Lovara and the Kaale had come
to an agreement respecting each other's territories of trade. The
*voivods* now assured Khantchi that they would not only barter
with the Kaale to ensure safe passage, but, if needed, buy assur-
ances of help.

"We'll reassure the Kaale," said one, "that all we want is to
pass through their territories in order to reach Sweden overland. "

That said, the Lovara and Sami shared Khantchi's powerful
homebrew. While drinking, the Laplanders fell into total silence,
a silence that made the Lovara grow uneasy in their skins, itchy
for escape.

"We couldn't be more different," Khantchi observed as he
and Dosha headed back toward Djemo's collective. "Yet outsiders
lump Sami and Roma together as one and the same. They think
of us as the same type of wizards and masters of the supernatu-
ral. This is especially true for those Finns and Russians born and
raised in the High North. They believe that, since both of our
peoples, Sami and Roma, train bears and dance around an open
fire beating tambourines, we should both be feared, yet consulted
at the same time, believing we can look into their future.

# 11
# The Thaw

As they traveled back toward the collective, Khantchi also told Dosha that at the first sign of spring she must move South with Djemo's traveling circus, as she had done the year before. Only this time, instead of traveling in a circle that would lead back home, she was to leave the circus and continue south, where Khantchi would find her. Together they would slip into Finland to join Patrina's *kumpania*, which by then would have crossed ahead of them.

On her first night home Dosha pushed all thoughts of the future aside. She and Jano fell into each other's arms and made passionate love. Afterward, as they lay side by side, Dosha took Jano's hand and placed it across her still wildly racing heart.

"Come spring I will have to leave."

He dug his head into her hair. "Forever?"

She nodded. "Khantchi told me it has to happen no later than this spring." Jano remained silent, but kissed her so deeply she thought he would drink her soul out of her body.

"We will have to part," he uttered sadly.

"You could always flee with us."

"If I were caught, it would only increase the danger to all of you."

She held his body tight. "At least we have till spring," she whispered. "I have come to love you." He turned and pulled her up to lie on top of him. He encased her face with both his hands. In the faint light of the kerosene lamp, with eyes linked, they were learning each other by heart.

"I hope it's not forever," she whispered, moving next him, where, intertwined, they lay open-eyed for much of the night.

In 1956 the "Thaw" that Khrushchev had initiated three years after Stalin's death raised great hopes, along with troubling after-shocks. Political prisoners were released, only to be forced, upon their return, to live in accusatory silence side by side with those who had victimized them, triggering new waves of trauma. As for Khrushchev's liberalization of the creative arts, it resulted mostly in widespread demonstrations and outcries for freedom. Shaken to the core, the new leadership reversed tactics and shifted public focus back to the sciences and the more easily manipulated areas of performing arts and sports.

To add to the existing program of international Olympic sports, a call was issued to revive the once world-famous Russian High School of Riding. Valuable horses and carefully selected breeding stock had fallen victim over the decades to wars, revolutions, and the famines caused by collectivization. Now highly trained military riders fanned out to all known collective and stud farms to round up suitable mounts for what was to be an equestrian team of international caliber.

It was, however, the introduction of electricity into backward areas that put the spotlight on the small, unregulated breeding-farm established by Djemo and his followers. The foreman of an installation work-crew was climbing a newly-raised electric pole when he first spotted Dosha's stallion pacing along the fence line of a field with his smooth, elastic walk. The rose-gray stallion was twice the size of the rugged ponies running free on adjacent land. The foreman promptly wrote to his superiors, asking that his find be reported to the Committee for Sport and Physical Culture in Moscow.

The first snow arrived unusually early that year. Daylight had already shrunk to a dusky two hours a day. The Soviet work crew was long gone, and with it the short-lived "magic" light of the electricity. It had not withstood even the first mild arctic storm. The sky bulged with snow like a featherbed ready to rip open. The winds swept in from the bare hills, driving all living things toward the shelter of dwarfed and gnarled fir trees.

As always, Dosha and her father had worked the horses inside the shed that morning. But sensing the impending storm, the horses had been jittery and too jumpy to perform well. Dosha herself felt nervous, uneasy, as if she too picked up a vague threat in the air. The stallion had acted up all morning in his makeshift stall, striking out at the walls that kept him apart from the rest of the herd. By the time Dosha turned him loose in his enclosed field, flakes of snow were flying at last. She had barely slipped the

108

lead from his rope halter when the stallion broke free, bucking and bolting, racing across the long but narrow pasture. It set off a stampede among the herd of Siberian ponies on the other side of the fence, as they headed toward a forest further south.

Dosha closed and then leaned across the gate to the pasture. The stallion had come to a sliding halt by the fence across from her, close enough for her to see his body shiver with suppressed power as every instinct urged him to catch up with the fleeing ponies. Several times their size and strength, he had no chance of surviving in their hostile world. He was born to sun and gentler climes. But Dosha had no way to take him further south till spring.

She wondered if Khantchi could be persuaded to let Jano come with them. She also wondered how she might convince Jano that his presence among them could no more endanger the tribe than Khantchi's. Wasn't her grandfather the most hunted Gypsy of all?

Jano had left the night before with a group of musicians to play at a Russian wedding. They had not yet returned. Soon they would be cut off by the storm. If they'd gotten drunk and fallen asleep, the Russians would simply throw them out into the arctic night. Their bodies would be found frozen after the storm. It seemed that ever since the last war, Russian peasants had nothing but mistrust for all outsiders, including the ones they called *tzigani*.

With a growing sense of foreboding, Dosha stared down the dirt road, long after the ponies had disappeared. Snow stung her face and the cold bit at her eyes, making her blink. That's when she saw the truck. A huge van equipped with a snowplow came roaring toward the encampment. Its headlights swept the snow ahead. The van was new, white and shiny. It had long narrow windows along both sides. *Is this a van to transport horses?* she wondered. The oversized vehicle skidded to a precarious halt right in front of the stallion's field.

The stalled engine's backfire rang out like the crack of a training whip. Then, to her horror, Dosha watched the treasure of her life arch his powerful neck, and, as if she had given him his cue, canter off, mane flying, with strides that seemed to be floating on air.

Djemo, who was still in the riding shed when Dosha had led out the stallion, must have heard the commotion. He came running outside, bullwhip in hand. Dressed as usual in Russian peasant attire, he appeared just in time to see the Gypsy dogs crowd the cab of the van like a pack of wolves. He cracked his whip to call them off. But the driver of the van was already standing on the steps of the cab with a drawn gun, ready to shoot.

Djemo lifted his hand, shouting, "They're good. They're under control." His Russian contained not even the trace of a Romani accent. He sounded completely Russian.

"Get them away, then!" the driver cursed.

The dogs cringed at the sight of Djemo's still raised whip. But when he calmly lowered it to the ground, the dogs, never taking their eyes off the whip, slowly turned and, with shackles still raised, cautiously slunk off to gather below the overhanging eaves of the shed roof.

Three more men emerged from the cab of the van. All four were dressed in military coats and riding boots. Dosha watched the smallest of the group, a bowlegged Tartar, walk close to the fence. The stallion, his panic at the cracking whip not fully dissipated, watched his owner from mid-field.

The Tartar soldier turned to Dosha. "Is this your horse?" he asked in a high-pitched, imperious voice.

She nodded.

"Bring him here."

Dosha felt as if a bomb had dropped. Djemo stood frozen in place. She knew she must fetch the stallion as ordered. The stallion sensed her anguish. He would not approach on his own, but tensely waited for her to walk up to him and grab his halter.

Confronted with this sudden, unexpected danger, Dosha's mind was racing. With deep breaths, she willed her thoughts to slow down as she led the stallion through the gate and then followed the intruders, at a safe distance, into the shed.

A crowd of Gypsy kids, drawn by the drama, had collected like flies along the low sides of the shed. Kerosene lamps, dangling from the support beams, threw an uneven light toward the center of the dark structure. Having just finished working with the young horses, Dosha herself was dressed in pants and riding boots. *That's a small stroke of luck*, she thought. *At least the bastards will take me for a Finn and not a Gypsy.* Gypsy women, even the equestriennes, wore only tribal attire, a custom Dosha had been allowed to breach while riding.

One of the soldiers now took the stallion from her by attaching a lead to his rope halter and quietly holding him. *They know horses!* The thought struck her with terror. *These are riders. Have they come to...?* She forced the very idea out of her mind, but then thought: *Where are Djemo's rifles? Did he barter all of them?* With a sinking feeling, Dosha realized they were defenseless. Besides, where these Bolsheviks came from, there were more, many more. Killing them would serve no purpose.

Meanwhile the Tartar had lit a cigarette. His brownish eyes, set in yellowish skin, gleamed like a cat's. His bowlegs indicated a man accustomed to the back of a horse, and his sinewy physique marked him as one who had grown up on a horse. He spoke to Djemo: "I see you've got lunge lines there," he said, pointing to the long leather leads hanging from hooks along the wall. "Let's see the best horses you've got."

"These are the only three we work during the winter." Djemo pointed to the stallion and his two horses, still in their stalls. "Our pony stock is already turned out for the winter," he said.

"Start with those," the Tartar said, pointing to the two horses in the stalls.

Djemo, without further comment, lunged his second-best horse first, then his favorite mare.

The Tartar, sucking on one cigarette after another, said nothing but watched with narrowed eyes. When both horses had been lunged, he turned back to the stallion. While the Tartar had been observing Djemo's horses, one of the other soldiers had run a hand over every part of the stallion's body, had flexed each front leg, then the hind legs. Now he was trotting the horse around the perimeter of the shed, where the roof was so low that the stallion had to drop his head to proceed.

Djemo, hands folded behind his back lest he betray his Gypsy origins by the busy hand gestures of a Lovari horse-trader, moved to Dosha's side. She had placed herself amid the Gypsy kids who, always ready for flight when confronted with strangers, now stood by the exit gate.

The Tartar flung his burning cigarette butt onto the frozen dirt of the arena, dug it in with the toe of his well-worn boot, and said, "Let's see him under saddle."

At once one of the soldiers who had been standing by the stalls ran out to the van, returned with a saddle and bridle — they had obviously come prepared — and moved resolutely to the center of the ring. First he expertly bridled the stallion, and then he slapped a flat, hard military saddle onto the horse's back. By then the animal's eyes were rolling wildly in their sockets.

"They'll never be able to ride him," Dosha whispered in Romani, stepping closer to her father.

"That won't much matter," her father answered in a sullen tone. "They're clearly here to confiscate. They'll sort it all out later. I'm surprised they even bother to ride."

That's when Dosha and Djemo got to watch them fly, those Soviets. One of the soldiers barely had his second foot in the stirrup, when he was bucked off. Another bashed his head against a beam as the stallion bucked upwards. That rider dropped like a stone. The stallion, his bridle hanging free, bolted.

"Damn!" the Tartar cursed, while one of the first of the dumped soldiers tried to block the circling stallion's way.

"Serves him right," Djemo swore in whispered Romani. "Goddamn Tartars! Here they just got their civil rights back, and what do they do? Swoop down on us Gypsies to take away ours. It's the old Bolshevik seesaw system all over again."

"But they'll just catch him again," Dosha whispered. "There's nothing we can do, is there?"

The horse had again been caught and brought, trembling, back to the center of the ring. Handing his coat to another soldier, the Tartar prepared to mount and take possession of what was not his to take. He began by pulling on the bridle to bring the stallion's close his own body, so as to restrict any impulse toward flight. The groom remained by the horse's head as the Tartar mounted, using a mounting block. He now pulled the stallion's head up high by shortening the bridle. Dosha could see the stallion grow more and more frantic. His feet scrabbled. He was breaking into a sweat. The Tartar let himself drop into the saddle like a 140-pound ax. The stallion was ready to explode but felt his head held up by the reins as if by a noose. With one swift kick the Tartar moved him forward, but the stallion's stride was so shortened, he appeared almost ordinary.

"They'll take him anyway," Djemo whispered. He sounded convinced.

"Never mind!" Dosha could stand it no longer. She handed her coat and fur hat to one of the Gypsy kids and stepped forward. She gently placed one hand on her trembling stallion's neck and told the Tartar, as one horse-lover to another, "Please, comrade, let me do it. It's the only way he'll respond."

For a moment the Tartar nailed her face with his hungry cat's eyes.

"All right then." He jumped off the horse. Dosha quickly loosened the girth by one hole, then walked the panting animal once around the arena on a loose rein, talking to him softly, one hand in his mane. Then the Tartar actually offered to give her a leg up. Dosha mounted, lowering herself into the saddle ever so gently, before leaning forward to embrace the stallion's neck with both her arms. She could feel his heart pounding under her hand. As she lifted herself into an upright position, the stallion softened his poll and collected under her. And from a standstill they struck off in a canter as fluid and rhythmic as waves rolling toward a sandy beach on a quiet day.

The Tartar watched, again with narrowed eyes, and then called his men. "We take the stallion and the mare!" he ordered. Turning to Djemo, he added, "They are drafted by the State!"

Dosha jumped off the stallion. A soldier stepped forward, removed the saddle, and slipped on a military halter and lead shank. He was in the process of leading the stallion toward the exit gate when Dosha rushed over to Djemo. "Can they simply steal our horses?"

Djemo had retreated closer to the wall, "There's nothing we can do," he said, "other than get out of here as soon as we can, or we'll be next."

That's when the Tartar pointed to Dosha. "Her too, in the name of the State. She is hereby drafted to help with the stallion's transition to a proper rider."

"And you better go," Djemo warned his daughter in a barely audible voice, "or your life is not worth living." She stood stunned.

"Go on. They want you too, and maybe, just maybe, you can protect our horses and us from further persecution—hopefully, till your grandfather can spring you." For a moment Djemo took Dosha's hand in his and held it tight. It was the first time he had touched her in a reassuring way since she had arrived.

"Jano," she whispered.

"Jano's not back yet."

"Tell him … Say good-bye from me. Tell him … I thought we'd have till spring."

And for the first time since her arrival she looked deep into her father's eyes. Confusion, anguish, longing — for what, she could not define — overtook her. Just at that moment, the Tartar pulled her by an arm. She had barely enough time to grab her coat and fur hat back from the Gypsy kid before she was half-led, half-dragged up the open back ramp into the van. She heard the striking of hoofs against wood, as a flashlight flared up in the Tartar's hand. It illuminated a row of narrow box stalls built diagonally along the left length of the van. Waving the flashlight, the Tartar motioned her toward a box stall up front. The narrow stall stood empty between the stalls of the riled-up stallion and the kicking mare.

# Part Two

# 12
## Drafted

Thrown like an afterthought into an empty box stall between two thrashing horses that had never before been confined to a moving vehicle, Dosha's first thought, as always, was to try and calm them down by softly talking to them. But this time her voice was lost in the thrashing and whinnying and the roaring of the engine that filled the dark space. She heard the stallion working himself up into all-out panic as he yanked the chain that tied his halter to a hook in the wall. The metal snapped and clanked but did not give way. He reared, his feet striking the wall up front. Coming down, his left hoof struck the dividing wall; his right caught the chest bar of his stall.

Dosha held her breath and started praying out loud — "Please *o del*, send us a miracle! Safeguard my horses and myself, *o del!*" — Until she heard the stallion land back on all fours. Quickly she reached across the partition, and grabbing his ear, she pinched it as hard as she could, in an attempt to distract him by inflicting pain.

"Shh, shh," she crooned to the sweating, frightened horses. The stallion stood still, quivering under her now gentle touch and soothing voice. Meanwhile, on her right side the mare kept rocking back and forth striking out at both the wall to her right and the low sidewall that separated her from Dosha.

The narrow windows that Dosha had noticed running along the length of the van were boarded up with wooden planks from the inside. The interior was as dark as she imagined the night to be by then, for the sky had already been clouding over when, earlier that afternoon, she had first set eyes upon the Soviet van. She imagined how the unbroken darkness would flatten the smooth

hills and gentle elevations of the vast landscape they were crossing. Only the freshly fallen snow would cast a ghostly glow.

Her thoughts flew to Jano. Would she ever see him again? If
he were on his way home by now, he could easily lose his way —
especially, she feared, if, giving in to his weakness for vodka, he
kept toasting the bride and groom with home-made brew. *I just
hope,* she thought, *that the others don't leave him behind.* For unlike
them, Jano did not have the instinct of the road. If he were left
behind, drunk, he might stagger off and freeze to death in that
trackless nowhere.

Exhausted, Dosha slid along the wall into the corner next
to the stallion's stall. Like the other box stalls in the van, she assumed, hers was bedded with straw. There was hay in the corner
next to the mare's stall. *They must have been looking for more horses
to fill the rest of the stalls,* she thought. Or maybe they'd be drafting
more along the way.

Dosha pulled her knees up to her chin and buried her face between her legs. Suddenly she felt every bump and rut of the dirt
road. Only then did the realization that she had been taken from
the security of her own people come crashing down on her in dev-
astating waves.

Memories she had boarded up and tried to forget suddenly
came rushing back. The snow crunching under the wheels of the
van sounded more and more like the chugging of freight trains —
the trains marked with the dreaded Nazi swastika that had carried so many of her people to destinations of no return. *Like cattle
shoved into rolling coffins at the mercy of forces that knew no pity.* She
covered her eyes with both her hands.

"Please," she prayed, "don't let this be a Soviet version of a
Nazi train." She remembered Patrina's warning, so many years
ago, that the Bolsheviks would surely one day hunt down and
persecute the Russian Gypsies. "It is inevitable," Jano had told her
as they clung to each other, alone in the dark. "Sooner or later,
they'll hunt us Gypsies down."

The horses, fortunately, had grown calmer as they grew accustomed to the motion of the van. Breathing deeply in and out,
Dosha tried to concentrate on their peaceful munching. Little bits
of hay dropped onto her head and face whenever they bent their
heads as far as their chains would allow them toward where she
sat. What would happen to them? She had no more power to
help them than Gypsy parents had to protect their children, once

trapped in concentration camps. An uncontrollable panic threw her into a wild confusion where childhood memories, hearsay, and all she had most feared broke over her again, submerging and drowning her. She tried to rise above the confusion. Instead she sank deeper and deeper into her past.

Dzumila's face, stark and ominous, stared at her like a face seen in the window of a train racing through the night. Beyond her image, reflections of the Roma arose: men, women, and children, lining up along the raised cement platform of a country railway station, dimly lit. The Roma stood there eerily still and silent. *Move! Run!* She prayed. They, however, remained frozen in ghostly positions. Until — a snapshot flared up in Dosha's mind and remained there, clear as a picture on a wall — she saw three smiling *rom*. They were young, their arms slung across one another's shoulders. They were about to be photographed by a fourth. All four were dressed the way of city Gypsies, in suits and hats. The fourth moved, bringing the still image to life as he lifted a camera. He was about to shoot the picture, but instead a shot rang out. At once everything in the vicinity sprang to life. The camera flew aside. So did all the Roma. Like birds frightened in a field, they rose and scattered in all directions.

The clack-clack of jackboots reverberated through Dosha's mind. She covered her ears with her hands. The clacking sound increased in speed. Of course they had been there all along; they must have been, buried somewhere in the still life of that scene. The firing of shots, warning shots fired into the air, further shattered the silence that had reigned before. The scattering of the Gypsies turned into a wild stampede. "*Schuss … Halt!*" Bullets sprayed like water from a faucet. The Roma, killed in midflight, dropped like dead birds across the platform and the tracks below. Gestapo soldiers prowled among them, shooting the dying and kicking the dead.

*But wait! This is Russia.* Dosha was bathed in sweat. Hadn't many other elders assured her, when they sat around fires in the evenings, that Russia's Gypsies were part of Russia's soul? Most Russians accepted the ways of their *tzigani*, loved their music, their dance, the freedom of their lives. Mother Russia would never betray the people who had joined her fight for freedom.

*But then again,* she thought, *with Gadje you never know.* She ran her hands along her coarse riding pants, down to the leather riding boots her father had insisted she wear while working with the horses. *At least,* she thought, *dressed like this, nobody will take me for a Gypsy.* Just as, during the war years, she had worn the dress of a Polish peasant girl to protect her from suspicion, she was again wearing camouflage.

Her fight was now to stay awake. After hours of jolting travel in the dark, Dosha could not resist the growing heaviness of her limbs. She stretched out on the straw-covered wooden floor of the van and closed her eyes. *For a moment only,* she thought. Instead, almost instantly she drifted into an uneasy half-sleep, where, between dream and wakefulness, she felt Jano soothingly move close to her, just as he had every night since she had accepted him as her *rom.* Although the shape of his face remained undefined and the shape of his eyes indistinct, the eyes themselves were languid, fluid. His lips were parted, touching her as fog tinges the tips of grass. Her mind nestled into his.

"Those who hunted you," she whispered, "have captured me instead." His shadow spread across her like a love embrace. She touched her face, trying to capture remnants of his airy touch. Instead, tears were running down her face, warm to the touch, salty to the taste. His absence struck her like a physical pain. Finally she slept.

She awakened to the sound of the truck engine revving high. Through the floor of the van, Dosha felt the front wheels spin — was the van stuck in the snow? The engine backfired, and died. She sat up straight.

The door of the van's cab opened and slammed shut again. Voices outside the van started to converse. One among them, louder than the rest, shouted angry orders which she could not understand. Not knowing what to expect next, she jumped to her feet and tried to pierce the darkness in the direction of the voices outside. The horses — the stallion first, then the mare — started to pee. Urine came gushing out like streams. Although Dosha could smell and had heard the droppings of manure, this was the first time since they had left the collective that they actually peed. Once finished, the stallion started to paw the ground furiously.

The small side door by the mare's head swung open to the outside. A blast of icy air hit them as a flashlight flared up, pointing to the ceiling. The light, lowered, ran along the chest bars that kept the horses from crashing to the front. Dosha noticed only then that her stall was the only one not equipped with a chest bar.

One of the military riders entered. He climbed under a round iron chest bar into the mare's stall, where he quickly lowered his flashlight to the floor. In his other hand he was carrying a bucket swooshing with water, which he poured first into the mare's water bucket, attached to a corner of her outside wall. He then made his way to the stallion's stall and bucket. The horses eagerly sucked up the new supply of water.

Through the still open side door Dosha was able to see a small fire burning in a portable iron fire pit a few feet away from the van. Next to it stood the Tartar. He was packing snow into a skillet — melting snow for water. The night was windless and muffled by the silent fall of heavy snow.

A second soldier entered and said, "Here!" In his outstretched hand he held a slice of bread and a small jug of water, which Dosha, getting to her feet, took while keeping her eyes focused on his hand, trying hard to avoid any type of physical contact with this stranger. The soldier then walked behind the beam of his flashlight to the bales of hay and metal cans tied to both walls of the closed ramp at the back of the van. He extracted a bale of hay, cut the baling string, and proceeded to refill the almost empty nets with hay for the horses. The other soldier re-entered and walked to the back of the van, where he grabbed one of the cans of what Dosha guessed must be petrol and left. For a moment she considered asking for permission to go outside to relieve herself, but she decided that for now her safety, among these men, probably lay with her horses. When the side door was again shut and bolted from the outside, she climbed into the stall of Djemo's mare, lowered her pants, and relieved herself.

Something big dropped from the front of the van with a loud metal clang. The noise was deafening. *They must have lowered that plow*, she thought. For now the van was traveling at a slower speed, as if clearing a path. With a reverberating clatter the snowplow kept bouncing off obstacles which threw the van every which way. The bumpy ride kept the horses stepping in place in a constant balancing act. They had stopped eating. Dosha could smell the sweat rising from their coats. Whatever water was left in their buckets was swooshing, even spilling at times. Only then did Dosha realize that the inside of the van was heated. Despite the bitter cold that had hit her from outside, the inside of the van kept an even heat. The horses wore no blankets. Soon the noise of the plow stopped and travel turned smooth again. The horses resumed chewing their hay.

Calmed by the familiar sound and the sweaty odor of horse, but exhausted from fear and uncertainty, Dosha curled into a fetal position and nestled deep into the thick layers of spread-out straw. At once an odor of dryness and trapped sunlight assaulted her senses, reminding her of the smoke of healing herbs. Once again, she softly drifted off into sleep. Her mind let go of her body and for a moment remained afloat. With a sense of peace, she watched the darkness around her shift, then lift. She found herself in a field of blazing yellow where she started to walk down a straight but narrow path — she started to skip. Suddenly faces she had known and loved shot up around her like flowers in the spring. Petal by petal, they opened toward her, as if she were the sun; they stretched, they interlinked, they reached, they touched her, chatting away and laughing, alive with joy.

But gradually the yellow that engulfed them started to dim. The faces receded, shrinking to the size of the black seedpods of blood-red poppies, now growing helter-skelter throughout what had turned into a darkened field covered with wild wheat that rippled in the wind.

Dosha ran here and there, bending down whenever she came across a poppy, and picked it, poppy after poppy. She stopped and stood intertwining them with the stalks of wild wheat, creating the bouquets of *patrins* for her road. Walking on, she tied them to tall stalks of wheat along her road of travel. *You must follow me,* she whispered, *for the journey I was destined to make since birth has now begun.*

She now raced ahead like a horse in full gallop, barely touching the ground. She was in flight — speeding toward the source of a light that suddenly appeared from beyond the lip of what she now realized was a floating sphere. The dawning light kept surging and receding, as if it were held back by a rubber band, when suddenly a sun popped up in full. Gusts of wind rose and circled. She heard the thunderous approach of a stampeding herd. The sudden light was blinding. Dosha tried to cover her face but there was no hiding from the light.

She opened her eyes with a start. A flashlight was pointed straight at her face. For a moment she did not know where she was; nor did she recognize the man who stood, bow legs spread wide, atop the open ramp, silhouetted against more of the same blinding light. The glaring light that poured in from the outside — floodlights — was partially blocked by other men in uniform who were climbing up the ramp. That's when she remembered the bowlegged figure: it was the Tartar who had captured her.

The horses were pulling at their halters, yanking their chains. The stallion snorted wildly, twisting and turning, striking out repeatedly with both hind feet. Then, when he both pulled back and rose half-way up, something gave way with a splintering crash. He had succeeded in ripping his lead shank, hook and eye, out of the wooden wall. Now loose in his narrow traveling partition, he threw himself against the divider that separated him from Dosha's stall. She heard the tail bar crash to the ground, and jumped to her feet. The stallion had broken free and wheeled around toward the open ramp. Soldiers flew or were kicked aside as the stallion exploded, bolting down the ramp into the flood-lit space.

By then the two riders who had fed and watered the horses before, had opened the small side door. The first rushed to the mare and positioned himself right next to the shaking mare's head. He started stroking her neck, trying to calm her, while the other rider stepped close, rattling an inviting bucket of grain. Dosha stepped into the aisle and ran down the ramp to catch her stallion.

In a rectangular yard, confined on three sides by low wooden barracks with metal roofs, with the truck blocking off the fourth, the stallion was running circle after circle. The Tartar, running ahead of an equally frantic Dosha, started shouting, "Don't shoot! Do not shoot!" as soldiers wearing long army coats and carrying tommy guns flew aside and sought shelter in the narrow alleys that separated the army barracks. Two or three had already dropped into kneeling positions, aiming at the stallion.

The panicked horse reared toward the streams of light that poured down from tall poles, rooftops, and high barbed-wired walls. Searchlights from watchtowers chased one another across the sky; crossing, they stopped like an X, creating a target mark on the stallion's side. He reared again in fear. For a moment the soldiers stood still, like cardboard figures. Again the Tartar shouted, "Stop! I say stop!"

Dosha, sidestepping the Tartar, kept her eyes solely on her stallion. He had come down and now stood on all fours, trembling and blowing hard. His breath was visible in the freezing air. Dosha approached him with outstretched arms and a soft hum. "Please, *o del*," she started to pray in a low voice, "I beg of you, don't rob me of what has brought beauty and magic into my life."

The stallion's eyes were rolling wildly when suddenly he spotted her within the melee of scurrying soldiers. Dosha linked her own desperate eyes to his. She knew she now must regain her calm and send assurance and love into his being. She approached him with tiny steps, whispering and humming. "Calm down. All is well. Don't be scared," she sang to him. Her focus never wavered — just as behind her, the Tartar, ramrod straight, never let his eyes waver from her every step. Gently, she touched the stallion's withers, then took his halter and dug her face into his mane. The soldiers at last started backing away.

They had traveled beyond the line of heavy snow, for the ground was hard here but bare. A fine icy drizzle moistened the air. The pitch-black night enveloped the lit camp like a cave. The odors of human confinement lingered and smelled as if trapped under a blanket of moisture and darkness.

A soldier approached. He handed Dosha a long army coat. "For you," he said.

# 13
## The Tartar Osap Tossuk

The Tartar, Osap Tossuk, had wondered right from the start at the girl's know-how with the horse. He had watched closely the instinctive way in which she handled the headstrong stallion. Were she not dressed in man's riding pants, and had she not been caught in such a random way, he would have labeled hers the Gypsy way, although she did not look like any Gypsy he'd come across. Besides, he knew from experience that Gypsy women did not give up their skirts, even when offered new clothing, free from the State. They clung to their skirts like soldiers to their rifles. Why? He had no clue

But the Tartar was no stranger to Gypsies. When, after World War II, Stalin accused the Crimean Tartars of having collaborated with the Germans, almost the entire Tartar population was deported to Uzbekistan and Kazakhstan. Osap was one of the few who had been saved from this fate by his lover, the Bolshevik revolutionary Galina Petrovna Popov. The night before a lineup, to prevent Osap's deportation, she had hidden him on a collective stud farm in the Urals. This *kolkhoz* was worked mostly by Gypsies who, as punishment for some transgression or other, were condemned to forced labor by Soviet law.

Only after leaving the stud farm, many years later, did Osap realize that although the Gypsies — men, women, ragged kids alike — had learned to play him like a violin, he was no wiser about what they did or what they felt than when he had first arrived. One other thing he knew for sure. He had never seen a Gypsy woman, old or young, ride a horse. All he had personally seen the women do was lead the horses down to the river at the end of the day to splash them down with water and rub them clean; women also helped with foaling.

Osap had left the stud farm a few months ago when, under Khrushchev's de-Stalinization program, the Tartars regained their civil rights. Once again, Osap gained a further advantage through his enduring association with his former lover, Comrade Galina Popov, now in her late fifties. Galina happened to be a loyal relative — a distant cousin, through her peasant mother — of Nikita Sergeyevich Khrushchev, the rising new Red Czar. The Tartar hoped to ride on her coattails to take advantage of this wave of new possibilities. One such venture — an idea which Comrade Popov proposed to her cousin Nikita — was the notion of reviving the once famous Russian High School of Riding. The initiative's first test had been the hasty entry of Soviet dressage and stadium jumping teams into the Summer Olympic Games of 1955, the first time Russians had participated since the Great Bolshevik Revolution. The experiment proved to be a disaster, which Comrade Popov had survived by explaining to her cousin, "It was merely a test. We will succeed in the end. It's merely a question of finding suitable horses and riders." So the search went on.

In his former position as a dressage trainer for Russia's most elite cavalry division, Osap had made it his priority to please his boss and now former lover, the formidable Galina, and as a result he was promised the position of head trainer of the new dressage team. In addition, he had been dispatched to hunt down the stallion that the sharp-eyed electrical worker had discovered and reported to the State. Even before he mounted the towering horse, Osap knew, by just laying his hand on its withers, that the stallion would resist him. But he was a consummate horseman. *That*, he reassured himself, *has nothing to do with me. This horse is used to one rider alone and will object to any stranger on his back.* He then witnessed the brilliance which the girl had brought out in the talented horse, which stood taller and better muscled than any he had seen so far on Soviet soil. *Of course*, the Tartar decided, *"it won't do for some unknown, a young girl to boot, to ride a stallion of such caliber. This glorious beast brings back memories of Russia's fighting past. Rus! That's it, for a show name to summon Russia's glorious origins! Galina will go for that.* Not only would the name be symbolic, it sounded patriotic. Of course the girl, whatever her background, would have to be exchanged at the earliest opportunity for another rider, one favored by the party and preferably male.

Back at the collective, he had looked into the stallion's mouth to get an idea of his age. Osap judged him to be nine to ten years old, *in his prime,* and whoever had given him his basic training had done so flawlessly. *Although,* Osap thought, *that in itself is suspect, given the godforsaken corner where I found him. Better to forget about that for right now.* Osap needed the girl's help with the transition to a different rider, or they might not get the stallion back to his full potential within the time frame of this officially declared "five-year plan."

The Tartar walked up to the girl, who was holding the stallion by his long white mane, and introduced himself. "My name," he said, "is Osap Tossuk. I am your new trainer." Seeing no need to inform her that she was about to enter the world of formal Soviet training and competition, he merely added: "We'll be spending the night in this officers' training camp."

The drive to this camp — Dosha later figured out that it was near Petrozavodsk, on the western shore of Lake Onega in Russian Karelia, the farthest Northern point of the Soviet railroad system — had taken them twenty hours. "Tomorrow," the Tartar said, "we'll load the horses onto trains to continue on to Leningrad."

"To where?" she asked.

"Leningrad," he repeated. "The old Saint Petersburg?" He wondered whether, despite his suspicion that she'd been exposed to more sophisticated training grounds, she may in fact never before have gotten out of that hole of snow and ice. "'Pearl of the Baltic,'" he added, cracking a smile that in no way relaxed her. One of the military riders came up behind them, leading the tall, big-boned mare. The stallion nickered in welcome. It occurred to the Tartar he as yet knew nothing of this girl.

"What's your name?" he asked.

She stared back at him as if this simple question had caught her totally unawares.

"Ana," she said, after a long pause. "My name is Ana." She turned her face back to the stallion.

"Ana what?" he asked. She turned back toward him and again gave him that look of one who had swallowed her tongue. "Father's name?" the Tartar asked with growing impatience.

"Dalova," she said, "My father is A — Alex," she stammered, "Dalova." It was the name her father used when dealing with *Gadje.*

"Ana Alexandrevna Dalova, then." The Tartar held her eyes. "That wasn't so hard now, was it?" *More like dragging it out of a Siberian woodchuck,* he thought. *Maybe not the brightest candle in the*

126

*camp, but one of their hidden beauties — tall and blond with glints of red in her hair and that faraway look in her eyes.*

He took the mare's lead from his rider and walked ahead of this Ana toward one of the barracks that had been converted into a barn. They were walking along the dirt aisle, lit by a string of naked electric bulbs attached to the ceiling. To their right, bony army horses and confiscated circus horses, long broken by the Soviet System, stood quietly in narrow stalls eating hay. *Fellow future competitors for sure*, the Tartar thought, *but so much work to bring them up to par.* Unlike them, the fiery stallion had not been marred or broken by this System that allowed for no individual brilliance for man or beast alike. A new wind was blowing in the land of standardization. *One can only hope*, Osap thought, *that it's not another ill wind that blows no good.*

In the meantime, he would use the girl and indulge her. When she insisted on sleeping with the stallion rather than in the room assigned to her, he simply sent a soldier to guard her, sending along a plate of dinner: cabbage boiled with sausage, and some potatoes, a soldier's fare, and when the soldier returned saying, "She wouldn't touch the food," Osap accompanied the soldier back and personally handed the girl a piece of black bread.

"You've got to eat," he said. "At least some bread."

He watched her face as she turned it in her hands. She had eaten nothing beyond one other hunk of bread, during the twenty-hour journey, and he was curious to see how she would react. He knew that bread was one of the few things made by non-Gypsies that a Gypsy felt safe eating. Now he took the opportunity to add a little trap. "*Manro?*" He gestured toward the bread in her hands, using the Gypsy word for bread.

The girl in no way took the bait. She stared straight in his face as if she didn't know what he was asking her. He shrugged and turned away, annoyed.

As Galina's trusted hound, Osap was expected to be one of her many extra sets of ears and eyes. He decided to entail the aid of the engineer in charge of the next morning's train transport. "I need surveillance in the wagon with those two latest horses," he ordered. Then, before the engineer could question why, he added, "This has been a long trip for them. What with the change in feed, they could colic, go berserk. They've never been on a train before. I need to be able to keep an eye on them."

The Tartar himself supervised the installation of the two tiny cameras that would transmit the imagery to a screen located in the first passenger wagon, where he and his military riders would travel. The cameras were hidden behind bright electric bulbs installed in each of the two diagonal stalls at the front of the horse wagon in which the stallion and the mare would travel to Leningrad. One camera aimed toward the floor of the first stall, where Osap believed the girl would sit, right at the stallion's head, rather than in the empty space behind his tail bar. There were eight diagonal stalls in all, a narrow aisle and a heavy center sliding door across from the stalls.

He had judged right. Soon after the train had pulled out of the military station, Comrade Osap watched the girl duck under the tail bar into the stallion's box, and sit against the wall at his head. The stallion calmly bent down and nuzzled the girl's hair. She stroked his face. For quite some time nothing more happened. The girl sat motionless, staring straight ahead. The Tartar pulled a stack of forms that he needed to fill out for the newly acquired horses from his briefcase and set to work.

The next time he looked up, he noticed the girl had buried her head into her arms, and soon her shoulders started to shake. *There, he thought, she's crying. But only when she thinks she's all by herself. She'll break before she'll bend. Of that* he was sure. *And in a System like ours, where apathy is the only road to survival, such emotionalism will prove fatal in the end.*

As far as Osap was concerned, when Ana's usefulness to him was over, he would send her home. It would take three days and three nights by various means of transportation to get her back — though, truth be told, he didn't think anybody would go to the trouble of getting her there.

*She'll disappear in some gulag or labor camp,* he thought, *where the guards will pass her around for entertainment. It would be a shame,* he decided, and for a moment he felt a wave of pity, before returning to his forms. Then again, if his vague suspicions were correct, and she was in fact a Gypsy, they were the minority next in line to have their culture eliminated by proven methods of standardization and this girl, Gypsy or not, would be incorporated into some System or another anyway.

By the time they reached Leningrad, exhausted from the lack of freedom, the horses showed no resistance to being loaded from the train into a van that was to take them from the train station to their new quarters, the former Junker-Institut in the Hermitage. As before, the girl insisted on riding in the van with the horses.

Shortly after the Revolution, the Bolsheviks had turned

the Junker-Institut, which adjoined the Winter Palace and had housed the Imperial Guard, into a maternity ward. Since the establishment of this latest five-year plan, however, its riding halls, stables, and some of the barracks had been requisitioned by the Committee for Physical Culture to accommodate the newly formed dressage team. Now, as the convoy stopped a short distance from the entrance gate, women on stretchers were still being evacuated into waiting ambulances. They were followed by nurses dressed in blue, carrying babies in baskets like wares to market.

The girl emerged from the van, leading the stallion down the ramp. Catching sight of the women, who clearly had given birth not long ago, she turned to the Tartar.

"Is that where we're going?" she asked, recoiling.

His eyes narrowed. "Yes. Why?" He stared at her curiously. The expression on her face shifted from tenderness to something close to abhorrence.

*How about that?* The Tartar pondered. *She eats nothing but bread, and now she is reluctant to go into this former hospital for women giving birth?* The Tartar knew for a fact that for a Gypsy one of the the most unclean places, second only to a site of death, was a place of birthing. *Mahrime*, they called it. He had heard the word they used for pollution more often than he cared to remember. *Mahrime* was a barrier that no Gypsy he had ever known would cross.

The girl, by contrast, threw back her shoulders. An expression of grim determination hardened her still childlike features as she led the stallion down the ramp and into the street. No, Osap decided, he'd been around Gypsies too long. His suspicions must be all imagination. There was nothing Gypsy about her — not her dress, her voice, her name, especially her looks. She rode like a man, and if she refused an army meal — well, army food took getting used to, he had to admit and if she was appalled to see the women with their babies carried out on stretchers, well, why shouldn't she be? Who would expect to see a maternity ward turned into a training stable for dressage?

By then the morning had broken clear as glass. The horse barracks lay south of the Hermitage Theatre, where the van had stopped. Waiting by the Winter Moat, Dosha — now Ana to *Gadje* — could glimpse the cobalt waters of the Neva River. The air was still, and not so much as a ripple moved on the surface of the mighty river. A white-bellied bird lifted from the far shore. It flapped its widespread wings before sailing along the jagged, pastel outline of the city, and then rose up into a sky that she found deep and empty and of a melancholy blue. Her heart felt heavy. Was this an omen of things to come?

She was determined to enter these stables, even if they were *mahrime*. She would enter them courageously. She would follow her horse wherever they were forced to go.

# 14
# Quadrille

Once upon a time the image of Russia evoked in young dreamers notions of unparalleled romance, bravura, and ecstasy — reflections of fearless Cossacks and conquering Tartars chasing each other across endless plains. In those distant medieval days, Osap Tossuk's Tartar ancestors galloped free as the wind at breakneck speeds on their light and hardy ponies. Racing in killer waves across the steppes, they swept aside all efforts at defense in those territories they wished to conquer. They were short, gnarled, bowlegged men with broad faces and slanting eyes. Raising their wiry bodies fiercely upright atop their galloping ponies, they sent clouds of lethal arrows onto their enemies, then dropped sideways against their horses' flanks. There they hung by one leg like bats from a beam to avoid being struck in return. They ravaged and raped in passing, leaving in their wake terror and destruction, an ever-growing number of babies, and an unquestioning willingness by those conquered to pay tribute to the great khans.

To Russia they brought their wagons, wives, children, and herds to stay - subjugating Russian nobles and serfs alike to 240 years of the Tartar Yoke which branded the Russian soul as much as her great wide-open plains.

Traces of Tartar blood and temperament could be detected right up to the Great Bolshevik Revolution in the faces of reckless Russian aristocrats as they raced their fancy troikas across moon-lit plains of snow, lending truth to that oft-quoted saying: Scratch a Russian and you will find a Tartar. The conquerors had interbred with Russian peasants and nobles alike.

Czarist Russia had long since given way to the great Union of Soviet Socialist Republics, the U.S.S.R. A remnant Tartar, such as Osap Tossuk, although still bow-legged like his ancestors — the better to wrap around a horse– had been forced into servitude by these latest Russian overlords. He was looked upon even by the former serfs with hereditary hatred. As for the half-wild ponies of his ancestors? They had long since been hauled in and killed in the course of countless wars and revolutions — or else, like all other horses deemed unfit for work in the fields, consumed by the ever-hungry Soviet masses.

The sudden drive to revive Russia's once famous horsemanship most certainly did not stem from the idea of restoring the ancient Tartar tradition of freedom on horseback. It was about displaying the discipline and drills perfected over centuries by military cavalry all over Europe and European Russia. Born of warfare, classical dressage entails precise and difficult figures, circles and half-circles executed at increasing speed and increasing levels of difficulty: leg yields, leaps, and ballet movements of horses as strong, limber, and supple as gymnasts, and of riders so accomplished, they appear to give no signals to their mounts. The discipline of dressage was never intended for combat; it was developed to demonstrate superiority of horsemanship. Its latest aim, in Russia, was to conquer world opinion and to prove that the Soviet Communist System was capable of attaining the highest goals in life and art.

More than any other Russian city, Leningrad displayed the former glory and might of the czars, leaders of all the Russias. Dosha looked about her with interest. It struck her that, within the Imperial Hermitage, in its gilded winter riding hall adjoined by fancy stalls, amid riders, trainers, and their entourage of grooms and overseers, those around her seemed no more freed from bondage than they had been under the czars. They now paid tribute, instead, to the System.

Dosha, like most nomadic Roma, was accustomed to acknowledging leadership. Even the smallest vitsa, or clan, had a leader, male or female. The big tribes had one of each but these were leaders a Gypsy could see, talk to, and touch. They offered comfort in grief, advice and wisdom and protection when possible. In return, these leaders were entrusted with keeping and exhibiting the tribal wealth. This System that ruled here had no face, it had no voice.

Dosha's newly assigned roommate, Ekaterina Siglunov, the only other female rider in the group, impressed upon her that "Most of all, you must not break the rules."

They had been assigned a narrow oblong room on the upper floor of the Staff Building: two beds divided by a commode with four drawers, two for each. At one end of the cramped room — so small that only one person could move about at any given time — was a window with heavy curtains of a faded green, and at the other a closet curtained with the same fabric. There they were to hang their uniforms and riding habits. When Dosha drew the closet curtain for the first time, she heard a plaintiff "meow" from within a pile of underwear heaped up on the floor.

"A cat?" Dosha cried out.

"Please," Ekaterina pleaded, "I didn't have the heart to leave her behind. I know it's against the rules."

Dosha looked from the cat, a scrawny gray, anxious-looking animal, to the Russian woman. She was older than Dosha and on the plump side, with innocent, soulful eyes — eyes that now nervously searched Dosha's face. Gypsies consider keeping cats in living quarters unclean. But this was the first time since she'd left her people that Dosha found herself alone with another woman, one who was asking for her help. On impulse she stretched out her arms, and for the blink of a moment she held the *Gadji* tight. "Your secret is safe with me," she whispered. "I'll save you some of my food. Forget about the rules."

Besides, no one had spelled out these rules to Dosha. From what little she could piece together, these rules appeared to be more powerful and pervasive than any leader she had ever encountered. Whenever Dosha walked into the barracks-like dining hall, or along the narrow corridors leading to the communal bathrooms, the stalls, the riding arena, she felt invisible eyes following her every move. The walls seemed to press in on her. Yet whenever she raised her head while walking, or when she suddenly turned while taking care of her horses, she never seemed to catch any eyes on her: everybody seemed to be watching everybody else instead. Only at night, when she left the tiny bedroom she shared with Ekaterina and walked along a damp and deserted corridor toward the deserted toilet stalls, did she feel the omnipresent threat hone in on her. Only when one of the so-called "Officers of Morals and Behavior," representing the strong presence of the KGB, openly followed her every step with an unwholesome glint in his shifty eyes did she realize that she was a lone woman at the mercy of a System that was everywhere.

The compound assigned to the newly formed team consisted of cement-walled rooms and halls built within the pre-existing walls of this wing of the Hermitage, the former Junker-Institut. Dosha, like all the other riders, was given permission to visit the city but unlike them she did not dare leave the compound.

Alone and isolated in the alien city, she felt a pervasive anxiety, which extended to her horse as well. The Tartar had already requisitioned Djemo's mare for his own use. Dosha was certain that someone had designs on the stallion as well. The ever-present fear impelled her to insist on doing her own grooming. She left the stallion's side only to sleep, and then only because Osap hinted at the consequences if she did not comply.

"The only ones around at night," he said, and for once he looked sincere, "are young..." — he bent close to her ear — "*male*," he emphasized, "soldiers. Why risk unnecessary trouble?"

Then there was the problem of food — polluted through contact with *Gadje*. What was she to do? Day after day she ate mostly bread, although she had started to eat boiled potatoes and sometimes smoked meat. She kept losing weight. With a growing sense of helplessness, she wondered what the System was ultimately planning to do with her. From a tiny window in the stallion's stall, she watched van after van drop off more horses with their riders. Most of the horses were lean. The riders had vacant faces.

Despite the constant traffic of horses and their riders in and out of the stables and riding halls, and grooms pushing wheelbarrows loaded with manure, straw for bedding, and bales of hay and feed, the noise level in the compound was uncommonly low. There was no shouting, no laughter. The loudest sound came from Osap, as he passed through the aisles and riding halls, examining horses and their movements, and issuing orders and guidance in his high-pitched voice. The dressage team was being chosen, and Dosha knew that in order to survive she had to be one of its riders. Only that way could she stay with her horse. The dressage competition as well as exhibition riding would consist of no more than twenty-three riders and their horses, plus two substitutes. Two weeks after her arrival, the vans stopped coming.

"How many are there all together?" Dosha asked Ekaterina, who with her stout workhorse had been assigned the stall next to hers.

"Forty-five horses in all," Ekaterina replied.

Dosha walked her horse into the work arena where Osap Tossuk was watching a horse being lunged. Dosha walked up to him. "Is the selection for the new dressage team now complete?" she asked.

"The riders now chosen," he said, keeping his eyes on the one lunging before him, "are merely the picks from our initial search. They in turn are now here to train for the final qualifying trial, but whoever comes here, no matter how small the chance of success, knows it's worth it." He turned to face her. "A spot on the team guarantees the opportunity to travel abroad, and," he added with a sly wink, "the possibility of putting their hands on valuable foreign goods and bartering merchandise, items not obtainable by the average Soviet citizen."

"What about the horses that don't make it?" Dosha asked.

The Tartar shrugged. "Certainly some, like the ones that can be kept reasonably sound, can serve as school horses for the various riding clubs," he said, "As for the rest ..." He screwed up his eyes to hers.

Dosha caught her breath. "Horsemeat?"

Osap, seeing the girl turn pale, hastened to reassure her. "You have nothing to worry about," he said. "Our," he paused, "stallion is certainly assured a place on this team. He is far superior to the others."

*In other words,* Dosha thought, *if 'our' stallion performs well, we will survive.* She took a closer look at the obedient animals lining the brightly lit hall. All were emaciated, some to the bone. Their heads hung low. Some, especially the older ones, proved to be lame once they fell into a trot.

*They'll eat them,* she thought. *If only I had the powers to save them!*

The next morning, right after breakfast, all the riders were ordered to stand in front of their horses' stalls and receive instructions for the first training session. An older man in uniform lifted a bullhorn to his lips.

"We will divide and train," he bellowed, "strictly by sponsorship. First into the arena ..." His hand swept along the row of stalls along the right side of the barn. "The riders sponsored by our trade unions will train from six to eight a.m. Tuesday through Sunday."

The trade unions sponsored the largest number of riders. Their riders furthermore received the highest salaries. The trade unions also had the power to requisition as many soldiers as they needed to do extra work. So far, they had assigned one groom to each horse and rider.

"Second," the man in charge bellowed, "will be Central Army and Affiliated Military Riding Clubs. Time slot: eight to ten a.m.. As above, six days a week."

135

"They have the best instructors, and the most opportunities to ride," Ekaterina leaned over and whispered into Dosha's ear. "They're all former cavalry, which gives them an advantage. They were the only ones able to hold onto and take care of their horses during the wars and revolutions."

"Last," the voice continued through the bullhorn, "are the four riders and their horses sponsored by Comrade Galina Gregorovna Popov, chairwoman of the Committee for Sports and Physical Culture. Comrade Popov will make the final decision as to who will stay on the team and who will go. Theirs will be the last time-slot: six days a week, ten a.m. to midday break."

"And that," Osap stated in a low voice as he approached his two female riders, "is the most advantageous time slot of all. We have no time limit after. Finagled," he winked at them, "by your very own instructor. I have also procured the two best grooms. There are only two of them for the four of us, but you," he turned to where four stalls assigned to them began, "will like them."

Dosha glanced toward the two slightly built men in their early thirties, both looking ill at ease in their Soviet uniforms, and felt her heart leap. *Rom!* Did they recognize her as well? She wondered, for their eyes went right past her, locked onto the stallion, and stayed there. "*Gres.*" She coughed the Gypsy word for horse. One of the two took a deep breath; the other moved his eyes, but not his head, toward the ceiling. So Roma they were, but they were warning her that there was surveillance, and not to give their Gypsy origins away.

Training commenced that very morning. The Tartar proved to be the best user of a lunge whip Dosha had ever come across, even better than her father. He could touch every part of a horse's body with precision.

"That's because," Ekaterina explained, "he was a famous circus rider before the Great Patriotic War and, like Comrade Popov, a specialist in *haute école,* The High School of Riding." Indeed, as she watched Ekaterina's big-boned horse trot around on a wide circle, Dosha noticed it perk up and collect itself at each and every slight touch of that lunge whip like a Gypsy horse at the sound of grain.

Then it was Dosha's turn to enter the ring. "Next!" Osap's voice rang from the arena. Dosha, awaiting her turn by the entry gate, was by then accustomed to the saddle she had been allotted. She trotted the stallion energetically into the arena. Osap's mastery of the lunge whip, however, proved an unwise art for the

136

stallion. Upon feeling the whip snap at his heels for the first time, instead of collecting his gaits, he leapt forward like a deer clearing a fence. The sudden jolt would have unseated a rider of even greater experience than Dosha, except that from early childhood she'd developed a flexibility that allowed her to go instinctively with whatever unexpected movement the horse made.

"Well done!" shouted the Tartar from the center of the arena. "So he's not used to being trained with a whip from a distance. But now," he said. "it's time to sit back up in the saddle, straight! Eyes up! Look straight ahead between the horse's ears! Only then," he shouted, "will you look like a classical dressage rider. He's got to learn," and once again he snapped his whip on the stallion's hindquarters. This time, as she had been told, Dosha remained sitting stiff and straight. Up went the stallion and this time he took off, plunging and rearing until once again Dosha relaxed and followed his motions.

"Forget about the lunge whip then," Osap told her, when the stallion finally slowed down. *Nobody else would have stayed on,* he thought. Besides, he knew for a fact that the brilliance of many famous dressage horses was often matched by their explosive temperaments.

"And forget the grenadier seat," Ekaterina whispered minutes later as she and Dosha held their horses side by side, awaiting further instructions. "Because on that power engine," she nodded toward the stallion, "it could get you killed."

"It's not the sound," Dosha whispered in return. "He's used to that. It's the being touched by it that he's not used to."

"They picked that up from the Germans and the Austrians, I was told …"

By then Osap had walked up to Dosha's stirrup. He had wisely left his lunge whip on the floor in the center of the arena, and now he handed Dosha a long dressage whip. "All directions are given by your aides — your heels, your seat, and your legs. Not with the reins. Any disobedience," he said, "on the part of that horse, such as not responding to the slightest touch of your heel or pressure of your lower leg, and … *crack!* You reinforce the command at once, and I mean at once, with a tap of the dressage whip."

The flexible leather whip, as he now demonstrated, was to be carried in her still hand and placed lightly across her outside thigh. With an almost invisible flip of the wrist, it could reach all the way to the hindquarters of the horse.

"The 'rider's frame,'" the Tartar said, "has to give the

impression of the rider's total control over the classically trained dressage horse. Yours, on the other hand," he added with a frown, "has a long way to go if you are to achieve a classical seat."

Dosha, by contrast, believed that the only way to establish true harmony between horse and rider was through inner contact with the horse — a combination of thought and instinctive body movement. To her, the training to which she and her horse were now being subjected, threatened to turn what had been joy and ecstasy into forced labor, especially since the stallion had never before failed to respond to the slightest shift in her weight. Sometimes all it took was a single word. At times he seemed to anticipate and respond simply to her thought, as if reading her mind.

She was also well aware that she had to go along with this military severity. However, she found to her surprise that the regularity of the work built up both her own and the stallion's muscles. After only a few weeks, he felt incredibly light to her hands. He started to execute the difficult, tight movements with greater ease. With increased elasticity he progressed from exercises on the compulsory figure eight to trotting on the oblique. He two-tracked and performed the shoulder-in and haunches-in while seemingly following the direction of her eyes. With floating gaits he rode serpentines, *traversades*, and changes of lead, from three-time changes to tempi changes. He pirouetted down to the *piaffe* — trotting in place as if he had studied to be a Grand Prix dressage horse all his life. He executed his movements with ease, although they were by no means perfected as yet. But throughout the training sessions, Dosha also felt a tension in the horse that never went away. Only when she sat by his head in his fancy stall, as he ripped his well-earned hay out of the shiny copper manger, with little pieces of hay dropping all over her, did she feel that they regained the peace and happiness they had always felt in each other's company.

The months passed. The bony horses gained weight, developed muscles. Then one day quadrilles were introduced in afternoon sessions. These were to include all forty-five horses under the direction of the head trainer of the military, Comrade Colonel Nikolai Plankov. Dosha breathed a sigh of relief. She was still on her horse — she'd passed another hurdle.

At exactly two o'clock, each rider mounted his horse. After they had lined up along one wall of the enormous indoor riding hall, each was inspected from the rider's head to the horse's hoof.

"A quadrille," Osap informed his team, "is the equivalent of ballet on horseback." He explained that, in their final stages, the quadrilles — encompassing figures and formations, circles, half-circles, parallel *traversades*, and carousels, all executed simultaneously — would be performed to music in teams of only twelve horses.

In their afternoon training sessions, they started to incorporate *pas de deux* and *pas de trois*, against the background of, or within the circle of, the rest of the team.

What emerged at once was the difference between the horses, resulting from their prior experiences. The army horses, like wooden carvings on a carousel, performed with the steadiness of wind-up toys. The circus horses snapped to at the sound of the whip. The younger horses, horrified at the sudden close proximity to other horses within a walled-in space, shied or bolted, scattering in all directions. As for the stallion, his volatile temperament and powerful build made him look as out of place as he had been among the Siberian ponies up north.

Dosha, although new to quadrilles, had seen her father work 'liberty acts' with the half-wild Siberian ponies. These acts consisted of rhythmic figures executed at a trot or canter guided by a lunge whip. Djemo's riderless ponies had moved in harmony like tall grass in the wind. By contrast, the quadrille sessions in the Soviet training hall were stiff and labored, and punctuated by the cracks of much whip-snapping. The stallion tensed up, and Dosha had a hard time keeping him in line and preventing him from kicking at whichever horse moved up too close behind him.

"I think my stallion should be either up in front or the last one in line," she confessed to Ekaterina. *Given,* she thought, *his dominant personality and long strides.*

"If I were you," Ekaterina Siglunov replied, winking, "I would keep all such suggestions to myself. That is," she whispered, leaning in, "if you don't want to end up in a cage. Or worse ..."

Dosha looked Ekaterina straight in the eyes and smiled. "Yes. Thank you."

Again she was struck by the kindness and honesty of the heavyset young woman, who was strong and muscled like a man, yet tender-hearted enough to smuggle a scrawny cat into their room. Not only was it *mahrime* for Dosha to live in the same room with a cat, it turned out the cat made her sneeze. She decided she must ask Osap after all to transfer her to another room. But that was before she heard the other woman crying at night. And when

DOSHA

Dosha had asked, "Why are you crying?" Ekaterina turned on a small lamp by her bed. "Oh, Ana," she said, knowing her of course only by her *Gadje* name, "my horse was stocking up last night. His legs are all swollen. What will happen if he goes lame?" Ekaterina nestled her face into the body of her cat.

Dosha hurried to her roommate's side and, between fits of sneezing, reassured her. "You let our grooms handle that," Dosha said, knowing full well that nobody can fix lameness faster than a Gypsy.

By then, after weeks of working together, and despite the vigilance of the KGB, what had emerged among all the riders — and not just Dosha and Ekaterina — was a subtle but unmistakable bond that knew neither ethnic nor political borders: the bond that unites lovers of the horse. This bond, however, excluded the Tartar, Osap Tossuk. Everyone distrusted him — the Russians because he was a Tartar, Dosha because she believed he was a slave to carrying out orders, whatever the consequences.

Ekaterina's horse was not the only one having trouble. Every night the grooms had to wrap the swollen legs and tendons of the tired army horses in linseed mash, and when the young horses colicked in their stalls from lack of turnout, the grooms walked them around the arena for hours on end to prevent a painful death. Yet Osap Tossuk — frightened of the System, as were they all, but also greedy for success, kept pushing the horses to the limit.

He was especially demanding when it came to Dosha's stallion. Hours after the other horses had retired to their stalls for a night's rest, the Tartar insisted on teaching Dosha "the airs," as he pompously called them, of *haute école:* "the *levade*, the *courbette*, and lastly, the *capriole*." Whereas the *levade* came almost instinctively to the horse, the *capriole* required hard training. It involved intricate jumps and movements requiring the stallion's utmost control — first rearing up, forefeet off the ground, then leaping into the air while striking with both hind legs. Made famous by the white Lipizzaner horses of Austria, these movements had originated as military exercises, as maneuvers useful in war.

Osap insisted on pushing the stallion to perform these complex procedures over and over again, first on a lunge line, freestyle, then between two posts placed in the arena for guidance. One day, late in the evening, the Tartar said, "Ana, get into your saddle!"

"With all due respect," Dosha replied, "I don't think either he or I are ready for this circus trick."

"In the circus and in Austria they teach their horses fast. Your horse," he insisted, "has that kind of talent." *And so have you,* he thought. But knowing that, in the end, he would still be ordered to replace her with a politically suitable rider, he knew it was wise to keep that opinion to himself. "Besides," he added, "when Comrade Popov arrives from Moscow, this is what will impress her the most. She is a highly accomplished dressage rider in her own right. She was one of the original founders of the Burevestnik Riding Club of Moscow and remains an honorary member of this highly selective group." The club, he explained, was originally established to divorce the art of riding from its purely military use. "As a young woman," he concluded with visible pride, "Comrade Popov was privileged to observe the Spanish School of Riding in the city of Vienna, in far-away Austria. I am sure she would be more than happy to share with you photographs of horses doing these intricate movements."

But Dosha could no longer endure the torturous training of her increasingly obedient horse. "I'm concerned that if we persist," she said politely, "this amount of work will kill this stallion's brilliance and turn him into just another broken-spirited work animal."

The Tartar stared at her. His dark, slanted eyes turned to pointed drills. "You may think so," he said, "but I'm in charge. We'll do one more practice session now."

Though he did shorten the extra session that evening, from that moment on, his interactions with Dosha became guarded and impersonal.

After weeks of training in solo sessions and quadrilles, the horses were considered ready. The day of the final selection trial arrived. The riders lined up in the aisle outside a different riding hall, one reserved for demonstrations and special events. They would ride into this arena one at a time, each accompanied by his or her trainer. Once in the main hall, they were to ride, in prearranged patterns, the compulsory ten- and twenty- meter circles: half-circles along the long sides of the arena, followed by figure eights and serpentines at walk, trot and canter. At the end, they were to ride down the center line at an extended trot, to a hault at the center of the ring, remove their hats, and bow to the judges, then exit at a trot to wait, still mounted, for the quadrille that was to occur immediately after the solo tests. The two women riders, Dosha and Ekaterina, were instructed to bow without removing their hats, as was customary in the show ring.

The stallion was scheduled to perform third from last. Nervously, Dosha studied every rider's demeanor as he emerged from the riding hall: she was looking for signs of success or defeat. But their faces were impassive — except for that of Ekaterina, who gave her an encouraging smile. Finally it was Dosha's turn. Osap walked ahead of her into the ornate gilded riding hall lit by three lofty crystal-and gold-chandeliers. Lifting a bullhorn to his lips, he announced: "Ana Alexandrevna Dalova and the stallion Rus."

Across from the entrance gates, the white-and-gold-columned spectator galleries were filled with important officials wearing dark coats and fur hats. Dosha noted a tall, imposing, buxom woman standing by herself, to one side, in the front row. *That must be Galina Popov,* Dosha thought. The woman's straight gray hair was swept up into a slight wave across her forehead and pulled back in a twist at the nape of her neck. She wore an unbuttoned light gray winter coat with a fancy fox collar, under which could be seen a dark blue suit, like a uniform, with rows of decorations pinned on her left lapel

The woman turned to a colleague, who at once raised his bullhorn and blasted, "Commence!" into the otherwise silent riding hall.

Dosha froze. She had performed every day for months, yet as she entered this unaccustomed festive hall, instead of concentrating on the job ahead, her mind flashed to a Gypsy legend, one that every Gypsy child knew by heart: Of when Gypsies still had wings like birds. That was until they, too, had been lured into a palace made of glistening crystal and gold. There, black ravens greeted the Gypsies who still had wings. The ravens showered them with precious metal and glittering stones, and for a moment the Gypsies wallowed in the wealth, until they longed to return to the sky. That's when they realized that, in exchange for the gold and glitter, they had bartered their power to lift off into freedom and fly.

The stallion picked up Dosha's fear. He froze in place.

"Commence, Comrade Ana Dalova," the bullhorn repeated but Dosha was gripped by a stage fright so absolute, she could not think. She had forgotten everything she had been taught. Her head filled with a black buzzing, and the stallion, though confused by her increasing fear, pushed forward into a wooden trot. He seemed to be moving on stilts as they rode a lackluster and wooden test.

The Tartar, dumbfounded, waited by the entrance gates.

"Ana! What the hell happened?" he growled but Dosha was too ashamed and humiliated to answer.

"What's wrong?' Ekaterina asked. Dosha merely shook her head.

Afterwards she could not recollect anything that happened between the time she left the silent arena and the time she reentered with the whole team to perform the quadrille. Suddenly she found herself in line again, the horses moving at a smart trot into the hall. With the appearance of the first horse, the small orchestra perched on a high-up balcony picked up the music. She felt her horse moving under her, and suddenly her mind snapped alert.

*Tchaikovsky*, she remembered. *Entrance of the swans — of course.* They had practiced this as a team and she remembered all the times they had ridden to this fast sweeping melody. She was third from last as they entered in single file at a sitting trot. They rode a figure S before grouping into pairs, then picked up a slow canter for the start of the configurations they were about to perform. Suddenly the flash of a camera flared up from among the officials.

The young horses flew into all directions. The older horses mechanically continued on. The stallion stopped so suddenly and completely in his tracks that the two horses behind him barely avoided crashing into him. *Noooo*, she screamed silently. *Not now*, but the stallion, snorting and shaking, reared on his haunches, forelegs striking the air. Then all his pent-up tension exploded. Ears flattened to his skull and nostrils flaring, he bolted into the panicking herd. He avoided them at the last minute through a whirling pirouette, and then galloped from one end of the hall to the other, and back again. Dosha, although remaining securely on the horse throughout, knew a fear she had never known before.

In desperation, she closed her eyes and let her whole being fill up with the sounds of Gypsy voices and music mingling with the winds sweeping across open plains. She was not Ana, the Russian, but Dosha, the Gypsy. When she opened her eyes again, her horse had slowed. She noticed Osap scurrying toward the spectator gallery. By then her inner music had come to life and the stallion picked up the change in her. After a few more strides he came back to her hands as light as a feather. His body in full and easy collection, he arched his neck and, with flowing mane and floating hooves, incorporating all the prescribed movements at the highest rate of perfection of classical dressage, they danced as if in memory of the beauty of the life they had left behind.

At the end of her performance, Dosha and the stallion came

to the center of the arena. The horse extended one front leg and bowed, the way he used to before an audience of backward peasants and lumberjacks. The other horses, meanwhile, had scattered to the edges of the arena, the quadrille in disarray.

In the resulting silence the Tartar rushed to the horse. His face grim with anger, he grabbed the reins. From the way the horse's head went up in a movement of avoidance, Dosha knew the bit was cutting into the stallion's sensitive mouth. Without a moment's hesitation, she bent over and tore the reins out of the Tartar's clutching hand. "Comrade, I beg of you, let go," she whispered. "He'll just rear up again."

She could see every muscle work in the Tartar's weather-beaten face. At that moment the bullhorn bellowed, "Resume the quadrille!" The team regrouped in its initial formation. Dosha fell into place again, her face red with embarrassment and joy.

# 15

# The Bolshevik Revolutionary
# Galina Popov

Galina Gregorovna Popov, the natural daughter of a count and a liberated serf, was seduced by the Glorious Revolution and its powerful ideas at a very early age. Born to walk the unbridgeable divide between servant and master class, accepted by neither, Galina had sought refuge among her father's horses and grooms. Seeing Russia's horses being devoured by the Great Bolshevik Revolution she helped launch ultimately caused her more pain than the suffering of Russia's people. It broke Galina's heart to see the finest breeds raised on the former elite stud farms yoked to ploughs or drafted into the Great Patriotic War, where they perished by the thousands along with countless Russian soldiers.

Arriving at the Hermitage to inspect the horses rounded up at random across European Russia, Galina was prepared to accept that the restoration of prerevolutionary standards of Russian horsemanship would be a slow process. She knew that it would take more than three months of training to synchronize a quadrille composed of aging army and requisitioned circus horses. What she could not have anticipated was the breathtaking sight of this young rose-gray stallion as he suddenly exploded out of the ill-matched formation and start dancing like a feather in the wind.

Galina's heart froze in her throat. She felt transported back to a way of life that she herself had worked hard to overthrow. She realized with a hollow feeling, long repressed, that in the end the Revolution had purged and killed all that had been beautiful and free in the country she loved.

Galina had survived the purging of all those fellow revolutionaries who had risen above mediocrity, only to find themselves punished for their initiative. She had recognized, early on, that the revolutionary forces were splitting in two — victimizers and victims — and that to survive, you had to kiss the hand in power. She chose survival. That choice had brought her not only recognition but many privileges — most important among them, security clearance for trips abroad. She had taken advantage of these official trips to keep abreast of the great passion of her childhood and early adulthood, one that had never let her down: her love for the horse and the art of dressage.

In 1923, as part of its goal to expand the revolutionary cause beyond Russia's borders, the Party smuggled Galina into Austria so that she might make contact with and recruit more agents and sympathizers. Having mastered the German language as a child — she had learned it alongside her father's legitimate children, all of whom had paid for their noble birth with their lives — she had proved perfectly suited for the role of infiltrator.

Later, as a designated official assigned to travel with the Soviet athletes to the Olympic Games, she watched with envy as their former enemies, the Germans, losers of the Great Patriotic War, now led all the other nations in the international dressage competition. Russian competitors had once shared that place at the top. But that was before the Revolution had put an end to a noble pursuit now labeled a bourgeois frivolity.

In her mind's eye, Galina visualized the international headlines:
"SURPRISE VISIT BY NEWLY FORMED RUSSIAN DRESSAGE TEAM,"
— featuring, in the lead, this slip of a girl riding this Soviet phenomenon. Such a spectacle would equal the quality of their great Russian ballets, still the best in the world.

Of course, this new Russia, the USSR, could no longer boast high-caliber pre-revolutionary trainers. On the other hand, it wouldn't be that difficult to smuggle in training movies from the High School of Vienna. There was nothing to prevent the Russian team from imitating Europe's best. 'Russify' it — that was Galina's plan. Instead of performing to Spanish Gypsy music, the way she remembered, they would perform to the famous tunes of their own Gypsies. Instead of Viennese waltzes and German marches, they would perform free-flowing formations to "Meadowlands," the electrifying anthem born of the Revolution as it swept across the land, blowing the old Russia off her foundation.

As the quadrille continued, Galina feasted her eyes on the

perfect proportions of the muscled-up body of the stallion. She pictured him surging and galloping into the liberated vastness of the motherland, and all to the musical beat of that revolutionary song.

*And that girl!* she thought, taking a closer look at the rider. *So naturally upright! Those legs — long and elegant.*

Comrade Popov leaned across the balustrade toward the Tartar, who stood just outside the spectator gallery "The girl," she observed, "has unmistakable propaganda value."

Galina surmised that this was by no means some simple girl from some unregulated collective. She sensed a common ground with this girl. This girl was like herself, full or part aristocrat — of that, Galina was sure. Maybe she came from a family that had sensed in time when to quit and where to disappear to. If so, they, unlike Galina's father, had escaped being slaughtered by their former serfs. *These people,* Galina concluded, *must have been smart enough to clear out in time.* They, through foresight, must have avoided not only being hauled off to Siberian gulags, but what was worse, to Galina's way of thinking: being sent to one of those State loony bins for the recycling of the nonconforming mind.

For a moment Galina toyed with the idea of sending her emissaries to where the girl and the extraordinary horse had been found. But she suspected that the discovery of the horse had served as a wake-up call to the rest of what — she was more and more convinced — would turn out to be a pocket of survivors of the Revolution. By the time the authorities could return to their hiding place, they'd have disappeared long since.

*'Ana Dalova,'* Galina pondered. *That's who that Tartar believes her to be but then paper is patient, you write on it whatever strikes your fancy, my friend.*

"When you picked her up, this Ana Dalova," Galina asked the Tartar, who stood by attentively, his face upturned, "did she have official papers?"

The Tartar's eyes narrowed to slits. Was it a trick question? He took his time to answer. "She's the one who told me the details," he said at last, turning his body fully toward Galina. "They were mere peasants, way off in the middle of nowhere, well beyond any regions that could be supervised."

"No matter." Galina watched him squirm. "Relax. You're probably right." But from what she could see from afar, this looked like no peasant to her. This was a classical Russian beauty. With proper grooming, a task Galina would undertake in person, this Ana could turn out as valuable a propaganda asset as Russia's international ballet stars.

Although she'd been born into the precarious social position of just another bastard of a Russian aristocrat, Galina had been favored by the fates with more brains and horse talent than all of the count's other children combined. More toy than daughter to her noble father, she had nonetheless been allowed to partake of the same training by fancy German and Austrian dressage instructors that he provided to his legitimate children.

In prerevolutionary days, not only did aristocratic riders have the advantage of being able to select from among the best-bred horses, they had the leisure to train their horses patiently, toward a goal of freedom and elegance of movement. The military, by contrast, had to make do with whatever horses were available, and training was achieved by means of iron discipline and persistence, the result of which was generally known as the "grenadier seat," stiff and unforgiving to the horse. This was the seat that prevailed among the riders presented to Comrade Galina Popov on this day, except, of course, *this girl — Ana or whoever she truly is,* Galina thought. Hers was the style of dressage seat once favored by Russia's most privileged — a mixture of techniques imported from the finest riding schools in Europe combined with a Russian's innate feel for a horse. The amalgam had made them top international competitors in the past, and could do so again. But for now, of course, Galina knew she had best keep such reactionary, antirevolutionary thought strictly to herself.

"All riders," the bullhorn bellowed once again, "are to line up along the side of the hall for inspection by the Chairwoman of the Committee for Sport and Physical Culture, Comrade Galina Popov."

Galina slowly rose from her chair on the viewing balcony. The darkly clad apparatchiki of the various unions and members of the military promptly followed suit. With the Tartar at her side, she slowly made her way down a winding set of stairs toward the riding hall.

In physical appearance Galina Gregorevna Popov was a tall woman in her late fifties. The parts of her legs that were visible were strong and muscular like an athlete's. The heavy bosom was that of a Russian peasant matron. She had an imperious air with her strong high-boned facial features.

Halfway into the hall, Galina stopped as the Tartar rattled off her various titles: "Chairwoman of the Committee for Sport and Physical Culture, distinguished member and lead rider of the Bureveshnik Sport Society of Moscow, leader of the woman's section of the Party Central Committee, chairwoman of the Moscow Trade Union Committee ..."

Then, after a measured pause, Galina gave her motivational speech. With the help of the bullhorn, she started out by stressing the interrupted history of the Russian horse in international competition — "a sacrifice that was necessary at the time for the good of the Motherland," she emphasized. "But now" — she enunciated each word with great care — "the opportunity to return Russian horsemanship to its prerevolutionary status is within your reach. Not only that, but" — she scanned each rider's face and paused for effect — "you have been given the honor and privilege of representing abroad the superiority of our socialist ways. We have already proven our mettle with our sciences, our weapons, our performing arts, as well as many sports categories — to which we will now add horsemanship.

"The Russian horse," Comrade Popov continued in a clear and penetrating voice, "is as much a part of the Russian plains as our endless Russian sky. With this magnificent example of Russian breeding in the lead" — she pointed to the rose-gray stallion — "we cannot fail."

Her speech met with rhythmic applause from the gallery.

"His show name will be ..." — she raised her voice dramatically, stretching her right arm straight out to the stallion — "Rus!" Her announcement prompted further applause, prolonged this time, from the gallery.

Then Galina walked up to the riders. Like a general inspecting his troops, she went from horse to horse. Each rider saluted her by doffing his tophat with his left hand, dropping his right hand along his side, and giving a quick bow of the head.

When Popov arrived at the stallion, positioned third from last, Dosha went through the rehearsed formal greeting procedure, which for a woman consisted merely of inclining the head and dropping her right hand to her side. At that point she noticed with great apprehension that the woman in charge was extending an open hand right toward the stallion's mouth.

Ever since he was rescued from the Russian soldiers as a colt, the stallion had never trusted anyone but Dosha. He was known to either bite or strike out at approaching strangers but in this instance, to Dosha's utter amazement, she felt no sign of tension whatsoever.

"Relax the reins," Comrade Popov ordered. Dosha let go of the reins. Astoundingly, the stallion, without hesitation, stretched his head toward the woman's hand, where Dosha now noticed two lumps of sugar. With soft lips the stallion gently took the sugar lumps from the outstretched hand of this stranger. He trusted this mannish woman. Taken off guard, Dosha lifted her downcast eyes and stared straight into what struck her as the sly, probing eyes of a she-bear.

Galina's focus remained on the horse alone. She ran her hand down the powerful neck to the wide chest. Whispering terms of endearment, she now ran a hand all the way down his front legs, with particular attention to the tendons of his lower legs. She went so far as to lean against his shoulder and pick up a foot, examining the hoof. Handing more sugar to the totally relaxed stallion, she stroked the front of his face. With a short acknowledging nod to Dosha, his rider, she then moved on to the final two horses.

As Galina headed back to the center of the arena, the Tartar, seeing his discovery singled out for all to witness, attached himself to her heels. Making sure he was out of earshot of the riders, he whispered into the ears of this stately woman — his erstwhile lover — "It was that flash! Somebody took a photograph and the horse panicked. But the girl, his rider?" He studied Galina's face for reaction. "Instead of pulling him up, she simply gave him free rein!" And how therefore the fault for the botched quadrille lay with the girl, and was not the fault of the horse.

"I've been trying hard," Osap whispered, "to find a suitable replacement rider." Getting no word in response, not even a facial expression, he added, still sotto voce, "You have to understand, this girl is not malleable. She will not blend in with the rest. Ever!"

It had been a long time since Galina had allowed the scrawny Tartar to feed on her ample body like an animal frenzied by need, back when free love was the revolutionary thing to do. To her surprise at the time, something between them had clicked. Their prolonged affair had turned into an alliance of mutual protection, which persisted long after the sexual attraction had faded.

For a moment she toyed with the idea of berating the Tartar for not having the foresight to realize that, before a horse is set

loose on a field of international competition, it must be trained to
withstand not only the flashing of lights, but a host of other dis-
tractions as well. Far more serious, however, was Osap's failure to
recognize that this stallion would never bond with another rider
to such an extent. Rus and 'Ana' were the perfect fit — the kind of
optimal combination of horse and rider upon which Russian dressage, in its prime, had been based. Clearly the Tartar was out of
his league. Galina needed help, and it wouldn't come from those
rendered brain-dead through Soviet indoctrination.

"We need to succeed" — Galina turned and stared the Tartar
down — "and for that, it would hardly do to lower excellence to
mediocrity, don't you agree? The trick is to bring the rest up to her
level of excellence. Wouldn't you say?" Galina spoke to her former lover if she had unwittingly stumbled upon the village idiot.

The very next day, what had started out as three distinct
groups of horses and riders, divided by sponsorship, were united under the sole command of Comrade Galina Gregorovna
Popov. Over the next week, twenty of the poorest horses among
the pre-selected group were dispatched to state riding clubs across
European Russia — or so their riders were told. The remaining
twenty-five horses and riders were divided by proficiency level.

In contrast, all of the trainers were retained, except that now
they were handed worksheets with specific exercises and work
drills, and assigned to changing groups of horses and riders
formed for that specific day only.

Under Galina's leadership, the training turned scientific. And
selected like the choice pick out of a show litter, held high above
for all to see, were Dosha and her stallion, now known to all as
"Rus." They were the only pair to receive this degree of individual
attention. For both the individual and group sessions, they were
assigned the topmost military trainers. Their group sessions consisted of no more than three horses and their riders, versus six to
seven for all other groups. During the afternoon sessions, when
the whole team worked on quadrilles and free-style formations,
Dosha and Rus were either in the lead or chosen to perform solo
amid whatever formation was being perfected — all under the
watchful eyes of Comrade Popov. She sat in a balcony overlooking
the arena, with the Tartar standing at her side. He held a bullhorn
in his hand, through which he called out Galina's instructions or
directives for corrections.

On the first day of the reorganization, at precisely 4:00 p.m.
— drill time in the riding arena had been increased by two hours

— riders and trainers alike were marched, without ever setting foot outside the Hermitage compound, to an office within the General Staff Building. There, installed behind a gleaming desk against a background of red silk curtains, sat Comrade Popov. With a wave of her hand, she indicated that they were to sit in two rows of chairs arrayed in front of her. A portrait of Lenin, mounted on the wall behind her, dominated the room. Popov, in full uniform and decorations, was positioned between Osap Tossuk, who sat to her right, and two KGB officers in blue uniforms, standing to her left.

As soon as riders and trainers had quietly taken their seats, the Tartar, cued by a nod from Comrade Popov, stood up.

"As you know," he stated, "the official countdown of the projected five-year plan to restore the Russian/Soviet Olympic Equestrian Team back to the international foreground began during the Summer Games in Stockholm. We have subsequently completed the round-up of the horses chosen for the, this time successful, implementation of this plan. Our next projected deadline will be the International Competition of Dressage and Stadium Jumping in Aachen, Germany, in July of next year — 1957. This will also be the first international qualifying trial for the 1960 Summer Olympics in Rome, our second major deadline. The dressage team will continue to train in Leningrad. The Soviet jumping team will continue to train in Moscow."

"Thank you, Comrade Osap." The Tartar took his seat again, as Galina, remaining seated, continued in a monotone. "Aachen is less than one year away." Her voice slowly rose. "The pressure from up high for us to succeed remains unrelenting," she announced in a voice clearly trained for public speech and indoctrination. "Efforts have to be tireless. The unpredictability of the horse cannot and will not serve as an excuse for any type of ... failure." The final word, pronounced after an ominous pause, descended upon the hushed assembly of riders and trainers with the sharpness of an ax.

In reality, no one present was more threatened — should this latest highly propagandized plan fail — than the woman delivering this speech. All her life, Galina had believed in ambush rather than open warfare. Yet now here she was, at the height of her career, sticking out her neck. After Khrushchev's de-Stalinization speech in February of that year, she had allowed herself to be caught up in what had been labeled "The Thaw." It had swept across Russia, drowning out years of repression like a symphony of liberation. Suddenly the arts were thriving. New housing for the working masses arose gracelessly in huge cement blocks on the outskirts of major cities, the first concrete sign that the triumph of Communism was materializing under this new leadership. For once Galina had allowed her heart to lead her brain, as she concentrated, not on her own survival, but on the fate of the Russian horse.

Another hour passed in directives and directions, each rider receiving personal criticism and notes on what areas required more concentrated attention.

"That's all. It's up to you." With a nod, Galina dismissed them for the day. She watched them closely as, one by one, they left silently and in an orderly fashion. They exchanged no words, no smiles — behavior that would have been unimaginable among fellow riders before the Revolution.

*Are they all afraid?* Galina wondered. *Is the KGB too much in evidence? There's not a thing I can do about that. Have I myself frightened them? Whatever the reason,* she concluded; *the System is in place, leaving them dead from the hairline down.*

Galina felt irritated with the team, and discouraged. There was no reason to imagine that the horses were any better than their riders. Years of neglect, both of training and breeding, could not possibly be remedied in only a few months' time — neither by the carrot nor by the stick. *What have I gotten myself into?* She asked herself.

"Stay!" she ordered the Tartar, who was the last one present and making motions as if to leave.

*If I dump my ill-conceived plan now,* Galina reasoned, *I myself will be dropped like a rock from a peak, right into one of those Siberian gulags.*

Khrushchev had opened the gulag gates, and most of his predecessor's victims had been freed. The camps were almost empty. On the other hand, he had issued no orders to dismantle them. *At least to my knowledge he hasn't,* Galina thought. *Maybe he's merely waiting to fill them with enemies of his own. After all, a snake can change its skin, but never its nature. Well,* she decided, *two can play that game. I need to start a purge of my own.*

Galina had inspected the room to make sure there were no hidden cameras, no recording devices in this office of the Junker-Institut, but just in case, she now found a military news station on the radio on her desk and turned it up loud. "This group of trainers won't do," she whispered to the Tartar. "Some will have to go.

I will instruct our Soviet embassies in Paris and Rome to extend grandiose invitations to top European dressage trainers — preferably from Communist states, of course — to come for an extended stay in Leningrad, cradle of the Bolshevik Revolution."

What she didn't tell the Tartar, whom these days she trusted only as far as she could keep an eye on him, was that she had already asked seven trainers — three from East Germany, four from Italy and France — to come to the rescue of the new Soviet dressage team.

Within a week, they were on the job. During their first exposure to a morning and an afternoon session, Galina kept her eyes obliquely on the imported trainers as they in turn observed first the team as a whole, then the individual riders. When the girl entered riding Rus, their eyes lit up.

"I knew it," Galina whispered to Osap. "That horse with that girl is Olympic gold."

"What about the rest of the team?" Osap Tossuk inquired humbly.

"The plan must succeed," Galina answered. "There is no other option." She rose and left.

Galina had organized a welcome luncheon for the newly arrived dressage delegation at the Hotel Astoria, one of several Soviet showplaces reserved for the benefit of foreigners and high-ranking Soviet officials. She dressed for the occasion in civilian clothes, the kind only available to the elite in special government stores. Once seated at a large table with the trainers imported from abroad, she dropped all traces of Bolshevik rhetoric and adopted instead the language of one horse expert to another. After much food and drink and a display of good old-fashioned Russian camaraderie, she took the plunge.

"So," she addressed the group, "you were impressed by the stallion Rus. But what about the rest?"

The foreign trainers squirmed. The Italians and French meekly shook their heads, but not one of the four said a word. It was the head trainer of the East Germans, one Ernst Schneider, who finally screwed up his courage to speak.

"Indeed, there is cause for concern. The rest of the horses, without intensive training, will find it hard to compete against the West Germans and the other Western countries as well."

"So, Herr Schneider," Galina asked the head trainer of the East Germans with a frown, "how do we proceed?"

Herr Schneider twisted his wine glass pensively. "You have

one option," he said at length. "You could have the girl alone, on her talented stallion, represent the Soviet Union — in which case, you could enter her in the qualifying trials. They'd probably do well. That way she would gain mileage in the international arena, keeping the Olympic Games in mind. You'd have three more years to get the rest of them ready for the Olympics." He politely glanced up at his hostess.

*Except that in Soviet eyes,* Galina thought, *a plan catering to one individual, and a girl to boot, would hardly qualify as a plan.* And Galina, who, more than most, had witnessed firsthand how idealists and the intelligentsia had been overcome by peasants and butchers, swore to herself right then and there that *if, by some miracle, I survive this midlife folly of mine, I will never stick my neck above the crowd of anonymity again!*

However, Galina was a problem-solver par excellence. She also knew that there was no choice but to continue on this road, once taken, simply because in the Soviet System, retreat meant a bullet to the back of the neck for sure.

"A team of one would never do," she said, her thoughts racing. *She must find a way out!*

There was the mare that had come with the stallion, the one that the Tartar kept fit for her own use, as well as for his own but the mare was too old for international competition. Galina had kept a close eye on equestrian Olympics for years, even though Russia had participated in only one such international event since the Revolution: the 1955 Summer Olympics in Stockholm, where Soviet participation had been dismal.

"To tell the truth," Gallina admitted to the multinational assembly of trainers, "I have no firsthand knowledge of the organizational structure of such an event. I've only recently been put in charge — since Stockholm, to be precise."

"To work, then!" said Ernst Schneider. "We have four years till the next Games. Germans train some of their best dressage horses in only three."

# 16
# The Training Of The Olympic Dressage Team

The next day nearly all of the Russian trainers were demoted to exercise riders (although they maintained their official title of trainers). In private conversations with Comrade Galina Popov, Ernst Schneider referred to them as *die Bereiter*, German for exercise riders. There were two exceptions: Osap Tossuk was appointed assistant trainer to Ernst Schneider, and Colonel Plankov, lead rider of the Central Army and Affiliated Military Riding Clubs, retained his position as trainer of all military riders because of his rank and party affiliation.

Galina, stationed for the time being in the Junker-Institut, kept the Tartar close by her side. She never doubted that, sooner or later, he would pick up on the precariousness of her position, and that if given the slightest opportunity to further his own interest and solidify his position as the discoverer of the stallion Rus, he would denounce her, his former lover, in a heartbeat.

Ernst Schneider very quickly emerged as the leader of the foreign trainers. At his suggestion, the time allotted to training was tripled. Lectures on the logic of dressage were added, as mental preparation, along with specific equestrian exercises on the ground meant to help the riders to loosen up.

"*Eure Steifheit*," Ernst remonstrated. "Your stiffness," Galina translated.

"*Beine los!*" Schneider screamed at the top of his voice. "Let your legs dangle free," Galina translated, as her riders were lunged for hours on end without stirrups and with reins loose in their hands.

"*Eleganz ist das Ziel!*"

"Elegance is the goal," Galina repeated in Russian, thinking it a bit much, coming from a former enemy, a *Fritz*, who stood commandingly upright in the center of the riding ring as if he'd swallowed a broom.

Increasingly, Dosha found herself singled out. Working solely with the stallion and two young grays selected from among the military horses, she was now completely segregated from the rest of the riders. Her work time was actually reduced, as if her status had been raised, approaching that of a trainer.

As before, only she was allowed to ride Rus. The two other young stallions were first warmed up by two former trainers, now demoted to *Bereiter*. These warmups consisted of riding the rambunctious young horses in straight lines, using long but firm reins: walk, trot, and canter, for about twenty minutes. Then the two were handed over to Dosha, for what Ernst called "finesse," or fine-tuning. He remained close by, as both instructor and ground person. Osap was relegated to a corner of the arena, where he was allowed to observe.

As a young revolutionary infiltrating Austria in the 1920s, Galina had had the privilege of studying the methodology of training the world-famous Lipizzaner stallions in the Stallburg in Vienna. She had closely observed the training of the carefully selected riders from all over Western Europe and had marveled at the results. Yet in all her experience over the decades, Galina had never witnessed such raw talent as this girl exhibited in the riding halls of the Hermitage. Ana's gift was all the more evident when she took these two poorly trained and bad-mannered young stallions in hand.

Ana showed neither fear nor hesitation when she first walked up to the horses. She gave each, one at a time, her full attention. To start with, she stood perfectly still at some distance, then stretched out a hand. She let the young stallion, still held by the exercise rider, approach her first. She let the youngster stretch toward her hand and let it sniff her before she stroked the front of its face, all the while talking to him softly. When she turned, not looking at the horse, it followed her. The exercise rider, still holding his reins at that point, stepped to the front of the horse, and the girl proceeded to walk around the young stallion, talking, touching, her eyes on the horse's ears.

*She is reading their feelings, their fears and apprehensions — reassuring them.* Galina watched as the girl now took the reins from the exercise rider, ran them across the young stallion's neck, and ever so gently, used a mounting block to lift herself onto his back. She took her time before slowly lowering herself into the saddle, still keeping most of her weight in her feet, placed — heels deep — in the stirrups.

Then, to Herr Schneider's horror — he exclaimed "That is crazy! That is not acceptable!" — the slender girl gave the stallion complete freedom of head and neck, holding the reins just by their buckle to prevent them from drooping too low.

For a minute or two she let him buck and whirl. When he started to rear up, she calmly leaned forward and embraced the horse's neck with both arms. At all times her body followed his, without clamping, as if they were one. Only when the horse came to a stop, breathing hard, did she sit up, patting the animal's neck for reassurance, before picking up the reins, very loosely at first. She engaged in every movement and action as if it were in play, before she started to ride briskly forward, at first in straight lines. Then, to loosen up the horse's body head to tail, she began bending his neck right and left, before leg-yielding him by imperceptibly shifting her weight to the opposite side of movement — first toward the center of the arena, then back to the wall. She progressed to shoulder-in and working on the circles — walk, trot, and canter — and on and on, playfully, perfectly.

"Still," Herr Schneider turned to Galina, "this is not what we in Germany consider training."

At that point Galina couldn't help herself: she could not hold it in any longer. She leaned close to the German's ear. "Actually, Comrade Schneider," she said, "what you have just witnessed here is the latest dressage training technique developed right here in the Union of Soviet Socialist Republics. A method," she added, "that incorporates not only talent but *feel*." This shut up, to Galina's relief, Comrade Schneider's comments about the superiority of German training.

After a few weeks, the young stallions started to collect. They came more willingly and lightly into Dosha's hands. "It is best at this point," she suggested to Comrade Popov, "to get the stallions used to just one rider — just for the time being. They will find it less confusing. They need muscling up and stretching out before they get assigned their permanent riders." She went so far as to insist on doing their grooming herself for the time being — "to bond further," she said. Galina acquiesced. All other riders were ordered off the two young stallions' backs.

It was not long, though, before Galina, who had kept her focus on training the selected horses, began to notice that something else was happening. Her principal rider, Ana Dalova,

158

seemed to have entered a state of mental darkness. Galina knew from experience that many horse-people, especially women, have a tendency to withdraw from humans, often feeling awkward and ill at ease around them. But this girl seemed to have withdrawn a notch even beyond that. She had removed herself from all interaction with the other riders and now interacted solely with the horses she rode and groomed.

It occurred to Galina that, by giving the girl preferential treatment, she had not only set her up as a prime target of envy and denunciation, she had separated her from her fellow riders like a leper from the healthy. *She wouldn't be the first case of some outsider from the hinterlands cracking under this sort of regulated pressure*, Galina thought. She had seen with her own eyes highly intelligent political prisoners, when subjected to solitary confinement, go wild or withdraw into madness and of course any obvious mental deviation would turn this girl into a security risk rather than a star. She would never be issued authorization to travel abroad and without the girl, Galina realized, her grandly publicized plan would be headed for another international disaster.

For the first time Galina considered the advice volunteered earlier by Osap. He still believed it was in the team's interest to replace this unknown young girl with a seasoned and proven male rider in order for the stallion to compete internationally. Observing the girl's mood, Galina was prepared to yank all three horses away from her — except that the dark melancholy expression that overcast the girl's classical features further enhanced her beauty. Given her unusual closeness to her horses, her riding reached such levels of fluidity that it turned her movements as lyrical as a *valse triste*.

Ana's performances reminded Galina of that other Anna, the legendary ballerina Anna Pavlova. No one had ever danced a more perfect dying swan. This girl on horseback performed with the same poetic movements, the innate magic and inborn glamour. *She is a born artist.* Galina's resolve returned. She would turn Ana Dalova into the first Soviet star of international dressage.

Galina had two weeks left in which to indoctrinate this rising star with the necessary Soviet values. At the end of that time, Galina was scheduled to return to Moscow headquarters; she would visit Leningrad only intermittently.

One afternoon, after the quadrille session, Galina asked Ana Dalova to accompany her in a black government limousine carrying the seal of the KGB. Shielded from the outside by tinted glass, the sleek Mercedes dove into the streets of Leningrad, dividing the streams of weary workers heading homeward.

"Where are we going?" the girl asked.

"I'm going to introduce you to the discreet world of the privileged few," Galina announced. "We're going to visit the Soviet Union's largest department store, the GUM."

Ana Dalova looked astonished and a little anxious. The limousine came to a smooth halt right in front of the department store's main entrance. Grabbing the reluctant girl by the hand, Galina marched ahead, past long queues of vacant-eyed shoppers who waited in silence. She made straight for the elevator, which took them to Section 100 on the third floor. Here a smiling saleswoman with tough features and subservient manners greeted Comrade Popov of the upper *nomenklatura*, a high official of the Communist Party, familiarly, by name.

Galina clearly knew the proper protocol in this mirrored, gilded, and empty showroom. She at once sank into a plush chair and motioned for Ana to do the same. After a short exchange with the saleswoman, other, younger salesgirls brought out dresses and shoes from Paris and Florence. "We have them in all sizes," the tall, well-dressed, heavily made-up salesclerk assured Comrade Popov.

Galina chose several dresses. "Go on," she ordered her visibly subdued young rider, who was still dressed in riding pants and boots and a heavy woolen shirt. "Go — follow the saleswomen into one of the changing rooms!"

When the girl reemerged, she looked tall and striking in a simple black dress with shoes to match. The saleswoman had smartly pulled the girl's heavy red-blond hair away from her face and had braided it halfway down her back. Her dark almond-shaped eyes, which never looked Galina straight in the face, now overpowered the pale, unblemished skin of one barely out of childhood. Galina was struck by something wild, untamed — an otherness that contrasted with the purity of the girl's finely sculptured features.

"Turn around," Galina said. "Let me have a closer look." The girl obediently spun, and again Galina, who had only seen the girl on a horse, was surprised that her legs were not bowed from early riding, but straight and well shaped.

"Walk back and forth!"

The girl's walk, furthermore, was not awkward, like that of other full-time female riders, but fluid and graceful.

Galina chose several dresses and pairs of shoes, and a fancy winter-coat with a fox collar and matching wool hat with fur trim. Back in the limousine, Galina Popov tried to engage the girl in conversation. "So," she asked, "the clothes? You like your new clothes?"

"They are very beautiful," the girl answered. She blushed. "Thank you, Comrade Popov," she said, shyly turning her face toward the city passing by.

"And the city?" Galina asked. "Would you like to see more of the city?"

"I would, Comrade Popov. This is my first time outside the Junker-Institut since I arrived," the girl said, as the limousine was racing along deserted streets, past rows of dimly lit lanterns that rushed by like rows of lone, forgotten sentinels. "I was starting to feel locked in," she said.

Only the moon, sailing in and out of fast-moving clouds, kept pace with the speeding car. Its cold, fleeting light briefly illuminated the green and silver metal roofs, the sweeping design of the city, which appeared deserted at this early time of night. The fluid light touched the girl's profile, as exotically alluring and delicate as an orchid in open bloom. If the girl were to apply for papers to go abroad without the proper escort to protect her, Galina feared, she would crack like glass at the first true attempt by the KGB to break through this shell of her mysterious origins. *What are those origins?* Galina asked herself once again. *What sets this girl apart from the average Soviet citizen?*

Galina, whose aristocratic mind inhabited a peasant body, wondered what it would be like to possess such beauty: the glowing skin, the firm flesh, the glorious hair braided down Ana's back, like the image of a beautiful and virginal bride of a powerful *boyar*, a Russian noble of the Middle Ages. The girl seemed unaware of the power of that beauty. Galina felt a sudden, irresistible urge to lean forward and caress that hair. The thought ricocheted back as if it had hit an invisible shield, striking Galina to the core. Unbearable feelings and memories of deeds left deeply buried rose to her mind like a nightmare in progress — forbidden urges and betrayals of self. She felt an acute disquiet.

Later Galina could not remember whether she had spoken the girl's name, or whether the girl had read her mind and picked up on her anguish. The girl had turned and fastened her dark eyes on Galina's. Like a steady, powerful flow, those black eyes invaded Galina body and soul. Mesmerized, she saw reflections of her own past rise up. Galina, the unwanted child, sweeping on horseback across the vastness of the Russian steppe, convinced that God was a horse with wings — God was freedom.

Little by little, Galina returned to the present, almost as if from a trance or some temporary exile. From deep within her subconscious a vision arose of the present drive to haul Russia's Gypsies off their ancient treks, the latest group to be fed into the grinder of standardization. She pictured a growing list of grievances brought against those Gypsies: Peasants charged that they'd been robbed by Gypsy women after being hypnotized into a state of frozen powerlessness and yet how rarely these peasant women reported such robberies, for fear of curses placed as revenge upon them and their kin! Galina, being of a scientific mind, attributed the phenomenon to the enduring superstition rife among backward Russian peasants — part of their need to kiss the icon, the deep seated ancient belief in God that even the Communist dogma could not erase — rather than to the supposed powers of those entrapped Gypsies. Yet Galina couldn't help feeling that she had just emerged from just such a trance.

The car stopped at the immense Palace Square. The driver in his blue KGB uniform hastened to open first Galina's door, then the girl's. It had started to snow. The snow covered the geometrical stone patterns of the gigantic square. Galina motioned the girl, dressed in her fancy new coat, to run on back into the barracks and her horse. She watched absentmindedly as the girl disappeared through the colonnades of the Staff Building.

The enormous square was empty except for occasional men in uniform, walking alone or in twos. The falling snow muffled the hollow silence and emptiness of the square.

It was almost right at that spot where Galina, as a young revolutionary, had heard the blank shot from the battleship *Aurora*, anchored nearby in the Neva River. This was the signal that had called forth the masses of sailors and Red Guards that had stormed the Winter Palace — "In the name of freedom!" That was the rallying cry. Under her breath Galina started humming "Meadowlands," the song that had epitomized the subsequent rush of revolutionaries across the great Russian plains, a revolt toward freedom and a better world.

She remembered again the thought that had taken shape in her mind all those weeks ago in the preselection training arena. What better way to export that rush of idealism and longing for a better society, the promise of Communism, than to combine superior Russian horsemanship with the spirit of that song? Moreover, she was certain now that nobody could enact it better than this girl, Ana Dalova, and the stallion Rus. They would start six months from now in Helsinki, the gateway to the West, where Comrade Khrushchev was planning a state visit.

# 17
# The Round-Up Of The Russian Gypsies

On October 5, 1956, the Soviet edict that Jano had predicted a year before was officially decreed: the motion "On Reconciling Vagrant Gypsies to Labor" was signed into law. Ironically, it was Nikita Sergeyevich Khrushchev, hailed as "the Liberator" after Stalin's death, who ordered soldiers to round up the Roma and confiscate their horses, caravans, forges, and tools. Open fires, the center of Romani life, were forbidden. Many Roma were shipped in freight trains to Siberia, already deep into winter by that time of year. All over Russia, those Gypsies unlucky enough to be captured in the roundups were handed shovels and picks, and ordered to break earth or ice for housing projects, ditches, and railroad tracks. For this labor, men, women, and children were paid too little to survive.

For over a thousand years the Roma had lived by the horse and the open road. They had made their living by trading horses, working iron, weaving baskets, telling fortunes — and mostly by dancing and singing. Nowhere had their artistic achievements reached such brilliance and been met with such appreciation and applause as in Russia. They were not accustomed to using shovels or working the land. Land had no meaning to the nomadic Gypsies. Now many were about to perish of hunger or exposure in what was to become known among the tribes as the "The Great Halt."

Although Osap had his suspicions, but was never sure, nobody else seemed to suspect that the tall, red-blond rider of the stallion Rus might be a member of the latest ethnic minority marked for cultural extinction. Locked away for months with her horse in the gilded equestrian quarters of the Hermitage, Dosha had by then learned to live with the deep loneliness a Gypsy feels when separated from his own. Recently, however, her dreams had been filled with screams and panic — with images of Lovari men and women grabbing their children and invalid elders while scattering in horror in all directions. Horses reared, neighing, and thundered off into the distance. Campfires flared into wildfires and spread, burning out of control. Echoes of the nightmarish screams pursued her into her waking hours. And above the upheaval that now dominated her mind hovered the image of Patrina's face. The familiar image, transparent as air, was like a beckoning call that would not let up.

It was at the height of this acute feeling of foreboding and powerlessness that freedom was suddenly thrown Dosha's way in little pieces — as if, during the brief moment of eye contact with Galina in the limousine, she had planted a tiny seed of freedom into the *Gadje* woman's mind and that seed had started to bear fruit.

Every week Dosha was to have two afternoons off to enjoy random walks through the city. One evening soon, she was to join Galina at a performance by the world-famous Kirov Ballet — "in order," Galina had said, "to apply elements of ballet to the performance of quadrilles." But even more exciting, all of the riders, plus thirteen horses, were to be transported by train to the former estates of aristocrats south of the city for a "weekend out in nature." The goal was to restore the spirit and alertness of the hardworking horses by breaking their routine.

In doling out these morsels of freedom, Galina, for her part, intended to train her elusive star rider like a falcon to the glove. What she did not know was that she was trying to train a Gypsy, and although a Gypsy can turn a tired, old nag into a horse that shines, can teach a bear to dance, a goat to climb a ladder and perform tricks, birds to fly free yet willingly return to his hand, the Gypsy himself is like the wolf. He can be trapped but not tamed. Nor will he ever love his captor. He'll never comprehend the glory of owning and working a plot of land, nor the happiness in remaining chained to some structure the *Gadje* call home. A Gypsy will always prefer the road, where two days are never alike and if he is trapped, all it takes is to open his cage a crack, and he will escape back to freedom.

Dosha, however, was tied to her cage by her horse. Leaving the barracks for her first afternoon of freedom exploring the city, there were only two people she could entrust him with: the two Gypsy grooms. They had made it clear to her from the start that any communication with other *Roma* would not only increase the danger of uncovering her true identity but place them in danger as well. Even so, the time had come to take that risk.

She approached them as they stood among other grooms and riders lined up the length of the aisle, preparing to saddle up horses attached to cross-ties. She was last to lead her stallion out and put him on the cross-ties in front of his stall. While starting to curry him down, she said to the *rom* next in line from her, "Guess what?"

He had just placed a saddle on the horse he was grooming. He slowly raised his eyes to her face.

"I just got special permission to walk into town. The question is, Where to? On my first time out, that is. Where is the liveliest spot?"

"The Nevsky Prospekt," the Gypsy groom said, his eyes reading her face. He was tightening the girth of one of the two young gray stallions that Dosha had handed over into the Roma grooms' care.

"That's Leningrad's main thoroughfare," said the other *rom*, who was saddling up the other stallion tied further up the line and for a short moment, with voices that seemed on a race against each other, they described in great detail, the best way to get there from the Hermitage. It was the quiet, never-wavering look in their eyes that told her they understood: She needed them to watch over her *gres*, her horse, the stallion Rus, but from the persistence of their stares, the almost imperceptible shaking of their heads, she guessed they had answered the question she had not dared ask, namely, where she would find people of her own.

Now bridling the horses, they turned their back to her. There was to be no further exchange of words. Their caution confirmed her fears, her nightmares — it was dangerous to be Roma here, even more dangerous than before. Yet it was Osap who had brought the two Roma grooms here. Wouldn't he have known? She herself had picked up snatches of the Romani they spoke to each other while mucking stalls and the Tartar must have done so as well. It was not Lovaritz they spoke. Their names were Ado and Hissen, and she believed they must be Kalderash. Did the Tartar know their tribe? She had noticed that the two *rom* appeared relaxed in his presence. Was Osap Tossuk secretly protecting these Gypsies?

Several hours later that day, released into what Galina proudly called Russia's Glorious Window to the West, Dosha, for the first time all by herself, stepped through the arches of the Staff Building onto Palace Square. She took a deep breath: Alone in the city, for however short a time, she could be Dosha again. It was barely past noon on a gray Soviet Day, yet the immense check-ered square appeared swept clean of human activity. Every now and then a lone person carrying shopping bags or a twosome with linked arms walked across the Palace Square, their figures look-ing tiny and lost on that chessboard of superhuman size.

Blasts of arctic air had been pouring in from the Baltic since the early morning hours. Freezing drizzle clung like black ice to the walls of the surrounding palaces, from the greenish-bronze statues placed along rooftops down to the ornate forged-iron lan-terns below. The frigid wind drove the misty vapors off the still open waters of the Winter Canal and made them waft like smoke toward a black limousine with tinted glass that squatted like a si-lent predator at the end of the wide square.

To find her bearings on this first day out on her own, Dosha decided to retrace the steps of the day of her arrival. But crossing the deserted, frosty square toward the Winter Canal, she felt more than ever like a moving target in a relentless hunt. Accustomed to listening with all her senses, she was convinced she was being watched even before she set eyes on two soldiers who had been standing on the other side of the massive dark base of the tall pink granite column of Czar Alexander that dominated the square. They were young conscripts, still in their teens, blond and blue-eyed, with the serene faces that only seemed to grow on Russian soil, but fully armed with machine guns and gun belts. *Barely reached full manhood*, she thought, *and already trained to kill.*

They lowered their eyes to their feet as Dosha drew close, as if she had caught them idling, yet remained in place like senti-nels as she walked by the stationary limousine toward the covered passageway connecting the Hermitage Theatre to the rest of the Hermitage complex.

Here she paused, close to the spot where they had unloaded the horses upon her arrival. Stepping under the arch of the Winter Canal to gaze at the Neva's widest span, she was again struck by how quietly the water of the massive river flowed, how smooth-ly it forked around rocky islands jutting out of its midst. On the far shore, houses stood enshrouded in shifting masses of fog and pollution, with only the spires of an enormous cathedral piercing through, as if poking the sky. Except for two empty tourist bus-es parked some distance away, by the entrance of what she had been informed was the Winter Palace (the official entrance to the Hermitage Museum), the Palace embankment looked even more deserted than the Square. Other than an occasional car driving by in each direction, and the shrill whistle of a steamboat cutting through the river fog, all was silent, as if city life had been diverted to another part of town.

Dosha lifted her face toward the beclouded winter sun, pale as the moon, and listened to the sweeping sounds of wind gaining strength. Suddenly the cackling of a flock of geese resounded from above the arch that spanned the Winter Canal. The geese dipped down onto the river but rose at once and continued their flight in V formation, spearheading the rising storm. *They're late,* she thought, contemplating the coming winter. *Did somebody hold them back like me? At least nobody separated them from their own. Only vadni ratsa, the lone goose of Romani legend, flies alone, on her mission to alert Roma that the time has come to flee and that she will show the way.* Dosha had been swaddled in this legend since birth. Had the time come for her to find a path back to freedom, not only for herself but for her people?

Dosha stepped out onto the embankment and turned her face into the icy wind blowing from across the Gulf of Finland — *where the world is still free,* she thought wistfully, *and where my path must lead.* Only how could she, without leaving the stallion behind, escape a system that had infiltrated every pore of Soviet life? How could she escape without the help of those she knew and trusted? In order to survive, she needed the secret contacts spread along the worldwide web of Lovari treks.

A man in a dark winter coat and a gray felt hat started to walk toward the empty bus from the side of the Winter Palace, holding on to his hat with one hand. Before climbing into the parked bus, he briefly turned his face in her direction. With growing anxiety — she could not shake the feeling she was being observed and followed — Dosha reversed direction and fell into a brisk walk. She decided to follow the suggestion made by the Roma grooms back at the barn and make straight for the embankment of the nearby Moika.

The arctic cold was settling in. Below the handsomely filigreed wrought-iron balustrades, a green rim of frozen water glittered along the river's granite shores. With one quick backward glance Dosha noticed, at some distance, two soldiers following the direction of her walk. Were they the same two conscripts from Palace Square and had they followed her all this way? *They*

*all look alike,* she thought, continuing past rows of former aristocratic mansions, their grandiose design and once-brilliant pastel
colors long turned shabby from neglect. Elegant street lamps with
embossed bases and fancy brackets chimed in the driving wind.

Cars honked as, ignorant of pedestrian rules, she turned left
across an arching bridge onto what the grooms had told her was
the main thoroughfare of Leningrad, the Nevsky Prospekt. The
soldiers were gaining on her. Turning right, she dove into a heavy
stream of pedestrians which moved like two massive assembly
lines on either side of the wide avenue. She allowed herself to be
swallowed up by the anonymous walking masses.

She walked at a faster pace than most and had covered a good-
ly distance when suddenly, for the first time since since she'd left
the Junker-Institut, her anxiety settled and her mind took flight.
That's when she started seeing them — Gypsies!

The first one was an old Gypsy woman. She stood pressed
into the entrance of a house, holding out her hand to beg. Then,
as Dosha approached the entrance to the Metro station, she saw a
heavyset Russian woman cornering two Gypsy girls. The woman
stood between them and a policeman, gesticulating and yelling at
the top of her voice, "Tzigani!" This was followed by a string of
Russian curses. " Vagrants! Thieves! Asking me, a hard-working
Soviet citizen, for money! As if ..." she yelled. "Look at them!
They're now sending out their kids!"

The policeman turned his full attention to the Russian woman, top heavy in her winter coat. He raised both hands in an attempt to calm her down.

"Good-for-nothings!" The woman turned toward a small
crowd that had started to gather. "They should be locked away!"

The Gypsy girls, as if her tirade in no way concerned them,
stared with vacant eyes past their accuser and right through the
cop as if he were made of air.

*Must be city Gypsies,* Dosha thought. *But what is happening to
them?* To a Gypsy, begging or stealing is a means of last resort
and although they were barely past childhood, the faces of the
girls looked hollow and drawn. Kerchiefs covered their hair, except for the ends of their dark braids, which dropped below the
triangular end of their colorful head scarves, indicating that they
were married. These were young *bori,* brides, probably of the tribe
of Kalderash, but certainly not Lovara, not even of the city.

Those she came across much later. Having zigzagged down
mazes of narrow alleyways and across canals via gracefully arching

bridges, she arrived at St. Isaac's Cathedral, a squatting mass of tarnished marble and granite. Its golden dome was catching the dying light when she at last saw what she had been searching for: a group of Lovari women, some clutching babies to their hips, entering the square. Their colorful skirts fell below their heavy sheepskin jackets, almost sweeping the ground. The long, flowing hair of these bori was only partly covered by colorful kerchiefs. They walked with loose strides, freely, like heedless royalty, fanning out into the crowd of pedestrians. People tried to ignore them by looking the other way. Unperturbed, the women went ahead and chose targets as if they'd been preordained.

"Let me see your hand!"

"A fortune? Do you want to know your fortune?"

They picked the hands of women passing by, seemingly at random. Ever so swiftly, they removed the gloves of those selected while nailing their victims with darkly gleaming eyes. They formed tiny islands of two within the moving crowd, as, with great intensity, they bent over outstretched palms.

Dosha's first instinct was to run right over and embrace them. Instead she took a deep breath and stepped into the path of one. "Lovara sym," she whispered. "I am Lovara! Pick up my hand! Pretend I am Gadje. Talk to me."

The *romni's* glance took in her dress and the fine coat, the fur-trimmed hat, before resting on Dosha's face. She picked up her hand. "What are you doing here?" She spoke with an accent like Jano's.

"I am a *diviliyo,*" Dosha answered, indicating a nomadic Lovara.

The woman's head snapped up. "And you're here? Don't you know?"

Dosha froze in place. "Know what?"

"They've started to round up the wild Roma. They are shipping them to *o del* knows where. You must not be seen talking to us." The *romni*, the Gypsy woman, squeezed and then dropped Dosha's hand. "It could give you away."

She brusquely turned and joined her friends. Dosha watched them disappear, holding themselves proudly upright as they cut with sweeping steps across the crowd. *They may look haggard,* Dosha thought, *but their spirits remain undefeated. Those city Gypsies will survive. But,* she shuddered, *for us nomads it's starting, just as Patrina and Jano predicted.*

Back in the Junker-Institut, safely ensconced in the barn aisle, she breathed in the smell and warmth of horses. The two Roma grooms were sweeping the aisle. They looked up when she approached, then dropped their eyes. No one spoke.

# 18

# Recreational Freedom

Soon the day arrived for the promised weekend in the country. On a Saturday, the thirteen horses were loaded into vans, driven to the nearest railway station, and led onto railroad cars equipped with standing stalls. The riders and the grooms were shown into passenger cars, where, amid much bantering and camaraderie, they were served *butterbrot* — sandwiches from a basket and hot tea in tin cups.

Dosha, knowing she had no choice but to follow orders, found herself seated across from Galina, in a more luxurious compartment apart from the rest. They were served tiny sandwiches on fancy plates and tea in china cups. To avoid Galina's penetrating gaze, Dosha leaned her head back against the soft headrest and kept her own eyes on the passing countryside. The land was flat and marshy, and already covered with a fine cover of snow.

After a two-hour train ride, they stopped at a rundown provincial train station, where a brief look out of the window confirmed her worst fears. Behind barbed wire that extended as far as the eye could reach, above a multitude of the low, squat tents of many different Gypsy tribes, rose the lofty summer tents of the nomadic Lovara.

"Yes," said Galina, moving close to her side, "it seems we are finally gaining control over these wild parasites. We are turning them into civilized workers and solid Soviet citizens like ourselves. Those *tzigani*," she emphasized, "are being standardized at last." Shaking her head, she added, "Come along, Ana."

With that, Galina marched off the train, leading Dosha onto a wooden platform where the other riders already milled about waiting for the horses to be unloaded from the freight cars farther down. The station itself appeared to have been hastily erected:

172

it was merely a wooden platform set between two sets of tracks, protected from the elements by a tin roof. Instead of a waiting room and ticket counters, two one-room wooden barracks with the same tin roof had been built side by side. A wooden sign on one of the barracks listed the number 189, instead of the name of a village or town.

Dosha was struck by the number of soldiers, guns at the ready, standing guard or walking back and forth along the chain-link fence topped with concertina wire that surrounded the tent encampment. She could see that, inside the camp, Roma of many different tribes had been randomly thrown together. — *as if,* she thought with growing anguish, *we were all alike.* In reality the various *natsijas*, the Gypsy nations, were as different and as incompatible in custom and beliefs as the countries of Europe.

Since childhood, Dosha had been taught that the Lovara were the noblest of them all, for their lives revolved around the horse. The Kalderash, the most numerous of all Roma tribes though less unified, were metal-workers. Dzumila had impressed upon her the fact that the Kalderash didn't have a single leader who, like Khantchi, had the powers of a king. Also, unlike the Lovara, Kalderash men paid gold for their brides and brought their young wives from far away into their own tribes, where, separated from their own kin, the brides were placed under the control of their mothers-in-law. As a matter of respect, the Kalderash women never walked in front of their men. The Romani spoken by Kalderash was so different from Lovaritz that they could not understand each other, although Roma of all tribes always found ways to communicate.

There were other tribes in the encampment, of which Dosha knew nothing. On second glance she noted, however, that there were clear divisions in the camp after all — indicated by the way the openings to the tents were positioned. Gypsies of all tribes are opposed to mixing or, worst of all, to intermarriage with tribes outside their own. *There will be feuds,* she thought, *first among the women, who will immediately be backed up by their men.* The feuds would spread. The different tribes would never truly unite and for the first time Dosha realized that the fatal danger to all Roma lay not only in the external enemy they shared, but in those deep-rooted divisions among themselves.

"They're horrifying, aren't they? Sticking to that primitive way of life! We have heard reports that these savages are hypnotizing peasant folk and then robbing them blind," Galina said, coming up beside her. "They're waiting here, in transit before being shipped off. One can only hope that Siberia will achieve what we Soviets have been unable to manage so far — to weed out the willing from the idlers. This time, they'll work or die."

*What she doesn't know,* Dosha consoled herself, *is that Roma have crisscrossed Siberia as far back as memory can reach. With their knowledge of the terrain, maybe they'll find a way out, an escape. Maybe they'll even find some friendly souls, some allies, and not just peasants who faint at the sight of strangers just because they're dark.*

The late afternoon light streaked the sky with pink and purple. It tinted the blanket of freshly fallen snow a frosty blue. This was the time of day when a normal Gypsy camp would have been in full swing. Instead, those in this forced encampment moved about like shadow figures devoid of life. Normally rambunctious Gypsy children were clinging to their mothers' skirts, their big blank eyes fixed on the halted train. The air was still and crisp. The purity of the freshly fallen snow shone in sharp contrast to the dark fate of these Roma.

As the grooms started to lead the blanketed horses down special ramps off the freight train and handed them over to their respective riders, Lovari men silently gathered to watch. They moved closer to the concertina wire atop the fences, eager to see the lovely horses. The stallion was the last to be lead out. At the head of the ramp he froze, then suddenly shot away from his groom and jumped onto the platform, pulling the groom along. A momentary panic spread through the horses already unloaded. Up to that moment the animals had stood obediently beside their riders — although to judge by their pricked ears, the nervous turning of their heads, and their snorting breath, visible like steam from boiling water, they were clearly alert to their unknown surroundings.

A lively interaction of words and gestures now sprung up among the interned *rom*, before their eyes turned to the one Roma groom and the expertise with which he was handling the now, kicking stallion. The groom lost neither nerve nor patience, until he was able to walk the stallion into increasingly smaller circles. When they both stopped, facing the other horses, the *rom* on the other side of the fence nodded their heads in approval.

Only then did Dosha notice that there was not one single horse among the trapped Roma — and no fires, no wagons, no horses. Just tents, with snow bearing down upon the tattered multicolored canvas they had stretched between wooden poles. Her only relief came in the realization that she did not recognize any of her own kin. She wondered how they had escaped the roundup.

"Follow me," Galina ordered with a wave of her hand. "Over there!" She pointed to the opposite side of the tracks, which bordered scrubby open land stretching as far as the eye could reach. "Blankets are to be left on this platform!" she ordered. At once the grooms pulled off the blankets that had covered the horses head to tail, folded them, and, walking across the still lowered ramp, piled them up inside one of the freight wagons.

The horses had traveled fully saddled and bridled. Halters with lead shanks had been slipped over the bridles and looped reins. The riders now removed the halters, handed them over to the grooms, and unlooped the reins. Then, in single file, leading their horses by the reins, the team marched on foot toward the open field beyond the railway tracks. There they spread out in a straight line, shoulder to shoulder.

For the first time since their induction into the newly formed dressage team, the horses were facing open space. Even the old army horses perked up at the sight and smell of land. Some dropped their heads and pawed the ground. Some stretched their heads up high, neighing with excitement. Only the slightest breeze swept across the snow-covered plain, but it seemed to pour the instinct of flight back into the deadened souls of the weary animals. They would probably have leapt forward and given in to their suddenly recovered instinct to up and run, but their movements were severely restricted by the bridles and reins held securely in their riders' hands.

"Mount!" Galina shouted. The riders promptly tightened their horses' girths, lowered their stirrups, checked the bridles, and allowed the grooms to give them a leg up onto their skittish mounts. The heavyset Galina needed two grooms to heave her onto Djemo's mare, positioned opposite the lineup. Once on top of the mare, however, she sat deep in the saddle and secure, looking more at home than when sitting behind her desk. The mare at once grew calm, and Dosha marveled at how one so in tune with horses could seem so indifferent to the fate of a whole people — men, women, and children.

They were all mounted when one of the grooms handed Galina a bullhorn. Raising it to her mouth, she blasted, "Our quarters...." The sudden violence of her magnified voice set the already riled-up stallion and several other horses off. They were on the brink of exploding again. With Dosha on his back, soothingly patting his neck, the stallion soon quieted again, but now he arched his neck and she felt his hind quarters quiver with irrepressible power. Left to her own devices, Dosha would have let him gallop into the open field ahead of the team to let him get rid of built-up tension. Galina, however, either did not register the stallion's impatience or chose to ignore it.

"Our quarters are an hour's leisurely ride from here," she blared through her horn, even louder than before. "However, this ride is not for—"

By then the stallion had gathered so much steam, it was beyond even Dosha's control. Her body flew forward as he leaped straight toward Galina, who dropped her bullhorn, shouting: "Pull him back!"

Dosha, knowing how the stallion would react to having his mouth yanked at such a moment, nevertheless did as she was told. Rus rose like a meteor into the icy blue air, high up toward the brilliant pink-streaked sky. Dosha could feel his blood rush through his trembling body. When the horse turned his head ever so slightly, what she glimpsed in the corner of his eye was the wild joy of facing free open space again.

"I'll have to let him run!" she yelled and allowed the stallion to explode through his dressage frame. With winged speed he fiercely swallowed ground. Standing in her stirrups, her back out of the saddle like a jockey's, Dosha leaned forward, stretching her hands along his neck. They were racing across the flat, snow-covered plain toward a black-and-white birch forest that rose like an island out of the shimmering sea of white.

Giving herself over to the ecstasy of his flight, Dosha buried her face into the stallion's flying mane. The only sound left in the world of winter silence was that of his breath, coming fast and hard, and the rhythmic fall of his barely touching feet. As they approached the birch wood, the stallion veered, now skirting the forest line. Suddenly he slowed, shied, and jerked to a spinning halt. His hind end tucked under and his head snapped up, he listened to whatever sound must have touched his keen ear.

The next moment Dosha saw a Gypsy woman and several children dragging dead branches out of the forest. The woman, suddenly confronted by Dosha on her horse, stopped as if shot. The children dropped the branches they had been carrying and rushed to her side. Dosha's heart stopped. The coincidence was almost too great to believe, for she saw that, under the woman's long felt jacket, the *romni* wore the colorful skirt of a Lovara. She glared at Dosha with stinging eyes — ready to attack if necessary, to defend her children.

Dosha pulled up the stallion alongside. "*Lovara sym.* I am Dosha," she whispered, "of the Khantchisti."

The woman dropped her wood and approached but Dosha stopped her with a motion of her hand. "I am being followed by a band of Bolsheviks. You can't see them yet," she turned back to where she'd come from, "but they can't be far behind. Hide in the woods until we are gone."

The romni did not move. "Patrina," she said, "our phuri dai . ... " The words gushed forth like a waterfall. "They've captured our tribal mother. She was camped along the road in her death tent, surrounded by her own. It goes without saying, they refused to leave her. So they took them too. Only instead of throwing them all into one of those death camps, the Bolsheviks took her to one of their hospitals instead, the kind they call a field hospital, nothing more than a tent. And there, with all her closest kin in tow, who once again would not leave her, they cut her open. The Bolsheviks cut our tribal mother open, and then they patched her back up again and, would you believe it, she made it out of there alive — only to find herself locked up, along with the rest of her kumpania, in some house that is in ruins. I'm told it's in the poorest part of Saint Pete." Although she knew the Bolsheviks would soon be upon them, the Lovari romni refused to move from Dosha's side until she had told her all. "She is waiting for her granddaughter, the one that is supposed to find a way out of this trap. Is that you? And if so, I don't see how one single....."

At that point her children, feeling safe with the two of them speaking in Lovaritz, intervened. Pointing to the horse, they shouted, "*Gres, baro gres.*" A horse, a big horse!

"They captured her with all the gold," the *romni* continued, unperturbed. "But Khantchi, once again, got away. They say he crossed the Finnish border with the help of the Lapps up North."

"*O del* be thanked, he got away yet again," Dosha said. "They have many reasons to want to catch him." Her grandfather himself had told Dosha that the Bolsheviks were afraid he had the power to spill many hidden events to Western journalists. "Secret uprisings and massacres," he had told her, "and not only of Roma." She paused.

"How can I find her?"

"Look for one called Larkin, the former partisan and *dopash rom* — the half-*rom* who was Patrina's friend, the one she adopted as her son. He fought at her side. He is well known among *Gadje*. They call him a master of dance."

Dosha spotted the rest of the riders racing toward them from across the field.

"Those are the Bolsheviks. Go! Hide!," Dosha whispered, waving the *romni* and her children into the woods and turning her horse to face what had become a stampeding herd. She looked back over her shoulder. "Where in Leningrad?" she asked, as the *romni* vanished into the trees. "How do I find this Larkin?"

But the *romni* had already disappeared into underbrush, where conifers among the birch provided cover.

For a moment Dosha felt an irrepressible urge to follow the fleeing *romni* and her children — the same impulse that drives a horse to run with its herd. Instead, knowing that flight would bring death not only to herself, she started to canter slowly back toward the cloud of stirred-up snow that marked the approaching horses. They were moving at a fast gallop in swallow formation. In the lead, riding as easily as if she'd been born on a horse, was a strikingly younger version of Galina. Rising in her stirrups, she was waving at Dosha and shouting, "Perfect! Perfect!"

With a commanding lift of her arm, Galina brought the herd to a sliding halt, her own mare almost nose to nose with the stallion. Breathing hard, her heavy bosom heaving with excitement, Galina straightened to her full height and waved a hand at the expanse of wide-open land behind them.

"Look at this!" she exclaimed, "A Russian plain, the charging horses — all you have to add is the sound of 'Meadowlands.' We will choreograph a horse ballet that will demonstrate the very essence of Soviet revolutionary power.

"In Helsinki, six months from now, we will show the West" — her voice rose to propagandistic heights — "that there is a new wind blowing in the USSR, a return to all that was glorious. Our ballet will be just like this charge."

For the first time since her capture, Dosha felt hope and lightness flood her being. Not only had she stumbled across her first real link to the "Gypsy post," Galina had just mapped out the time and route of her escape.

The rest of the weekend was uneventful.

# 19

# Galina's Gamble

In late December 1956, Comrade Galina Gregorovna Popov, in an impassioned speech, had laid out for the ideological committee of the Ministry of Culture her plan to introduce the new Soviet Dressage Team to the West. Nikita Sergeyevich Khrushchev, Secretary General of the Soviet Communist Party, presided over the closed session. His de-Stalinization speech of that same year had prompted a sudden explosion in the arts. A new generation of artists, writers, directors, and filmmakers were eager to secure approval for state-sponsored productions and exhibits; however, most of their proposals met with vigorous vetoes. Only Comrade Popov's presentation was greeted by Comrade Khrushchev as "Excellent!" He pushed back his chair, stood up, and declared with a roaring voice, "At last, an event of propagandistic and revolutionary value to be added to the other Soviet artistic performances! These will pave the way for my first state visits abroad since the restructuring of our Communist regime."

Galina suspected it was the idea of horses that appealed to her distant cousin. *It must remind him of his former lords and masters,* she thought. *What this new peasant elite really wants is to step into the boots of their murdered aristocrats. It's strange, though —* she threw a discreet glance his way *— that of the whole Gang of Equals hand-picked by Stalin himself to keep his personality cult alive after death, Nikita is the one who has managed to clamber to the top. That uninspired peasant with his smiling face and eyes of steel has managed to turn himself into the rising new Red czar.* What was clear to Galina above all was that she had underestimated her cousin Nikita, who now held her life in his hands.

Galina had survived Stalin and his purges by joining the chorus of yea-sayers that surrounded him. She had become one of the

179

few women ever to achieve real power in the all-male Soviet political system. She was now, at age fifty-seven, at the peak of her career, and her status endowed her with certain privileges — such as the ability to bypass the long lines of people waiting in the street outside the Kirov Theatre, formerly the Mariinsky, home of the Kirov Ballet. With her chauffeur holding open the doors, Galina led Ana Dalova straight into the gilded reception hall.

The foyer was filled to capacity with masses of theatergoers awaiting the bell that would allow them to enter the hall of the theater. Cutting through the crowd, Galina motioned to an attendant standing by one of the entrance doors, who at once rushed to take their coats and usher them in.

It was a Friday evening — "the most sought-after night," Galina proudly told the girl. They followed the uniformed attendant, still carrying their coats across one arm, all the way down to the third row in the orchestra, where Galina had reserved two seats on the aisle.

"With you seated on the aisle," Galina whispered, leaning toward the girl, "I can explain things to you, with minimum disturbance to others. Remember," she said, "you're not here to watch, but to learn." With that Galina stepped ahead of the girl and took her seat next to the Men in Power already filling the row.

"I was not much older than you — in fact I was a young revolutionary — when I was sent on my first mission abroad to Austria," said Galina as she settled into her chair, "There I was offered the great privilege of watching the Spanish Riding School of Vienna perform to classical music. During my observations I was informed by a fellow Communist that the trainers of the world-famous quadrilles drew their inspiration from the choreography of classical ballet.

"It is my longtime commitment to the Bolshevik cause," she pontificated, "that now allows me to offer you the opportunity to study and apply that same connection from the art of classical ballet to the graceful and perfected union of man and horse — only, Russian-style, of course."

Galina relaxed back into her upholstered seat and shifted her attention to the high-ranking Party members surrounding them. The first three rows were reserved for upper-echelon comrades, some bedecked with medals, and their wives. Now the theatergoers who had been patiently waiting out in the foyer and in the street poured in, emitting a steady, subdued hum of conversation as they proceeded to their assigned seats in an orderly fashion.

When the last seat was filled, the brilliant lights that had bounced off the gilded walls and crystals chandeliers dimmed. For a moment Galina allowed her eyes to climb up the gilded balconies and examine the crowd. She had not attended a performance in months, and she noticed with amazement the smooth, unmarked faces of a new elite. Like mushrooms grown in some dark protected corner, a new privileged class had suddenly popped up after Stalin's demise.

Instead of the grim faces Galina had long become used to in her professional surroundings, these young apparatchiki and their pretty women in foreign clothes and hairstyles were gently facing each other with an air of almost prerevolutionary romance. These young men and women of the new elite seemed to pick words off each other's lips as if picking cherries off a tree. They were nothing like the sturdy replicas of authentic Russian peasants whom Galina and her husband, perfect symbols of the Revolution, had represented at their age. Galina's husband, Comrade Andrey Popov, reluctant revolutionary but true peasant, had long since been dispatched to a permanent post in Novosibirsk, thus allowing her free rein as she climbed the ranks of power.

As for other such former model citizens, the more typical party members — proud of their status as peasants and workers — were still present, but they seemed suddenly to have been pushed into the background. Turning to look around, Galina noticed a few stout peasant couples strategically placed here and there, like rocks in a park. The women's hair was still cut in the standard way or else permed close to the skull. The couples, men and women alike, had impassive Russian faces that had seen everything: their eyes stared straight ahead like nails. Even in this relaxed new era, they still received state-dictated rewards for God knows what, whether they liked it or not. If given a choice, these former peasants would probably have preferred to reclaim their expropriated cows and their *izbas*, those tiny peasant huts with adjacent patches of land on which they could grow their own food. Galina knew that her peasant mother — rest her tortured soul — would have liked nothing better.

*They've got to feel out of place in halls like these,* Galina decided, *especially seeing this new elite, the offspring of our hard-fought revolution, grown soft. Do they also question what in the end it was all about?*

The controlled hum of the audience was cut off by the sudden shrill tuning of instruments. A moment's silence was followed by a

181

hearty round of applause performed in rhythmic unison by every-one in the audience; and this too was followed once again by total silence. Softly the overture to Tchaikovsky's *Swan Lake* poured over the quiet audience. Even in these heady times of change and contradiction, *Swan Lake*, a tale of good versus evil, still reigned supreme.

At the first sounds of the soulful music the mood of the audi-ence, old and young alike, showed that same hunger to bare their souls in religious rapture that their serf ancestors had exhibited while kissing icons in church. *In the end*, Galina thought, *nothing has changed at all.* The superstitions and religiosity that had kept the illiterate masses docile and obedient for centuries had been re-placed by Stalin's iron fist and to keep his unwavering grip, Stalin had ruthlessly purged all that was free and different. *What he has really left behind*, Galina thought, *is a nation of robots interspersed with schemers. And I, am I among them?*

At that moment Galina, rather than looking forward to a future of continued success and privilege, had to admit to her-self that as a youth, split between serfs and aristocrats, she had recklessy and idealistically joined the revolutionary forces of de-struction. *We hoped to build a world of fairness for all*, she thought ruefully as she listened to the soaring music. *Instead, we have ex-changed one dictatorship for another.* Yet fate had now handed her a key to turn back the clock and return to the passion of her life, the world of the horses and horsemanship. *And I will do everything in my power*, she swore to herself, *to return to Mother Russia some of her past beauty.*

The heavy, blue-and-gold brocade curtain lifted, and the spotlight shifted from the audience to the dancers onstage as they started to move to the romantic strains of uplifting music in a place glimmering with the pomp and glamour of a royal court.

Galina glanced sideways at the girl beside her. In the muted light, dressed in the classical black dress of French design, the young girl had the noble bearing and the flawless beauty of an aristocrat. Her luxuriant hair, twisted in a bun at the nape of her neck, shone like old Russian gold.

Instead of concentrating on the stage, as she had instructed Ana to do, Galina herself looked around at the spectators in the balconies to the side. There in the third balcony to their left sat a woman with black hair, a Gypsy, whom she recognized. The woman was cooling herself with an elaborate fan spread out like a peacock's tail.

"That," whispered Galina, drawing the girl's attention away, while pointing with a slight lift of her hand to the balcony, "is Maria Andreyevna. Years ago she was considered the most famous dancer of the Teatr Roman, our cultural effort to legitimize Soviet Gypsy art. She is actually married to our most famous choreographer. This is his production of *Swan Lake*, the most famous ballet of our great Russian heritage." *And nobody,* Galina wisely refrained from uttering out loud, *can breathe new life into this museum piece of former Russian art as he can.* Noticing the girl's keen interest in the Gypsy woman, Galina once again had a nagging feeling — the sense that something had been left undone.

*So be it,* she decided after a moment's reflection, for she herself felt swept up in these heady times of the Thaw. Perhaps Russia had at long last arrived at the final stages of Marxist-Leninist Communism, the promise that had driven all the young, angry idealists, herself included: the promise of freedom and equality for all.

*Besides,* Galina reasoned with herself, *Ana Dalova has been shadowed at all times.* It had been brought to her attention that the two soldiers sent out to follow and observe her on her first day had lost sight of her. But that had been in the heavy pedestrian traffic of the Nevsky Prospekt. The girl had returned to the Junker-Institut at the designated time. Subsequent operatives, from then on dressed in civilian cloths, had not observed her making any contacts or doing anything out of the ordinary. Ana Dalavo had not veered in the slightest from her commitment to her horse and her job as a rider and the added freedom and privilege had, if anything, resulted in improved performance. It had not only lifted the melancholy darkness from the girl's expression, but had resulted almost immediately in lighter movements among the horses she rode. Freedom and trust had definitely proven more effective with this girl than supervision and restriction.

In light of the girl's brightened mood and her own growing optimism concerning the coming International competition — inspired in great part by the girl's unusual talents — Galina decided to lift all further surveillance and provide the girl with her own private quarters within the General Staff Building. She would order the change the next morning.

Of course, just as she had dressed the girl to fit in with this newly emerged elite, so she would now have to teach her to navigate the System with its many treacherous undercurrents. The old guard would ensure its own survival at any expense. The girl's aristocratic bearing and aloofness would make her a prime target for those inclined to strive for advancement via denunciation. However, this girl would be protected. *By none other*, Galina thought, *than myself.*

At the first round of applause, she leaned toward Ana. "Tomorrow," she whispered as they clapped, "you and I will visit the studios that produce these lavish ballets, and you will meet the man in charge." She did not add that he had already been drafted to help choreograph the dressage free-style. "His name is Comrade Nikolai Larkin."

At the mention of the choreographer's name, the girl, who during all this time had kept her attention dutifully on the stage, suddenly turned to Galina. For the first time her face was as unguarded as a child's, eyes wide with surprise. It was for only a split second, and the girl's dark eyes returned to their usual impassivity, as impenetrable as the one-way mirrors Galina used in her line of work.

During the short intermission many audience members left their seats and moved into the aisles, where they stood about, greeting and talking to acquaintances and friends. The hall filled with the drone of low voices interspersed by coughs or the blowing of noses, until once again music as melancholy as the Russian soul resumed. The ornate blue-and-gold curtain rose, this time revealing the image of a lake. Galina leaned toward the girl and said, "Remember! It's choreography we're here to observe."

Her comment caused a fat-necked comrade directly in front of them to heave himself sideways with an irritated "Shh!" Turning his head to get a better look, he was quick to add, "Excuse me, Comrade Popov, I didn't realize ..." His deference indicated to Dosha, more clearly than before, that the mannish woman by her side was a *thagarni*, a queen among *Gadje*.

Onstage, dancing lights began to highlight the dark water of the make-believe lake. Across its undulating surface the silhouettes of graceful swans glided majestically toward shore against a background of painted images of wind-driven white birch and tall grasses, frozen in mid-motion under a bulging sky. Delicate ballerinas, almost uniform in size and looks, were next to enter. They blew in like swirling snowflakes, turning right and left in perfect unison.

Galina tapped Dosha's arm. "Ana! Follow the flow of movement of these dancers! Then transpose those formations to our horses."

To Dosha, a gift for visualizing horses racing and bucking in the wind, moving as a herd in all sorts of formations came as naturally as Galina's need to control. Ever since she had been confined to her mother's side while still a child, Dosha had dreamed up dances for their horses. She had visualized dances that imitated the spontaneous movements and the joy of Gypsies dancing to music that was always improvised.

*Like the riderless Siberian ponies*, she thought, thinking of the 'liberty acts' that her father had perfected, directing the horses by swooshing a lunge whip that imitated the shifting waves of storms and wind. As she watched these delicate nymphs wearing tiny crowns materialize out of the shapes of resting swans, she decided that they couldn't teach her much about the power of horses dancing to the sounds and upheavals of nature. Her mind turned from the blurred mass of mesmerized *Gadje* faces, back to the Lovari *romni* at the edge of the woods and her words in parting: "Look for one called Larkin!"

Could that Larkin possibly be that same half-Gypsy who had fought the Germans alongside Patrina and her band of Gypsy partisans? Dosha had been told that, before the war, Patrina's fellow partisan was a city dweller involved with dance. Dosha had presumed that he worked with the Gypsy dancers of the Teatr Roman. Now it turned out — if he was indeed that same Larkin — that not only was he married to the Gypsy woman sitting above her on that balcony, he was in charge of this elaborate show and tomorrow she would meet him.

Up to that point, just as somebody afraid of heights knows not to look down while walking along the top of a steep cliff, Dosha had kept her mind strictly on the road ahead, minimizing the hopelessness of an escape for herself and her horse. But when taken by surprise at the mention of Larkin's name, Dosha had let her guard down and looked straight into Galina's eyes, staring for the first time straight into the abyss that loomed under her at all times.

At that moment Dosha admitted to herself what she had known all along. One step in the wrong direction and she would be shipped off to a death camp or simply shoved alive into one of the many open mass graves already filled with millions of innocents killed in the name of the great Soviet cause. Stalin and his Bolsheviks may have kept the truth from his own people, who never ventured beyond where they lived and worked, but even the remotest countryside could hold no secrets from the eyes of traveling Roma, trained by the unpredictability of nature to be forever on the alert: lovers of life, they had witnessed the killings that the state strove to hide. As for the fate of Dosha's stallion, since he would never accept anybody but herself on his back, he would be left to the mercy of the ever-hungry Russian Gadje, who saw nothing wrong in eating horse flesh, even if the horse was as magnificent as the stallion Rus. Or would this woman, this powerful woman next to her, be able to intervene?

Dosha felt her breath coming faster. She threw a desperate glance at the woman up in the balcony, the Gypsy said to be Larkin's wife. She was dressed almost like a true Lovara, in a bright red top, with a colorful shawl across her shoulders. *If only you could come and talk to me — talk to me in my own tongue,* Dosha prayed in anguish. *Someone, anyone, tell me what to do! How long can I last, completely separated from my own?*

However, the woman on the balcony, her face half hidden by her elaborate fan, kept on gently fanning herself, her eyes on the stage. She seemed unperturbed, at ease. *As must I, as must I,* Dosha decided. To calm herself down, she tried to listen closely to the music that rose from below the stage but the music was foreign to her — *as foreign to me,* she thought, *as those stilted dances.*

Just then a single male dancer with feathered wings exploded onto the scene. The backdrop of dark water and white birch suddenly turned dark and ominous. The stage looked smaller as he leapt high up into the air, bursting through the frame of standardization that had dominated the elaborate scene.

"A talent," there was admiration in Galina's voice, "not seen since the great Nijinsky." The dancer, waving his winged arms, executed ever more powerful jumps and twists in midair. "He was proclaimed 'People's Artist of the USSR' this year," she noted. "Unfortunately, within the Ministry of Culture, he is considered politically suspect. He is the son," she lowered her voice to an almost inaudible whisper, "of Olga Karayeva, the poet. She died in exile in Novosibirsk. There is worse: His father was a follower of Trotsky. When Trotsky was deported, Dmitri Kutunov disappeared into thin air. To this day he has not been tracked down. Leaving their only son? Suspect, of course."

Transfixed, Dosha watched this winged demon unleash a force that seemingly nothing could stop, least of all himself. Muscles ran like elastic rope the length of his perfect body, the epitome of manhood. His fawn tights left nothing to the imagination. The corps of swans, sensing the power that would soon possess them, fluttered and closed in on themselves like flowers whenever his powerful wings hovered over their delicate bodies.

Dosha felt herself blush. Roma are prudish about exposing their private parts. *He's playing the stud*, she thought, *arching his neck and parading his stuff.* The dancer's masked face, with its protruding tongue, was meant to repel. But the eyes staring through the mask kept changing, depending on the angle of the stage lights, from the blue of ice to the darkness that lures at the bottom of the sea. The eyes of the masked dancer were calling to Dosha, pulling her in.

"He's dancing the role of the evil spirit," Galina explained with a dismissive edge to her voice, "part of the pagan beliefs and superstitions of the old Russia, the mystic faith that's now banned."

But that was the only part of Russia Dosha had been taught and loved. There was a time when the Russians of old and the Roma had understood one another's soul — memories kept alive through endless tales spun and repeated around burning fires at night, when the mind is prone to dream and absorb. Soothed, Dosha felt she was witnessing Russia's past and Gypsy legend join and fuse, like colors pouring out from different jars, on the canvas that was the stage.

And the dancing birdman, whose face was hidden behind his monstrous mask as he spread his darkly feathered wings across the dainty swans, he was no stranger to Dosha. Her mind's eye transformed him into the nameless King of the Locolico, the winged demon of Gypsy legend rising from the depths of the earth — the one whose people had been changed by *o bengt*, the devil, into terrestrial spirits condemned to live deep within the earth, to where the sun never rose. Far back in time, when myths and legends ruled the traveling Lovara's way of life, the winged demon king caught a glimpse of the pure and beautiful princess of the *Keshalyi*, the Good Fairies, as he skimmed her castle high on a mountain almost touching the sky and the King of the Locolico was seized by such immediate and anguished desire, he felt compelled to ravish the princess.

*"It is her name"* — Patrina's voice now rose to Dosha's mind — *"I offered you when you were a little girl: Ana. It is meant to protect you, should you fall into the hands of strangers.*

*"Beware then of winged demons"* — Patrina's warning reverberated through Dosha's mind — *"lest they carry you off the way the nameless king of the Locolico carried off the princess of the Kelshalyi.*

*She sacrificed herself to protect her people from the onslaught of his fe-rocious men, for they took by torture what was not given freely. He at once carried her to a dark corner where he fed her the brain of a mag-pie to drug her to his will, so that he might penetrate her virgin body and release his seed, again and again, although she could not bear to see his distorted demon's face. In the end, Ana of the Kelshalyi gave birth to nothing but powerful demons, sorcerers and casters of spells. Remember? It was her destiny to become the mother of Roma witch-craft and magic."*

Dosha's reverie was disrupted by the probing presence of the woman next to her, the one who held her fate in her hands.

Galina's lips moved closer to Dosha's ears. "However much we try to indoctrinate them, the Russian masses always seem drawn to the past, despite how harshly and unjustly they were treated then."

*But me, too,* Dosha despaired. *I also remain shackled to the an-cient myths and superstitions of my tribe, although I have tried to escape.*

She turned to look at Galina Popov, surprised to find a hint of warmth in the powerful woman's eyes. "I am too young to know the Russia of old," Dosha said, "but I often wonder what is was like."

Galina, nodding her head, gently patted the girl's arm. But the unexpected warmth of the *Gadji's* touch confused and fright-ened Dosha. She quickly escaped back into that mental space a Gypsy calls her own.

# 20

# Within The Hallowed Halls
# Of The Kirov Ballet

On a dreary, mid-December day when daylight was reduced to a few hours of muted light, Galina strode ahead of Dosha through the deserted hallways of the Kirov Theatre. They climbed a wide marble staircase up to the fifth floor, where the Kirov's most acclaimed soloists practiced with Alexander Larkin.

"The Ministry of Culture has already informed him that he is to help us choreograph our free-style horse performance," Galina declared." I imagine he's not pleased. It's up to us to get him truly engaged." *And if anyone can make him enthusiastic,* she thought, *it might be this beautiful girl.* Without bothering to knock, she opened a tall dark oak door onto a vast, brightly lit dance studio. Gray light poured through large half-moon windows across a floor polished like glass, where a whole ballet ensemble — reflected in mirrors that covered two entire walls — were engaged in various poses and movements.

Signaling the girl to stay put by the door, Galina walked up to a smallish, older man, who stood facing the dancers, his back to the entrance. He was the only one present not wearing ballet tights. Dressed in gray pants and a white shirt open at the neck under a sleeveless gray woolen sweater, he looked more like a petty functionary pushing papers in one of the many state-run offices than an artist of great renown.

Galina tapped his shoulder. Oblivious to the intrusion, the Great Larkin, as he was called by those privileged to be his students, remained fully focused on his dancers. "To maintain the flow," he continued in a soft but clearly audible voice, "you must keep in mind the coordination of movements: of the head, the eyes, down to the arms. And," he paused to emphasize, "most expressively, your hands!" He lifted his own hands to demonstrate.

189

"Your soul," he exclaimed, still ignoring Galina, "has to fuse with that of the spectator." He paused. What followed was a moment of total oneness with his students — broken by a second tap, harsher this time, on the Great Larkin's shoulder.

At that point the whole ballet ensemble witnessed their master's pale amber eyes slowly lose the trance-like look he assumed when drawing on his inner world. As he reluctantly turned away from his task, his hands, which had been extended over his head, faintly quivering like the hands of the most delicate of ballerinas dropped and became the sensitive hands of an aging man.

Observing him, Dosha felt her heart sink. He looked nothing like a Gypsy, not even a *dopash* or half-Gypsy. Ever since the woman out in the country had mentioned Larkin's name as the link connecting the web of Gypsy contacts in Leningrad, she had tried in vain to recall whether she had ever met him. All she could come up with were tales of Larkin's exploits in enemy territory, his daring escapes and brilliant maneuvers to rescue so many Lovara. Having been a little girl during the years of the Great Patriotic War, she could not conjure up a face to put to the name of Larkin, Patrina's wartime ally and adopted son.

The Larkin addressing Galina as "Comrade Popov" appeared to be pure Russian in looks and demeanor. Finding himself in such close physical proximity to Galina, he took a step back. Galina chose to ignore such tell-tale signs of uneasiness with the physical closeness she was imposing, not to mention his irritation at having his work in progress disrupted. Beaming with enthusiasm, her painted lips parted in a full and fleshy smile.

Dumbstruck, unbelieving, the dancers of the *corps de ballet,* who had been positioned as if on stage, halted in mid-movement. Not one single dancer among them had ever seen anyone interrupt a rehearsal conducted by Alexander Larkin. Not only were they incorporating several new dancers into the *corps*, but they were to perform that night.

Furthermore, nobody had ever crashed a work session without being specifically invited to do so — not even Party officials. Whenever visitors were to be admitted to rehearsals, the dancers were informed well in advance.

Even the accompanist, Madame Karnowsky, an old-timer in the studio, found herself in a quandary. Should she, or should she not, take five? Momentarily derailed from the strictly prescribed schedule, she decided to abandon the adagio to *Swan Lake* and let her fingers free-associate across the ivory keyboard of the old upright piano.

Everyone in the fifth floor studio had heard of Comrade Galina Popov, Chairwoman of the Ministry of Culture; known to be the only female member of the Politbureau. All eyes now watched in unison as she left the Great Larkin standing dumbstruck and returned to the open oak door.

"Come on in." Comrade Popov raised her voice and waved a hand, before turning her attention back to the most decorated choreographer of Soviet ballet.

"As you have been informed, Comrade Larkin," she said, "an effort has been launched to revive our great Russian tradition of horsemanship, which was interrupted by the Great Patriotic War. Part of that effort" — she moved closer to Larkin, as if the information were for his ears only — "is the establishment of a new Soviet international dressage team. In addition these riders will demonstrate the new Soviet High School of Horsemanship. This team will make its first presentation to the West on the occasion of Comrade Khrushchev's state visit to Helsinki next June. This initiative will also serve as a preparatory testing ground for the next Olympic Games, which will take place in Rome in 1960."

That was the extent of the speech she had prepared in advance. As far as Galina was concerned, that was all this man in charge of the Kirov Ballet, an important part of the Soviet propaganda machine, needed to know in order to put forth his best effort.

With a deep frown of annoyance, Alexander Larkin, head choreographer and number one balletmeister of the Kirov, took another step back. He had to. As his dancers knew, he was far-sighted, probably as a result of his advancing age. His attention was now fully riveted on the girl at the door. The maestro was known to his students as a man easily distracted by minute details and slow to start on the actual work at hand but once in a state of concentration, he forgot everything, including time and even hunger. Drawing on his inner world, his strong spirit would charge up his frail physique. At this moment, his focus was on this stranger approaching. Compared to the ballerinas, she was on the tall side. She had a beautiful stride, although hers was not a dancer's walk. She was wearing dusty riding boots.

"Has she ever danced before?" the maestro asked for all to hear.

The piano stopped altogether. The flabbergasted dancers wondered whether this might be a new pupil, one of those pulled from someplace way up north — talent that could not be ignored. The Great Larkin, after all, was known to look for the unusual in unlikely places. He himself had been only a mediocre dancer, but he was a man with an eye for talent.

The three male dancers, positioned at the barre that ran the length of the mirrored back wall, allowed themselves to assess this newcomer discreetly: after all, one of them might be required to lift her. Her fancy coat seemed at odds with the army-issue fur hat with earflaps that covered her head.

Dosha had been pulled out of the riding halls, without warning, right after working her horses. Now, with all eyes upon her, she felt self-conscious and out of place. Keeping her eyes straight ahead, she pulled off the hat. Her long braid dropped down her back.

"Ana Dalova," Galina introduced her. "She is the star rider of our dressage team. Through my offices, she has been assigned by the Ministry of Culture and the Central Committee's Cultural Department to study socialist-realistic choreography under the tutelage of Comrade Larkin."

After that the dancers seemed all but forgotten. The Great Larkin appeared to be mesmerized by the girl's brilliant reddish-blond hair. His rapt attention made Dosha's heart skip a beat. Had he been expecting her?

"And it is of course not up to any Soviet citizen," Galina continued, as if unperturbed — her voice carrying to all those present, "to question the motivations of our Party leaders, who are in the service of our great Soviet nation. It is our duty to cooperate to the very best of our ability, especially since this plan has been devised by none other than the First Secretary of the Communist Party of the Soviet Union, Comrade Nikita Sergeyevich Khrushchev himself."

Galina Gregorovna Popov lied easily. After all, she knew through long and hard personal experience that — as the saying goes — "A comrade should eat everything, but not necessarily know everything."

Larkin, his arms held stiffly at his side, listened calmly as Galina now mapped out schedules and shared responsibilities.

"I myself," she added, "unfortunately am obliged to turn my attention back to matters of the Soviet state."

*In other words,* Dosha thought, *she is placing all responsibility on this Larkin's shoulders. Amazing!*

Larkin had made no attempt to interrupt Galina's strident speech. He gave a little nod here and there and watched Galina absentmindedly, as if letting the whole idea sink in.

In the background the dancers had started to relax. There was much shaking of limbs, rolling of heads, stretching forward and back; dancers were flexing their feet, pointing their toes, lifting their legs. They all wore identical attire: the men in black tights and white sleeveless T-shirts, the ballerinas in black leotards. Only Valentina Kruglov, an aging icon of the Russian ballet, was dressed in a graceful beige tunic, and only she continued to dance. With one hand on one of the male dancer's shoulders, she lifted herself up onto full pointe, executed a *petit battement*, left foot to right *pointe*, and continued on, drilling in intricate twists and turns, and bends from the hip down.

"In other words," Galina Popov stated in conclusion, "I place the next segment of our ambitious plan into your capable hands."

By then, most of the dancers had started to leave their assigned positions. They spread out in the shape of an uneven horseshoe, chatting and giggling, smoothing back their hair, wiping off sweat with the back of their hands. One tall male dancer, whom Dosha recognized as having danced the role of the Prince the night before, stepped toward the shortest male dancer and started to talk in a low voice.

Meanwhile Valentina Kruglov, uncertain whether she was looking at a future rival, decided to establish her boundaries. Using the shorter dancer's shoulder like a barre to stretch once again toward extensions, she murmured into his ear — but in a voice loud enough for the strange girl to hear — how she, the prima ballerina, didn't need to be reminded about serving their great System, and how the dancers ought to be united in their efforts, how discipline was a two-way street, and that nobody had the right to interrupt — until the male dancer, young of body and short of patience, was ready to explode, but catching himself in time, he merely coughed.

Dosha, ill at ease and feeling out of place, as if somebody had cracked a whip, swung her head toward the source of the cough. For a split second she stared straight into the shorter dancer's brilliant eyes. *That's him!* She recognized him instantly. His were the eyes that had stared at her through the mask of the birdman, only this time they were unwaveringly blue.

The dancer, Vasili Kutunov, who more than anyone else had noted her beautiful walk, kept his eyes longer than was wise on what he perceived as a face of great beauty. It was a face, however, dominated by the burning dark eyes of what he figured to be a bona fide fanatic. He shuddered. *They grow in Russia,* he thought, *like poppies in a field of wheat. All those writers, poets, like my own mother, who had to pay with her life for being the brightest among them; all those idealists searching for meaning in Soviet life, amid a System that had promised justice and equality for all.*

Unlike the offspring of many of the Russian intelligentsia, Vasili had not paid for his mother's free-flowing brilliance and his father's objectionable politics by having his own life cut short in exile. Larkin had saved him from such a fate but even Larkin could not save him from major attempts to indoctrinate him — to "recycle" him and force him to reject all that his parents had stood for. "In order to survive," Larkin had impressed upon him, "you must at least pretend." But he knew that there were some who, no matter what the cost, and however much they tried, could not submit. To Vasili, the girl, despite being in the company of a Soviet heavy, looked like one of those feverish-eyed fanatics.

A moment later — he had quickly averted his eyes — the unexpected visit ended as abruptly as it had begun. Dosha and Galina left. As soon as the door closed behind them, Larkin stepped forward, raised his arms and called out, "Resume positions!"

# 21

# Alexander Larkin, Ballet Master

Before Dosha, pretending to be Ana Dalova, had followed her horse to Leningrad, nature had dictated the rhythm of her life. Schedules and regularity of any kind were completely foreign to her, as they would be to any Gypsy. Now Galina was handing her a wristwatch.

"I am about to depart for Moscow," Galina said. "I have to spend most of the winter months in my office at headquarters. If problems should arise, Comrade Tossuk will inform me, or so can you, should the need arise. This wristwatch," she continued, fastening it to Dosha's left wrist, "will organize your day during my absence.

"Mornings," she paused, "and mornings alone, you will work the horses assigned to you." She was still holding Dosha's arm with one hand; with the other, she tapped the watch. "Five times a week, precisely at noon, you are — until further notice — to present yourself at the fifth-floor studio of Comrade Alexander Larkin for the creation of an artistic 'free-style' program for the horses. Do you understand?"

When Dosha arrived at the studio for the first time, the noon bell for lunch must already have rung. She had to force her way through a rush of dancers toward Alexander Larkin who stood casually by the piano, watching her approach.

She heard the heavy door behind her close, muffling the sounds of feet hurrying down the marble stairs. Dosha hesitated, questioning again whether the frail, elderly man by the piano could be the one who had led many of her people to safety under the Nazi threat, at a time when hundreds of thousands of Gypsies were gassed or otherwise murdered during the *Porraimos* — the devouring, the Romani Holocaust. If it was indeed he, luck had not only brought her to him, but had given her this moment alone with him.

Dosha's heart beat faster. The moment was perfect — too perfect. She searched the walls and ceiling for signs of surveillance. After months of hiding her true identity, she felt an almost irrepressible urge to rush forward and blurt out her Gypsy name.

Something in his look stopped her.

Since the very beginning of their endless trek, Gypsies have crossed one hostile country after another, surrounded by languages they could not understand. They learned to rely instead on reading facial expressions and body language. They also learned how to hide their own feelings and fears by avoiding direct eye contact with outsiders. Dosha noticed that Larkin's eyes kept shifting away from her face the way a Gypsy's would in order to evade a pair of probing *Gadje* eyes.

Dosha turned around and only then realized that the door had been shut behind her by the matronly pianist, who now stood holding a tray with sandwiches and three cups of tea. "*Butterbrot!*" she exclaimed with a smile. *She must have been right behind me,* Dosha deduced, *following me with a cat's stealthy silence.*

"Comrade Karnowsky," Larkin introduced her. "You remember Ana Dalova."

"Indeed I do." The heavyset accompanist placed the tray on top of the upright piano. She selected a sandwich and sat down in her chair in front of the keyboard.

"Help yourself," she said to Dosha, pointing to the platter. "We're donating our lunch break to Comrade Popov's project." Dosha looked at the platter, but made no move to take a sandwich.

"No?" The woman's eyes flickered from Larkin to Dosha and back in an attempt to decipher the awkward silence that had fallen.

Larkin handed Dosha a cup of tea and took a sandwich himself. "Our task," he said to Madame Karnowsky, "is to apply the principles of ballet to a sort of artistic performance for dressage horses." He took a sip from his cup. "This is new to us, but I understand it has been done abroad. According to Comrade Popov, they used to be called 'horse ballets' hundreds of years ago. It's what the Germans call *Kuer*, one of those German words that stick, like *Butterbrot*." He winked at the pianist, who raised an eyebrow and stopped chewing. "We shall refer to it as 'musical freestyle,' similar to the approach of our world-famous Soviet ice-dancers.

"Our job at present," he continued, but addressing Dosha now, who was holding the hot tea cup in both her hands and drinking it in small sips, "is the selection of appropriate music. Your job" — he kept his head inclined toward Dosha — "is to figure out whether that particular music is suitable for horses to dance to: the tempo, the gaits, et cetera. During this afternoon session, you'll have the opportunity to observe the tempo and the configuration of our dancers, and then figure out what is applicable to the larger strides and capacity of the horse.

"The music, Comrade Karnowsky," he said, finishing his sandwich and licking his fingertips, "should have nationalistic relevance, both to the Soviet and the Finnish people. Both the Kirov and the dressage team," he emphasized, "will pave the way, culturally, for Comrade Khrushchev's first visit to Helsinki."

His briefing completed, Larkin positioned himself behind the piano and motioned Dosha to sit down on an empty stool to Comrade Karnowsky's right.

"We've got fifty minutes!"

Like twin hammers — *pah-PUM* - Comrade Karnowsky's hands descended onto her keyboard. Then, freely and expertly, her surprisingly slim, agile hands started wandering through various musical genres, ranging from gentle folk tunes to bombastic marches. From time to time she would pause to stand up and sort through stacks of sheet music piled on top of the piano. Licking her thumb like a bookkeeper going through receipts, she separated them into piles. A selected few she placed onto the reading stand above the keyboard, but once the music was placed there, she rarely glanced at it. She seemed to know every piece by heart. Her eyes rarely left Larkin's face.

Leaning both elbows on the piano, Larkin listened intently to every last melody, merely nodding. At times, he made a "so-so" gesture with one hand in the direction of Dosha, who remained quietly on her stool. Once again she was the outsider, and she felt a wave of relief when the bell indicated the end of the midday break.

At one o'clock, according to her wristwatch, the entrance door to the studio opened and the dancers came trickling back in. Larkin pushed himself off the piano with both hands. Dosha rose, feeling lost and out of place. Was she supposed to leave or stay? She didn't know. With a wave of his hand Larkin motioned her over to the row of half-moon windows that covered one wall of the studio. There, in an attempt to blend in, she sat down on a windowsill, molding herself against its curving frame, with one booted leg folded under her, the other dangling to the floor.

Still, she felt uneasy so close to Larkin. He positioned himself only a few feet away from her to coach that afternoon's session. He pulled a crumpled Russian cigarette from a shirt pocket underneath his sleeveless V-neck sweater and groped for matches in his pants pocket. He lit up the first cigarette of what would be that afternoon's chain, turned to the dancers and announced, *"Pas de trois!"*

Three young ballerinas stepped forward and linked arms. Seen close up, the delicate swans of the stage production looked tough and muscular. Heads and feet snapped into position. The three dancers picked up exactly where they had left off before midday break.

"Allegro!" Larkin commanded, coughing out smoke. Comrade Karnowsky at once picked up the tempo of the music, while remaining all eyes and ears, like a *dezhurnaya,* the watchwoman posted on every floor of the Junker-Institut dormitories.

Reverting to his more familiar raspy whisper, Larkin called out, *"Sauté!"* He lifted both arms, as if conducting an orchestra.

Dosha followed the rehearsal closely, taking mental notes of the various formations, especially when the whole *corps de ballet* started to create flowing ensemble movements, from which the principal dancers emerged as concertante soloists. This, Galina had impressed upon her, was a true specialty of the Great Larkin, and she should explore in her mind how the trainers could apply them to performances by the horses on the team.

However, no matter how hard she tried to focus on the various formations on view, Dosha's mind kept drifting back to what mattered most to her: Larkin. Was he or was he not the same *do-pash* Gypsy who had helped the Lovara in the past? Might he represent the first step in her escape?

When surrounded by *Gadje,* Gypsies of all tribes have a whole arsenal of secret signs with which to signal one of their own. From early childhood on they're taught movements of the hands, the eyes, and the body with which to interact secretly with other Gypsies, using signs that have no meaning to *Gadje.*

Dosha had recently used these nonverbal tools with the two Gypsy grooms as soon as Galina had informed her that she was to attend afternoon sessions at the Kirov for several weeks to come. Instead of trying to talk to the grooms in secret, Dosha had called them over to look at her stallion's tendons. Speaking Russian, she instructed them how to take care of the stallion's needs while she was absent, all the while indicating her concern by means of facial expressions. Not until the three of them were huddled close around the horse's hoofs did she warn them what never to do, and those words she whispered in Romani. In their faces, she read that they understood and could be trusted.

Larkin, on the other hand, had given her little indication that he could communicate in any way other than Russian — except during that one split second when she had first arrived, when the look in his eyes seemed to be warning her not to talk.

As the hammering of the piano drove the dancers faster and faster, Dosha felt her strength overwhelmed by a wave of anxiety. The lights around her seemed to dim and all movement faded eerily into the distance. She had to face facts: Her destiny lay irrevocably in the hands of total strangers. Even if this Larkin had once been part of Gypsy life, the all-pervasive System had turned him into a *mulo*, a mere ghost of his former self. He acted exactly like everyone else in power back in the Junker-Institut.

Dosha's growing panic trapped her breath. With horror she understood that what she had been assured was a temporary assignment, requiring only these few hours a day, could turn into a permanent separation from her stallion by the simple stroke of a pen and now Galina, her protector, whose love for the stallion she had come to trust, was far away in Moscow. Dosha felt lonelier than ever, lost in this musical world she did not understand.

# 22
# The Outsider

Through no choice of her own, Dosha was thrust into this dancer's universe, a hive of rules and regulations, where everything had its proper place, and all exits and entries were mapped out like roads. Five times a week, starting at noon, her mere arrival seemed to send the dancers swarming about like bees whose hive had been invaded.

Some actually stopped in mid-exodus and stood in clumps to watch as Dosha hung her Western-style winter coat alongside theirs. Like peasants in a village staring as Gypsies passed by, they gasped with disbelief that Dosha would enter the pristine world of Russian ballet dressed, underneath her fancy coat, like a worker in a horse barn.

It wasn't just that she had no time to change between her morning work with the horses and the Kirov appointment at noon. Dosha had no interest in acquiring new clothes, especially *Gadje* clothes, although she could have afforded them on the salary she earned as a state rider. With escape ever uppermost in her mind, Dosha looked forward to the day when, having rejoined her people, she could revert to the traditional ankle-length skirt worn by Lovari women. In the meantime she adopted a working uniform of a coarse white peasant shirt. It was buttoned at the side of the neck and gathered at the waist by a thin leather strap. These were worn by most riders during the morning working session. Her riding pants were army-issue but stuffed into the fine black leather riding boots — a gift from her father — that she had arrived with. Her outfit struck the elite dancers, accustomed to finer things, as eccentric in the extreme.

Dosha was surprised to discover that, although Galina had asked her to participate in choosing music for the exhibition ride in Helsinki, Larkin soon narrowed the choice down to three pieces, almost as if they'd been preselected.

"First, 'Meadowlands'!" he informed her, and Madame Karnovsky struck the opening chords on the piano, enthusiastically adding her voice. Dosha recognized it as the piece to which Galina had alluded during their outing in the countryside. "This song embodies the Russian Revolution," Larkin insisted. "It is a perfect overture for our horses and riders.

"To be followed," he continued, "by 'Finlandia,' composed by Finland's own Jean Sibelius to commemorate that country's tragic, bloody past." He explained that this piece would both accommodate a quadrille and incorporate a powerful *pas de trois* performed by the team's best threesome — which Dosha supposed meant the three grays she was training.

"And lastly," he concluded, "there is to be a solo, for you and the stallion I've heard so much about. Rus — that's his name?" Dosha nodded. "You will be dancing to 'Valse Triste,' also by Sibelius. It is a melancholy piece," he said, "but it will unite the spirits of Russians and Finns alike."

In preparing her star pupil, Galina had never really elaborated on the history of so-called "horse ballets." Instead, she had stressed that the proposed exhibition of freestyle riding would, while following the strict rules of classical dressage, offer Dosha — or rather, "Ana" — free choice in terms of the sequence of the various movements. It would be an opportunity for Ana to demonstrate her creativity while showcasing her innate gift for rhythm and show. She was to formulate a presentation that would demonstrate the magical harmony possible between rider and horse — a form of riding revived in this new, vigorous phase of the Soviet Union.

By the third session, they were spending most of the fifty minutes at their disposal discussing where to cut and splice the music at hand. "Slow the tempo here," Dosha would interrupt Madame Karnowski's playing — or then again, "Go faster here." The pianist would mark the changes on the score. "Unlike a ballet dancer, who is trained to follow the music," Dosha explained, "during this ride, the music must follow the natural gait and movement of the horse."

Dosha had no idea whether the dancers had been briefed as to why she was auditing their work sessions. Day after day she encountered the same wall of hostility as she made her way into the studio at noon, and day after day, upon returning to resume rehearsing at one o'clock sharp, the dancers would find the three collaborators in exactly the same positions: Comrade Karnowsky at the piano cracking her knuckles, the Great Larkin pulling a crumpled Russian cigarette from one of several possible pockets and lighting up his first of what would become the afternoon's chain, and Dosha already retreating to one of the gigantic half-moon windows.

There she would sit for the rest of the afternoon, an outsider looking in, wondering how she could possibly apply choreography designed for dancers trained like wind-up toys to the powerful movements of horses, especially a horse as dazzling as her own stallion. *His performance*, she realized, *has reached this level of brilliance only because I've never tried to break his spirit through excessive drills.*

When she danced with him, it was not the music of *Gadje* — their wars and revolutions, their memories of romance and lost love — that she heard. Dosha danced with her stallion to the sounds of nature which she carried within herself: the life of the forest rising with the sun, the sound of storms whipping the tops of trees in a powerful waltz while driving the tall grass below to bend gracefully this way and that.

Late one afternoon, upon returning to the Junker-Institut, Dosha informed Osap Tossuk that the music for their freestyle had been chosen, that she felt she understood choreography, and that she was ready to start applying formations to their quadrilles. The next morning, the Tartar informed her that, on direct orders from Comrade Galina Popov, she was to draw the formations on a piece of paper, but that she must continue to study Comrade Larkin as he choreographed his dancers. As of that day, however, the time she spent at the Kirov was to be cut back to three times a week. At the start of their next session, Larkin handed her several blocks of drawing paper and a box of multicolored crayons.

Even with the frequency of Kirov sessions reduced, there seemed to be no end in sight. Although she was now busy drawing formations (using brown, black, and light gray for the different colored horses), for Dosha, being forced to sit and watch the unrelenting grind of *Gadje* discipline felt like being trapped behind barbed wire. Once again she fell prey to doubt. What was she doing there? She always came to the same conclusion: *They are using these sessions as a pretext to separate me from my horse — to give some other rider the opportunity to learn how to ride him, so that they can replace me once and for all.*

Dosha closed her eyes. She had visions of her stallion striking out in panic, bucking and tossing off strangers. They would punish him with the whip, or worse, they would yank his sensitive mouth. He did not like men, let alone the rigid control of *Gadje*, but she had noticed, to her relief, that the stallion seemed to show a growing trust in one of the Roma grooms, the one called Ado.

The music stopped. Opening her eyes, Dosha noticed an attendant in a gray coat sprinkle the floor with resin. The dancers were standing about, shaking the tension out of their limbs. As soon as the attendant receded into the background, Larkin called out, "Vasili Kutunov!" and clapped his hands. "Pirouette! Da-DUM!"

The dancer at once drilled himself back into step, twirling with his customary boldness right toward the girl sitting against the leaden skyline of Leningrad.

Dosha thought back to the first time she had seen him, dancing the role of the evil spirit in *Swan Lake*. It had not taken her long to make the connection once the disguise of the mask was removed. It was his eyes — she continued to do her best to avoid his gaze — that brought back the memory, as he once again effortlessly launched himself into double and triple spins, soaring above everyone else. He seemed to dance to music deep within. When he landed in an arabesque right in front of her, Larkin turned to Dosha, whispering, "Simplicity is beauty!" Dosha, taken off guard, exclaimed "*Shukar!*" — the Gypsy word for beautiful.

That one word in Romani cracked Larkin's composure. For a split second Dosha glimpsed a much younger man. This was the *do-pash* Gypsy after all. Her spirits soared. For just a fraction of a moment they acknowledged each other as Gypsies.

"Continuez!" Larkin caught himself, quickly reassuming the persona of the world-famous choreographer of the Kirov Ballet. He beckoned Valentina, the prima ballerina, who with furious agitation spun after Vasili Kutunov, who remained posed in the same position near the girl. His partner placed a light, proprietary hand on his shoulder, and still the dancer's deep blue eyes lingered on Dosha, who was silhouetted against the fading light of the short winter's day.

Valentina, who had clearly assigned herself the role of Vasili's permanent shadow, leaned close to the dancer's ear, whispering, "Imagine — parking yourself cross-legged on a windowsill of the Kirov's most prestigious studio! She acts like a nomad blown in from some wasteland, pretending she doesn't belong?"

Valentina, wrapped in privilege and attention by the Soviet State, kept dropping invidious remarks like poison into her partner's ear. She went on, insisting that "anything that odd, suddenly pulled out of nowhere and planted smack into the elitist halls of the Kirov, is just that — a plant! No true Soviet citizen …" Still muttering, she yanked Vasili back toward the barre.

On some level, Vasili felt inclined to agree. There was a definite otherness about this intruder. Although the girl's reddish-blond hair and pale skin were certainly striking, she could still pass for ethnic Russian. However, her dark, almond-shaped eyes and classical bone structure hinted at more exotic origins. Nor, he noticed, was she used to being closed in. Her eyes kept escaping to the ceiling, where a gigantic round skylight offered a wide view of the sky. It gave the immaculate studio below — with its row of tall half-moon windows and columned walls reflected in mirrors — the feel of a cage.

Vasili was well aware of the danger of fraternizing with outsiders. After his parents and their friends were betrayed by spies and purged, his mother had died of exposure in Siberia. He could only hope his father was still alive somewhere and yet he couldn't help feeling drawn to the girl called Ana.

From that day on, when work was done, Vasili Kutunov no longer rushed down the stairs with his fellow dancers to join one of the groups heading homeward. Instead, he began to follow the girl, shadowing her when she jumped on the bus right in front of the Kirov Theatre. Sometimes, with the flowing motion of one used to walking a lot, she would walk past a stop or two before getting on.

Day after day, he watched, but he always stopped short of making contact.

# 23
# Bride Of The KGB

In their secluded world of motion reflected in mirrors and in windows facing the winter darkness outside, Vasili glimpsed the prima ballerina Valentina watching him as he watched the girl.

Vasili knew full well that in this place of privilege where the walls, the mirrors and the ceilings had eyes and ears, mixing lust with work could prove fatal. Right after he had won the gold medal in an international ballet competition in Moscow, Larkin had pulled him out of the Siberian Ballet Company as if picking a puppy out of a litter. Almost immediately, Vasili, at age twenty-one, found himself promoted to the position of prop — for that was then considered the primary function for male dancers — for the Kirov's prima ballerina, the carefully maintained but aging icon Valentina Kruglov

Vasili Kutunov, however, soared on wings of true talent. He was noble of face and godlike of body and although such sexual orientation was officially declared illegal, several of the other male dancers cast an unlawfully appreciative glance his way. When it became obvious that Vasili was attracted to women, some had spitefully urged him to take up with his dance partner — which, to his great regret, he had.

On this particular day, during the stampede to the dining hall, one went so far as to poke him in the ribs, laughing: "A little bird told me Valentina's expertise is such that she can give a dying comrade his last rise — true or false?"

Vasili threw a brief, backward glance to the top of the stairs where Valentina stood, waiting for the rush to subside.

Just as the Soviet ballet performance was packaged to represent an approved version of the Russian dream, so Valentina

Kruglov had likewise been improved upon. Her true age was guarded like a state secret. Perfected with every aid available in those still dark days of cosmetic improvements, she had been transformed to mirror the mysterious beauty of the Russian soul. Her dark eyes were deepened and further enhanced by shadows and long dark lashes. Her porcelain-white face, trained in the mobile mastery of silent screen technique, was firm and unwrinkled. Her limbs were rounded by years of unrelenting drills and the absence of true beauty was disguised by costumes that accentuated the fine arch of her back and the curve of her long neck. Her most acclaimed role was that of the black swan in *Swan Lake*, a role made famous by the finest dancer of all time, Anna Pavlova, whom she tried relentlessly to emulate.

Like many young men, Vasili was not exactly discriminating when it came to opportunities for sex, he found it helped him let off tension after his rigorous drills. So early on, he'd gone along with a quick and ardent tryst right on Valentina's makeup table. (She was the only dancer to enjoy the luxury of a private dressing room.) Several mutually convenient encounters ensued on matinee days, which in due time led to an invitation to Valentina's unusually spacious apartment in a yellow brick apartment building, the kind of housing reserved for the elite.

There, by flickering candlelight, Vasili — who had never thought to question Valentina's true age — for the first time peeled off all her clothes and saw for himself that the youthful curves he'd observed onstage and in their rushed backstage couplings were a mirage: seen up close and not in motion, the great ballerina's muscular flesh was riddled with lines, like the rind of dried fruit.

For a moment Vasili averted his eyes and looked around. He was young, but he had risen close enough to the Soviet elite to know about furniture called Finnish modern, the built-in cabinets and fancy countertops, all of which were unobtainable to the average citizen. Shelves and coffee tables were decorated with porcelain figurines, ivory sculptures, gilded china — the expensive memorabilia taken from murdered aristocrats. What he saw were all the outward trappings of one favored by the KGB.

Vasili's eyes instinctively started to scan for hidden cameras and bugs. For there was no doubt in his mind that in his youthful ignorance he'd been screwing a highly prized courtesan of the

KGB, and he realized — too late — that he had stepped into a trap.

Helpless, he watched Valentina raise her muscular arms theatrically toward him, beckoning him to where she lay, spread out in the nude like a queen on her oversized bed. What choice did he have but to obey? Once he was by her side, she sat up and ever so slowly proceeded to help him out of his shirt, his pants, and the rest, until they lay, as lovers do, stark naked side by side, with the mirrors positioned alongside her bed blocking any hope of mental escape.

At first Vasili just lay there, stock still by her side, flat on his back, as her teeth nibbled his throbbing neck — until, with bated breath (there was no escaping the tell-all mirrors surrounding her elaborate bed), he watched her starting to finger him like newly ripened fruit.

At the beginning of his unwise association with Valentina, sex had been the one aspect of Vasili's life that the Soviet State had left uncurtailed. At the very first sign of the mutual attraction, Larkin, bless his fatherly soul, had warned him over and over again not to mess with that one. Weren't there plenty of others around? And now, for the first time in his life, Vasili found he had to call upon fantasy to come to the aid of his sexual performance. So, with his eyes closed, his hand on her taut but withered body, he visualized her hair pulled loose from the ballerina bun and tumbling down thick and free. Mentally, he filled Valentina's face with youth, her eyes with sparkle and laughter. He willed her breasts to ripen like apples ready to pick off the tree.

When fantasy failed, he started to dream up other escapes instead — the way, as a boy, he had dreamed of digging tunnels out of the camps that had incarcerated him with his mother when they first arrived in Siberia, the land that sleeps. He tried more glamorous visions of riding fast-moving sleighs through sparkling snowfields. Only this time, Vasili's mind refused to come to the aid of his body. He watched with horror as the aging icon of Soviet ballet, using two fingers, their long nails lacquered a bright red, lifted his penis like a queen picking a dead worm out of a pile of rich manure.

That's when, as if struck by lightning, Valentina turned jealous of her young lover's thoughts. With blazing eyes, the star ballerina demanded, "Who is she?"

Valentina Kruglov had paid for the beauty and perfection of her technique with a youth sacrificed to work. Instead of letting herself fall in love, she had granted sexual favors to men in power in order to advance her career. Now that she had discovered, so late, the joy of love without an agenda — the thrill of a youthful body fused to hers — she was not about to give it up. She believed, too, that the liaison not only enhanced her personal wellbeing, but, more importantly, the quality of her dance. Her newly aroused passion was breathing life back into what, for her, had started to feel like the mechanized movements of a wind-up doll.

Now, whenever Vasili's eyes wandered to the girl, whose army shirt could not hide the fully developed body of a woman, he would feel Valentina's fingers dig into his shoulder.

"Relax," he whispered, annoyed, into her love-parched ear but relax Valentina would not. Vasili realized too late that he had blithely ignored what Larkin had been trying to impress upon him: the fact that when a ballerina — or any artist, for that matter — advances her career by sleeping with the KGB, she will be well rewarded. She will also forever be their tool to spy and to denounce. She will be their so-called "bride."

As the weeks went by, a web of undercurrents spun itself across the iron structure of the dancers' routine. Eyes lost their fixed focus and came alive, flashing like sparks. Emotions, long suppressed, lit up like stars in the sky.

Nobody was more stirred up than Comrade Karnowsky. Over the years, dancers may have defected — the worst possible crime against the Soviet state — but not on her watch. It was as a preventive measure, and not a tribute to her musicianship, that Comrade Karnowsky, a top human intelligence operative of the KGB, had been placed as pianist in the midst of this world-famous Soviet ballet troupe years before. She was less corruptible than one of their "brides," more efficient than the best of their electronic surveillance devices.

Within the structured lives of the dancers there was, and always had been, other means of expressing the yearnings of the soul. This nonverbal language, a matter of eyes and subtle gestures, now flared up among the company, as long-established relationships were shaken by the presence of the one person in their midst who stuck out by having escaped their own relentless training and indoctrination. The rider's languid presence, like the scent of a new female on the block, spoke to hidden longings, luring the dancers to emerge from behind the masks they'd adopted in hopes of ensuring their security.

Everyone was on the alert. Vasili's eyes kept darting about to see who was watching whom. Men were watching men watch women. The closeted "blue men," as Soviets disparagingly referred to homosexuals, were tenser and more confused than ever. Who was true and who was blue? The question was important, for beyond the protective walls of the Kirov, the wrong sexual orientation could earn a one-way ticket to Siberia.

Instead of hands or words, eyes linked. Vasili's eyes kept wandering back to this new girl, the nondancer, who sat in the window day after day, watching without making an effort to befriend anyone or to belong. Fantasy and reality merged, until he felt he knew this Ana, and that she knew him — that they had known each other all their lives. His eyes rested with wonder on the body of this rider, who sometimes stretched with feline grace, until the dancer experienced a sudden hormonal upsurge and quickly had to turn away, only to stare into the hurt eyes of ... "Lord!" he cried.

By then the Prima's timing was all but shot. She'd begun to miss her cues, and Vasili the catch. Once she almost crashed to the ground; Vasili barely managed to catch her and managed to lift her up. Now she was in tears.

"He's missing her jumps on purpose," one dancer whispered to another.

All of her working life, Valentina had subscribed to a system that valued technique above all: same steps, same time, same place. The younger ballerinas could set their watches by the precision of her pirouettes, her arabesques. Step by step, little by little, over time, Valentina had honed every movement until there remained no wasted energy, not a single loose end. She had achieved a stunning perfection in terms of standardized art but her accomplishment was soulless and now that her precision was thrown off, the other company members stood there, lost.

"Enough!" yelled Larkin in desperation. "Enough of this! Valentina, Vasili, everybody — we will start over!"

Valentina Kruglov was not inclined to cede her high and protected perch without a fight. Searching for a statement that would be politically wise, she uttered at last in a firm tone, "I find the presence of a nondancer at our daily practice highly unsettling. She impedes my concentration, and clearly others' as well. It's hardly in the best interest of the. . ."

She stopped her party-line diatribe in midsentence. Drawing himself up in front of the entire company, Comrade Larkin stood suddenly transformed into a political official, gray-faced and hollow-eyed. In icy silence he stared down the famous star. This was a Larkin the dancers had never encountered before. It suddenly occurred to them that, given the many different political tunes that had been playing since the last Bolshevik Revolution, he too might have danced multiple roles on the Soviet political stage. It raised the unthinkable specter of a purge within the sanctuary of their sequestered world.

"Overtime," Larkin spoke loud and succinctly. "We stay until we get it right! Valentina, if you can concentrate before an audience, you can focus in the presence of one young girl." There was nothing like a whipping, corporal or mental, to put the average, survival-bound Russian back on track. Everyone snapped to.

That same day, Dosha was experiencing increased anxieties of her own. The night before, Ado, the older and more experienced of the two Roma grooms, had not shown up for the obligatory night check of the horses. Junker-Institut officials had launched an immediate search, and Ado was found not only drunk, but smoking cigarettes in the section of the Hermitage Palace where the old imperial carriages were stored, right next to the stables. He could have set the whole ancient structure on fire. The guards dragged him out of the museum and into a wash-stall, where they sobered him up by hosing him down with ice-cold water like a horse as the officials interrogated him. He tearfully confessed, "It's the anniversary of the death of my wife and newborn son."

*That's what Gypsies do*, Dosha thought but could not say, when fellow riders filled her in. *They remember the first anniversary of their dead.*

To Ado's *Gadje* overlords, this was of course an inadequate excuse. They made him disappear that very night.

Now there was only one Gypsy left to look after the stallion. Hissen, the younger one, was a city Gypsy, who — like Jano — had lost his feel for a horse.

Dosha expressed her concerns to Osap Tossuk as soon as she arrived at the arena at midday. She begged him for more time with her horse, and complained that her presence at the ballet studio three afternoons a week had become pointless. Osap was obdurate. Galina had set that rule, he noted, and whatever Ana's preference might be, it was not up to her to break the rule.

By then Dosha had grown accustomed to those programmed

afternoons, much as she resented the time away from her horse. At 5:00 o'clock sharp, as the session ended, Larkin would join her at the windowsill and, shaking hands, exchange a few words. It was generally assumed that these comments were related to her work with horses but ever since their mutual recognition as fellow Gypsies, Larkin would manage — during these short, curt lea-vetakings, inaudible to the rest of the company — to impart some information about Patrina and her people, who were trapped in the city not far away. Her hope renewed, Dosha would pick up her coat, give a shy nod to the dancers, and, with a wave to Comrade Karnovsky, rush back to tend her horses.

Except on that day, when Valentina had her outburst, Dosha, along with everybody else, was kept from leaving. The hands of her watch approached 5:00 o'clock, then 5:15, then 5:30 — the time she was expected back at the barn.

As the minutes passed, Dosha became more and more fidgety. Horses, especially when held in captivity, have an inborn sense of time. Ever since the stallion had been captured, he had grown accustomed to the same routine as other horses — except that he was bonded to Dosha more deeply than any of the other horses to their riders. If for any reason she was only minutes late, he would impatiently strike his hooves against the walls of his stall and whinny for her. Also, she worried that it would take her longer than usual to get back to the stable. It had been snowing all day, and from her window, she could see deep drifts. The wind had come up: it howled against the windowpanes.

She was sure that Larkin, who had lived with the Lovara and their horses, understood her anxiety but whenever she made a move to ask for permission to leave, she found herself stopped by the forbidding glare and single raised finger of the pianist, Comrade Karnowsky, who for some reason seemed on high alert. Clearly, there was danger in the air, for Larkin had retreated back to being the professional choreographer, whom Dosha had first met, the man who had left his Gypsy ways behind. Her exit was barred.

# 24

# Metro Station

At 7:30 that evening, when they were finally allowed to leave, Dosha pushed her way through the exiting dancers in a frantic rush to get back to her horses. She was the first to open the heavy door to the outside, only to find that a snowstorm had buried the city alive. Howling winds had swept all signs of life from the streets. Not a soul stood by the bus stop, and for good reason: no attempt had been made to clear the trolley tracks.

Fearful that the highly sensitive stallion would get himself into trouble because of her unusually long absence, Dosha decided that on a day like this, her best chance was to travel underground, however much she dreaded that confining mode of transportation: this would be her first venture into Leningrad's new subway system, which had only been in operation for slightly over a year.

She plunked on her army-issue fur cap, closed the earflaps around her face for further protection against the biting cold, and made her way through the eerily deserted streets until she reached the brightly-lit blue letter M indicating the entrance to a subway station. Here the snow had been trampled down, but individual footprints had been effaced by snow drifting across and right on down the stairs of the metro-station.

Dosha made her way downstairs, where, in contrast to the raging storm outside, an eerie stillness reigned. Compared to the dilapidated grandeur that characterized the city above, the newly inaugurated Metro station looked like a hall of splendor. Along the length of the platform lofty columns of green marble decorated with heavy copper emblems supported massive arches. Light poured from ornately framed panels that resembled windows letting in daylight. Softly lit globes were placed at either end of the platform to indicate entrances and exits.

Today, however, even in this underground showpiece built to serve mass transportation needs, she saw no more than ten or twelve people moving about in the subway, each wrapped from head to toe in heavy winter gear. Most were walking toward the exit at the far end. Only one man with a small child was standing and waiting by the subway tracks.

Dosha walked up to a cashier's desk that showed both a map of stops along the route and the price of a ticket. At that very moment a train came sliding with a soft rolling noise into the station and came to a standstill, almost like an owl landing with quiet wings. She hesitated for a moment and considered going back up to the street.

That's when she saw him, the dancer Vasili. He must have followed her all the way through the storm, and now he stood there, poised between light and shade at the bottom of the stairs watching her. The color of his eyes kept changing from a blue of brilliance to the dark blue of night, like that first time she had seen him on stage.

*Only this is no fairytale,* Dosha thought with growing disquiet. This was the unyielding Soviet reality she had come to know. Where two members from different cultural groups chosen and screened to go abroad, who suddenly became romantically involved would more likely than not find themselves purged off the coveted list for performances abroad; a trip that for Dosha and her horse represented their only chance of survival through escape and she knew there were agents, men and women dotting every open spot of daily life on the lookout for just such potential deserters and defectors.

Dosha cursed the impulsiveness of the dancer Vasili, if indeed he was trying to initiate what would be an unwise association between them. Galina had warned her against just such a pitfall. Dosha quickly extracted the required kopeks from her coat pocket, bought a ticket, and barely made it into the train before its doors closed.

The train pulled out with the same smooth whoosh, but once out of the station it thundered like a meteor through the city's dark underbelly. Staring into the gaping blackness outside the train window, Dosha could not shake the image of the dancer's eyes. They followed her with the unrelenting, stark brilliance of stars in a midnight sky.

Mostly, though, her mind reached out for the stallion. She could barely remember a time when she had not known him. She and her horse had grown up together. She knew he would never willingly hurt her. She knew that she was safest on his back, just as she knew by instinct every move he made before he made it. When something flew out of the bushes or moved in the forest, her mind shied before he did. Whenever she rode or worked him, she could feel his every thought throughout her body. Whether she was on or off his back, his spirit stayed with her at all times. Whenever she looked into his dark and soulful eyes, she saw reflections of herself and right then, on the train, she felt with every fiber of her being that the stallion was in acute danger.

Growing more desperate, she willed the train to move faster. Getting out at the Nevsky Prospekt, the stop closest to the Hermitage, she raced up the steps, then along the wide but unlit avenue, through dark side streets, until at last — tearing past the guards into the Junker-Institut — she reached the stables. The aisle, usually cast in shadows, was flooded with light — light pouring from the high, vaulted ceiling, from along the walls, and from the flashlights being waved around in every direction.

The stallion, wild-eyed and with nostrils flaring, was cornered at the far end of the aisle. Blood trickled down his shoulder and onto the cobblestones. He reared, reaching high up toward the vaulted ceiling, his powerful front legs ready to strike those he perceived to be his attackers. He was like a stallion in the wild fighting for his life.

For the first time ever, Dosha felt the full-blown fury of a Lovari woman who perceives her own to be under attack. All fear, all caution left her.

"Back off!" she shouted. "All of you — back off!"

Osap and several grooms turned toward her. Among them was the Gypsy groom, Hissen, who helplessly raised his shoulders.

The stallion, recognizing Dosha's voice, came to all fours and pawed the cobblestone aisle. He was wearing a saddle with stirrups hanging down, and a bridle with reins snapped in two, that dangled along both sides of his shoulders.

"I could not prevent — " Hissen, the Roma groom, looked at her with despairing eyes.

"Comrade Popov will hear of this." Dosha's voice was icy.

They stepped aside at once, Osap and the grooms. Behind her, Dosha heard Djemo's mare whinny, her hoof striking against the wall. Most of the other horses, those that had never known freedom, were nervously wheeling and circling in their stalls.

Dosha advanced slowly, stretching out one hand toward the

overwrought stallion's face as she whispered softly in Russian. His eyes, still rolling, grew calmer as she approached. His breathing slowed. She touched his neck. She started to stroke it with both her hands, inspecting the wound. He had torn off a chunk of fur. The running blood was keeping, what looked like a superficial wound, clean. Dosha closed her eyes and silently thanked Sara la Kali, patron saint of the Gypsies that she had arrived in time. Still talking softly, she gently pushed the stallion's head under her armpit to let him smell her scent — the smell of her body that had bonded him to her when he was still a foal.

After some minutes she took off his saddle and slid it to the floor. The stallion was lathered in sweat. She removed the bridle with its torn reins from his bleeding mouth, and lovingly slipped on his halter. Then she walked him up and down the aisle to cool him down, all the while using towels handed her by Osap to rub him dry.

An hour later Dosha sat beside the stallion's head in his stall. Osap and the team veterinarian had stopped the bleeding and dressed the wound, but left it exposed to the air to heal.

"You have to understand," Osap told her in a conciliatory tone of voice, "at this point, after all the training, we should be able to put on another rider. He was experienced, too ..."

Instead of replying, Dosha looked at the Tartar with killer eyes.

"He had only one foot in a stirrup, when *bam!*" Osap whispered. "The stallion rode him straight into a wall."

"What did you expect?" Dosha hissed. "Couldn't you at least have waited for me?"

"The rider, a German, is hospitalized with one crushed rib and a broken ankle."

"He's lucky he isn't dead."

"They shoot horses for such aggression!" Osap protested. "The only thing that saved him this time is his talent," he muttered. "That and Galina."

"And she will hear of this! Look at his bleeding mouth! Who here is the victim?"

*And may* o del *bless Galina*, Dosha thought, standing up. She leaned her head against the horse's shoulder and placed her hand slightly above the wound. She could feel the heat from his wound rising to her hand. She tried to summon the healing power that, according to Patrina, had been passed on to her through her mother's line. Eventually, though, in a state of total exhaustion, she sank back into a corner, right next to the stallion's head. There she listened as the stallion rhythmically munched at his hay — a sound as soothing to her as that of the ocean licking a rocky shore. Tiny pieces of chaff gently rained down on her face. At times the stallion nuzzled her face and person. She could feel his breath on her face, as silently, amid the pungent aroma of straw, manure and urine of a horse held in captivity, tears started to run down her face. They kept on falling, silent and unbidden, as if they belonged to somebody else. She was crying herself to sleep.

At once, as if they had lain in wait, Vasili's eyes returned to her from the dark hollow of sleep, just the way they had stared at her with that brilliant intensity from the bottom of the stairs that had led her underground. Their brilliant blue contained none of the dark pain Dosha was used to seeing in her people, and yet something about them seemed so intimately, unavoidably familiar.

That night, sleeping in her horse's stall, Dosha followed those eyes into a dream. Atop a ridge that divided a desert into light and shade, she sat bareback on her gleaming white stallion. She was naked but felt neither cold nor shame. When the stallion turned his head as if he had picked up a sound, she followed the direction of his eyes and saw a long line of Gypsy mourners snaking their way through a valley in the shade. At the front of the procession, two men carried a white shroud stretched between two poles held up high. No wind stirred. Nothing disturbed the tightly stretched shroud. On it she recognized the imprint of Jano's bloodied face. It was the image of a tortured Gypsy Christ.

A dull pain spread through Dosha's mind and body. The loss hit her with such unbearable power that it melded her, as if frozen, to the back of her horse. She wanted to open her mouth and cry out for help, but her voice felt trapped within. Time stood still — until the ground split open in the very depth of the valley. A naked man rose to the surface. His powerful wings overshadowed and dwarfed the procession of Gypsy mourners, who halted in place.

This was no demon, but a man of beauty. His eyes ignited the sky with blue, but turned dark as he raised his wings to join them over his head. The ground must have swallowed up the Gypsy caravan. It was nowhere to be seen.

Dosha wanted to cry out Jano's name, vent her inner pain, but she was unable to get out a sound. Nor could she move amid the oppressive stillness, until the winged man spread, then flapped his wings. The motion sent a breeze her way. It caressed her like a gentle wind. The winged man rose higher into the air, where he hovered with the widespread wings of a hunting hawk right above her and her stallion. Yet there still was no sound. Then all motion stopped as well. The scene froze like a still-life caught on canvas. The only thing pulsating with life was his *ka,* his penis. Obscenely huge, it rose like a lance from the dark mass of his pubic hair. Suddenly all sprang to life. With the piercing noise of a dropping bomb, he dove down for the kill, sweeping her off the white horse and lifting her high into the sky, where, enveloping her with his powerful wings — again all sound receded — he ever so softly penetrated her.

Like smoke from fire, Dosha's mind lifted away from her body. Observing herself from up above, she watched herself arch her back and close her eyes as she gave her body to the purifying flames of the birdman's passion. Together they exploded into a cloud of brilliance that came raining down like shattering glass.

Once again, she sat on her white horse. Only by then the sand to both sides of the ridge high above the valley had turned into dust of gold. The glittering dust covered both her and the horse. The birdman was also straddling the horse, now clinging to her back. She sensed his despair.

Just then the ground beneath them started to shift and give way. They were teetering on a steep cliff. Almost immediately, the white cliff crumbled like an avalanche, tumbling into the plain below. The collapsing cliffside was pulling them along and under. She felt the winged demon-king lose his balance. His grip on her faltered, and she felt him slide off the horse. She turned just in time to see him raise his feathered arms above his head before he sank like a spear into the now raging river of golden sand. She herself was being sucked into the rushing sand slides. She was losing all sense of what was up and what was down, when the white horse underneath her began to round its back. Renewed power surged through the animal from head to tail. It collected and rose to her hands. In full collection like a grand prix dressage horse, it took two steps back, onto the last remaining piece of solid ground, to safety.

Dosha woke bathed in sweat. Around her all was dark and quiet, but for the soft, rhythmic chewing and occasional snorting of the horse by her side but she could not dispel a rising sense of disquiet and foreboding. In her dream she had pulled the card of death: the white horse carrying death across the valley of shades.

# 25
# The Gypsy Poste

Lately, whenever Alexander Larkin, ballet master and chore-ographer of the world-famous Kirov Ballet, left his fifth-floor studio at the end of the day, his mind invariably shifted to a dance of a different kind. By then the initial outbreak of jubilation brought on by Comrade Khruchchev's "Cultural Thaw" was fast turning into a day of judgment in the Red Empire.

"If only," he said to his wife, Maria Andreyevna, "I could choreograph present-day reality, a *danse macabre.*" They were walking along the deserted embankment of the Kryukov Canal, not far from where they lived.

Maria Andreyevna looked around. The embankment was deserted, but for a young couple walking ahead of them at a brisk pace.

"I can visualize the scene." Larkin turned to his wife. "From one side of the stage" — he pointed to that imagined corner — "enter a straggling line of emaciated survivors of Stalin's reign of terror — the prisoners, the *zeks.* They gather loosely in the shape of a half-moon. One by one, they start dancing stories of torture. Together they demonstrate mass murder. Next, to join the dancing *corps* of former *zeks,* enter the sons and daughters of those who never made it back — the dead. The music changes from dark and gloomy to shrill and piercing. The dancing *zeks* and the children of the dead, in unison, now raise accusatory fingers as, from the other side of the stage, enter those who denounced them, former friends and neighbors" — the ones, Larkin knew, who had sold out the others to save their own skin, or merely to acquire some minor privileges.

"The music stops, abruptly — " Here Larkin, noticing the stark worry in his wife's face, went silent. He retreated into his thoughts, where, with a brass ensemble striking up a somber tune, he visualized victims and persecutors linking hands on this new political stage, before, in hollow silence, they united in a ghostly dance of remembrance.

"The fantasy alone could get us locked away for life," Maria Andreyevna whispered. "Especially since the man who calls himself our 'liberator' is hauling nomadic Roma off their treks and shoving them into unheated cattle wagons. Just like those who went before them, they'll be dumped in Siberia with no food or drink or shelter — it's cheapest to let winter finish them off. Hopefully they'll find shelter somewhere, some friendly soul to take them in. For I have no idea what us city Gypsies can possibly do, other than wait for the right moment to come to their aid!"

"What about Patrina?" Larkin's voice was soft, in contrast to his wife's angry tone.

"Oh," she said, taking a deep breath, "they made an exception for Patrina and her immediate *kumpania,* at least for the time being. They've been rounded up but not shipped off. They're in a tenement on the dark side of town, as I've told you before."

"I wonder why," Larkin mused.

"I have no doubt it's because of Khantchi," answered his wife. "He has seen too much, knows too much, and they know he's apt to pass his knowledge on to the West. Also, some city Gypsy may have leaked to the Bolsheviks the fact that Gypsies never leave their own behind to die alone. So they figure that, sooner or later, the Gypsy king will come to the aid of his sister and those closest to her. The KGB is merely using Patrina as bait."

"The problem is," said Larkin, taking his wife's arm, "nobody other than the Roma themselves seems to care. Nobody even knows what's being done to the Gypsies, because they still have no political voice at all."

"At least," Maria Andreyevna replied, after they had walked on for a while, "unlike most Russians, the Roma know what's going on." For years she had trained young city Gypsies as singers and dancers. These performers now formed a Gypsy network of spies, dedicated to observing the elite in fancy Soviet restaurants and at party functions. They were well placed to pick up valuable information spilled in the course of heavy drinking. From them, Maria Andreyevna had learned what the Soviet State had planned for the Roma who were still freely moving through the countryside.

"I am the one who should visit her." Larkin said, more to

himself than to his wife. He'd been in Poland fighting alongside Russians when he first came across Patrina and her band of Gypsy partisans. After only a few days together, she smiled at him approvingly and said, "I bet you've got some Gypsy blood." At the end of the war, after he had rescued her from a concentration camp in the middle of night, she adopted him as her son. Her approval had allowed him not only to be accepted into their clan, but also to take Maria Andreyevna for his wife.

In fact Larkin's father had been Roma. His mother, a Russian ballerina, had raised her son alone in Leningrad. Larkin's encounters with his Gypsy father had been random, occurring only when the small circus that his father belonged to traveled through the villages surrounding what was then still St. Petersburg. Larkin had been drawn to his father and his people, and they had accepted him as one of their own — even more so after Patrina adopted him as her son, and he chose a *romni* for his wife.

"For you to show up there — you, of all people — would not only endanger them, but us as well," Maria warned her *rom* yet again. "Siding with the nomadic Gypsies at this point would give the Bolsheviks an excuse to turn their fury upon us as well, and get us all killed. Then who would the nomads have to turn to as an ally?"

Pausing on a narrow pedestrian bridge, they stared down at the sluggish water of the canal, which appeared dark brown in the falling darkness. "Besides," Maria added, "as I told you weeks ago, the one Patrina is waiting for is Dosha, Khantchi's granddaughter. The wild Gypsies believe that she is their new *vadni ratsa*, the one destined to appear when Roma find themselves trapped in inescapable circumstances, the one who they believe will lead them back to freedom. You know how they still believe in their old legends." She moved close and squeezed his arm. "And, after all, who really knows?"

Larkin had come to respect the Gypsies' refusal to be fooled by *Gadje* manipulations and propaganda. He had also witnessed, while fighting with them side by side during the war years, how their belief in miracles and the power of their myths had helped them survive. He had stopped wondering long ago whether such prophecies were self-fulfilling or not.

"And to think," Larkin marveled, "that Dosha and this Ana Dalova are one and the same!" He looked into his wife's darkly troubled eyes.

"There is no doubt," she said. "Besides, I told you long ago that I saw her with Comrade Popov at the Kirov. I caught this girl looking up at me with pleading eyes, and I figured out that it was because I was the only Gypsy in that hall.

"And then you wouldn't believe me when I told you that Comrade Popov's protégée could very well be the captured Lovari princess with her missing horse. You wouldn't listen, because of her fair skin and her red-blond hair. Yet, as I keep telling you, it's not that rare among the Lovara."

Larkin came to his own defense. "I just never thought a Lovari woman would strive to achieve such high levels of riding"

"Her father just happened to have been a circus rider before the war, a famous one."

Whatever the reason, Larkin had failed to make the connection between the young girl introduced to him by Galina Popov and Dosha of the Khantchisti, who had been missing for months. He remained in the dark until that day when he caught her looking at him with her guard down, and she uttered that one word in Romani, *shukar.*

After telling his wife about his discovery, Larkin had followed her instructions and, every day at the end of rehearsal during his brief parting conversations with the girl, dropped coded words of warning — words relating to nature, such as bark, leaves, cocks' feathers, and flowers — the items that formed the secret Gypsy code. "She's bound to go crisscrossing the city," Maria Andreyevna assured him. "Gypsies patrol their territory."

Whenever Larkin now turned to the girl to explain his dance instructions, he inserted barely audible Romani words. Using key words like *patrins,* the Gypsy roadside signs, he informed her of Patrina's location by mentioning landmarks along the way. He also mentioned birch trees, to signal the extreme danger of moving about alone. During one of their rare moments alone at the top of the stairs while everyone was preparing to leave at the end of the day, he warned Dosha that she must wait for a meeting, a plan was in place, and that the meeting would have to be very short, since Patrina was being used as bait to catch Dosha's grandfather Khantchi, the fugitive leader of the Lovara.

Meanwhile Nikita Khrushchev's state visit to Finland was drawing closer. Even more imminent were the projected departure dates for the various cultural groups intended to pave the way for a favorable reception not only by Finland and by representatives of Western embassies, but more importantly by members of the world press. Khrushchev was planning to use the opportunity of the state visit to present his new doctrine of "Peaceful Coexistence."

By then the turmoil that had followed his de-Stalinization program in the motherland was spreading abroad like the Russian flu. Anti-communist sentiments were gathering strength in the satellite states. Workers rose up against the communist regime in Poland. A revolution exploded in Hungary. Rumors flew that the Thaw was heading back to a deep freeze, along with Stalin's denouncer, Nikita Sergeyevich Khrushchev and in the land of sudden reversals, those who had profited from previous political advantage suddenly found themselves at risk. Many of the writers, artists, and filmmakers newly raised to international fame through Khrushchev's "liberalization" were already being denounced as enemies of communist ideology.

Larkin had suspected all along that his prima ballerina, Valentina Kruglov, was a KGB plant installed by Moscow's Bolshoi Ballet — the premier ballet company under the Soviets — in order to spy and to denounce. Larkin also presumed that, since Valentina had proved herself to be an expert navigator and survivor of many purges and upheavals, she would now be among the first to run for cover, especially since she had risen to her position through political influence rather than mere talent.

Yet Valentina's attention remained doggedly on the silent presence of the girl and her impact not only on Larkin, but more importantly on Vasili, Valentina's young lover. The irate ballerina seemed frustrated most of all by the fact that this newcomer of seemingly minor importance was shielded by the powerful Galina Popov, who was higher in rank than any of Valentina's own protectors in the KGB. In fact, whenever Valentina had tried to denounce the girl, this mysterious Ana Dalova, to one of her patron lovers, her suggestive words invariably hit a wall. "At least," she whispered into the ear of one of those fat comrades, this one a high ranking member of the Politburo, "allow me to return to Moscow, to the Bolshoi, if only for a while."

By then her initial mild annoyance had taken on the texture of hatred. As a countermeasure, she kept making overtures to Vasili, blowing little kisses in his direction. Larkin wondered at what point her lust for the young dancer had turned into obsession.

It was only when two solo dancers from within their midst vanished one day without a trace that Valentina seemed to come to her senses. Their disappearance was too reminiscent of Stalin's purges in the not-so-distant past. Alarmed, the prima ballerina at once retreated to the safety of her perfectionist drills. Her self-control returned with a vengeance. Larkin watched the precision of her movements grow sharp and brittle. Meanwhile, the pressure from Valentina's swallowed pride and venom kept mounting, and she at last gave in to the fundamental human need to trust someone, anyone. At which point this scheming ballerina, known best among her fellow dancers for her performance as the black swan in Swan Lake, hissed into the safest receptacle she could think of, Larkin's ear, simply because they both had crossed a perilous past and had survived:

"It's that goddamn Thaw," she spat.

*As if freedom were nothing but drifting packice,* a thought Larkin wisely kept to himself.

"So she's here on behalf of the Ministry of Culture, no less," Valentina continued sotto voce. "She's been here several times a week for months. Yet she does not talk to anybody other than you. She doesn't join in; she always walks off alone. What is she hiding? And from whom?" Concluding viciously, "Yet, despite all that, she's been approved to travel abroad! One has to wonder: Why has the KBG not subjected her to closer scrutiny, like everybody else?"

Larkin shuddered, wondering how many unsuspecting rivals this well-kept "bride of the KGB" had denounced on her climb up the Soviet Socialist ladder and he couldn't help imagining the infinite harm she could do Dosha if she set her mind to it.

At least life in the studio was once again chugging along like a train on a set of straight rails. Until one day the invisible powers behind the scenes suddenly decided to switch rails. Prima ballerina Valentina Kruglov was plucked from the Kirov, the Leningrad company that had made her name. To the great ooohs and aaahs of the whole corps she was called to dance the lead role in *Giselle*, back at the Number One, as per declaration of the Red elite, ballet theater of the Great Soviet Socialist Union: The Moscow Bolshoi. She would be dancing for the Bolshoi for the next month, but would return in time for the Kirov's final rehearsals of Swan Lake in preparation for the tour to Finland.

Larkin's first reaction was not without envy. After all, the opportunity to work with the Bolshoi was the greatest honor a Soviet dancer could achieve. The Red reign had made sure to reduce the Kirov, aristocratic cradle of Russian ballet, to a mere stepping-stone to the Bolshoi of Moscow, headquarters of the new elite. But his second, predominant, reaction was relief. With Valentina gone, the company need no longer rehearse and perform incessantly that showcase performance for the trip abroad: *Swan Lake*. Larkin at once put all the standard rehearsals and performances on hold till the return of his black swan/white swan shortly before their departure, four weeks away.

In the interim no more swans would flap their arms like wings, pining or dying! No more catering to the whims and anxieties of an aging icon, sent here primarily to keep an eye on him. A relieved Larkin closed his eyes and turned inward. Time to realize some of his own visions of what dance should be.

For *Swan Lake,* Larkin substituted a production of *Le Corsaire*, based on the poem by Lord Byron. *Le Corsaire* would be danced in Leningrad, he determined, *Swan Lake* would go abroad and no one in Russia danced the title role better than his solo dancer, Vasili Kutunov — although it was the role of Rhab, the slave, that had won him a gold medal at the international dance competition in Moscow, where Larkin had first spotted his future star.

Without the pressure from Valentina's jealousy, Larkin watched the talent of Vasili unfold into a liberated, dynamic *Corsaire*. The young dancer seemed to draw on music from within, attaining such fluid beauty and perfection that it energized the entire troupe. Even the KGB's remaining watchdog, Comrade Karnowsky, at the piano, melted under the energizing contributions of ten different composers and the brilliance of Vasili's rendition. She played the piano with renewed energy.

Larkin had assigned Vasili a new partner for the role of the heroine, Medora. She was a young upcoming ballerina, a fiery Georgian by temperament, yet delicate as a porcelain figurine. Still testing the movements of her nascent art, she elegantly yielded to Vasili's lead. Her eyes quivered, her translucent skin flushed as she came breath to breath with Vasili in their *pas de deux*. Her face lifted to his like a flower to a bee. But by then Vasili had grasped the fact that flowers can turn into Venus flytraps.

It was obvious to Larkin that, with the help of his newly

found prudence, Vasili kept the enticing young ballerina at the prescribed arm's length. Only when Dosha walked into the studio did Larkin notice Vasili swerve from his resolve not to mix work with romance.

*Maybe,* Larkin deduced, *that young fool is rationalizing that since she comes merely to observe, she is a* spectator *and therefore not part of his work.* At any rate, whenever Vasili paused, standing about shaking his limbs or waiting for his turn, his eyes were on her. To the best of Larkin's knowledge, the two had never spoken, never interacted with each other in any way. Yet their mutual attraction was palpable.

*Of course,* Larkin further reasoned, *there's no way Vasili would ever guess that this beautiful blond girl is a Gypsy.* Although there had been instances of Gypsy women marrying aristocrats under the czars, that was then. Now, especially in these times of Gypsy persecution, for a Lovari woman merely to interact with a *Gadje* other than for trade or fortune-telling, let alone consider loving a man outside her tribe, except under very special circumstances and agreement within the tribe, would lead her to face the Romani *kris,* the Gypsy court of law. It would condemn her to a life away from her people — the worst punishment of all. For a young woman like Dosha, groomed from birth to be a leader of the tribe, the notion was unthinkable.

*It is a love,* Larkin decided, *that must never be.*

# 26
# The Dostoyevsky District

The winter of Dosha's captivity in Leningrad had been the coldest on record. As brutal, she was told, as the winter of the Great Siege of '41, when an ungloved hand could freeze within seconds. Now, however, the deep arctic freeze had broken. Warmer air had started to sweep in from the Baltic, reducing the biting cold to a penetrating chill. Piles of sooty snow melted into dark slush that spread across the sidewalks and flooded gutters and potholes in the streets. A leaden mist rose from the pavements, billowing toward what was still a pale winter sun but higher and staying in the sky longer.

It was late April and Dosha had just walked out of what, Osap Tossuk had informed her, was to be her last session at the Kirov. Although the Tartar told her that Larkin had been informed, there were no good-byes that afternoon. No announcement had been made to the company that in two days she, and the entire equestrian team, would leave Leningrad for Finland, four weeks ahead of the other cultural groups. The required quarantine period for the horses necessitated an early departure.

Ever since her capture the year before, Dosha had lived for this moment, vacillating between despondency and the intense hope a Gypsy is capable of. Yet as she walked toward Theatre Square, just as the number 22 trolley came to a screeching halt, she felt compelled to turn back one last time to gaze upon the imposing façade of the massive Kirov Theatre and there she saw Vasili Kutunov, lingering amid a group of fellow dancers.

While the others mingled, chatting, Vasili seemed intent upon looking beyond his immediate surroundings. Head raised, he was scanning the steady flow of pedestrians, all the way from Ulitsa Dekabristov on his right to Theatre Square on his left, where he spotted her. Caught off guard, their eyes linked and held on to each other for the first time. Something that had grown precious to them both was about to be cut in two.

A car passed, then another, followed by an official stretch limousine that flung icy slush in all directions. The dancers jumped aside, leaving Vasili alone, standing by the curb. Dosha saw him hesitate, as if coming to his senses. After all, it was not that long ago that he had been liberated from his unwise romantic entanglement with the prima ballerina. Dosha had witnessed firsthand how his newfound freedom contributed to the breathtaking beauty of his dance. Yet now, as if she had called his name aloud, Vasili — without so much as a second thought and in full view of his fellow dancers — started walking toward her, winding his way through pedestrians and passing cars.

*What is he doing?* Dosha panicked at his impulsiveness. To prevent such an ill-omened encounter, she cut into the long queue of off-duty workers who were shoving and struggling to get on the trolley before the doors closed. The trolley departed before she could push her way on. Dosha broke from the remaining queue and quickly walked off, without a backward glance.

*He is risking everything! The trip abroad!* Her thoughts were racing. *And what about me? I won't let him jeopardize my only way out of this trap!* This was the night, after months of careful and clandestine planning, that she was to have her only meeting with her adoptive grandmother Patrina, tribal mother of the Lovara, in the company of other high-ranking members of her tribe.

She thought of all the effort and daring over the span of many weeks that the half-Gypsy Larkin had put into organizing the evening. He had risked not only his own safety and livelihood, but that of Maria Andreyevna as well.

"The fact that these Gypsies live in town doesn't mean that they don't look back to the lives they left behind," he had whispered to her. They had walked all the way down the stairs from the studio for the first time alone, earlier that evening. "They stay in touch. Especially since, without this recharge from time to time of true *romanija*, the Gypsy songs and dances they perform for the *Gadje* sound as standardized as the rest of Soviet art."

Larkin had also told her how many highly valued Gypsy artists were caught by surprise upon learning, amid the general jubilation over increased freedom for Russia's people, that their own nomadic kin had been targeted as enemies of the State. "Although they're not officially targeted themselves," Larkin had added, "many of these popular Gypsy artists worry that they are being followed. Not in their own parts of town, of course, where only Roma live, and where an outsider sticks out like a sore thumb. It's when they go beyond their Roma neighborhood out into the main streets and marketplaces, or when they take subways and trains."

The plan that evening was for Dosha to walk to where Larkin and Maria Andreyevna lived, in an apartment building at the edge of the Dostoyevsky district. "That's where it's safest," Larkin had impressed upon her, "A group of Patrina's men will pick you up before nightfall and take you to her."

Most importantly, in order not to raise suspicion by a longer than usual absence from the stables, Larkin had requested written permission for the rider, Ana Dalova, to spend the evening with him and his family to celebrate the successful end of her sessions at the Kirov. The Tartar Osap Tossuk, who was in charge of the girl's schedule during Comrade Popov's prolonged absence, had given his permission.

*Nothing must sidetrack me,* Dosha decided as she hurried on her way. *There is too much at stake. I have to stick precisely to the plan worked out by Larkin.*

Not only did the meeting with Patrina represent a long-awaited reunion, however brief, with Dosha's people, it was a vital part of the plan to organize her escape with her stallion, once they were on Finnish soil. Only with the help of Patrina and her grandfather, Khantchi, who hopefully would arrange for Dosha to join a Lovara *kumpania* awaiting her in Finland, could she hope to break free and travel further west. For although Finland was not under Soviet rule, her grandfather had warned her that it lived in the Soviet shadow.

"The Finns are walking a fine line," he had told her during their outing to visit the Sami. "They have no choice." He knew for a fact that Finland had complied with the demands of its powerful neighbor and had sent Soviet defectors back to Russia.

Dosha had been walking fast, hoping to shake off the dancer. Now she turned her head only to see Vasili still brazenly following her. She further accelerated her steps and moved farther and farther into streets smelling of mist and moisture. Red flags flapped and snapped away in rising winds that were gathering momentum for what felt like an approaching storm. The chilly mist swirled and dissipated as it rose toward banners of red hammers and sickles fluttering at the tops of tall townhouses and the towers of former churches.

It was the kind of early spring storm that on the steppes would draw renewed life from the frozen plains — a sign for nomads to move their fires once again to the outdoors and prepare for life back on the road.

Glancing back at the next corner, Dosha noticed that not only was Vasili still following her, he had almost caught up with her. There was no mistaking him. The exuberance of his walk made him stick out like a dancing light among the somber, slow-moving crowd. She observed with relief, however, that by then he had wisely wrapped a scarf around his lower face, clearly in an attempt to avoid drawing attention to what must be a shift in his daily routine. *And with his face and person highlighted by success and privilege, isn't he famous enough to be recognized even beyond the circles of the priviledged few?* she wondered and that meant, as she had learned by now, that out there in the massive stream of down-trodden anonymity there lurked, like vortexes in a mighty river, envious people ready to practice their denunciatory skills. There was always the hope among the many exploited that, by sucking down the lucky few into their own pit of despair, they could make a few of those privileges their own.

With a Gypsy's innate distrust of *Gadje* law and its enforcers, Dosha couldn't help noticing the great number of soldiers and uniformed policemen on the street — some walking alone, others in pairs, some with dogs.

In a final attempt to shake her pursuer, she quickened her pace, but stopped just short of running, which was forbidden within city limits. The dancer followed suit. He was about to catch up with her when Dosha dove into a narrow back alley that she knew would lead to a parallel street along the Kryukov Canal. Here the dampness, trapped in a narrow space, had turned to smog, and the gray light of early evening exposed the crumbling backsides of the city's grandiose facades.

The alley itself was empty except for a drunk, who lay peacefully asleep and rhythmically snoring among an assortment of banged-up trashcans and spilled garbage. He was clearly beyond caring that he could easily freeze to death in the puddles of dark melted slush. A smell of decay filled the chilling air.

But Vasili had seen her dodge into the alley. He called her name. "Ana Dalova!"

At the sound of his voice Dosha felt a lump rise in her throat, trapping her breath. *Two people from different groups destined for a propaganda trip to the West meet clandestinely in the streets at nightfall?* Terrifying images bombarded her brain like a shower of meteorites. She was sure many people had been purged from the desirable list of "trips abroad" for less and was the sleeping drunk really a drunk? The KGB always had some man or woman on standby, keeping an eye out for potential defectors.

Her fear was intensified by the knowledge that, if she were caught committing the slightest transgression against the Party line, she would have to hand her stallion over to Osap Tossuk, to be reassigned to whomever he thought fit. *One of those robots of the system!* She fumed. *They've been waiting for just such a misstep ever since I arrived, so that they could grab my horse.* For she knew that the stallion was every rider's dream — regardless of the fact that only she could ride him and that the powerful Galina was her protector. The Soviets would find a way, and with their unyielding discipline they would break the free spirit and brilliance of the horse she had nurtured since he was a foal. In return, when in isolation with her dying mother, there had been moments when the stallion had liberated her by allowing her to share the ecstasy of his powerful flight across open land.

Vasili must have thought she had not heard him — she neither faltered nor slowed her steps. "Ana," he called again, loudly, causing the drunk to struggle to his feet with a gurgling curse. His flailing arms set off a crashing of metal, as trashcans fell and rolled and smashed into walls and one another. Like bullets shooting from the barrel of a gun, rats sped from one side of the alley to the other, followed by cats hurling their cries.

Without breaking her stride, Dosha turned her head. "It was unwise for you to follow me," she said. Her eyes swept over the drunk, who was staggering toward the street they had just left.

"Why?" Vasili caught up with her. "Wait! I want to talk to you." But then he added, "Of course!" The words spilled from his lips. "You're being followed!" He glanced around. After all, this was hardly one of those free capitals of the "corrupted West", where one could stroll anywhere at any time. This was Leningrad, where anything and anybody that didn't fit the norm was scrutinized as if under a magnifying glass.

"No," she answered. "That is, I don't know." His hand still rested on her arm, sending shivers down her body.

He quickly rose to his own defense. "We're in the midst of a cultural thaw, you know. The iron rules have been relaxed — ever since last year," he added, "when Comrade Khrushchev promised us greater freedom, less surveillance."

Dosha shrugged and stared at him with narrowed eyes. What could she say? *Doesn't he care*, she thought bitterly, *that within that same year, Comrade Krushchev deprived the nomadic Gypsies of their freedom?* She knew that, as the son of an exiled poet, Vasili had grown up witnessing the murder and extinction of many of the country's brightest. *Doesn't he care that with the stroke of a pen the current bureaucrats are now purging the last remnants of a pure and ancient way of life?*

Out loud she murmured, "If what you say is true, about this thaw, how do you explain all the soldiers we passed out there in the streets? If we're free, why are they out in such force? Or maybe you didn't notice them." Without waiting for a reply, she hurried toward the other end of the alley, where every now and then the headlights of a passing car briefly flared up like flashlights in the shifting fog.

Vasili, noting the anger in her voice, wondered for a moment whether she might be on the verge of cracking up, remembering some of the fanatics exiled to Siberia to whom feeling persecuted became a way of life. Just then, as they were about to reach the canal, he spotted two fully armed policemen leading a muzzled German Shepherd at heel, a short distance in front of them. The embankment was nearly deserted: just a few random pedestrians, and the occasional car driving by. Even so, he noticed yet another guard, a soldier this time, posted at the corner of the next side street they passed.

"See?" Dosha whispered once they had passed the soldier. "They're everywhere. Nobody called them off. They're merely in a holding pattern, ready to pounce — like crows circling an open grave, waiting for the next corpse." *And here in Russia*, she thought, *they're still killing whoever doesn't march in line.*

As if she had lifted the veil from his eyes, Vasili started to perceive the oppressive menace that spanned the largely deserted embankment. He was relieved, though, to see that none of the sentries appeared to be following them. Dosha, too, seemed to relax just the slightest bit. She was no longer so adamant about not talking to him.

"You see those fancy buildings?" she whispered close to his ear. "They're nothing but tombstones — mere markers for the people who lost their lives while they were being forced to build those grandiose monuments."

As if paranoia were a communicable disease, Vasili looked up at the facades of the palatial buildings they were passing and felt the plaster masks and friezes from stories and balconies high up were staring right back at him. He felt a frisson of fear.

Reading his sudden anguish, Dosha stopped walking and turned to face him. "Why take unnecessary risk?" she asked. "Just in case … I mean, you never know." She knew that the dancers had not been informed that this was her last day. Larkin had impressed upon her that there were to be no official good-byes.

"There is just too much at stake," she said, turning away and walking on, "although I honestly don't think I'm being followed — not anymore. On my afternoons off, I walked the same route each and every time. I believe they got tired of watching me — too much work for some reluctant soldier yanked from the taiga. It's much easier to lean back and go blank, the Russian way. Besides Comrade Popov told me she had called off all my surveillance; maybe because different soldiers kept informing her of my unchanging walking habits. Of course," the girl concluded, "I have no delusions as to the price for breaking such trust — none at all."

They had arrived close to the Dostoyevsky district at the underbelly of the city, a section that as far back as czarist times had been a place of criminals and derelicts. According to Larkin, it was the unofficial dark side of the city, a place where, especially at night, even the KGB refused to patrol.

Dosha stopped in front of a renovated apartment building facing the gloomy Kryukov Canal. The three-story building was covered, almost in its entirety, with a canvas poster of Lenin. She turned to face Vasili. "This is where we part," she said. "I have to say good-bye."

"But this is where Larkin lives, with his Gypsy wife." Vasili had often been invited to their spacious second-floor apartment, to celebrate glowing reviews.

He raised his eyes to where the warm, blustering storm rippled and shook the canvas poster. The black image of Lenin in profile with his goatee and worker's cap stood out against the bright red background. Lenin was pointing with one outstretched arm — toward where, no one knew.

Vasili's gaze returned to the girl. There was an exotic wildness in her face, like that of a delicate flower blooming in protected shade. He stood so close to her, he could feel her breath on his face. He realized he had no idea how old she was, this girl-woman so vibrantly beautiful beneath the poster of the man of harsh angels and superhuman grandeur.

The dancer was at a loss. Ever since his early manhood, his physical beauty as well as the genuine pleasure he took in women had made him their darling. Most of them, downtrodden and abused since birth, yearned for love and beauty. They had allowed him access to their melancholy souls and his body had loved them in return. They had come flying his way like roses thrown in wild appreciation onto a stage. All he had to do was pick and choose.

This girl, on the other hand, he had followed as if he'd been waiting for her call. *"Like the flower of the sorceress,* he suddenly thought of Bizet's 'Carmen'. He couldn't just let her slip away. Desperately, he grasped at some means of bridging the silence that had opened like a chasm between them, growing wider and deeper.

"Today was your last time at the Kirov!" he said, taking a wild guess as to the reason she might be visiting Larkin at home.

"Yes. It was my last time. We leave for Helsinki the day after tomorrow."

The house behind them was quiet. It took Vasili a moment to absorb the shock of this news.

"But clearly Larkin and Maria Andreyevna aren't home. Look," he said, "there's no light on in their apartment. Stay with me a while?"

She looked around uncertainly.

"We're safe here," he said. "Larkin is married to a Gypsy, did you know? He told me that this whole section of the embankment has been inhabited by Gypsy entertainers, artists, and intellectuals since Czarist times."

The girl stepped into the entryway and he watched her fold her body into one of its dark corners in much the same way she had molded herself into the corner of the half-moon windows at the Kirov dance studio. In the darkening light he suddenly felt her fear. Her almond-shaped eyes, underlined by faint shadows, seemed darker, more apprehensive. She reminded him of a hunted, cornered doe.

For the first time since childhood, Vassily felt the urge to protect someone — to put another person's well-being before his own. He wanted to touch her face, reassure her. She was trembling. They had run out of words and now found themselves at the edge of intimacy, a divide as delicate and transparent as glass. Yet he knew that if he were to touch her, the moment would shatter and she would vanish like a dream.

Larkin, dressed in a dark winter coat and a gray fur hat, came walking along the deserted embankment. The couple had never been far out of his sight. He had witnessed Dosha's futile attempts to shake his persistent protégé. Among her people, a young Gypsy woman like Dosha would never find herself far from the protective presence of the males of her *kumpania*. Inappropriate behavior of any kind toward a Gypsy woman could spark a blood feud in a second.

As Larkin came within sight of his house, he leaned against the iron balustrade of the canal, wondering what to do next. The young couple was half hidden in the shadow of his entryway. He knew the girl was waiting for him, and he imagined that Vasili might be wondering why she'd come to the ballet master's house. Larkin had told his protégé nothing about the girl — to protect not just her but Vasili as well.

Unlike young men of noble birth, pampered by enormous wealth and unquestioned authority over the poor, who had openly courted fiery, beautiful *tzigani*, the dancer had grown up amidst the purging of Russia's brightest and her most courageous. Blessed with unusual talent but most of all luck, he was the exception to a fated rule. He had found an escape, a small state-run ballet school in Siberia, from where in turn Larkin had rescued him. Larkin loved Vasili like a son. But to tell him that, to a Gypsy girl like Dosha, he would be *mahrime,* unclean, would be to offer him knowledge that could endanger them all.

Besides, even if love and youth were able to overcome all other obstacles, the minds of *Roma* and *Gadje* could never truly meet. The Roma's ways and customs, their taboos and loyalties, often remained a mystery even to those as close to them as Larkin, husband to a Gypsy and half-Gypsy himself.

Maria Andreyevna had told him the story of the great Tolstoy's sister-in-law, a Gypsy whose singing had been known to reduce audiences to tears, and who had married Tolstoy's brother. Once her youth and her passion for her *Gadje* husband had faded, the tiny *romni* silenced her voice. She spent her remaining days sitting alone, smoking her pipe, by the entrance of the vast Tolstoy estate, her eyes lost in the distance. She was waiting for her people to come and take her back.

At the outbreak of the Great Revolution, the aristocrats had been the first to pay for the excess and frivolity of their past behavior. Next in line to be eliminated were the idealists among the revolutionaries, for at least trying to stick to their past promises, and then came the brightest among the intelligentsia, for being brighter than their new overlords. The only constant in the Great Red Promise so far had been the killings and Larkin knew that, although Vasili had thus far escaped his parents' fate, his life was a ticking time bomb; his freedom hung by a thread and to connect his destiny to that of Ana Dalova, a member of the latest group to be suppressed or eliminted, was like exploding that bomb.

As he stood lost in thought, Larkin's eyes followed the flight of a white-breasted bird as it soared from the opposite embankment and started circling the gloomy canal. He watched it spread then fold its wings as it dove like an arrow down between the ice floes, dipping in and out of shifting layers of mist.

Suddenly, from the crown of a tall tree on the opposite bank, a whole flock of birds rose into the air like particles of dust. A small crowd of young men emerged from under the bare branches of that same tree. They continued on to a footbridge arching gracefully across the canal. At its apex they paused, loitering. Some stood up straight, others leaned over the ornate iron railings to peer through the mist at the piled-up ice that still blocked the free flow of water.

Larkin counted seven of them. They were a miserable lot, fidgety and nervous. They wore dark, wide-brimmed hats above shaggy dark hair that fell down to their shoulders. They wore no coats over their loose pants and jackets. They appeared overly slender — sharp and angular, like Spanish Flamenco dancers, silhouetted darkly against the mist. These were the Roma he had been waiting for.

Spotting Larkin with darting eyes, the young *rom* drew into a circle on the footbridge, leaning toward one another with bent backs. Cupping their hands against the wind, they used a lighter resembling a miniature flamethrower to light cigarettes, which, as they straightened up, sparked in the darkness like fireflies and like a change from day to night, the gloomy scene along the quiet canal suddenly came alive.

The girl was the first to move. Leaving the protection of the entryway to Larkin's apartment building, she stepped into the middle of the street. There, as if shaking off an assumed identity, she pulled off her squirrel hat and, with one hand, tore her heavy hair loose from the twisted bun at the nape of her neck. Gusts of wind tossed her long, glowing hair wildly about her face as she assumed the bold stance of a nomad facing a storm sweeping across open land.

Like actors in a play, the same play, everyone present came

alive. The men on the bridge converged toward the girl in a loosely connected group. The girl, her open coat billowing behind her like a cape and her fiery hair waving about her laughing face, looked back at the dancer with glistening eyes. Then, half walking, half running, she advanced toward the approaching *rom*.

Vasili, infected by the sudden upbeat movement that had sprung alive, appeared to be ready to join in with the rejoicing Gypsies, as if he too were part of this reunion.

The time had come for Larkin to intervene. *Doesn't the fool realize,* he cursed, *that although his departure is still four weeks away, he's sure to be under heightened scrutiny? And that dancers more famous than he have been bumped at the slightest hint of defection?* So, just as the men from the bridge approached the girl, Larkin stepped into the dancer's way.

"It would not be prudent for you to be spotted in this side of town, only weeks away from your departure to the West!"

"What about her?" Vasili shot back. "She's only one day away from her departure." He tried to get around Larkin, his protector and mentor, who had directed every aspect of his life, professionally and emotionally, ever since discovering him.

"This is her chosen good-bye."

"From Gypsies?" Vasili asked in disbelief. Memories rose in his mind of the hordes of Gypsies he'd seen hanging about the railroad track when he and his mother had been sent into exile on the Siberian Express. The Gypsies had camped out in tattered tents right by the tracks, half starved and as intently focused as wolves on the prowl. They had huddled together on the overcrowded Siberian Express as well, staring with hauntingly sad eyes at the desolate passing landscape. Then suddenly they'd start to talk and laugh, taking comfort in one another's company. Someone would strike up a song on a violin or on one of their seven-stringed guitars, melodies that pierced though the layers of Russian apathy and stirred up feelings that were better left untouched. To the small boy, their laughter and joy had seemed out of place, for, young as he was, he was quite aware of the pain and misery that surrounded all of them, Russian and Gypsy alike. Their camaraderie only served to deepen Vasili's fears of that Great Unknown they were relentlessly approaching, in a train that offered no escape.

"What would link her to them?" he insisted, catching Larkin's arm.

"She probably just happened to live somewhere close to them, way up north." Larkin lied. "Plus, they are known horse dealers. Who knows? Maybe they found her that stallion of hers."

The group from the bridge had opened up like a mouth and swallowed the girl into their midst, they quickly moved off. Larkin continued to block Vasili's way. Together they watched her and the *rom* disappear.

"Has it ever occurred to you," Vasili asked with horror in his voice, "what could happen to her in a place like this? This is the very worst section of Leningrad! Women, especially young ones like her, have been known to disappear here, and nobody ever bothers to ask what happened to them."

"That was under Beria," Larkin said, alluding to the former head of the secret police. "He was shot three years ago."

"There are others like him ..." The dancer's voice trailed off, but he obediently remained by his mentor's side.

Dosha ever since she had been granted permission to take walks alone had never ventured into this part of town. Now, walking deep into the Dostoyevsky district, surrounded by Patrina's men, she watched all signs of civilization peel away like dead skin from the once glorious city that was still proudly referred to as "Russia's Window to the West."

"These houses," the one called Pulika told her, "were inhabited by *Gadje* poor, even before the time of the last Czar." Chipped yellowish paint was peeling off in huge chunks, allowing pitted red brick to show through. Wide cracks ran across crumbling walls and sagging balconies, boarded-up windows pointed like milestones to a miserable history. No effort had been made to glorify the past. All the pockmarks of war had been left untouched — *a monument*, Dosha thought, *to human suffering, and survival.*

But as they walked further into this derelict neighborhood, Dosha detected a pulse of life she hadn't felt in other sectors of the city. Even at this hour, when the second work shift was officially in full swing, all sorts of people — men, women and children — and the occasional dog on a leash walked about at leisure. This world of supposed dissenters and subversives seemed to be in no great rush. Every now and then someone in the crowd threw a brief glance at the Gypsy band moving quickly through their midst.

The *rom* kept her close at all times as they sped around street corners, into back alleys and out again, until they arrived at a cluster of residences centered — like most buildings in Leningrad — on a square. There were no indications as to who lived there — no nameplates or lists of apartment numbers or tenants' names. The place looked as if it had been condemned and abandoned, and that therefore the census-takers had walked right by.

"Are we there?" Dosha asked.

They were standing before a stone archway leading into a messy courtyard. Dosha stepped out of her circle of guides. At once she was surrounded by children in rags. She reached into the pockets of her pants, and dropped candy into their outstretched hands.

"I see you came prepared, Dosha of the Khantchisti," Pulika laughed, addressing her respectfully by her formal name.

"I bought those as soon as the half-Gypsy told me of this plan." She waved at the children, who were cracking the candy with gleaming teeth and stretching out their hands for more. There were children everywhere, jumping off piles of firewood stacked all across one side of the dilapidated inner courtyard. Children were climbing on and off an outhouse that had a cutout in the shape of a heart on the door. Half-rotted, the door dangled unevenly on loose hinges. Emaciated mongrels roamed about like giant rats. During the early evening hours, when Soviet children were supposed to be inside their homes eating dinner, these hoards of no doubt hungry but happy children were laughing and tumbling about all over the place.

"Like fleas on a hot peasant stove!" said grinning Pulika. "These *xurde* — our children — may not be decked out in uniforms like the children of this new Russia that suddenly refuses us our ancient way of life," he murmured thoughtfully, "but they are and always will be the Gypsy's trump card for survival. Nobody breeds better and more children than us Lovara — in fact, all Russian *tzigani*. Don't you agree?"

Suddenly a stranger came walking up the street behind them. He at once found himself singled out by a pack of mongrels. Like wolves, their teeth bared and hackles raised, they surrounded him in a threatening half-circle. For a moment the children stopped playing to stare intently at the stranger.

"Leave it to those Gypsy dogs," Pulika whispered to Dosha. "They can pick out a non-Gypsy the way a crime victim picks out his attacker in a lineup."

The stranger made an abrupt about-turn and took off. The dogs at once backed away, driving the children to peals of laughter as they resumed their play.

Pulika ducked into a building on the left, and Dosha followed.

# 27
# Patrina, Tribal Mother

Shortly before Russia officially decreed the Gypsies' ancient nomadic ways illegal, and just days before the first detachments of soldiers were dispatched to enforce the Great Halt, Patrina had received a message from her brother Khantchi. The leader of the Lovara advised his sister to head straight for the Finnish border — specifically, to the swamps north of Lake Ladoga. There, during the dark hours before dawn, she was to slip across to the West.

Patrina at once split up her large clan, her *vitsa*, into smaller *kumpaniyi* to avoid detection and headed for that uninhabited stretch of Russian Karelia. As she neared the swamps, however, a numbing cold invaded her extremities. Within an hour she was doubled over with abdominal pain. She urged her *kumpania* to leave her and cross the border to safety without her. Her fellow Lovara, however, refused what to them seemed unthinkable, to abandon the tribal mother of all Russian Lovara as she lay dying. Instead they erected a death tent at the edge of a small clearing fringed by birch trees and built the customary fires to burn through the night.

In their grief, they ignored the whimpering of their dogs. The horses were restless with their heads lifted up high, ears pricked, as if sensing the approach of a storm. In their defense, the Lovara were still within the boundaries of Russia, where they had never before been directly targeted.

Suddenly, out of the darkness that surrounded the camp, the double headlights of army trucks flared up from opposite sides of the clearing. Soldiers pointing flashlights stormed the campsite. They came swarming into the circle of parked caravans and around the death tent, where most of Patrina's kin sat cross-legged on the floor. Flashlights lit face after face and finally shone directly into the face of the dying old woman.

239

Lovara always chose the wisest and bravest of their women as tribal mother. These leaders were hardly birds that freeze at the flare of a light. In an instant Patrina rose above her pain and tried to peer beyond the glaring light to the aggressor who held it, an officer.

"Who exactly are you looking for?" she asked.

"Khantchi," the officer replied, "the one known to authorities as the King of the Gypsies."

"Oh, him," Patrina whispered, closing her eyes as if relieved. "He'll come back for me," she added, curling back into a fetal position like a child in pain, "as long as I'm alive, of course."

The Lovara believed that with those words their wise leader, who knew the ways of *Gadje*, having fought as a partisan among them, willingly turned herself into live bait. Although she knew, as did any other Lovara, that Khantchi would never walk into such an obvious trap.

After conferring among themselves, the soldiers reappeared with a stretcher and loaded Patrina with care onto one of their trucks. They transported her and all of her followers, truckloads of them, to an army field hospital a day's travel away. There she was put, as Patrina later described it, into "a long and dreamless sleep." When she came to, she had been cut open and, to the Lovara's surprise, patched right back up again. The *Gadje* doctors, in whom no Gypsy had ever placed any faith, had saved the life of a Lovari queen.

On the day they were captured however, the Lovara of Patrina's *kumpania* lost their horses and their caravans. All their gold was confiscated. At least they had not been massacred on the spot, as had so many other minorities and dissident Russians before them.

"Patrina believes," Pulika informed Dosha as they entered the building, "that someone out there is bent on betraying us — one of our own. Even back near the Finnish border, only another Gypsy would have known that, by trapping our tribal mother, they would trap us all.

"We believe," he continued, "that they never bothered to look for the rest of our tribe, those who had been traveling apart, because they thought the others would follow us into this cage on their own, as soon as they'd find out where we'd been dumped. Instead, the rest of the different *kumpaniyi* retreated into the woods, beyond their reach, preparing for the day when we can reunite.

"Thankfully," he concluded, "they allowed the kids to bring some of our dogs. At least now we have a kind of early warning. They come knocking on our doors at all hours of the day and night."

"Who do?" Dosha asked.

"The KGB," Pulika answered. "They're in uniform, too. Our children and the elders don't dare close their eyes at night, waiting for that cursed knock. Although it's rare they come at night. There's too much crime here for them. Too hard to control, even for the KGB."

The interior of the stone building felt colder than the night air outside. It had the lingering smell of wet coal and the grimy semi-darkness of an abandoned mineshaft. The only light came from a partially boarded-up window half a story up. Pouring down the cavernous stone stairwell, from the floors above, came the din of many voices and the strumming of guitars.

Dosha climbed the hollowed stone steps up two stories toward a swaying light that turned out to be a bare bulb dangling by a wire. Underneath it stood a young *rom*, a boy still, watching their approach. His dark face was tense with worry.

"She's been waiting for you," the boy said to Dosha, as if he knew her.

All the doors on the landing had been removed. In a room to her left, Dosha noticed a group of *rom* of all ages asleep on the floor. They were fully dressed, a sign that they were on high alert, ready to leave at a moment's notice. To her right a small corridor was lined with neatly stacked felt boots and shoes. She started to pull off her own boots, but the boy said, "You better carry those along with you. You have to be able to leave in the blink of an eye."

He lifted an Oriental rug that hung across an empty doorframe and motioned Dosha in the direction of voices that mixed with the gentle picking of guitars and the tuning of violins.

What had once been a spacious apartment, consisting of several rooms, now looked like the waiting room of a railway station filled with wartime refugees. Whole sections of walls had been knocked down, leaving what was left posed like rough-hewn columns.

Here were the women of Patrina's *kumpania* — *romni*, young and old, all of them in traditional dress. Some wore kerchiefs on their hair, indicating their married status; young girls let their long hair fall loosely down their backs. Some moved about, some sat cross-legged on the floor, snatching at the smaller children who were toddling about. Next to neatly stacked piles of what looked like doors cut up for kindling, two homemade iron stoves burned just short of red hot, their pipes extending through boarded-up windows. A samovar hissed on one stove; on the other a young woman with a baby clutched to her hip stirred an enormous pot of stew.

After her long absence from her people, Dosha was struck by the unifying effect of a Gypsy feast in progress. The hall-like space had the spotless cleanliness of the inside of a tent or caravan. But there was no chopping of herbs, no kneading of dough, no peeling of vegetables or plucking of birds. As Dosha entered, the kitchen fell silent. Some of the younger children stared at her hair, her height, and most of all at her riding pants. To Dosha the hollow, hungry eyes of those Lovari children reflected the horror of this latest dark passage of the Romani trail.

Patrina, beloved tribal mother and queen of the Lovara, had been placed on an elevated podium in a corner of what must previously have been yet another small room. A wall had been torn down to give her a view of the whole central living area as well as partial views of the rooms to either side. The space crudely resembled the nave of a church. There, open-mouthed and toothless, Patrina lay asleep on a pile of colorful featherbeds and blankets. Her sunken lips moved peacefully with every faint breath. Her upper body was propped up against a multitude of colored silk pillows salvaged at the last minute from the abandoned caravans.

A mixed company of men and women, all high-ranking members of Patrina's *kumpania*, sat cross-legged in small groups on the floor, talking and smoking with a quiet reverence that recreated the timeless aura of Roma living in the wild.

Patrina, like most Russian Lovara, had always been tiny, but in the orange glow of the kerosene lamps, her body looked so shrunken that it seemed lost within her voluminous Gypsy skirts. She wore a red silk blouse embroidered with silver thread that left her forearms bare, exposing her dark and weathered skin and her fine bones.

By her head sat a plump, middle-aged woman with haunting eyes. "I am Bugumila of the Loboski," she said, motioning Dosha to sit by her side. "I saw you when you were still a little girl, when we all met with Patrina at the end of the war.

"She's been waiting for you," she said. "Patrina has been waiting. She kept saying 'Dosha — where is my Dosha?'"

Several very young women approached and, without a word, placed a wooden crate upside down in front of Dosha. One placed a cover of fine lace on top of the crate, and another offered her a plate heaped with potatoes and roasted chicken. A third arrived with tea, which she poured into a fine porcelain cup held by yet another romni.

Dosha realized that they were offering her food that they themselves had little of. She said to the woman who was holding the plate,"Chaves! Give it to the children!"

At once the children moved close and eagerly grabbed the offered food with both hands. They ate with great haste, lifting their eyes every now and then to look at Dosha. For the first time she saw them smile.

Turning to Bugumila, she said, "I've been well fed. I come with money, too. I saved it for Patrina."

Bugumila took the folded bills, placed them into her lap, and said "Look at her!  Look at what they did to her! Our *phuri dai* lost all her teeth. Gypsies don't lose their teeth!" Her voice had a repetitious drone to it, like that of someone selling wares in a marketplace. "Our tribes used to spread from Poland all the way to Spain, through White Russia all the way to the Caucasus," she continued in that same wailing monotone. "All Patrina of the Khantchisti wanted was to die by the roadside, as her ancestors had done for as long as memory can reach and there she lay stretched out in her death tent, writhing in pain, when we were betrayed. Betrayed!" she repeated. "And not by some Soviet clodhopper either, but by one of us — of a different tribe, to be sure. A lower *natsia,* for no Lovara would ever ..."

As if seeking confirmation of the faith she had in her tribe, Bugumila searched Dosha's face while, absentmindedly, stroking the wad of bills. "Then, against our will ... We never asked for this! The Russian soldiers took her to one of their cursed hospitals, cut her open, and patched her up again.

"*Appendixi,*" she droned on. "That's what they call it. So now, instead of dying by the roadside like her ancestors, she's losing her life force ever so slowly here in this trap.

"Her mind," Bugumila whispered. "It comes and it goes. She tells me that when she first opens her eyes, everything — walls, people, objects, all of it — is flat as a sheet of ice. Then suddenly things pop up again."

Only then did Dosha notice that her great-aunt's eyes were

resting upon her. However, Patrina's focus looked broken. She seemed to be staring right through Dosha, her unseeing face filled with pain and anxiety, as if she were witnessing something horrific, invisible to the rest of them.

At once Bugumila leaned toward her tiny queen. But Patrina, weakly lifting an arm, gestured her to move aside. In the process the old queen managed to lift her neck and face off the pillows with a strength that only seconds before had seemed all but gone. Dosha witnessed life invade the old woman once again with extraordinary force. Her pain-filled face broke into a toothless smile from ear to ear. Her eyes sparkled with joy as she stretched a trembling hand toward the girl, whispering, "Dosha!"

Dosha moved close to her great-aunt and took both of the old woman's hands in hers.

"Look at her!" Bugumila at once resumed her monologue. "She has lost all her teeth. Gypsies …"

Patrina, her eyes warm and fearless and suddenly in full focus, waved a limp hand in a somewhat commanding gesture toward Bugumila's droning voice. "Enough already," she ordered in a cracking voice. "Nobody's listening. You lost your audience way back and long ago," and then, in that half-whispered but still commanding tone, she ordered, "I need a smoke!"

The plump, middle-aged Bugumila slowly rose to her feet. Mumbling inaudibly, she walked toward the group of young women and girls who were busy by the stoves.

"Cracks me up, the way she goes on and on," Patrina said, her eyes never leaving Dosha. "You have to understand, the poor thing is the only member of a once large *kumpania* to have survived Auschwitz. We came across her in the woods and took her along, of course. She has sworn a blood oath of loyalty to me. She's my closest servant now and she means well, but it's like having the bird of doom stuck to your ear. Talks and talks and doesn't listen; doesn't worry that nobody tries to understand.

"I feel I have to warn you," Patrina, emphasized, "just in case she starts singing the song of Auschwitz. It cuts right through you. It's worse," she whispered, "than the call of the owl."

Bugumila returned with a long pipe already lit. After taking a deep, long puff herself, she handed it over to the *phuri dai*. The old woman at once hungrily inhaled, her paper-thin cheeks sucking like bellows as she sank deeper into her pillows and her face relaxed behind a cloud of wispy smoke. In a moment she started coughing out smoke. In between gasps, her eyes returned to Dosha.

"Khantchi's waiting for you," she said. "Those Soviet clod-hoppers, those land-bound former serfs, think he'll be coming for me. They're wrong, as always but you must not go looking for your *papo*, your grandfather. You must give him time to find you," she whispered between drags from her pipe, hollowing her cheeks with each intake and closing her eyes with rapture. "Give him the time to find you — else you'd be placing all of us in even graver danger."

"How do you know?" Dosha leaned close to Patrina's face.

For a moment it appeared as if the old woman's mind had again left her withered body: her eyes remained wide open but unseeing. Finally she spoke in a steady voice: "Patrina knows what Patrina knows and it's not just what we've learned from the city Gypsies. Of course, we can't completely trust them. After all, haven't they walked willingly into this trap and stayed in it all along? Right now, though, they're the only ones willing to help us. They're actually feeding us, keeping us from starving to death."

She gripped Dosha's hand with another spurt of force. "You must tell Khantchi that Patrina sends him wishes of good fortune and wealth. Our roads are not meant to cross again. Tell him Patrina has grown very tired. Sometimes I think ..." Patrina sighed as a wave of pain crossed her face. "Sometimes I think my bones are held together by this dress alone. It gets so loose, I can hardly find myself. Dosha, would you believe it? My mind cannot find my body at times. *Merav*," she whispered. "I'm dying."

Hearing her words two women hastened over with morsels of food and a bottle of liquor.

The old woman pushed their offerings aside with a faint movement of her bony hand. "Go, quit your worrying and your whining!" she shouted the best she could. Turning to Bugumila, she commanded: "Go put some flame to this one instead." Patrina held out the pipe, which had gone out. Clearly, she did not have enough strength to both scream and smoke.

"This, my Dosha," she whispered with weary eyes, "is the last stretch of Patrina's road. But," she raised her voice toward her women, "I am not dead yet. So you should save your moaning for when I'm actually gone, the Lovari way." With that, she took her relit pipe from the returning Bugumila and triumphantly took a drag that must have reached all the way to her feet.

"I'm not coming back as a mulo, no threatening spirit, either," she spat, exhaling "Not as long as you stay trapped in this heap of stone. I am sure the owl is calling my name, back where I belong, wondering where the hell Patrina's gone to. How would it know that Patrina is buried alive in this coffin of cement, where no one can hear me call?"

She placed a hand light as a feather on Dosha's arm, motioning her to move closer. "What the others don't know," she whispered, "and I know for a fact, is that Khantchi made it across but the less they know, the less the Bolsheviks can torture out of them and as long as he doesn't show up, my people here will be hungry but safe."

Patrina pushed her mouth to Dosha's ear, "The one whom the Lovara accept as our King, the Bolsheviks think of as a racketeer. When many of the high-ranking comrades started fearing for their lives under Stalin, Khantchi was the only one who could smuggle their stolen wealth across the border, just in case."

Patrina settled back, again exhausted. "You must wait for him," she repeated. "He will get in touch with you. He will get you and your horse to safety. Don't try to contact him." She patted her granddaughter's hand. "I'm glad to see you again before I die."

At that moment, the entire configuration of the room abruptly changed, like colored chips shifting in a kaleidoscope. Only the *phuri dai* remained central. The elders who had sat cross-legged on the floor suddenly rose to their feet, and the *bori*, the young brides in charge of the household chores, busied themselves clearing away pots and plates, glasses and bottles. Dosha felt Patrina's hand grip her arm with desperate strength.

"Remember," she whispered, "the best picture lies in the soul. Take my image back to open space."

Dosha had been so intent on Patrina that she hadn't heard the first knock. The second one now reverberated through the room, as the leader of the group who had led her to Patrina now pulled her away, rushing her through back doors and basements and out into the alley behind the building. There were no soldiers there, only scurrying cats.

The dreaded knock followed Dosha into her dreams, suspended like a guillotine above her subconscious mind. Her final two nights in Leningrad billowed with nightmares of Lovara with haunted eyes living in darkness, poverty, and fear. Waking on the appointed morning with a start, Dosha felt with a hollow emptiness that with the dousing of the Romani fires, Russia had lost the last remnants of her vast and ancient soul.

# Part Three

# 28
# D-Day

The day of Dosha's departure from Leningrad, a strong April sun rose like a ball of fire and spread a gigantic halo of scattered light in a cloudless sky. The summer of 1957 exploded suddenly, without spring. The rapid meltdown of the remaining pack ice along the Neva and of the frozen ground at its shores caused the swampwater under the city to rise and the earth to heave. The brackish water forced itself through every crack in the foundations of houses and palaces alike. Tender green tufts of grass had broken through cracks in the sidewalks. On that early morning the surging dawn drew fetid moisture off the streets; the mist rose in waves of orange steam, too thick almost to inhale. To Osap, the buildings on the far side of the Neva appeared to float between steaming water and blazing sky. *As if,* he thought, *they could rise and dissipate with the morning mist, or slowly sink and vanish into the swampland that this city has never truly conquered.*

Parked in a straight line along the Palace Embankment were thirteen ZIF 150 military trucks painted in shades of camouflage. Osap, awaiting Galina's arrival (she had been scheduled to return to Leningrad the previous evening), stood next to the last one, which was parked across from the Winter Canal. From where he stood, he could keep an eye on the outer edge of Palace Square.

Osap was surrounded by the twenty-three selected riders and their trainers. Riders and trainers alike wore riding boots and gray uniforms with matching caps. They waited in silence. The only sound was the click-clack of marching horses, which reverberated all the way from the Palace Square, still deserted so early in the day. The horses arrived in single file, each led by a groom. Upon reaching the street along the Winter Canal, they tightened into pairs, thirteen in all. The stallion Rus and the mare from the same collective were in the lead. Each pair of horses was now flanked by two grooms. In addition a soldier accompanied each pair on the street side of the canal.

The departure had been planned with military precision. The trucks had been transformed into two-horse vans by building solid wooden stalls, painted to match the cabs, onto their flatbeds. The boxes, eight by twelve feet in dimension, towered several feet above the truck-cabs. Their darkly stained interiors had been divided into two standing stalls by a chest-high wooden divider attached to an iron pole installed four feet in. The trucks were lined up one behind the other, but with plenty of space left in between. Their heavy wooden back-loading ramps had been lowered for the horses' imminent arrival.

The departure moved along as planned, until the stallion Rus spotted the first of the line of open ramps that gaped like dark traps in the heavy orange mist. He pulled back so suddenly that the lead shank flew out of his handler's hand.

"No!" Osap cursed out loud. "Not now," he muttered as he ran toward the horse. "Goddamn stallion pulls a fast one every chance he gets!" This time, however, the horse did no more than simply stand there, feet planted, snorting and eying the open ramp.

Unfortunately, the echo of his shoes striking the pavement set off the ever-present instinct of flight right down to the last horse in line, causing a general slipping and sliding of hooves and causing several of the horses to shy into the street. While grooms pulled lead shanks in an attempt to bring the plunging animals back into the line, some of the soldiers, at the first sign of this sudden unleashing of herd-power, flew aside in fear.

From beyond the last truck in line, Osap heard a man shout, "Enough of this! Somebody crack a whip!"

Osap whirled in the direction of the voice. *Now that*, he thought with disbelief, *is bound to cause the stallion to rear and bolt across anything and anybody in his path.* It was only at that moment that Osap noticed that the groom who had let go of the stallion's lead was not Hissen, his one remaining Gypsy groom, but a blond, blue-eyed kid whom Osap had never seen before.

"What happened to his regular groom?" Osap cried, turning back to the blue-uniformed officer who had shouted the command and was now striding past Osap toward the Winter Palace, where a limousine, a fleet of motorcycles, and a second group of men stood waiting.

"Ilya Petrovich Krematov," the officer introduced himself. "And you must be Comrade Tossuk."

Osap's mouth tightened. He had heard only the night before

that, instead of Galina Popov, this high-ranking KGB officer from Moscow had been appointed at the last minute to oversee the trip to Helsinki. He was now acting like the man in charge.

"Comrade Tossuk," Officer Krematov continued, "you must have been aware that the groom in question was a *tzigani,* a Gypsy, and therefore a flight risk. Especially," he emphasized with a bite in his voice, "now that we're finally getting these parasites under control."

Before Osap could hold her back, Ana Dalova stepped out of the group of riders and advanced toward the stallion, who now was doing nothing worse than eyeing the open ramp and refusing to walk on. Yet without hesitation, as if the horse were about to fight or bolt, the girl spread out her arms, her eyes never leaving the horse, as she whispered softly—the way, Osap believed, only a nomadic Gypsy would go about hauling in a horse.

"You foolish girl," Osap Tossuk cursed under his breath. Didn't she realize she was possibly revealing to the rest of those present what he, Osap, had long since guessed? Namely, that she was as Gypsy as the groom who had just gotten himself bumped off the trip abroad. At times, from a distance, he had watched the girl communicate with the Gypsy grooms in the manner of these nomads: they seemed to be able to communicate with each other without uttering a word. However quite some time back, and more than once, Osap had overheard them randomly drop Gypsy words, when they thought nobody was paying attention or near enough to overhear.

*Mind you,* Osap decided in the next breath, *it's unlikely that this KGB robot will ever suspect that one so beautiful and blonde, so Russian in looks, could possibly be a Gypsy.* Under this new regime, all nomads, including Gypsies, were supposed to be dark and dirty, they begged, they stole.

The next moment Osap changed his mind again—for who had not heard of Krematov? Unfortunately for the girl, she was not dealing this time with the likes of Comrade Galina Popov, who, although a staunch Bolshevik, was a lover of horses and admirer of horsemanship above all. This time Moscow had sent a butcher. Comrade Krematov came with mile-long credentials, programmed to root out subversives. He was a known specialist in achieving results through torture.

Osap glanced around him and for the first time noticed the extent of the changes since the day before. He cursed his blindness. Clearly these extras, both the KGB commander and the new grooms alike, had not been chosen for their expertise with horses. The commandant lacked horse sense, and even the alleged extra grooms acted like city folk when confronted for the first time with a panicking horse.

Osap cringed. He realized that any delay in departure at this point would mean closer inspection of those leaving on this trip abroad, and that neither he himself, a Crimean Tartar saved from previous ethnic persecution primarily through Galina Popov's intervention, nor his star rider would pass muster under torture.

What was uppermost in Osap's mind, however, was the unexpected replacement of Galina Popov by this high-ranking officer of the KGB. In the not-so-distant Stalinist past, the sudden reshuffling of those in charge had always signaled the start of a major purge. Furthermore, the person who had been supplanted this time was Galina Popov, his protector and the only woman ever to rise to such a position of power within Party ranks, a rise attributable in part to her cousin, the newly ascended man in charge, Comrade Khrushchev himself.

For a moment Osap's slanting eyes swept across the second group still waiting by the limousine and motorcycles. He counted eight agents of the KGB. *Of course*, he thought, *they always come in pairs, one to keep an eye on the other.* They were dressed in civilian clothes, although, with their dark hats and raincoats over two-piece suits and shoes polished to a military shine, they might as well have been wearing the customary blue uniforms of the KGB. The night before, these same agents had entered the team dormitories and collected everyone's money and traveling documents, issued a week earlier, in preparation for what one them had referred to as the "Propaganda Mission." As Osap struggled to quell his panic his star rider stood at the stallion's head. Holding him loosely by his lead shank, she kept stroking and tapping his neck with her free hand. The horse was starting to relax his poll. His eyes soon lost that wild, roaming look. *He's come a long way*, Osap thought. *He's high-strung but smart.*

The animal bent his head to nuzzle his rider's hand. She chose that moment to walk him closer to the open ramp, only to have the stallion's head come up again, tensing up as he eyed the object of his apprehension. To distract him, she resolutely walked the animal in tightening circles right in front of the ramp. To avoid any further delay Osap now signaled to the mare's groom that he should move her right up alongside the stallion, in preparation for loading. Osap himself hurried to open the narrow side door to let in more light. Grabbing a metal bucket full of grain, he started to rattle it. Both horses pricked up their ears. Osap watched as both horses, with Ana Dalova in the lead, climbed the wooden ramp without any further hitch.

Everybody, including the soldiers who had kept a safe distance up to that point, gave a sigh of relief, and general loading resumed without further delay. Instead of returning to his limousine, however, Comrade Krematov lingered near the stallion's van, like a hound on a scent. Stepping close to Osap, who still stood by the open side door of the truck, Krematov pointed with his head toward the ceiling above the horses' heads and asked in a low voice, "See that hook up on the ceiling?"

Osap turned from Krematov to look inside the truck. A pole supported the stall divider at its front, and also supported the iron chest bar, which left a large undivided empty space in front for the horses' heads. Nets filled with hay hung from opposite corners of the two stalls.

The mare's groom hooked her halter to a metal tie-down positioned at the height of her head. There was an exchange of words as the groom hooked her tail bar to the center post in back. He then jumped off the ramp and back into the street. The girl still had not tied the stallion's halter but remained by his side, stroking his withers. Osap glanced beyond the mare's hay net and for the first time noticed an oversized iron eye hook screwed into the ceiling right above the stallion's head.

"Any more trouble out of that horse," Comrade Krematov stated, "and that beast's head gets tied up high! The more he pulls, the more he chokes."

*So,* Osap thought, *the bastard has been briefed on Rus's volatility.* He was still standing between Krematov and the side door of the van, covertly watching the girl. He wondered if she had heard Krematov's remarks. If so, her face betrayed nothing. She stood in the semidarkness of the trailer, erect and brave. But suddenly, with her blank, steady eyes, she looked much younger, barely out of childhood. *It's the mask she wears in public,* Osap thought, not for the first time. He knew, though, that if she were to be caught up in the merciless grind of the Soviet system, she wouldn't stand a chance.

Out in the street, a soldier helped the mare's groom to raise the heavy wooden ramp and lock it shut. Still holding the stallion's lead in her hand, the girl climbed under the chest bar at the front of the stallion's stall and positioned herself between the two horses.

Osap's thoughts drifted back to Galina. With a sinking feeling, he decided that Galina had been denounced, and a deep sadness rose from the bottom of his soul. He had to suppress tears that threatened to rise to his eyes. Change was in the air, and in Russia's long and tortured history, change was always for the worse. Ever since the Glorious Revolution, Russia's magnificent horses had invariably been among the first to fall victim to slaughter or neglect. Second in line were the true idealists, like the amazing woman he had come to respect and love. *Yes, love.* Osap surprised himself as he realized that what had started as a one-night stand during the heady revolutionary period of free love, for him had turned to love. *But then,* Osap reasoned, *many a Tartar nomad would have admired a woman of Galina's strength and loyalty. Wasn't she like the strong Tartar females of their distant past, owners of their own vast herds of horses?*

But Osap was a survivor above all. He knew he had to be careful not to allude in any way to the one who had previously been in charge. From now on, anyone who openly stood by Galina Popov would go spiraling down with her. Osap knew that a man in his modest position could in no way come to her aid. He could, however, try to save the stallion she had so admired.

With a quick sidelong glance, Osap assessed his former boss's replacement. Boris Krematov was in his forties, of slight built, but with the upright posture of a Prussian officer. His blue cap hid dark, thinning hair, and stark, icy eyes peered out from behind Trotsky spectacles. Krematov had a reputation for having interrogated and deported thousands of so-called "enemies of the people." This was a face that knew no mercy. His gaze kept shifting from the girl to the stallion, as if both were of special interest.

"With all due respect Comrade Krematov," Osap stated in a firm and confident voice, for any sign of intimidation was like a flag signaling guilt, "I don't believe harsh treatment of this stallion will result in improved behavior. Any horse professional will assure you that this stallion will prove to be a valuable international propaganda asset to our Soviet cause and his only requirement is the presence of his rider, Ana Dalova."

She must have heard him, for she looked up and met his eyes.

Dosha, known to her *Gadje* captors as Ana Dalova, had awakened that morning filled with all the excitement of a nomad breaking winter camp, her mind focused solely on the road ahead but her euphoria switched to apprehension the moment the stallion shied at the open ramp, which in turn sent a chain reaction of panic down the line of marching horses and among the grooms she had never seen before, some of whom were clearly afraid of horses. With a quick count she realized that these newcomers outnumbered the horse grooms she had worked with and come to know over the past months. Ekaterina Siglunov was not among the riders, she had not made the cut. Most importantly, she realized that Galina, the woman who had protected her and her horses, was nowhere to be seen.

Dosha dropped back to earth like a migrating bird shot in flight. This was no propaganda mission, no so-called "friendly exchange" of cultural and sports events, as she and her teammates had been led to believe. This was a covert military operation, and she was part of it. Furthermore, she suddenly realized there were no outsiders to witness the send-off. The area had been cleared of all pedestrians. Even the usual sightseeing boats were anchored down the Neva, farther away than usual.

She was about to step into a trap. Still, there was nothing left to do but walk the still shaking stallion up into the waiting van, where she remained, on the far side of the chest bar, one arm around his neck, her face buried against his mane. He nickered as the mare, led by a groom in military uniform, one she had never seen before, climbed up the ramp behind her and into the stall on the other side of the divider. The groom hooked the mare to a trailertie. Then, noticing Dosha standing in the headspace, still holding the stallion by his lead, he asked with a wave of his head toward the open ramp, "Coming?"

"I'll be riding with them," she said, glancing toward the side door, beyond which Osap and the man from the KGB stood talking in hushed voices. Shrugging, the soldier hooked up the tail chains before exiting down the ramp. A soldier helped him lift the heavy wooden ramp and fasten the locking bar to brackets on the outside of the van. With a thud, the bar dropped into place. Except for the open side door, where Osap was still talking with the KBG Commander, Dosha was locked in.

*At least we are together,* she thought, feeling blessed. She hooked the stallion to his tie, then closed her eyes and prayed sotto voce to Sarah la Kali. "Black Madonna of all Roma, safeguard us on the road ahead." Then, with the same mental intensity Gypsies use to place a curse on an enemy, she spun a protective shield around herself and the animals entrusted to her care.

Dosha was called back to her surroundings by the sound of motorcycle engines revving. Looking out the narrow window beside the stallion's head, she saw four motorcycles go by, heading toward the lead truck of the convoy; clearly they would soon be on the move. At the same time Osap's face appeared in the opening of the side door, below the mare's head. He did not step up into the van; he merely tapped the mare reassuringly on the shoulder but his slanted Tartar eyes sought out Dosha's own. She was taken off guard by the deep grief she saw in them. Tears sprung to her own eyes. *O'del protect us, we have lost Galina.* Their eyes remained locked in common grief. "Please let her stay alive," she wanted to say, but instead she lifted her gaze to the ceiling, searching for surveillance. The Tartar gently shook his head, to indicate that she should not speak. He understood.

*What if Khantchi had the power to spring Galina from whatever jail was holding her?* Dosha wondered, as she watched Osap turn away. She listened as the door clicked shut, and to her relief, she heard no heavy locking bar fall into place on the outside. *He is leaving me an escape hatch!* she exulted. *But by now he must know I'd never leave without the horses.* For the time being, Dosha was safe, alone with her horses.

The misty light falling through the two windows by the horses' heads now softened the inside of the wooden box stalls to a soothing chiaroscuro. She heard a car drive up alongside the truck and stop. Through the window she recognized the black limousine that had been parked beyond the last truck lined up in front of the Winter Palace. A young soldier jumped from the driver's seat, ran to the other side of the car, and, saluting, rushed to open the back door. Comrade Krematov stepped up and climbed in, followed by another agent in civilian clothes. Next, Osap opened the front door on the passenger side and got in. The chauffeur saluted as he closed both doors and returned to the driver's seat. Sirens blared up and the limousine, preceded by its motorcycle escort, moved to the front of the convoy and took off, spearing its way through the early morning traffic that was just now beginning to stir. Once the convoy moved beyond the Palace Embankment, it had to make its way through the first waves of workers funneling toward the bus and subway stations. Cars moved over as the convoy sped by.

Having crossed a wide bridge over the Neva, they passed

through streets Dosha had never seen before. The vans sped on, rounding corners so sharply that the top-heavy wooden stalls swayed from side to side. The horses tried to keep their balance by fast-stepping in place. They were working themselves into a sweat.

The speeding convoy was moving farther and farther from the city Dosha had looked upon as her cage. Yet now, as the city faded into marshland, her heart felt torn, for that cage not only held some of her closest kin, but with them the links to those displaced elsewhere and even those lucky enough to have escaped the Red net altogether.

Dosha had overcome many of the obstacles thrown her way. She had tried her best not to get polluted. She had kept personal contact with *Gadje* to a minimum. Yet she had to confess to herself, she was not leaving her prison untouched, for however much she tried to focus on the future, she could not shake the image of the dancer Vasili. He had breached her resolutions the same way he had broken through the rules and confining regulations of the Kirov—by rising to heights of freedom and ecstasy within his dance. For the first time in her life, Dosha felt that same urge to break away—to escape not only the ever-present danger of Gypsy life but above all her special role within that world, a role that had condemned her to loneliness. Could she possibly consider leaving it all behind and—like two birds without a flock—fly off with the man whom she believed to be a kindred soul? *If only he were Roma.*

Looking out the little window by the stallion's head, Dosha noticed that the convoy had reached a long, straight, two-lane road. By then both horses were tearing hay out of their nets. The mist had evaporated, and now the sun, high in the sky, was pressing down on the heavy wooden box stalls. The trapped heat within grew stifling. The horses were sweating. Dosha slid both side windows open to cool down the heat that rose like steam from the horses' rumps, sides, and chests.

The convoy was moving slowly now. There were no houses in sight. Even under the bright sun, the land looked desolate and forsaken—just forest, a mixture of spruce and birch, interspersed with swampland dotted with stunted or dead trees. Except for the purring of the motorcycles in the lead and the drone of the truck engines, she suspected the landscape was wrapped in the eerie silence of a landscape charred by war. It reminded her of the villages that, following the hidden roads of war, her *kumpania* had crossed in the aftermath of massacres that had left nothing alive behind.

The forest thickened, walling in the narrow road but what might have seemed impenetrable to an untrained eye was home to the Lovara, who knew how to read the forest like horses, they knew terrain by instinct. Dosha hoped and prayed that somewhere in that dense forest Khantchi was waiting for the right moment to spring her, the same way the Lovara had rescued Patrina from a Nazi camp. Then they could cross the border at some lonely spot, unguarded if only for a moment. Hadn't she been told that her grandfather was one of the few people capable of smuggling the wealth of the new elite across the iron border? It was wealth stolen from former artistocrats, which they in turn had gained through the labor of serfs. Dosha had heard that this new corrupt elite paid a high price for Khantchi's services. She wondered if through his connections he could help gain access to Galina and smuggle her across the border as well.

Meanwhile, the convoy was heading ever deeper into a border region steeped in blood and human suffering. Gypsies, unless in flight, did their best to stay away from this region crossing into Finland. They knew that it was surrounded on three sides by water and that the escape route into Sweden was far away, up north. More importantly, this stretch of land was *mahrime*, inhabited by *mule*—the spirits—of masses of the dead.

They were crossing what before the wars had been Finnish Karelia. In the course of two hard-fought wars, tiny Finland had lost a large chunk of its territory to its mighty Soviet neighbor. Thousands of Finnish citizens had been deported and dropped without food or shelter into hostile regions of Siberia or the largely uninhabited High North. The Finnish Karelians, whom Dosha had gotten to know in her father's encampment, had been the lucky survivors of that last wave of deportations. Most of their fellow Karelians had perished. Yet Khantchi had told her that Finland, this small, resilient nation wedged between East and West, remained the only nation along the Eastern Baltic coast still breathing free.

Now the enemy was knocking at Finland's door again. And Dosha had to pretend to be Ana Dalova, one of them.

# 29
# Under The Thumb Of The KGB

An hour out of Leningrad, Krematov pulled back the opaque, soundproof glass divider that separated him from his chauffeur and Osap Tussuk. He ordered the convoy to stop. They had reached the outskirts of Vyborg, the former capital of Western Karelia, when the entire region was Finnish. After the last Finnish-Russian War, in 1944, part of the region, including Vyborg, had been ceded to the Soviet Union. .

"Comrade Tossuk," he commanded, "go fetch the rider Ana Dalova out of the horse van. I want to question her."

When Osap returned with the girl, they found Comrade Krematov standing by the limousine, holding what must have been her traveling documents in his hands. He was talking to the KGB agent who had been riding with him in the back of the limousine. Both men scrutinized Osap and the girl as they approached.

"Comrade Dalova," Comrade Krematov said, "we have been studying your traveling papers."

The girl stopped a few feet away, facing the two men in front of her.

"You identify your mother as one Kylikki Tervo," he said.

"Yes."

"That is a Finnish name."

"Finnish Karelian, yes."

"You speak your mother's tongue?" Krematov persisted, looking from the documents to her. "You speak Finnish, then?"

The girl took her time. "Enough to get by, Comrade Commandant," she said at last in a calm, firm voice, looking straight into Krematov's face.

Osap felt a cold chill run down his back. He was the one who had taken the girl to the Ministry of Registration to obtain her first international papers serving as passport. He had been present when she listed her mother's name as Kylliky Tervo. He had not given the matter a second thought.

Without moving his head, Osap looked beyond the two men to where the silhouettes of small houses spread out from both sides of the two-lane asphalt road. The houses looked deserted, as did the road. *Why the sudden stop?* Osap wondered. The spot was perfect for a last-minute interrogation, with no one about to witness the outcome, and they were still on Russian soil. On the other hand, it didn't seem suitable for use as a dumping site for assassinated undesirables. They were too close to both the Finnish border and to Leningrad.

Suddenly Krematov's steely eyes were fully on Osap's face. "Am I right to assume," Krematov grilled Osap, "that comrade Dalova is to continue on to the city of Aachen in Germany for the first Olympic Games qualifying competition along with the other riders on this team?"

Krematov's stark eyes did not blink. The Tartar's skin crawled. He remained at attention, sure that Comrade Krematov, as the new man in charge, had been briefed as to their precise schedule. Osap's mind whipped back and forth over details. His answer could mean his life. What did Krematov want? In four weeks' time, the day after their exhibition ride in Helsinki, the troupe was scheduled to travel to Aachen for the first qualifying competition for the Summer Olympics of 1960.

"Yes," Osap stated in a firm voice. "Ana Dalova is our star rider."

"I am told you are the one who discovered her?" Comrade Krematov asked.

"Discover is perhaps the wrong word," Osap hedged. *Which was best,* he agonized, *the truth or a lie?* "We merely followed a lead about a magnificent horse up in the High North—the most remote area I've ever been to. Once there, we found that the girl was the only one who could handle the stallion with ease. We had to beat a blizzard to get out. It seemed simpler to take her along and since then, she has proven her worth."

"You must have met her people, then?" Krematov dug on.

"That was not part of my assignment," Osap said. "The tip about the horse came from a worker on an electricity crew: he spotted the stallion while extending lines to the isolated area. In fact, we got two horses there. The place turned out to be an unofficial collective—nothing but makeshift huts and one run-down farm building. We were driving into the biggest snowstorm of the season and we had to get out fast. So we hurriedly grabbed the horses and left. The people in the collective could have been Karelians; they could have been ethnic Russians," Osap conceded. "It was dark," he added, his fists tight with tension.

"No recollection in retrospect?" Krematov would not let up.

"No, Comrade Krematov. It was dark."

Osap knew full well that the man from the KGB might track down other witnesses to the conscription of the stallion and the mare. Yet he left out the fact that at least some of the people occupying that collection of huts and farm buildings had been Gypsies. They had stood by the equipment shed, frozen with fear, as the Soviet soldiers appeared out of nowhere and made off with their two best horses. Only the girl had confronted him. When it became clear the stallion was leaving, no matter what, she had not resisted his command to accompany what seemed to be her personal mount. Of course, at that time Osap had every intention of weaning the stallion away from the teen-aged girl, for he believed that a stallion of such size and power demanded the upper-body strength of a man. Only later did he come to respect her extraordinary courage and talent as a rider — just as, after a while, he had come to agree with Galina that the combination of the stallion and the girl was the kind of match that every horse lover dreamed about.

"I assume she was properly screened for this trip abroad by my predecessor?" Krematov asked.

Osap shrugged his shoulders. "My assigned role," he said stiffly, "is that of trainer. I was not involved in the screening of those selected and cleared for this trip abroad."

At that point the girl, with an impulsiveness that made Osap catch his breath, took it upon herself to interrupt the interrogation concerning her role.

"Comrade Krematov," she stated in an almost accusatory tone of voice, "my father Alexander Dalova is, and always has been, a patriotic Russian and a firm believer in our Soviet System. My mother was an early Communist of Finnish/Karelian origin, and my father insisted that she speak Russian to me, not Finnish. Contrary to his wishes, however, she did teach me some Finnish.

"Up until the collectivization of the stallion"—her face remained impenetrable throughout her speech—"our sole ambition was to prepare the stallion, with me as his rider, to qualify at the state-run competition for the circus in Murmansk. During the training period, we made the stallion available for breeding to help the local population improve their small, pony-sized horses. We have at all times kept the interest of the community and, above all, of the motherland uppermost in our minds."

Osap lifted his eyebrows. *Convincing,* he decided. *She's picked up a thing or two since I pulled her out of that godforsaken squatter camp.* She sounded as if she were telling the truth. But Osap knew from experience that, to a Gypsy, truth is as flexible as a rubber band—and that when it came to dealing with non-Gypsies, Gypsies stretched the truth any which way they needed to. After all, he had overseen the paperwork for Gypsies condemned to forced labor; he had worked with these people long enough to know that Gypsies were adept at inventing new identities for new occasions. From birth on, they made sure to leave no paper trace, or else they collected as many false birth and residential certificates as they could lay their agile hands on.

*Then again,* Osap thought, *our man from the KGB can't possibly know he's dealing with a Gypsy.* The Gypsies, the nomadic ones, had been smart enough to stay far away from Soviet control. Only now were they coming under the jurisdiction of the likes of him. *It will take him a while to decipher their diversionary tactics,* he decided.

*Then again*—he weighed the other side—*the girl's not dealing with some easily duped Gadje either, but with a highly trained officer of the KGB, and if she's caught in even the tiniest untruth, there will be no way out. Not for her, and I'll be next in line.*

Krematov remained standing there without uttering a word, but his eyes shifted as he lifted the knuckles of his clenched fist to his lips. The KGB officer was taking his time, weighing his options. *He must tread cautiously,* Osap decided, *because, with the latest power structure in the process of being overturned, so is the replacement order still in flux.*

"At the border," Krematov pronounced at last, looking straight at the girl, "you are to come forward and make yourself available for formalities." Then, with an abrupt turn, Krematov climbed back into his car. "We'll see how well you speak Finnish," he said in parting.

Osap watched the girl walk back to the horse trailer and climb in. The driver of the van closed the side door and dropped the locking bar into place. This time she was fully secured.

Osap returned to his seat next to the driver. The convoy

continued on, winding its way through the center of Vyborg, the last Russian city before the Finnish border. Before it was annexed to the Soviet Union, the city, then called Viipuri, had been the bustling cultural center of Finnish Karelia. Now its grandiose marble train station and elegant townhouses looked gray and neglected. Having fought in Finland with the Soviet army, Osap knew that, right after Finnish Karelia was annexed, Stalin had purged the area of all surviving Karelians and resettled it with Russians to make it look as if the land had always been part of Russia. Now, however, the few pedestrians in the streets looked like squatters. Children dressed in rags stretched out their hands to beg as the convoy traveled along the main road of what looked like a ghost town.

Osap couldn't help thinking of his own people, wrenched like weeds from their Crimean homes and flung out to perish in Soviet hinterlands. Now he had to wonder whether his own fate—which had kept him exiled from his own people—had been merely delayed by Galina's protection.

In the end, Osap thought grimly, there would be no winners, merely survivors of this regime. Ever since Comrade Khrushchev's "Secret Speech" on February 25, 1956, the dam of absolute Soviet suppression at home and abroad had been cracking; now it was giving way like ice in spring. In condemning the excesses of Stalin's tyranny, Nikita Sergeyevich Khrushchev had unleashed cries for freedom and upheaval of such unforeseen magnitude that they could only be quelled by exerting a renewed, even harsher repression. To save their own skins, these latest leaders bargained for time by attempting to show a new face and, in the process, generating some good press from abroad.

For the time being the new rule from the land of the hammer and sickle was rumored to be soft. No hammer would be swinging from Nikita Sergeyevich's fat hand, not yet. The fist that had crushed Hungary without hesitation, less than a year before, now came bearing flowers, trying to persuade tiny Finland to maintain an amicable working arrangement with its neighbor to the East. So far the mighty Union of all Soviet Republics had allowed Finland to escape the closing fist and, like some tenacious fly, remain free and buzzing right in Russia's back yard.

But among those in the convoy whose lives were about to be reshaped by events they could not foresee, only Krematov knew that the new First Secretary's political perch was already rumored to be swaying amid a rising storm of opposition. Back home, powerful forces were hard at work trying to topple Comrade Khrushchev, who, while denouncing his deceased boss Stalin, had not succeeded in whitewashing his own reputation as the Butcher of the Ukraine.

As the convoy left Vyborg behind, the forest again began encroaching upon the road, which showed worsening signs of neglect. Osap worried that the deep potholes would send the horse vans flying. He wondered if he should express concern, but sat silent: one confrontation with the formidable Krematov dissuaded him from embarking on another so soon. As the city receded in the distance, he once again conjured up the strong face of his fallen lover, Galina.

No words were exchanged among the four occupants of the limousine as the convoy, led by motorcycles, approached the checkpoint at the Russian-Finnish border. On the Soviet side, the border control consisted of a run-down military outpost. Here, the motorcycles peeled away and parked behind the checkpoint barracks. Four Soviet border guards stood at attention as the convoy continued on alone.

By contrast, the Finnish side, separated from the Soviet outpost by a narrow strip of no-man's land, consisted of four modern cement booths complete with yellow-and-black-striped tollgates. They were connected by an overhang that stretched the width of the road. Beyond the booths lay a vast paved square edged on one side by low buildings and on the other by a railway yard with an array of parked freight trains and one passenger train with a locomotive attached.

Osap was struck by how, on the Finnish side of the border, crossing guards—dressed in gray uniforms with red epaulettes—seemed to be all over the place, although none were posted in the booths. They were climbing in and out of trucks (incoming and outgoing), and using mirrors on rollers to examine the undersides of flatbeds and cabs. All the doors were left open, for inspection. The drivers waited alongside, holding papers and awaiting approval.

The horse convoy came to a slow halt in single file, lined up in front of the booth farthest to the right. The noon sun beat down mercilessly. Krematov ordered the windows lowered as two Finnish guards approached the limousine.

*This,* Osap thought, *is where that girl will get caught.* In a moment she would have to prove to their new boss that she could speak a language that had absolutely nothing in common with

Russian — nor, for that matter, with any tongue spoken within the Soviet Republics, except perhaps among some minor tribes in Inner Mongolia and should she fail, which Osap thought likely, those papers of hers—the ones Osap had considered a mere formality—could not only prove her downfall, but threaten the whole team. Her traveling documents, if invalidated, could throw their whole venture onto the dreaded "operation aborted" pile.

Osap inhaled deeply and for a moment held his breath. Before they'd even crossed the border, would they find themselves turning right back to where they'd come from?

Glancing at his side-mirror, Osap watched the Finnish soldiers proceed from van to van, unlocking the side doors. The minute her door was unbarred, the girl jumped down and approached the limousine.

She wore no cap and her hair fell loose down her back. Nor did she wear her jacket, part of the required uniform for riders and trainers when out in public. She had unbuttoned her shirt almost to her high, fine breasts, and now she leaned toward the open window to address Comrade Krematov.

"Permission to water the horses," she requested in an insistent tone of voice.

The agent on the other side flung open his door and jumped out. He rushed to open the commandant's door and held it open while standing at attention, as his superior slowly emerged. Osap joined them, as did three more agents from the limousine behind them. The whole group now faced the disheveled girl. Glancing sideways at Krematov, Osap observed as a look of admiration for the girl's beauty flashed across the KBG commandant's thin-lipped face. *This*, Osap thought with horror, *would be the worst outcome of all.* He'd heard rumors that those who were in the business of state-condoned murder and torture also had a taste for violent sexual acts, and such men had been trained to leave neither trace nor victim behind. Everybody knew that young girls, some still children, had disappeared by the thousands under the rule of Comrade Beria and his cronies.

"It feels like a furnace in those wooden boxes!" the girl protested and indeed her face and breasts gleamed with a fine layer of perspiration.

*The balls on that girl!* Osap thought. *Or is she acting out of ignorance?* Didn't she realize that already, by having declared herself half-Finnish as they approached the border, she had pronounced herself a flight risk? She might as well have admitted to being a Gypsy, and this right after her Gypsy groom had been dismissed.

"Those horses will colic in this heat," the girl went on, raising her voice. "I guarantee it." She didn't seem in the least bit intimidated.

*As if,* Osap thought, *a butcher like Krematov would have the slightest concern for the well-being of a horse—any horse.* The year before, Krematov's colleagues in the KGB had caused an uproar during the horse show in Stockholm, when they insisted that the Soviet riders withhold water from their horses and tie their heads up high to control unruliness and possibly, to increase their scores.

With a dismissive wave of his hand to indicate his lack of concern for border formalities, as well as the horses' welfare, Krematov motioned the girl toward the approaching Finnish guards. "Ask them!" he ordered. By then whatever sexual glint had seemed to lurk in Krematov's icy eyes was so completely gone, Osap's heart lifted. Had he merely imagined that gleam of desire?

They watched and listened as Ana Dalova addressed the two guards in a soft, almost pleading tone. When the guards replied, she translated, "They need to see passports or other documents, then certificates of health and inoculations for the horses."

Upon viewing her passport, one guard asked "Tervo?" to which she replied "Kyllae." There followed a rush of words in that staccato-sounding language, until she yelled in Russian toward the first truck in line: "Buckets! Everybody bring buckets for watering the horses."

Comrade Krematov followed the ensuing activity with cold-eyed intensity, like a snake fixated on prey. Osap had no way of knowing how good his rider's Finnish was, but he was relieved to see that she was fluent enough to persuade one of the Finnish guards to accompany her and two Russian grooms into the closest building on the Finnish side of the border. The other guard helped to initiate a bucket brigade between the office and the horse trailers.

To Osap, both Finnish guards looked no older than the typical young Russian recruits pulled straight out of boyhood into war or whatever other service their government had in mind. However, he was not fooled by the look of untried innocence on those young Finnish faces. These were the sons of the same soldiers Osap had fought during his own youth, when each and every Finn had turned into a ticking time bomb. Dressed in white like ghosts, occasionally working alone but usually in small groups, they had appeared in the middle of the night on fast-moving skis, typically with deadly consequences. Centuries of being overrun by marauding enemies from both east and west had ingrained in the Finnish character a strong yearning for self-reliance. Whereas many unwilling Russians had fought merely to keep from being shot in the back in the event of retreat, the Finns had fought for freedom—their own.

In the end the Finns had lost the battle, but not the war. They had kept their freedom—*but at a price,* Osap thought, *and they're still paying it.* In exchange for independence, Finland was required not only to forfeit a third of its territories and pay the USSR more than $225 million in reparations, but to follow Soviet dictates as to who and what was permitted to cross their common frontier. This border was a sham—which, Osap surmised, partially explained Krematov's disdain for the proceedings. The border was set up to monitor not what was entering Finland, but what was leaving Russia.

Suddenly, as if a bell had signaled the end of midday break, a replacement crew of border guards strolled out of one of the nearby buildings and spread out to the four previously unmanned booths; a fresh set of guards replaced the guards at the tollgates as well as those inspecting vehicles. The two Finns who had been helping with the watering saluted Krematov and withdrew.

Krematov ordered all Soviet personnel, including the girl, back to their places. As the motors roared to life, he waved away the KGB agent who had been sitting by his side earlier. "Go sit in front with the driver," he said. "Osap, you'll ride in back with me." The tollgate was raised, and the convoy drove into Finland.

Osap sat uncomfortably on the black leather seat, waiting to be grilled. Instead Krematov remarked, in his cold, detached voice, "The girl managed to sidetrack a bunch of foreign border guards from their assigned tasks simply by asking for water for a bunch of thirsty horses. Amazing, don't you think?"

What was Osap supposed to do? Give an answer? Voice an opinion? The prolonged silence imposed by the man in charge unnerved Osap. He was aware that his very future might hinge on how he answered the further questions that were bound to follow. Yet he could not speak.

"Of course, they must have been distracted by the girl's beauty. Still, did she know what she was doing, or was it all unintentional? Tell me, is this girl intelligent?"

The question took Osap by surprise. "I've been focused solely," he said, "on her abilities as a rider. I found her to be less submissive than our military riders, it's true, but as for her mind ..." His voice trailed off. "I've never really given it much thought."

"Hmm," Krematov said, "I think there is more there than meets the eye. I wonder if she could not be of use, other than as . . ." He didn't bother to finish his thought. Instead, he picked up a folder from a stack in the back pocket of the seat in front of him.

They were driving along winding, minor country roads now, rather than on a straight major highway. Mostly the roads were walled in by forests of fir, pine, and birch. At times the trees would open up to expose the occasional small farmhouse surrounded by well-kept, freshly plowed fields, or vast stretches of marshland which, Osap knew, spilled into lakes and streams that in turn stretched all the way to the ocean. Rocks and boulders, hundreds of them, lay strewn everywhere, as if dropped from the sky.

Osap felt more and more like a man condemned. His eyes lingered wistfully on the fine fuzz of green that covered a landscape ready to burst into life after the long Nordic winter. Krematov, distractedly drumming his fingers on his thigh, spoke again.

"Her Finnish," he said at last, "is good. On the other hand, I'm concerned about that strident behavior of hers. Her disrespectful attitude toward her superiors ..." His cold voice grew heated. "Namely me!" he sputtered. "It's unbecoming in a Soviet woman of her age, especially one so lacking in rank."

*Why is he telling this to me?* Osap wondered with surprise. After all, now that he no longer enjoyed Galina's patronage, he had become as expendable as any other Soviet soldier. His worth lay solely in his expertise in managing the show horses and their riders. He was well aware of the dangers posed by the on-again-off-again problems he'd had with his star rider. Ana Dalova was as hard to handle as her stallion.

"With all due respect," Osap made a feeble attempt to come to her defense, "an athlete of her caliber, a mere girl at that, riding a stallion of the size and strength of the stallion Rus, cannot afford to be timid and ... "

Krematov interrupted him with a "hmm" and a smirk. "Well, that boldness could certainly come in handy," he observed. He jabbed Osap with his elbow, as if they were two buddies sitting in a steam bath. "Women, especially young and pretty ones, can serve many functions, don't you think? They can distract men, young and old—and most importantly old men, the ones with power and knowledge. With the proper training these still child-like girls can extract important information, if—and this is a big if—they are taught properly beforehand. And of course, they must be trainable to begin with."

Osap felt the blood rise in his face. *You bastard*, he thought. *You want to turn my star rider into one of those "brides of the KGB," a whore by any label. First you'll pass her around the KGB, and then you'll use her as bait and a human listening device.* There was nothing Osap could do. He had no power.

"We're approaching the former Soviet military base on the Porkkala peninsula," said Krematov, glancing out the window, "sixteen miles from Helsinki."

The landscape had turned scruffy and nondescript, as if they had hit an invisible border of scorched earth. Sparse grass, tree seedlings, and tiny tufts of shrubs thinly covered open land consisting mostly of rocks and brown, lumpy earth. Spiky little yellow flowers had broken into bloom at the base of a far-reaching wire fence, tall as those surrounding the gulags Osap had inspected when accompanying Galina and her entourage during Stalin's reign. The fence was topped with coiled razor wire, further fortifying the enclosure. There was no mistaking the fact that this had once been a military post. Beyond the strips of barren earth and rocks, abandoned watch-towers punctuated the fence at 200-meter intervals, disappearing into the distance.

When they reached an open section of fence that had either been cut out or had once contained a pair of gates, the driver turned onto a much wider road that led into the former Soviet enclave.

Krematov visibly relaxed. He rolled down his window and sank deeper into his seat. "It seems as if we barely left," he said to Osap. "I was in charge here, you know."

The limousine sped through small clearings cut into the high pine forest within the enclosure. They passed the empty shells of two huge burned-out Soviet tanks. The roadsides were littered with army debris—junked vehicles and overturned garbage cans rusting in the open. The condition of the base testified to a hasty departure after a prolonged presence.

"Graciously returned to our Finnish friends," Krematov intonated, "and long before the lease expired, too. A gesture," he smiled sourly, "of Soviet good will."

Osap surmised that this site would be off-limits to foreign journalists: it would not have been politically wise to reveal further evidence of the contamination left behind by a Soviet army in retreat. Nor had the Finns bothered to clean up the mess. Perhaps they expected their former foe to return, sooner or later.

The convoy was now approaching a small village, a cluster of old Finnish farmhouses which the Soviet occupiers had requisitioned as barracks and painted a standard Soviet bright blue. Left open to the elements, what had once been the homes of Finnish farmers were now mere skeletons. The empty window frames gaped like eye sockets in a skull.

At the center of what had once been the village square stood a simple wooden church surrounded by a graveyard. The roof had caved in, and the walls looked as if they'd been battered by the butts of rifles.The graves were overgrown with weeds, the headstones broken and scattered.

The convoy drove on. At the edge of a vast field beyond the church stood a gigantic wooden arch announcing "STADION" in bold Cyrillic letters. Evidently, the stadium itself, like so many other Soviet projects, had been abandoned soon after the planning stage. Behind the arch, two rows of thirteen tents awaited the horses. The field was bordered on three sides by dense, impenetrable forest.

"You'll only be here for two weeks," explained Krematov with a cold smile, as if he had read Osap's dismay. "It's part of the agreed-upon quarantine for the horses."

Osap kept staring at the tents, the solid forest wall, and all he could think was that, at age fifty-seven, he had finally landed in a prison camp. *Any of us who think they're now in the free West, where all it takes is a dash for freedom,* he predicted, *will find themselves shot down like deer crossing a clearing.*

# 30
# Under Quarantine

"Until a year ago the ancient Finnish territory of Porkkala was leased to the Soviet Union as a military and naval base. It was one more concession to yet another Soviet victory; this one the war of '41-'44." Comrade Krematov addressed the Soviet equestrian team, who had been asked to assemble for a briefing in the open field in front of the horse tents.

"During our occupation," the commander drew himself up, his hands folded behind his back, "Finnish trains passing through were forced to lock all carriages and draw blinds, while our soldiers guarded the tracks with Raskolnikov machine guns at the ready during the crossing. Now, since we have no security barriers," his eyes swept the team, "I suggest you keep away from those railway tracks. Comrade Tossuk will post a schedule of Finnish trains passing through. Till further notice, then," he added, dismissing the team.

"We're only 30 kilometers South-West of Helsinki," he caught up with Dosha as she walked back toward the horse-tents ahead of the other riders, "a distance you will travel five afternoons a week, back and forth, for briefings and planning with our Military Attaché, Major General Alexander Raskov. He is in charge of the horse event, until we can move the horses out of this quarantine camp."

"And when will that be?" Dosha asked. "How long is the quarantine?"

"Two weeks from now," Krematov replied, "The Finns have agreed to cut the quarantine from six to two weeks. Maybe," he said more to himself, "because they haven't as yet bothered to decontaminate this place of our prolonged presence. It's exactly the way I left it behind."

It was the morning after their arrival from Leningrad, the grooms and riders were in the process of getting their horses adjusted to the change in schedules and conditions. The nights were still cold and frosty, but during the day, once the sun was up high, temperatures could climb to almost 60 degrees. Back in the stone buildings of the Hermitage the combined body heat of the horses had kept the barns warm, but here the heat escaped through the canvas tents, and the horses needed extra blankets. Furthermore, the unaccustomed noises of the forest that surrounded them on all sides kept the animals on the alert. They snorted and nickered all night long, allowing their riders and grooms an uneasy sleep at best.

As the only woman left on the Soviet team selected for this equestrian tour abroad, Dosha had requested that her sleeping bag be placed apart from the men in an empty stall next to the stallion. Both she and the stallion had grown up with the sounds of the forests. They both slept through the night.

The days were growing longer. Riders and grooms rose at sunup between 5:00 and 5:30, with the forest already wide awake and shrieking. Heat was rising from that night's manure as it was carted in wheelbarrows out of the tents and toward the forest line. The fields around them were covered with hoary frost that soon burnt off under the rising sun, leaving the grass a springtime green.

The horses, fit for competition and smelling that first growth of grass in the early morning hours, were on the muscle and rearing to go even before their heavy blankets were pulled off. Unfortunately their temporary quarters had been organized by bureaucrats and not horse-people; there were no fenced-in paddocks where the horses could run free and get the bucks out of their systems in the invigorating morning air.

"How about rigging up a temporary paddock?" Dosha asked Osap.

"It is never wise to make requests" Osap answered

Instead, the skittish horses had to be walked in hand, or the younger ones put on lunge-lines and lunged in twenty-meter circles for extended periods of time. Only Dosha jumped bareback onto her stallion and let him race and buck and play, allowing him to discharge excess energy before the highly concentrated work session that began one hour after morning feeding.

At 6:30 precisely, the team started their work under Osap's supervision, warming up with the usual compulsory figures: Flexing the horses in shoulder-ins, haunches-ins, riding twenty-meter circles and figure eights, before regrouping into pas-de-deux and pas-de-trois. Most importantly, they were finally able to work on what, due to the limitations of an indoor arena, they had only practiced piecemeal up until then, the highly choreographed running stampede. They now executed the fluid patterns of the stampede beginning at one forest edge and cantering diagonally across the open field to the opposite corner. As for the music, the 'politically significant music' that Dosha had spent so much time selecting at the Kirov with Larkin and Madame Karnovsky, no musicians were put at their disposal during the two-week quarantine period. Instead Dosha directed the rhythm and changing movements of the freestyle with one lifted arm which she used like a maestro's baton. The riders had been assured that the selected music would be played by the Red Army Choir and Orchestra, as soon as the musicians arrived in Helsinki one week before the actual performance.

Meanwhile many of the grooms who had joined the team just before the departure from Leningrad now stood with weapons at the ready along the forest edge or else they strolled, weapons in hand, between tents. They wore the uniforms of the Soviet Army and, instead of taking care of the horses, they kept their stark eyes on the riders night and day. Of the original grooms only roughly half were left, so each now had an increased number of horses to take care of, and many riders did their own grooming.

On the fourth morning three unmarked limousines, two black and one white, drove into the encampment. The two black ones were stretch-limousines. They discharged eighteen more Soviet soldiers, fully armed. The riders had just finished their work session when Dosha, still astride her stallion, saw Krematov walking toward her from the nearby village, where he had established his headquarters. He stopped at a respectful distance from the massive animal, which was bathed in sweat from his work-out. Heat was rising from his flanks and neck, and his nostrils were flaring.

"Prepare yourself to leave within the hour," Krematov ordered. "We're going to the city. Wear city attire."

"How long will we be gone?" Dosha asked.

"Who are we?"

"Us riders, of course."

"You are the only rider leaving," Krematov seemed taken aback by her questions. "You're the only one speaking Finnish, a rarity," he said, "and definitely a help in our present situation."

She dropped her eyes to her hands. The stallion, feeling her sudden distress, tensed up.

"You will always be back by night, leaving after morning practice," Krematov stated in a cold dispassionate voice, and turned on his heels.

She watched him walk away. So she would "always" be going to Helsinki? She would "always" be back by night? Ever since Hissen, the remaining Roma groom, had been dismissed, Dosha had found only one person she trusted with the care of the stallion. That person was Osap. She had noticed the change in the Tartar since their departure from Leningrad—ever since it had become clear that Galina would not return to them. In his free moments she often caught him eyeing that solid line of forest, looking more and more like a prisoner longing to break out. Now, after settling the stallion in his stall, she tried to track him down in the stable-tents. If she were once again ordered to work for The System she cursed and despised, instead of doing the riding work she loved, she needed him to safeguard the stallion in her absence.

She found Osap at last, leaning against the arc to the stadium that was never built, smoking a cigarette.

"I never knew you smoked," Dosha said.

"You've never seen me away from the horses," he replied with a grin.

"I need you to look after my stallion," she took the bull by the horns.

"You're going somewhere?" He threw the cigarette into the dirt, and stomped it out with a foot, as if he'd been expecting something of that sort.

"I've been ordered afternoons into Helsinki."

"How often?"

"I don't know how often. It might be five afternoons a week, or more, or less for that matter. He didn't tell me. But," she impressed upon Osap, who was looking straight into her face, "you must never, I beg of you, ever manhandle this horse," and for the first time she saw the aging, bowlegged Tartar smile. "Give me your hand." She reached out for Osap's hand. He looked up at her. He put his hand in hers and allowed her to lead him forward, their hands joined, to greet the stallion. In his stall, Dosha lifted their joined hands to the stallion's nostrils to let the animal know she trusted Osap. They remained there, indulging in that moment of shared warmth, allowing it to linger.

"It's all about feel," she whispered, still holding on to his hand, "about establishing trust and mutual respect. Brute force will get you nothing but resistance and resentment. And nobody," she emphasized, "other than me, should ever get onto his back again. Please, he's highly intelligent," she emphasized again. "He will either buck that rider off and forever have the upper hand, or, what is even more likely, some rider will insist on breaking him, and this time it will ruin the stallion's brilliance."

With Osap at her side, they remained in the canvas stall that was heavily reinforced with steel on all sides. She wanted to spend the time before leaving camp to softly talk to the stallion, nuzzling his neck. "What will happen to me?" She looked at Osap, whose eyes had not left her.

"Nothing, I hope," he answered gravely. "That is if you're careful. But you better go now. You need to change your clothes."

With a last grateful nod, she left the horse in Osap's care.

Exactly one hour after Krematov had approached Dosha that morning, eighteen of the soldiers who had traveled with them from Leningrad were packed into the two black stretch-limousines like rows of dead fish. Only Dosha's limousine, the third and white one, had the luxury of space. As she was about to enter the car, Krematov eyed her up and down with such uninhibited perusal that she cringed.

"That," he said, "is not proper day-time attire,"

She had changed into the black dress and black heeled shoes that Galina had provided for her, clothes suitable for theatres and restaurants in Leningrad. "They're the only clothes I own," she replied.

"I will see to it that you're provided with suitable clothes at the Embassy then."

After that Krematov never said another word as he ducked into the back seat of the car, but she could feel his mind on her. She was seated between him and a KGB agent. A second KGB agent sat in front beside the chauffeur. The car took off, moving swiftly out of the encampment, across the railroad tracks, then along the wide paved road straight toward the missing gate and exit. Once outside the former military base, Krematov placed his hand, his fingers tapping the leather, on the seat so close to Dosha, he was almost touching her thigh. Dosha shrank back, feeling she sat next to the raised head of a snake, ready to strike should she move. She forced herself to remain calm and immobile, keeping her eyes on the passing landscape, while every nerve in her body quivered. She was cornered, intensely aware of his nervously busy hand, inches from her leg. For the first time she felt grateful for the presence of a KGB officer, for she had figured out by then, that one of their primary functions was to keep an eye on his colleagues.

Dosha had not stepped beyond the encampment since their arrival from Leningrad four days earlier. Although the Soviet military had left this base close to a year earlier, the feel of a hostile foreign presence remained, and once again Dosha was shocked at the Soviet army junk that defiled the thick woods—and then, once they passed the dismantled gate and the abandoned man-towers, she saw the way the land must have looked before the Soviets took over.

They were now driving on dirt roads through a vast expanse of dark forest and gently undulating hills and again rocks of all shapes and sizes were strewn haphazardly wherever the forest opened to expose the finger-lakes that stretched like arthritic hands towards the ocean. There was little evidence of human habitation—an isolated hamlet here or there, consisting of a few one-room farmhouses. It was no more populated than Russia's High North, only here the hut-like houses looked well-kept, and the small fields surrounding them were neatly plowed. Nonetheless, seen through the dark, tinted glass of their limousine, this sparsely inhabited wilderness appeared shrouded in a layer of gloom.

As they approached the outskirts of the city, two of the three cars peeled off. Only Krematov's limousine joined the light urban traffic moving on the wide avenues. There were a few pedestrians here and there, but nothing like the masses that pumped through the streets of Leningrad during working hours. Here the few people walking along seemed easy-going and unhurried. Passengers stepping out of trams or getting on were few.

"Is this a holiday?" She asked the KGB agent next to her.

"Why?" answered Krematov

"It looks so empty."

"Despite the size," Krematov said, "they've got only five hundred thousand inhabitants here, a fraction of Leningrad's," he said, "let alone Moscow. It's more like a prop of a city, a show place." His words sounded derogatory and dismissive.

But Dosha marveled at the clean house fronts they passed, the towering churches and massive government buildings adorned with columns. They appeared unscarred, almost new. Once beyond what was clearly the center of the city, they were approaching the forbidding façade of a gray palace facing the sea.

"That's it." Krematov turned to Dosha. "This is the Soviet Embassy in Helsinki, Comrade Dalova."

The limousine slowed as it took an alleyway toward the backside of the embassy. Two armed guards high-stepped forward and then opened a heavy iron-forged double gate. The car drove into a square, walled-in, cobble-stoned courtyard, along a circular driveway and came to a halt in front of a set of tall oak doors. At once the agent beside Dosha jumped out, leaving the door open for her, while the agent from in front opened the door on Krematov's side.

Krematov and Dosha proceeded into the Embassy, where Krematov handed her over to two other uniformed guards. They must have been expecting her, for without a word, they marched her through an enormous, stark but gleaming marble reception hall. The guards were older than most soldiers and unusually tall and muscular. Their steps echoed through the high-ceilinged space, deserted except for two soldiers standing guard at the foot of two curving staircases that led to galleries on the second floor. Dosha, pinned between her guards, lifted her eyes to the elegant iron-forged balustrades of the galleries. Her escorts with eyes ahead, made straight for a row of gleaming steel elevators half hidden behind the twin staircases. The door of the elevator at the center of the row gaped wide open.

*I'm being processed.* The reality struck Dosha like a thunderbolt. Once inside the elevator, the guard to her left pressed the number four. The elevator smoothly lifted off. They stood so tight-packed in one row in the narrow elevator that she could feel their bodily warmth through the fine wool of her dress. Their faces showed no emotion. When the elevator came to a halt, the one to her right was the first to exit, before together in a row again, they marched through a long, brightly lit corridor with few doors. When they reached the last door on the left, one guard opened the door and motioned her in; the other told her to "Stay!" They left, closing the door behind her. She heard their steps fading away. There was no further noise.

*But then,* she decided, *all sounds must be muffled here. They're probably standing close by somewhere, making sure I can't escape.*

She found herself alone in a space that, although furnished, looked as if it had never been inhabited. Ahead of her stood a heavy wooden desk with one ornate armchair behind it, further back three upright chairs were placed in front of three sets of open windows. The windows were wide and high and from where she stood, Dosha could see the sky. It was of a deep uniform blue. *Not at all like our Russian sky*, she mused, often overcast, always melancholy. This sky, although of a glorious blue, looked hollow, eerily devoid of life, just like the office they had confined her to.

The office reminded her of one of those rooms in Russian monasteries, the ones built into rock. The Lovara, seeking shelter, had found them sparsely furnished, with a stone slab for a bed, a table made of stone, sometimes a few dilapidated wooden stools that the monks had left behind as the Soviets put them to death or had chased them out.

Dosha stepped closer to the massive desk, looking beyond the three chairs positioned at a precise distance from each other by the three identical open windows and there, under the blue light, she beheld the Baltic Sea stretch toward a distant horizon. A flat expanse of the deepest blue, dotted with tiny islands of gray rock or tufts of trees. There was no wind, not a ripple, as if nature were taking a deep prolonged breath. A beauty painted on glass, shattered for an instance by the piercing cry of a seagull sailing by. The silence resumed.

Time stood still. *I'm about to have my soul extracted*, the thought took hold of her. *They won't kill me, not yet.* She straightened up and took a deep breath. *And that with freedom in full sight, no farther than the other side of that windowsill.* But no sooner did she step toward the window than the door behind her flew open.

She turned. The first to enter the office was an old man. His face was round, his eyes squinted. His thinning, steel-gray hair was cropped close to his balding skull. *He must be vain*, she thought. His dark, gray-striped suit was surprisingly well-fitted to a man of his considerable girth. His step was resolute and energetic. He was followed by Krematov and the two guards who had led her to the office. The guards closed the door and took a stance, inside the office this time, on either side of the door. The old man strode past Dosha without acknowledging her and heaved himself into the chair behind the massive desk. He motioned Krematov to the seat to his right, and then to move the chair closer. He left Dosha standing.

Dosha took several steps back toward the entrance door. For a moment, with the shifty eyes of a shrewd peasant, the fat man looked her up and down.

"I am General Alexander Raskov, Military Attaché of this

Embassy," he introduced himself. "And I have been informed that you are Ana Dalova, the lead rider of our new dressage team. I have been assured that you have the talent and the trained ability to redeem our failures of ...."

Dosha had been subjected many times over to this speech concerning an event she could not be faulted with, namely the failure of the Soviet team at the 1956 Summer Games in Stockholm. She decided on pure impulse that it was in her interest to block out the rest of what he was about to repeat from previous sources. Although she suspected that this time, the previous failure she had no part in, was probably being used as a form of intimidation, some veiled threat, should she fail at turning her ride into an international success. Divert her from her only hope of escape? For a moment she merely let the words of this latest Soviet bureaucrat wash over her and focused instead on the aging man's face, trying to read his expression.

*Something*, she thought, is *protecting me*. This was no all-out assault. Why was the fat man not simply dictating to her what he wanted her to do? She knew the System that had kept their lives rigidly in place, had been shifting and moving as of late. Now in this room, she at once felt the lack of trust between Krematov and this man who must be his boss in this city of the West. They were seated side by side, yet separated as if by a wall. *Is their world crumbling?* She wondered, and instinctively grasped that not just her life but that of everybody in this room was up in the air. The slow, grinding Soviet machine was malfunctioning. It could blow up any time.

Dosha's eyes wandered back toward the hollow sky, partially blocked by the old man's bulky shape, when his hand suddenly struck his desk with unexpected violence.

"You," he addressed her, as if she were accused of an intended crime, "do not seem to understand that your riding program is risky. It's as risky as the one in Stockholm, and that was our first Soviet equestrian participation since the Great Revolution. I remember how heading for Stockholm too, the Ministry of Culture assured us that the brilliance of our Soviet horsemanship would enhance our image abroad. Instead they failed. They didn't measure up to the horsemanship of even some of the minor European countries. What do you have to say for yourself, Comrade Ana Dalova?"

She stifled an outcry. "With all due respect," she hastened to defend herself. "I was drafted Comrade Raskov—drafted—'taken along like an afterthought, so to speak, on account of my horse. This was never my idea, Comrade General. You may ask our trainer Osap Tossuk. He's with the horses back in our transition camp."

General Raskov's face flooded with red. He was ready to explode as he directed himself with mounting impatience to Krematov. "Before entering this office, has the rider Ana Dalova been briefed, or has she not, as to what is expected of her?"

Krematov had the trapped look of a rabbit in a hole.

But Raskov went in direct pursuit of Dosha once again. "Have you, Comrade Dalova, been instructed on what is required of you at this point?"

There was no escaping the general's fuming face. The axe was about to fall. Dosha shook her head.

"Your role has been expanded, beyond riding your horse. You are being recruited," the old Bolshevik shouted, "as a street agent to mingle with the locals. Not all is as it appears out there. On account of your knowledge of the Finnish language, you will be sent out into the streets of Helsinki to act as the eyes and ears of our great Soviet Union. To feel the pulse of this host nation and report it back," he shouted, "to me! For which you need,"—he added, turning to glare at Krematov, "a cover."

There followed a lot of back and forth about who or what she should pretend to be. Should she be a student? A visitor from abroad? A Russian tourist? An Embassy clerk?

Until: "With all due respect," Dosha objected with all the courage she could muster, "I am a horse person, Comrade General. I can read and I can write, but not enough to qualify as a student. I am an athlete. Horses have been my life. Back in Leningrad I was trained, at our famous Kirov, to work on the performance on horseback to politically significant music. I. . ." and then she proceeded, with heated and passionate words, to sell the program she had equally been forced into, with all the eloquence of a Gypsy selling a spruced-up nag as an expensive horse to an earth-bound farmer at a market.

Raskov pushed back his chair, stood up and pronounced his decision.

"If asked, be what you are, the show-rider Ana Dalova. Meanwhile," he turned to Krematov, "she'll be made to look like one of them, a Finn, a tourist, whatever. Dress her up and turn her loose into the city this afternoon. Let's see what she can do!" And without further explanation General Raskov, Military Attaché to the Russian Embassy, stormed out of the office followed by the two guards.

Krematov stood up, pushed the chair back to where it had stood before, and shrugged. Dosha's understanding of what had unfolded was that she had just been demoted from 'People's Athlete of the USSR' to human bait out in the streets of this gleaming city of the free West.

# 31

# A Crash Course In Spying

In no time at all a female official in her thirties, tall and slender, dressed in a Western style suit and high heels came to fetch Dosha.

"I am Olga Askunov," she saluted the KGB Commandant. "I have come for the briefing and outfitting of Comrade Ana Dalova."

Krematov stepped up to the desk just vacated by General Raskov, and ordered, "Follow Comrade Askunov! Go with her and carefully absorb her instructions."

Olga Askunov's heels reverberated like striking hammers as Dosha followed her down the same corridor that had led her to Raskov's office. Short of the elevator, she ordered Dosha to walk ahead through a narrow doorway and down several stairwells to a landing with a single metal door. There the official stepped ahead of Dosha and opened the metal door to a room that was windowless but starkly lit. *Some kind of bunker,* Dosha shuddered. There was not a hint of sky.

Ceiling-high rolling racks were lined up along three walls. Some contained clothes for both men and women on hangers, others all sorts and sizes of shoes on metal shelves. The fourth wall was covered from floor to ceiling with large mirrors similar to those in the Kirov Ballet Studio. The center of the room was taken up by a large cutting table, framed with a narrow metal frame. It was covered with maps, bags, and with what appeared to be items used for hair. There was a stack of hats as well.

"Step over there," Comrade Askunov ordered, "right in front of the mirror."

Dosha started to shiver. "Is it cold in here?" She asked without looking at Askunov.

"It's the heavy walls," Comrade Askunov replied and stepped close to Dosha. From her right hand she dropped a rolled-up flexible cloth tape to full length. With her eyes on her task, she started to take measurements of Dosha's figure from all sides, before eye-balling her reflection in the mirror. Then, with the expertise of a saleswoman with an eye for size, she selected an armload of garments, which she held, one at a time in front of Dosha's body, before ordering her to change into a summer dress of fine natural cotton with big whirling designs in pale green. The dress had long wide sleeves and buttoned up front like a coat.

"It's a Merimekko," Comrade Askunov said, and in response to Dosha's questioning look, she added, "one of the finest Finnish designers." There was no changing cabin, so Dosha turned her back to the mirror, hastily pulled of her own dress and slipped into what Comrade Askunov was holding out for her.

"It suits you, hein, Comrade Dalova," Askunov stated and for the first time looked into Dosha's face. Her features softened with a smile.

Dosha looked at herself in the mirror. The dress was beautiful in its simplicity. It fell loosely from a buttoned collar down to mid-knees, the soft cotton embraced Dosha's body like flowing water whenever she moved. The official now turned toward one of the shelves lined with shoes.

"Sit over there," she pointed to a metal stool in front of the mirror, while she herself stepped over to the shoe shelving, from where she returned with two boxes of shoes. Dosha pulled off the black heeled shoes Galina had bought her, and took a pair of low-heeled open sandals from the official's hand which she slipped on.

"They fit perfectly," Dosha exclaimed and looked up at the official, who once again was eyeing her in the mirror. For a moment she thought she detected a flicker of pride in Comrade Askunov's matter-of-fact eyes and face.

"Training," she replied, "the best. Get up and walk. Your assignment will require extensive walking,"

Dosha walked back and forth. The sandals not only looked elegant, but felt wonderfully comfortable. She couldn't stop looking at herself, transformed into a *Gadji*, she had to admit of unusual beauty, with her braided hair falling below her shoulder blades.

"It's that hair!" Comrade Asunov said and stepped between Dosha and her mirror image. Grabbing the metal stool with her right hand, Comrade Asunov placed it to Dosha's side and stepped on. She looked into the mirror and said, "Turn sideways!"

Reaching for Dosha's hair, she lifted the heavy braid and held it high as if she were lifting a horse's tail.

"Extraordinary," she stated with matter-of-factness, "the color of it. On the other hand," she dropped the braid, "last thing you want is to stick out in this kind of work." She pulled off the little brown ribbon that held the braid in place and proceeded to unbraid, then rake Dosha's long hair with bony but agile fingers. When the hair was loose, she pulled it tightly to the back of Dosha's head and, twisting the length of it expertly first around her hand, then into a bun, she fastened it with pins to the nape of Dosha's neck.

"There," she stated. "That's how girls your age wear it over here." She climbed off the stool and motioned Dosha to join her at the cutting table. There she picked up an open money purse and briefed Dosha as to the value of the Finnish coins and the paper money it contained. "You will need to take trams," she said, "a bus. It may prove opportune for you to visit a coffee shop for refreshments. You must make every effort not to appear like an outsider. Things are done differently over here," the official looked straight into Dosha's face as she went into detail, instructing her on how and where to pay in a tram, on a bus, in a restaurant or coffee shop," and then there is the capitalist habit of tipping."

The last item of that day's recruitment consisted of the study of the maps spread across the cutting table. First they examined streets and intersections at the center of the city, as well as the names of department stores and smaller shops. On a transportation map, Dosha was instructed to learn by heart the local tram system, with their destinations and various stops. She was then handed a folded pocket map, on which was marked a route in red ink for her to follow, which shops to enter, which parks to visit or cross. It included her drop-off point at the railway station as well as the time and place where a car would pick her up again,

The official placed the folded maps, the purse with money, but no identification papers into a shoulder bag, an item Dosha had not owned before, and placed it around her neck as if she were a mannequin in a window store.

"Now, follow me," she said. The whole training session had taken no more than an hour, and before she knew it, Dosha was being driven in a small, foreign car that looked indistinguishable from the others out in the streets of Helsinki.

No tinted glass this time. Comrade Askunov drove slowly along a park, past a church, into the center of town. Not far from a row of taxis lined up along one side of an enormous railway station built of sand-colored stone, she stopped. She left the motor running.

"This," she said, "is your drop-off point. It's where Comrades Khrushchev and Bulganin will make their official entrance into the Finnish capital three weeks from today. Your assignment today," she added, reaching over to unlock Dosha's side of the car, "is simply to blend in with the general population. Walk around. Get comfortable moving about the city. Don't go in the station but have a café in the bookstore. See what you can see. Follow the route we planned out for you. See if you blend in. Tomorrow we start planning how you make contact with the local youth, specifically how to infiltrate the local student population. That shouldn't be a problem for a girl as pretty as you, should it?"

"What am I looking for?" Dosha asked.

"Raskov has not briefed you?"

Dosha shook her head. "Not precisely."

"Radicals, of course. Objectors! They're festering, as we speak, in the local student population. You will have to find a way to infiltrate, at least get close enough to hear and witness. Meanwhile, I expect to see you, Comrade Dalova, in two hours back here. You'll see my car parked over there." She pointed to a corner diagonally across from the entrance to the railway station.

Dosha climbed out of the car and closed the door. She watched Askunov lean over and heard her click the locking button back down. The car drove off and disappeared into the thin trickle of traffic, back into the direction of the embassy.

*The only thing I have to find,* Dosha swore, *is a way out, a way back to my own people. I will never be your whore or that of anyone in your cursed System.* Besides, for now, for however short a moment, she was free.

Relieved, Dosha took a closer look at the impressive railway station. Her eyes climbed the pairs of muscular giant statues that were holding translucent lanterns to either side of a colossal set of doors. The square-jawed giants were sculpted of the same blocks of sandy stone as the rest of the massive, square structure.

Dosha walked out onto the railway station square. Contrary to her strict directives, she wanted to enter the railway station and have a look around before starting out on her prescribed route. Gypsies liked railway stations. She knew that those who had been forced to relinquish their horses and wagons had easily switched to riding what they called 'the iron horse,' the Siberian Express, visiting distant relatives and markets. Besides, railway stations, at least back in Russia, were packed with masses of *Gadje*, providing the kind of setting where the *romni* together with their children felt safe to offer readings of good fortunes, sell lace to travelers to take along as gifts, as well as flowers, real in summer or made of paper in winter.

She walked up to the massive doors, one of which stood open and peered into the inside. She saw at once that the enormous railway station here in Helsinki served many fewer travelers than those in Russia. Only a few pedestrians were leaving or entering the railway hall. She shouldn't go in. Not, she decided cautiously, when somebody from the Embassy was sure to be watching her, especially on her first day out. It would be somebody like herself, dressed to blend in—or probably several spies—who had been given her picture with instructions to never lose sight of her. *Best to stick to the plan today,* she concluded.

So, eyes ahead, Dosha walked on, trying to look Finnish among the few other pedestrians, whose numbers grew even sparser once she left the station square. Trams stopped along pedestrian islands to let off no more than two or three passengers at most. Few passengers were waiting to get on. Dosha kept to her route along the wide Helsinki avenues. They were sun-drenched under the mid-afternoon sun, but utterly bare of anything green or growing. She saw no queues of people waited anywhere. This white city of the High North felt like an empty stage setting. Raising her eyes to the pale, granite house-fronts, gleaming in the light, she was struck by the absence of hidden arch- or alleyways, of recessed doors or portals. This clean-cut place offered no routes for escape, no easy way to slip in and out. In a place like this a Gypsy like herself felt center stage.

That was only until she reached two parallel tree-shaded avenues. She had studied them on the map, where they were divided by a stretch of green, the Northern and Southern Esplanades. She came however unprepared for the sudden profusion of springtime colors splashed about as if by a painter gone mad within the confinement of all the architectural purity and newness of the city. This stretch of park stood out like an oasis of color in a desert of man-made stone. Here the city came to life. People were strolling, sitting on benches, conversing, although even here the animation of these Northern folks was low-key and discreet.

*Still*, she thought, *aside from the railway station, if I am to find Roma, this is the place,* but among the Finnish populace, all dressed for summer, only three men stood out. They wore black suits and black hats. *Dzut,* she decided: Jews standing in front of an octagonal kiosk reading the front pages of newspapers and announcement posters of coming events.

In Leningrad Dosha had never spotted religious Jews dressed in black. She knew that apparel was considered an expression of their religion and therefore forbidden in the Soviet Republic but back in Belarus and in the hinterlands of Russia where the Lovara had and still traveled, she had seen Orthodox Jews still dressed like these men at the kiosk. Back there they still stuck to their ancient ways, like the Lovara themselves. The Roma used to erect their tents and park their caravans close to the villages of these Jews, the ones they called shtetels. The Gypsies felt safe and welcome there. Furthermore, the music of the Jews was so similar in sound and feeling, that Gypsy and Jewish bands at times exchanged musicians to play at the village weddings *of Gadje,* the ones the Jews called *goyim,* but come night the Jews locked themselves in. They said it was to protect them from sudden outbursts of persecution. For the same Russia that had once loved its Gypsies, had never stopped viciously persecuting its Jews.

*But here,* she thought, *in this white city, the Jews are free to walk openly in their dark clothes.* She had to admit they stuck out. *Just like us Gypsies,* she thought, *whenever we enter the world of Gadje.*

One of the three men turned to watch as she approached the kiosk. His face was very dark. Unlike the men in the *shtetel,* he wore no side-locks—a fact which she would recall only later in the day, for right at the moment she stood stunned by the face of the dancer Vasili staring down at her from a huge color poster. It announced the arrival of the Kirov Ballet and its performance of *Swan Lake.* At once all those feelings she had been trying to smother since her departure from Leningrad ignited like a dying flame in the wind.

For a moment she just stared at the poster. It showed a bare-chested Vasili who held a fragile Valentina with one strong, muscular arm. The Kirov's prima ballerina in her role of the dying swan folded her feathery head gently against his chest. Their closeness raked Dosha with sharp pain. Had the aging icon of Russian Ballet taken possession of the young dancer once again? It was then that Dosha noticed right next to the Kirov poster a smaller poster of horses racing in swallow formation with a powerful

white horse in the lead. The poster announced: In Russian with
Finnish subtitles:

SOVIET EQUESTRIAN OLYMPIC TEAM.
INTRODUCING RUS, ELITE STALLION OF THE USSR.
MEADOWLANDS, SONG OF THE REVOLUTION.
AN EQUESTRIAN FREESTYLE RIDE
AT THE OLYMPIA STADIUM UNDER THE MIDNIGHT SUN.
JUNE 5, 11:30 P.M.

Close to midnight! Dosha gasped, whoever was in charge
had chosen the time, special to all peoples of the High North,
when worshippers of the midnight sun gather to celebrate the
sun's slow descent into an ocean of self-generated fire, a fusion
sending shock-waves of glow and afterglow high into the sky, before falling out of sight beyond the boundless horizon leaving a
twilight of glowing dusk.

The poster made no mention of any rider's name. There would
be no recognition for Dosha, and she shuddered. She knew only
too well that back in the USSR people without recognition could
vanish without a trace. She turned from the image of the horses,
back to the dancer, then to those who were either quietly walking
by or sitting on benches in that space of green and flowers. There
were dogs on leashes, and children playing ball on grassy areas.
The three Jewish men were disappearing down the street.

She reminded herself, once again, that for the time being her
only safety lay in following her prescribed route. That route led
her next to a large department store called Stockman. Here she
was to spend time looking at the window displays before moving on toward a large bookshop called Akateeminen Kirjakauppa,
which she was to enter. The bookshop was several stories high,
and she remembered it had an upstairs café where she was to take
refreshments. This, she had been instructed, would probably be
the easiest place to make contact with university students who
were known to gather there after classes to talk and debate.

But Dosha could not chase the image of Vasili from her mind.
She wondered what kind of fate and strength had allowed him
not only to keep afloat, but to thrive in a system that turned live
human beings into robots. How could she herself possibly survive
if she were unable to flee?

She found that the clean and quiet atmosphere of the streets
she was crossing, the wealth of the clothes, the hats and shoes

displayed in huge store windows only heightened her anxiety at being different and alone in a place more alien than any before. She hurried toward the bookstore like someone seeking shelter.

To her amazement the inside of the building was the size of a GUM department store, with story upon story full of shelves and tables laden with books. Dosha took a stairwell to the second floor where she paused, right by a section labeled FRANÇAIS.

Jano, the husband she had left behind for what seemed so long ago, in reality not even four full seasons, had taught her how to read and write in both the Russian Cyrillic and the Western alphabet. She had believed at the time that the reason Dosha's father had insisted on her learning some French was because Lovara were known to travel and operate in France. Although Jano under the Bolsheviks had left behind the Gypsy ways and had turned into what *Gadje* called an intellectual, Dosha had insisted he teach her mostly the words and phrases a nomadic Gypsy like herself would need to survive in a land such as France: words like *le cheval* for horse, *le marché* for market, *je suis une femme des Lovara*, meaning *I* am a woman of the Lovara.

Jano had been impressed by the ease with which she learned a language, as well as reading and writing, although she had used the Western alphabet mainly for reading the Finnish language to which she was exposed in the encampment of her father Djemo, and not to French, which seemed of no immediate use.

Now she leafed idly through big picture books marked FRANCE. Pictures of cities with big cathedrals like Leningrad's, parks, streets, pedestrians, lots of them, like in Russia, pictures of lush countrysides, valleys, hills, winding streams, but the face of the dancer kept filling her mind as if they were having a clandestine meeting in those green pictures of a far-off country, away from prying eyes. She saw him not the way he looked on the poster, but the way he had looked at her the last time she'd seen him— with longing eyes, with eyes that spoke of a dream, a life in freedom, and maybe, just maybe a life together?

Somebody bumped into her from behind. She turned, a young man in a bright pink shirt took a step back and said "pardon", before hurrying on toward the stairs.

*Must be French*, she thought, and turned back to her pictures and her thoughts.

At the end of her third day "out," as her assignments in the heart of Helsinki were called, Dosha was told to walk back to the embassy by herself, instead of being picked up by Comrade

Askunov at the railway station. So far her schedule had consisted merely of strolling from one to five o'clock, reconnoitering the city in an effort to make contact with the local student population. At five o'clock promptly she was driven back to Porkalla by Krematov in his limousine. So far the Commander had kept his promise, every evening Dosha was reunited with her stallion and slept in the tent beside him.

Every time back in Helsinki, the same female official, Comrade Askunov dressed her with that same eye-balling intensity, each day choosing a different outfit. Each day the outfits grew tighter, as if increasing the lure.

Yet so far Dosha had not managed to attract a single soul, let alone infiltrate the local student body, and now she began to be afraid, for she was certain that if she were to fail at this, the Government could easily scratch her horse event. For which purpose they could invent a variety of last minute causes, such as — the stallion Rus has unfortunately colicked, he broke a leg. The Bolsheviks had deceptive answers for every question up their sleeves.

Dosha felt an attack of all-out fear. However, while still a little girl, the war had taught that fear froze the instincts of survival—fear could kill. So she tried to fight against the invading thoughts, but her senses could not brush aside the impression of unusual listlessness in this first Western city she'd ever known. More and more the quiet reminded her of the empty skies during times of war, in the hours before the fleets of aircraft roared in for an all-out attack, a final battle, when survival on the ground turned into the toss of a dice. Yet nothing could have been more peaceful than her surroundings at that very moment.

She sat on a bench in the rock strewn park called Kaivopuisto, within eyesight of the Soviet Embassy. Trees in the park were in full summer growth, lots of bushes and flowers were in bloom. The almost church-like peacefulness was broken only by the occasional passer-by, walking along well-kept paths, among them again a religious Jew. As he walked by her bench the Jew in his long black overcoat averted his face. He was an old man with a graying, beard, trimmed short. He stopped at some distance away and stood watching gray squirrels scurry back and forth on the grass. He had come prepared too, for she saw that from his coat pocket he withdrew, then threw morsels of bread their way and watched the alert little creatures race away, across the rocks or up a tree, their loot in their mouths.

Dosha smiled. The squirrel, called *roman morga* or Gypsy-cat, was considered a lucky mascot. As if the old man had picked up her thought, he turned in her direction and for the split of a second looked straight into her eyes.

*Khantchi! Papi!* Overcome by relief and joy, Dosha wanted to rush toward her grandfather, hear his voice and feel his closeness but he had already turned his back to her. With deliberate slowness he strolled across the grass toward a clump of birches. There he stopped, touching one of the three, slim, white tree trunks with one hand like an old man steadying himself. He had touched the *patrin* indicating danger. At once she recalled Patrina's warning that she must let Khantchi initiate all contact, or else she could place all fleeing Lovara in danger.

Back in control of her emotions, Dosha rose from the park bench and turned toward the Soviet Embassy, a mere stone's throw away, and from where, more likely than not, several pairs of binoculars were directed straight at her. Her heart was racing. She knew Khantchi's appearance had served the sole purpose of making his presence known. He was sure to pick a spot — perhaps among an anonymous crowd — when he would communicate with her, a place like the park in the center of the divided Esplanadinkatu, or a tram stop. For now she would report back to the embassy and return to the horses in Porkalla for the night.

Just then a low whistle stopped her. It was the kind of whistle a Gypsy uses when trying to catch the attention of a fellow Gypsy in a forest or in a market place. Dosha turned around, thinking it was Khantchi. Instead there stood a young man with brown hair and eyes. He looked neither like the tall, blond Scandinavians nor the small and dark-haired Finns. He was dressed differently from local men, in his white pants and a short-sleeved white shirt open at the neck. To her surprise he came jogging up to her, almost as if he knew her.

He was not much older than Dosha. He stopped in front of her and smiled. She was about to turn and walk away, when he stretched out his hand.

"Akateeminen Kirjakauppa," he raised his voice almost to a shout. "The bookstore! Remember? I saw you at the bookstore!" His Finnish sounded foreign and almost not understandable. "The French section?"

Dosha, still excited about Khantchi's sudden appearance, was caught off guard.

"Remember?" the young man insisted, moving one step closer. "Mademoiselle?"

Her mind raced. Was this the kind of student she was supposed to attract?

"Of course," she smiled at the young man. "I remember now. You were wearing a pink shirt then."

Could I invite you to a *café*?" he asked, eagerly studying her face.

She hesitated, torn between her schedule and this first opportunity. "How about another day," she replied, "I must return home right now."

"Tomorrow then?" He called after her as she started to move away. "What's your name?"

"Ana Dalova." She waved back to him, and hurried on back to the embassy, where the encounter with the young man had not only been observed, but brought straight to the attention of the Military Attaché himself. She had barely stepped into the reception hall of the Soviet Embassy, when a guard led her straight to General Raskov's office.

"Perfect! You have captured the attention of none other than the son of the French Ambassador himself." Raskov beamed at her, "And we have a file on him the size of 'War and Peace'."

"A professed Marxist-Leninist!" added Krematov, seated at Raskov's right, "with links to other radical students at Helsinki University."

"The concept of Marxist-Leninist Communism is nothing but a fad among the corrupt French élite, of course," countered Raskov. "Nothing but fluff."

"Nevertheless, next time out you are to encourage him," Krematov stressed. As usual they left Dosha standing before Raskov's desk. "Furthermore, you don't have to bother to pretend to be any other than yourself. You are half-Finnish, with freedom to roam about in the spirit of our Soviet détente and you will find him taking to a bona fide Soviet like a fish to water."

To her relief there was no mention whatsoever of Khantchi dressed as a Jew. It was at that moment that the picture of that other, the young Jew by the kiosk returned in full clarity to Dosha's mind, no side-locks. He too had been a Gypsy in disguise. Lovara, disguised as Jews! They had kept their eyes on her since her first day out.

# 32

# The French Ambassador's Son

With so many eyes focusing on her comings and goings, Dosha felt like a lone bird released above a field of hunters. It took the son of the French ambassador no time at all to meet up with her again. Finding her in the French section of the Akateeminen Kirjakauppa, the bookstore, he stretched out a hand, and said,

"Jean-Marie de Bonneville-Graves."

The hand Dosha shook was soft and moist with perspiration. She felt an immediate revulsion, but kept her hand in his, and replied,

"Ana Dalova, member of the Soviet Equestrian Team."

The officers at the Soviet Embassy clearly knew the kind of bait he'd take, for when she added the lie that her mother was an early Communist of Finnish descent, and that in the spirit of Soviet détente she was now allowed to explore the country of her mother's origin, and do so freely, the Frenchman became highly agitated and spoke to her in a mixture of Finnish and Russian.

"I admire Marx," he gushed. "I admire Lenin—and how the Soviet Union has managed, at long last, to mobilize the Great Russian masses as no government before."

It took Dosha a while to get used to Jean-Marie's unusual accent and the cadence of his speech in what for him were both foreign languages. What she pieced together in the end was that, although he was the son of a diplomat representing a country that was ruled by members of the "haute bourgeoisie," he himself believed idealistically in the triumph of the Socialist masses over the forces of capitalism and bourgeois escapism.

"I am dying –," he concluded in a whisper and with a choice of words Dosha found prophetic, "to join the young Soviet State. I'm a Communist back in France," he boasted. "There are many of us, back in universities all over France, where young people feel as I do."

Dosha could have told the young fool that, were he to actually carry out such an ill-advised inclination, it would bring him nothing but hunger, hopelessness and barbed wire. But her job was to turn this encounter into an introduction to the alleged frenzied, anti-Soviet activity of the local student population. Therefore, when Jean-Marie started to talk about his fellow students and Finnish friends here at Helsinki University, she murmured enthusiastically, "Oh, I would so much love to meet them, this new generation of my mother's people."

"Now?" Jean-Marie laughed.

"Could you introduce me now?"

"No problem," he said. "Come with me."

He walked ahead of her from the bookstore a short distance along the Mannerheim Avenue to Vanha, "also known as the old student house," he told her. There, taking her hand in his, he climbed a wide flight of steps, where some young people in summer clothing lounged in the sun, reading and talking. Nobody paid attention to Jean-Marie and his new companion as they walked into the building. Still leading her by the hand, he walked along dark corridors, past closed offices, some with doors wide-open but empty, smoke-filled reading rooms and cafeteria-style eating halls. In the two latter, the students mostly stood about in small groups, a few stood alone and some sat on randomly placed chairs. Talking was sparse and intermittent among these students, but they passed bottles and glasses around, and all of them seemed to be smoking. Dosha was struck by the fact that no one spoke to Jean-Marie, or moved to greet him.

"They're not too communicative, not the way we are in France," Jean-Marie told Dosha with a crooked smile. "Instead they drink a lot. It's the long winters, I suppose."

"Where are we going?" she asked, extracting her hand.

"Shsh," he whispered."Wait and see. Here we are." He pushed open a pair of swinging doors and led her into a central lecture hall where a young, blond Finn stood at a podium and was addressing a packed audience.

"The time has come," his voice boomed, "to cut our ties with our oppressive neighbor to the East, and –" he paused—, "line up with the democracies of the West, at last!"

To Dosha's astonishment, this declaration was followed by deafening applause.

"I can't believe it." She turned to her guide, meaning the openness with which the speaker voiced his dissent, but Jean-Marie took her remark another way.

"I know," he whispered close to her ear. "It's so unrealistic. I just wanted you to see this stupid anti-Soviet side. They're of course totally misinformed." Noticing her surprise, he explained further, "You have to understand, these people, and I'm sure you must be aware of this, on account of your mother—these people, the Finns, they came from Inner Mongolia, you know, centuries ago and from the time they got here they've been constantly over-run. From land, by sea –, and always outnumbered.

"What do you learn to do in such a situation?" He kept his eyes on hers. "You ambush, of course, and you negotiate, which was how their elders fought in previous wars when they found themselves cornered. This is probably the first generation to stand up and bare their chest to the enemy. They want," he stressed, "open confrontation—they're asking for it. Of course," he added, leaning close to her ear, "it has turned this tiny nation, here at the end of the world, into a live, political minefield. Foreign diplomats have started to evacuate their families."

"What about you?" Dosha asked. "Aren't you from a diplomatic family?"

"*Moi,*" Jean-Marie stated, "being *majeur,* I told my father that I would stay behind. You must understand that, unlike these young Finns, I am a Communist. I believe in the Communist way of life. I believe in egalitarianism."

*Which is maybe why,* Dosha thought, *his fellow students seem barely to tolerate him.* Those young Finns, she observed, kept him at the fringes like a stray dog trying to join the pack. Nobody addressed him. Some gave Dosha, his new companion, a brief glance and quickly turned away. *These young Finnish men,* she decided, *are not fool enough to get sidetracked by some young female, not at a time when their freedom is hanging by a thin threat. And here I am, supposed to denounce them, gather names.*

The blond young Finn, even before the applause subsided, stepped off the podium and was at once surrounded by fellow students.

"Unfortunately we came in too late," Jean-Marie whispered to Dosha, pulling her back into the empty hallway. "I'm sorry you couldn't hear the whole speech. Problem is, they think of the Hungarians and the Estonians as their linguistic brethren, the only people on the European continent they feel connected to, and that because of what I consider an unfounded theory: common origins. So when, only months ago, the Hungarians demanded to regain their right to self-govern, the Finns' own arch-enemy from the East, your Soviet Union, without a moment's hesitation, sent tanks as a response. The Hungarians got crushed. Yet, if only to make a stand, this new generation of young Finns unwisely wanted to join the Hungarian revolution, a revolution that was doomed from the beginning. Furthermore, these students actually believed that the eyes of the world were upon them. They firmly believed that, this time, the West would come to their aid."

This was Dosha's first exposure to Western youth. *No Gypsy,* she thought, *was ever that young, nor so trusting.* If the student union were a Gypsy camp, a stranger like herself would have stirred up the whole *kumpania* like a flock of geese. The women would have seen to it. They would have poked their way to any hidden truth in seconds. But here, in the darkened student halls and hallways of the University of Helsinki, most of the students barely gave her a glance. Their shouts of "Russak go home!" rose like the foreboding beating of a drum; boom-boom-booming from all sides, reverberating, Dosha feared, right through the heavy stone walls and open windows of the central lecture hall of the old student-house out onto the Mannerheimintie, for all to hear.

*And to think,* Dosha marveled, *all of this unrestrained agitation is taking place right smack in the back yard, so to speak, of the great Union of Soviet Socialist Republics, that giant abuser of power!*

Dosha felt a mounting thrill of excitement, tinged with fear. She knew that Russian Intelligence—the spy-masters, the moles, sources, collaborators, the agents and double-agents, right down to the operatives, including small-time informers like herself—had to be honeycombing every nook and cranny of this gleaming white Finnish capital, looking for just this sort of agitation. The signs weren't hard to find, all Dosha could think was that, if this 'State visit' were to turn into an invasion, these golden youths, hatched by their hard-earned Finnish independence, would be the first to be crushed. The Bolsheviks had created a legal stamp to quash just their kind of "impermissible liberalism." It was engraved into the soul of every Soviet-branded Gypsy man, woman, and child: the notorious article 70 of the Soviet penal code, which condemned all "Anti-Soviet agitation." It would get them stuck in a hole in the ground with a lid on top that would prevent them from ever seeing the sky again.

Upon returning to the embassy, Dosha, knowing that an invisible gun was pointed at her head at all times, had no choice but to report, almost verbatim, all she had heard and seen, to those who held her own fate in their hands. *Forgive me, o'del!* She prayed in anguish, at the same time, cursing the fate that had put her and her horse in the power of these evil forces. There seemed to be no place left for her to withdraw to and regain enough strength to plan her way back to her people. Even when she sat on the back of her stallion, escaping into the work she loved, she found Krematov watching her every move. In his eyes she saw glints of a man who visualizes a woman in the act, naked in his arms.

"About that young Frenchman," he said the morning after her visit to the student house. "Having sex with the young *franzuski* would dry up that well of information for sure. He's young and spoiled. Only an old man," he paused, as if savoring the image, "would come back for more."

Indeed Krematov had intuited the Frenchman's train of thought. The two men's intentions were running along parallel tracks, for the very next day the Frenchman, Jean-Marie, shifted his focus from politics to the personal. He intercepted Dosha before she entered the bookstore. He pulled up to her in the street in a sporty, low-riding, white convertible.

"Hop in," he said. "I am going to show you *la nature*. Out in the country."

Dosha smiled and shook her head. "Not the country," she said. "Not yet," adding a timid smile to give him hope.

'Where to, then?" Jean-Marie asked with gleaming eyes.

"*Le marché*," she said, employing one of the few words she knew in French, "the market in the South Harbor." She was grateful for this unexpected opportunity to escape her Soviet watchdogs for a little while and use the Frenchman for her own purposes, and if all went well....

Jean-Marie leaned over and opened the door of the running car. Dosha climbed into the low seat and Jean-Marie gunned the engine of what he fondly alluded to as his "little British thing." His eyes turned to the road.

*Finally an opportunity to get there,* Dosha exulted, *and what better place to come across local Gypsies than on the marketplace!* Her hair had come undone and was blowing in the wind. She felt young. Krematov would be furious. He would say that driving in a car alone with a man was too high of a risk. But Dosha knew that although words came easily to Jean-Marie, courage with women did not. Should he get any ideas, she'd be able to stop the young pup with a glance.

Right by the open marketplace that spread from the quays of the South Harbor toward a solid line of house fronts, Jean-Marie brought his car to a screeching halt. Lines of canvas-topped stands covered the market square. On wooden and metal tables food and textiles were offered for sale. Boats lay anchored along the ocean side of the quay. On wooden benches the boats displayed fresh fish next to baskets filled with potatoes, onions and apples. Buckets with flowers were placed in between. Bunched in a far corner were a group of what appeared to be minorities with their tents and tables.

Dosha strolled through the market with Jean-Marie, doing her best to disguise her excitement. Selling their wares from within the last anchored boat were three Laps. They wore the red embroidered felt hats that identified them as Sami, although their white cotton shirts were of Western style. Right next to them –"Look at that," Jean-Marie exclaimed, "*des tsiganes*! We have them in our country as well, you know. They're colorful, but a nuisance, really."

Dosha of course had spotted them right away: Gypsies in front of a bright orange tent with closed sides. Three grandmothers were exhibiting lace on a flat cart. More lace was thrown over a baby carriage. The older women were wearing lace collars below and above their sweaters, and they held lace pillows in their hands. They wore colorful skirts, and despite the warm weather, their sweaters were buttoned down to their ample hips. They smiled at the passers-by, all the while talking and laughing among themselves.

Dosha's heart sank. There was no sign of Khantchi. Of course, Lovari *rom* never sold wares in marketplaces, but sometimes they accompanied their *romni*. Lovari *rom* sold horses, and that activity — from the trip to the marketplace to the handshake that clinched the deal — was wrapped in strict and ancient rituals. Besides, Patrina had informed Dosha back in Leningrad that, these days, Khantchi was trading, not horses, but secrets of the new regime, information they did not want leaked to the West. The Soviets were intent on his capture. They knew he crossed this border at will. Khantchi would avoid the company of Gypsies out in the open, as must she. Still, Dosha had hoped against hope to catch a glimpse of him, albeit in disguise.

Jean-Marie must have guessed at her distress, for his hand,

cool and clammy, now touched her bare arm to comfort her and remained there, lightly, tentative. "We call them *voleurs de poulet*, chicken thieves, you know," he whispered. "They are parasites, really. The Germans, of course, believe they are born with criminality in their blood, another one of those theories of theirs."

For a moment Dosha nailed the Frenchman's shifty eyes into place, watching them grow expectant. *If this Gadje knew he is touching* tzigani *flesh*, she wondered, *would his hand shoot away as if he had touched the burning coals of hell?* The Gypsies themselves never tried to enlighten outsiders as to the true nature of their lives. They preferred to protect and keep pure their traditions and the life in freedom that they cherished above all else.

*Prejudice*, Dosha decided, looking into the Frenchman's questioning eyes, *is like a solid wall preventing entry to the mind. It will force all independent thought to halt and stay outside and we Gypsies are no different.*

For a moment she remembered the touch of that other *Gadje*, the dancer Vasili. He sprung to her mind so vividly that she could almost feel his presence and once again, she thought of Russia, the vast country that she and her people had crossed and loved, the country she was trying to leave behind. *And that only if I am lucky*, she thought.

"Would you like to go somewhere else now?" The Frenchman asked, at last dropping his hand.

"I must get be back to the embassy early today," she said. The words came out sharper and colder than she had intended them to. "Look for me by the Esplanadinkatu, tomorrow," she added in a softer tone.

It was a lie. Krematov had told her that morning that the horses were about to be moved from Porkalla closer to the 'Olympiastadion' on the outskirts of Helsinki, where training would intensify, from now on with live music from the Red Army Choir. "As of the end of today," he had told Dosha before dropping her off at the embassy, "Your work as an infiltrator and street agent will be suspended."

Lingering for just a moment longer with the Frenchman, whose eyes were not leaving her, Dosha was grateful that most of what he had divulged was information of himself; he'd passed along almost nothing of value about his fellow students. She had come away with descriptions of the students involved, bits and pieces of speeches she had witnessed, descriptions of the radicals delivering those speeches. They could have fit hundreds of other students—but no names, only words.

Strangely, the embassy officials hadn't pressed her for more, and she had not pushed the issue. In the case of the Frenchman, she expected that back at the Embassy they would wait for the right moment to exploit his misguided ideology in some way and use his connections, whereas the lack of previous results on her part could still put a noose around her own neck. *As soon as the State Visit, or whatever it will turn out to be, is over. If not –,* the thought trapped her breath—, *before.*

Dosha wondered, not for the first time, how many others from the equestrian team had been recruited as street agents, informers on their host country. Certainly no one had alluded to any secondary duties. In fact, any exchange of information other than about problems directly related to the training of the team was strictly forbidden among fellow comrades, especially while abroad.

"I must go," she told Jean-Marie, taking a deep breath, "I am needed early today at the embassy." With a short wave of goodbye, she walked past Jean-Marie's fancy open sports car and, striding briskly, took the coastal road back toward the embassy. Before she turned a corner, she looked back. The car was gone. He must have driven off in the opposite direction.

# 33
# Helsinki's Olympic Stadium

By sunrise the next morning, the convoy was on the move. The vans carrying the horses and their equipment had already pulled out of the former Soviet military base on the Porkkala peninsula. The riders and other personnel, assigned to trucks and limousines, were just starting to leave when Dosha heard a loud noise coming from the sky. Looking up she saw, like birds descending upon a dump, two, three, five helicopters heading toward the meadow of the camp. They landed midfield and stopped their engines.

In their wake a flock of men on motorcycles and in small armored cars swarmed the field. Men leading muzzled dogs spilled out of the cars and spread out among the tents just vacated by the equestrian team.

*A field for sport is turning back into a field for war,* Dosha surmised. The Soviets appeared to be taking over once again, even though no Red star identified them as such. Men and vehicles alike were decked out in anonymous camouflage.

Dosha was sitting to Krematov's right next to the window, with Osap Tossuk on Krematov's left. Their limousine made up the tail end of the convoy of trucks and cars. As Dosha's eyes swerved back from the field to the road ahead, where the horse vans had already moved out of sight and hopefully out of earshot, she realized that Krematov had been watching her watching. She knew that undue curiosity was regarded as suspect in a Soviet citizen, especially one screened to travel abroad. But instead of reprimanding her, Krematov spoke sharply to Osap.

"Comrades Khruchchev and Bulganin are scheduled to arrive only eight days from now," he said, "so the time to intensify your training is now. From this point on I will be preoccupied by increased duties at the embassy. As of today, I am putting you in

302

full charge of the equestrian team. Much depends on your performance, Comrade Tossuk!"

The cold and formal tone of his voice left no doubt as to the consequences should Tossuk deliver anything less than a flawless performance.

As Krematov leaned forward and ordered the driver to move to the front of the convoy, Dosha shot a glance at Osap. He sat frozen like a man condemned.

"As for you, Comrade Dalova" — Krematov leaned back, his body unnecessarily close to hers "it would be wise to focus strictly on your horse and on your performance from now on. That goes for all the equestrians. You are to absent yourself from your quarters only when summoned by the embassy to attend special occasions, such as performances put on by our various cultural groups. They are arriving in the Finnish capital as we speak."

Dosha said nothing in reply. *However*, she thought, *if this is the first stage of my flight to freedom, it feels more like a trip to the gallows.*

Once again her mind leapt to the dancer, Vasili. Would he know her if he saw her at the theater? What about Larkin? Would he be in Helsinki? Or had his exit visa been withdrawn at the last minute, like that of Hissen, the Gypsy groom?

The journey continued in unbroken silence. The driver followed the customary route from Porkkala toward the Finnish capital, only this time he skirted the western edge of the city. After crossing Mannerheimintie, the limousine approached a curving white structure with harmonious lines. A tall white tower rose from the center of its outer walls like a sharp needle toward the sky.

"Their Olympic Stadium," Krematov informed Osap. "And that" — he turned to Dosha, pointing out the dark granite statue of a naked male runner, caught midstride atop a gigantic white pedestal — "is modeled after a famous Finnish runner, I'm told, although I can't think of his name."

Dosha felt herself blush. Was there some significance to the fact that he had pointed out the naked male statue to her and not to Osap? Her skin crawled when, on the pretext of pointing out the statue, he leaned toward her, placing his other hand on her leg. She nervously shifted away from him, keeping her eyes directed to the outside.

Krematov pretended to take no notice of her obvious discomfiture. He turned his attention back to Osap. "As you will discover," he said, "the barracks are located within riding distance, to facilitate your daily drills."

Driving eastward, they entered what appeared to be a combination nature preserve, amusement park, and open-air theatre. A dirt road led away from this open area into dense woods. After a short distance, they came upon another clearing, this one with a row of bungalows and a row of horse stalls arranged in an L shape.

"Cavalry barracks," Krematov explained, "vacated for us compliments of the Finnish government—horse barns and all."

Two transport trucks that Dosha had not seen before had pulled in just ahead of the limousine. As Soviet soldiers rose from wooden benches in the truck beds and jumped to the ground, others began removing musical instruments and passing them down. She surmised that these were the musicians of the Red Army Choir.

Krematov looked them over as he climbed out of the limousine. He turned back toward Osap. "They will accompany you every day, Comrade Tussok, traveling to the stadium by truck," he informed his new first-in-command. "From now on, every drill is to be a full dress rehearsal, complete with music. However" — and now his eyes slid from Osap to the girl — "your interaction with the musicians, as with any of the other cultural groups, is to be restricted to professional matters. There is to be no personal contact whatsoever between the separate and distinct groups representing our Soviet government abroad. Is that understood?"

Dosha needed no reminder that the System liked to keep its citizens — even those not yet confined to the vast prison and gulag system — in line by sowing fear and enforcing isolation. Krematov had raised those mental prison bars around both herself and Osap. She knew that Osap, now that he was in charge, would be subjected to heightened stress.

To Dosha's surprise, however, as soon as Osap was on his own, instead of assuming the dictatorial stance of a now high-ranking member of the supervisory staff, he began to address the members of the equestrian team with the voice of a caring father. Dosha wondered whether this was because, as a horseman, he knew that instilling fear in his riders would only result in their horses executing wooden movements. Or was he experiencing the relief a man feels when he has nothing left to lose?

From then on, every morning right up to the night of the

performance, the orchestra and singers of the Red Army Choir were transported in two unmarked trucks to the back entrance of the Olympic Stadium. The riders followed on horseback, along a bridle path that cut through the woods.

The upcoming horse event was widely publicized. Dosha hoped that Khantchi had his own spies tracking her every move. Still, out of habit, and in accordance with time-honored custom, she would have liked to use *patrins* to indicate to her tribe her comings and goings, and the degree of danger lurking in this hostile territory, but when she tried to drop back and ride singly in the rear, telling Osap, "You know how that stallion is likely to bolt," Osap agreed, but insisted on riding right next to her. So she had no choice but to place her trust fully in her grandfather's inventiveness.

"Last time I was here," Osap told her as they rode for the first time side by side to the stadium, "I wore the uniform of a Soviet soldier. It was during the war. They fought like Tartars, those Finns did. You've got to admire them for their guts. They must have known they would lose in the end but before all was lost, they negotiated for their independence. The costs were high. The defeated Finns were still paying exorbitant war debts to our Soviet Union when they decided to invite the world to Helsinki for the 1952 Olympic Games, four years ago. That's when they built the stadium. It's truly a symbol of their fierce determination to remain free."

Dosha was astonished that Osap would talk to her so freely about political events. It could endanger them both. They continued in silence to the back entrance of the stadium. Its double metal gates stood open, in expectation of the team's arrival. The riders ahead of them rode without hesitation through a long, tunnel-like cement passageway that led to the open arena at the other end. Only Dosha halted, holding her stallion back. Osap looked at her with obvious concern.

"What now?" he asked in soft voice. "What's frightening you?"

Dosha had underestimated Osap. Wasn't he after all a nomad by origin like herself? Underneath his submissive official behavior he, too, must experience an instinctive fear of closed-in spaces. For Dosha, a Gypsy, having to ride through a dark tunnel into a wide open arena, visible at the other end, with tiers of seats rising like the slanting walls of a fortress high into the air, knowing that during the actual exhibition all doors and gates would be sealed off, brought forth that age-old, instinctive fear of being trapped like a crab in a barrel. She couldn't breathe. The stallion, feeling her distress, started to snort and tighten up.

"Come now," Osap whispered. "There's nothing around us, no threat, at least not right now. There's only woods. Besides, this whole area has been carefully secured. Nothing can happen to you, I promise. After the ride I'll hold your horse, and you can go climb that tower and see for yourself, okay?"

With her heart in her mouth, Dosha urged the stallion through the tunnel and into the arena, where the musicians were already tuning their instruments. Once there, she walked the stallion around the perimeter. It took a long time, though, before she had herself in hand, such was her fear of being trapped.

Then the practice began, and she forgot everything but the performance. Once again she became one with her horse as they wove through the carefully choreographed patterns of their free-style exhibition ride.

True to his word, after completing their first full program to music—with much stopping to fine-tune movements—Osap dismissed the team.

"Ride ahead back to the barracks," he told them. "I'll give you further instructions there. Ana, stay." He motioned for Dosha to dismount and took her stallion's reins. "Go on," he urged her. "Go up the tower. Look for yourself."

From the opposite side of the stadium a maintenance crew entered, carrying rakes; they were followed by a large, red tractor, dragging a tine rake. With a backward glance at Osap holding the stallion's reins, Dosha strode hurriedly across the arena. She opened a low wooden gate onto a passageway that lead between two tiers of seats toward the stadium tower.

A man from the maintenance crew approached her, and when she pointed wordlessly to the tower, he led her to the elevator and held it open for her. Once inside, she pressed the button for the very top, where she stepped out onto a platform affording a magnificent view of the city and coastal islands.

The land around them was mostly covered by dense, dark-green forest. Toward the east she recognized, carved into the forest, the amusement park with its open-air theatre and its fenced-in arenas for rides and carousels. It was a larger version of those she'd known in the remote areas of Russia's High North, where she and her circus companions used to perform during the summer

306

months. Her heart stood still: Here, too, at the very edge of the amusement park, spread out in a wide half-circle, stood a caravan of covered Gypsy wagons. They were so close to the cavalry barracks that she suddenly understood why, late at night in the barracks, she'd sometimes awakened to what sounded like the yapping of the half-wild dogs that accompany Gypsies of all tribes. Falling back asleep, exhausted by the day's drills, she'd dismissed the noise as just a wishful dream.

Now there was no doubt in her mind, the presence of the wagons was no coincidence. Khantchi had found her. He had moved close by. He was waiting for the right moment to connect with her.

Dosha's heart raced with excitement. She took the elevator back down and had started toward Osap and her stallion when another, older, portly maintenance man approached her. In an instant she recognized that walk, the energetic step.

"Khantchi," she whispered in disbelief. "You're working for the Finns!"

"Some of these guys are actually agents," he whispered, nodding in the direction of the maintenance crew, busy raking in the wake of the tractor. He had blocked Dosha's path and now held out one hand as if indicating where she should walk to avoid disturbing the area already raked.

"We made a deal, the Finns and I," he murmured in Romani, "Soviet secrets in exchange for tickets to freedom—for both you and me."

"But they're holding my horse hostage," she whispered. "I need to get him out, too."

"That's why we're splitting the escape in two," Khantchi said.

"How?"

"You've got to buy an accomplice on the inside," he whispered, again indicating the path she should take, in case they were being observed. "What about the man who's holding your horse? Isn't he the one who allowed you to come out here alone?"

"Osap."

"Where's he from?"

"He's a Tartar."

"Crimean?"

"I suppose so."

"Old enough to have been in the war?"

"Yes."

"Perfect," Khantchi said. "When the Tartars returned home

after fighting in the war, Stalin had trainloads of them deported as traitors. Many perished—women, children, old men and women. Ask him what he'd want in exchange."

Up until that moment, Dosha had looked upon Osap as one of her jailers. Now, in retrospect, she realized that his behavior toward her had changed over the past few months. He had become protective of her and the stallion.

Dosha stared at Khantchi, her mouth open in surprise.

He winked and turned on his heel, hailing the other maintenance men as if returning to supervise their work.

Back at the barracks, Dosha had just started to hose off the sweaty stallion when Osap walked by.

"Can I speak to you?" she asked in a low tone, and when he paused, she nodded toward the other riders who stood laughing and talking nearby "Alone?" she whispered.

After she had rubbed the stallion and settled him in his stall with an armload of hay, she went to find the trainer. He was leaning against a tree, smoking a cigarette while observing the horses being walked and washed. His slanted eyes took her in with speculative interest.

"I have a question," she said.

"What is it?"

"It's private. Personal."

"All right." Osap took his cigarette out of his mouth, and kept it between two fingers by his thigh.

"What would it take to have you help me and the horse escape?" she asked in a low tone of voice.

Without a moment's hesitation he answered, "A Gypsy wife."

Dosha was caught off-guard. "Gypsy women don't marry non-Gypsies," she whispered, aghast.

"I may be *Gadje*," Osap answered, unperturbed, "but I grew up a nomad and as such I can turn out a horse as well as any *rom*. I am not asking for a virgin, either," he continued in a calm voice. "In fact, I'd love a woman with children, one not too old, one with small children, I mean. Besides," he raised his cigarette back to his lips, and took a puff, "if I stay with the Soviets, whether we succeed or not, I'm eventually doomed, as are you. The only a question is, when. So, since you came to me," he turned and for a long minute stared straight into Dosha's face—"how will you carry it off, this escape?"

"I don't know yet."

"The man I saw you talking to in the arena?"

She flushed. It wouldn't do to hand Khantchi over to Osap, not yet. She shook her head. "I'll figure out a way. But I'll need your help."

That help came in an unexpectedly inventive way during their next training session in the stadium. The maintenance workers were in the bleachers, repairing seats. "Comrade Dalova," Osap ordered, "please use your Finnish to instruct the crew to delay the tine-raking of the arena by one hour, from now."

Dosha calmly walked her horse over toward the maintenance crew. Khantchi at once came clambering down from the upper tier of seats. "Officially I'm to ask you to postpone the tine-raking with the tractor by one hour from now on," she said, adding under her breath, "He wants a Gypsy wife."

The news took Khantchi by surprise. "What does he know about Gypsies?" he asked.

"He somehow figured out that that's what I am. He dropped a Romani word the first day they took me and the stallion. I ignored what I thought might be bait, hoping it was some random word he'd picked up but I figured there must have been some connection sometime, somewhere. He even brought in two *roms* to work with the horses under his care."

"He'll get his wife," Khantchi answered after a pause. "She'll have to be Kaale, a *romni* from here. The Tartar won't know the difference."

"You want to meet him?"

"Not now, not till the escape."

"How will it take place?" Dosha asked.

He answered without looking at her, his voice so soft that she had to lean forward to hear him. "It will be after your performance. All you have to know is to follow whatever Roma are there, whenever they leave. Remember, the timing has to be exact: you must not hesitate."

"But what if –?" At that moment, she became aware that the stallion had calmly stretched his neck toward Khantchi's face and was about to nuzzle him in recognition. She quickly lifted the reins and gently, with her seat and legs, started to pivot the stallion back toward the group of riders. Osap stood there, arms akimbo, as if eager to get his reply and get on with the drills.

"Tell him," Khantchi called after her in Finnish, "he'll have his extra hour before we start to rake."

So the lengthening Arctic summer days — their fleeting nights set aglow by the rising midnight sun — moved close and closer to that first Friday in June. No one at the barracks openly transgressed the rule of no communication between the different Soviet cultural and sports groups. Only professional matters concerning joint performances, as was the case with riders and the Red Army Choir, were allowed. However, tongues wagged and rumors flew nonetheless. Dosha learned that the Kirov Ballet had arrived in Helsinki on the same train as the Red Army Choir.

Three days were left before the arrival of Comrade Khrushchev. The team was only two days away from their exhibition ride. The tension among the athletes was palpable. Their fear of failure was reflected in the increased jumpiness of the horses. The Finns they met as they rode their skittish horses through the recreational area from the stables to the stadium glared at them with ill-suppressed hostility, as if they were intruders, unwanted enemies on their soil, although so far only the Soviet cultural artillery had besieged the city.

In prominent first place of the Soviet cultural barrage was Leningrad's Kirov Ballet performing Tchaikovsky's *Swan Lake*, a trusted staple of the Soviet propaganda machine. "The most likely performance to capture the minds and hearts of this nation of lumberjacks and peasants," Comrade Krematov murmured into Dosha's ear as they drove in his limousine to the Helsinki Opera House. He had ordered the whole equestrian team to attend the Kirov's opening-night performance, but only Dosha was asked to go as his personal guest.

In the Opera House Dosha found herself once again in one of the rows reserved for high Soviet officials. This time she sat wedged between Comrade Krematov and General Raskov. It was the latter who pulled her attention from Krematov.

"This venue, Ana," Raskov leaned toward her, pronouncing her name as if it were a caress, "here in Helsinki, provides exposure for our rising young stars, such as Vasili Kutunov. He's a great talent, to be sure. On the other hand," he whispered with almost paternal confidentiality, "he unfortunately happens to be the son of a poet who turned enemy of the people. There were some who said we should not bring him to Helsinki. Instead he is under constant surveillance. He will be a hit—just watch. He dances the part of the prince. You'll be amazed by his leaps."

When Vasili, in the very first scene, walked onto the stage with springy steps and open arms as if to embrace the audience, Dosha was struck once again by how he stood out among the others. He had an aura of brilliance, of ease, of genius. *Shukar*, she thought—*beautiful, in mind and body*, and however forbidden the thought was for a Lovari *romni*, she had to admit that she had been waiting to catch a glimpse of him, was waiting impatiently to see him perform. Yet even before Vasili started to dance, Dosha knew this was an even more polished version of the man she had left behind in Leningrad.

The public was on the edge of their seats as he danced the role of Prince Siegfried, paired with Valentina Kruglov, lifting and enhancing the performance of that world famous icon of Russian ballet, in her famous double-role as Odette/Odile. Like hers, his performance was flawless, but he seemed to have grown wings: his body flew up with breath-taking leaps and twists, as if his energy were feeding on itself. Dosha was enraptured and when their eyes linked ever so briefly during his last curtain call, amidst thunderous applause, what Dosha read in those glittering eyes was the purest form of ecstasy and passion.

The headlines in Helsinki's major newspaper the next day extravagantly praised Vasili and the entire star-studded cast. "Our Soviet ballet," Krematov informed the equestrian team next morning, "is a triumph of art and a propaganda coup for the motherland." The Kirov's triumph was followed the next night at Helsinki's National Theatre by a performance of the Red Army Choir. Soviet voices trained to sound like those of Russia's former peasants and serfs. Their voices lifted like twirling mists from imagined endless plains, escaping the bonds of earthbound heaviness and exploitation to unite and soar like birds of beauty in glorious harmony.

To keep the momentum of this cultural siege going, the ordinarily secretive Soviet Embassy flung open its gates to receive foreign dignitaries and diplomats. The marble reception halls offered a taste of prerevolutionary Russian hospitality: tables were laden with Beluga caviar, sturgeon in aspic, roasted baby pigs bearing apples in their gaping mouths. Vodka and Champagne—a Russian version of France's Champagne—flowed like fountains in a royal court and the feasting was accompanied by Don Cossacks all wound up, singing and madly kicking their booted heels while balanced on their haunches or catapulting up like pogo-sticks to perform splits in mid-air.

However, Dosha knew how to read an audience. What all Roma had in common, beyond the professions that divided them into tribes, was the gift of music and dance. The Lovara counted among their own many famous dancers and musicians. It didn't take Dosha long to realize that, with the exception of Vasili's dance, what she was witnessing in Helsinki was nothing but the usual museum pieces of what had once been the expression of Russia's soul and spirit. A rehashing of what was gone forever.

Furthermore, she suspected that the foreign invitees were well aware that, although the Russian swans still flapped their wings and died with great perfection, for the most part the dancers' feet were frozen to the lake, and, when in response to a standing ovation, the comrades from the Red Army Choir threw in "Granada" for an encore, and the lead singer put so much yearning into the rendering of the one non-Russian song in the show, Dosha doubted that anybody could help noticing the choristers' ill fitting uniforms, the purely rehearsed past. It was clear for anyone to see: These comrades had been singing from behind invisible but clearly defined bars, just as it was obvious that all the abundance of food and drink at the embassy was off limits to the sweating Cossacks, servants of the State. And no Finn joined in the dancing.

"They're not the dancing type, you know," General Raskov told Dosha, trying to explain away the awkward diffidence of the assembled guests at the embassy. He took her arm in a fatherly fashion. "Besides," he added, "in a land of endless winters and darkness, booze not only paves the road to oblivion, for many it's the only form of entertainment they know. And oddly enough," he added, laughing, "it doesn't seem to lift their spirits — unlike us Russians!"

To Dosha that evening, the unusual sobriety displayed by the Finns and their Western allies alike stood out like a united front.

# 34
# Under The Midnight Sun

The Finnish Ministry of the Interior received information and Russian intelligence confirmed it, that a group of Czarist fanatics, not only alive but thriving on this side of the Iron Curtain, were going to form a human pyramid around the statue of Czar Alexander II in the Senate Square. Their plan was to shout, in unison, 'Long live the Czar!" at the very moment the Soviet delegation's motorcade was scheduled to pass by. Some reports included the possible presence of hand grenades and bombs.

As far as tiny and beleaguered Finland was concerned, still forced, although not publicly, to follow many dictates of its powerful neighbor, this was the kind of hare-brained eccentricity it could do without. Besides, in these times of national threat, there were limits to the tolerance that even the purest of democracies could muster. To the eyes of the Finns, these fallen Russian aristocrats who had come through the revolution alive but mostly broke, although tolerated in their midst, were merely the sons and daughters of previous generations of usurpers. They were and always would remain Russian, first and foremost, and as such, these exiles were treading on thin ice.

However, the threat of sabotage, ludicrous and weak as it was, served as a further wake-up call for a population already on high alert. Dissension and disapproval of the Russian visit began to spread to the general population. Their Finnish leaders had never considered the possibility of any type of interference of their plan of action from within their own borders, a plan that had been adopted by consensus of its freely elected leadership. Let alone the possibility of demonstrations of protest by their own youth against the official position of their tiny nation surrounded on all sides by forces that far exceeded their own military capacity.

Finns and Russians were old adversaries in the deadly game of war and peace. The Finns, experts in confronting armies many times the size of their own, had learned it was best to wait for the enemy to make a wrong move first.

To limit the stage for such unforeseen yet possible terrorist action on the part of Finland's own citizenry, the Finnish Minister of the Interior issued an immediate change of plans. The speeches by high officials of both countries to the Finnish people were now to be confined to the inside and to the front of the railway station, where the delegation was due to arrive. In addition, the final Soviet performance, the free-style equestrian event, was shifted at the last minute from the Olympic Stadium, perceived as too confined a target, to a large open field in that same, highly secured, green zone on the outskirts of the city, making it less of a confined target. The area of the performance would be further protected by a cordon of Finish security guards in civilian clothing.

No stage-setting could have done more justice to the spirit of the horses and the chosen program than that particular meadow. Without visible boundaries it stretched like a flat plain toward the skyline of Helsinki, outlined white and stark against a deepening orange midnight sky. No trees, no shrubs — just wide-open space rippling softly with tall meadow grass and all of it flooded by the light of the blazing midnight sun.

A crowd of several thousand milled about in small groups. The mood of the crowd appeared somber and subdued, as if they were awaiting a service honoring fallen heroes, rather than what Finns usually engage in at this time of year, to gather for an almost daily celebration of the midnight sun and there was no escaping the magic and the spell cast by the flaming light, it had the presence of a pagan god.

A big, bright green tractor with a raised front-end loader, also bright green, chugged back and forth with a steady rumble. In wide swaths, it mowed a gigantic square at the city side of the open field. A group of Finnish soldiers, carrying waist-high white metal stakes and a roll of yellow cord, proceeded to rope off a performance arena in the shape of a half-moon, open to the side whence the horses would arrive.

Its mowing completed, the tractor drove off toward two Soviet personnel transport trucks parked at some distance. There the tractor lowered its mower-deck and its front-end loader down to the ground. The engine stopped.

At once, like a choir liberated of its soloist, the pulsating humming and buzzing and chirping of cloud after cloud of insects rose to deafening heights. The infamous Finnish midge was at the height of its life-cycle and maybe in part to escape their unrelenting attacks, maybe out of caution for not knowing what exactly to expect, the much put-upon crowd — they had kept stepping back to allow the tractor to do its job unhindered — now moved out of the tall grass and closer to the yellow rope and mowed area, all the while maintaining their clear divisions into groups.

Liveliest among them were the Czarists in exile. They spoke a Russian no longer heard in the Soviet Union, one sprinkled with French and German expressions. They had placed mosquito netting over their hats, hair, and faces. Their voices sounded high, their laughter defiant and out of place. Most of them had belonged to what had been the lower aristocracy. The upper aristocracy, with money in Swiss bank accounts, had chosen exile in more cosmopolitan centers, such as London or Paris, often with summer places overlooking the Mediterranean Sea. It was however, the lesser aristocracy who had contributed the greater numbers of officers fighting the Reds. It was they who now had nothing left to lose and therefore posed the greatest threat of terrorism.

Near them stood a group of haughty-looking diplomats, representatives of various embassies. They milled about with cocktails in their hands, provided by staff members of the Soviet Embassy, the host of the event.

Then there were the various groups of Finns. Not talkative by nature, even when drunk, they remained quietly wherever they happened to stand without much moving about, except to shift position, fold and unfold their arms, or swat bugs here and there. They had brought their children, who ran about some, never straying far. No mosquito netting in that group: dressed in short-sleeved shirts, they seemed to endure the bug attack stoically. They were tough customers, these Finns were, and the Reds knew it.

Even one of their minorities had come to watch the much-advertised equestrian event: a band of Gypsies. They were Finnish Kaale — dressed in festive clothing. The women wore wide ornate skirts and V-necked lace blouses displaying their gold jewelry. The men, wrapped in cigarette smoke, stood apart from the women and children. They wore puffy white shirts under black vests, and loose black pants stuck into knee-high black leather boots. Here as elsewhere, the Gypsies kept themselves separate and apart, they stood, loosely dispersed, along the side of the tall grass and their children, which was unusual, stuck close to their parents and elders.

Several Soviet soldiers jumped from the cabs of the two army personnel trucks parked near the tractor and started to roll back green tarps from green metal hoops covering the flatbeds of the trucks. The flatbed of the first truck held ten musicians seated with instruments across from one each other on long wooden benches; the second had transported two rows of ten singers each. Musicians and singers alike were dressed in Red Army uniforms. They remained seated as the trucks now drove slowly closer to the open side of the spectator area. The rolling vehicles dispersed several groups of young girls in folkloric dresses and wreaths of white daisies in their straight long hair. Performances of ancient Finnish dances and songs to celebrate the midnight sun had been planned long before their invasive neighbor had chosen to violate that sacred moment with a program of their own.

The young Finnish dancers, who had been sitting in circles in the grass, at the approach of the two trucks, jumped up and for a moment swarmed about like stirred up butterflies, freshly hatched, before settling back into clusters, heightening the dreamlike texture of that scene, where the pagan power of the midnight sun dwarfed all other life.

Cultural events from the Soviets had been imposed upon the Finns ever since the establishment of "friendly cooperation" between the two countries. However, this was to be the Finns' first exposure to Russian horsemanship since the Bolshevik Revolution. The Finns understood that it was in their best interest to attend. Nobody knew what to expect: whether this would turn out to be yet another moth-eaten performance brought back to life from the distant and dead past - dressage ridden by the military with their stiff grenadier seats, or acrobats doing some old-hat circus trick. Nobody knew. Nobody cared. The Finns in the crowd wanted the performance to be over with. Get the Red bastards out of there. Have life return back to normal. Enjoy the light, while it lasted before darkness once again returns the land of the High North into its protracted sleep.

Suddenly from the benches that lined the two Soviet flatbeds two conductors, in uniform like their musicians, stood up tall. There was one in each of the two army trucks, one for the musicians, one for the singers. Their heads stuck out above the uncovered metal hoops. They raised their batons high, for all to see. All conversation stopped, followed by, ever so faintly at first, the clapping of spoons imitating the sound of hoof beats approaching from the distance.

The cry of a single violin, followed by the whole orchestra, was soon joined by the voices of the choir, softly mingling with the da-da-da-da-da of spoons-playing, swelling in volume, like the wind of an approaching storm, feeding on itself, gaining momentum.

Meadowlands! It was the song born of war and revolution! The Czarists, stilled by memory, froze in place. This was the song that had turned into the heartbeat of the Revolution that had overrun their world; a symbol of the forces of upheaval that had ripped their ancient world off its deep rooted foundations. Mesmerized, they stared into the open distance, from whence the sound approached—for real this time — of galloping hoofs. The music swelled and billowed as, like specters of the past, a stretch of horses — seemingly rider-less — moved neck to neck, their heads rising and falling to the rhythm of their speed, racing like freedom reborn across the open field.

Little by little, a single horse, rose-gray, its white mane and tail catching the burning light, moved to the fore, swallowing ground. The rest of the galloping herd, both light and dark, spread out loosely behind the lead horse in the V-formation of migrating geese. The herd swayed lithely back and forth, as if sailing the waves of the wind.

As it neared the crowd, the V-formation tightened. Files closed behind the rose-gray horse, crashing through the music as they approached the roped off area like a spear. Instinctively, the crowd shifted, scampered out of the way, in case there was no stopping the onslaught of the stampede.

The lead horse came to a sliding halt. Dosha could feel his hindquarters tuck way under her. Sod flew. The music stopped as if by the flip of a wrist. At once the rest of the herd fanned out to both sides of the rose-gray stallion, and the other riders, wearing white Cossack fur caps and each dressed in the color of his horse, lifted their faces out of their horse's mane and sat up straight.

There were twenty-three horses in all: three massive light grays at the center, flanked on either side by ten chestnuts of medium size. *Red and white*, Dosha wanted to shout, *hardly an oversight on the part of those in charge of Soviet propaganda, with the Reds in the majority.*

Presenting. . ." a loudspeaker blasted from one of the trucks: "three elite stallions and twenty international dressage horses of the Soviet Union of Socialist Republics!" The announcement

317

was repeated in Finnish, in Swedish, and—diplomatically — in Russian last. The announcement was followed by silence. The music had stopped a while back. Nothing but the sporadic clinking of bridles, the swooshing of tails, and snorting through still flaring nostrils of the beasts; their eyes rolling wildly after a chase cut short at its height.

"Especially presenting..." — the loudspeakers flared up again, this time in Finnish only — "making his first appearance in the West, the Soviet Elite Stallion, Rus."

The magnificent stallion, though only slightly taller than his two companions, dwarfed them through the awe-inspiring spirit of his presence. Of perfect dimension: the deep chest, the strong legs, the fine head, rose-gray rather than white. *If anyone among you knows horses*, Dosha prayed and hoped, *it's the Soviet brand that you should take issue with.*

Even the assembled spectators with no knowledge whatsoever of horseflesh, might question whether a horse like this could possibly have risen from the ashes of a revolution that had fed on its horses. The Czarists, once owners of Russia's finest horses drew closer to each other. Russia had her many breeds: the Tersk, the Budenny, the Ukranian, the Latvian riding horses, their Orlov trotters, to mention some good looking grays, the Toric, the Akhel-Teke, and so on and so on.

"But have you" — one of the aristocrats raised the question in a whisper —, "ever seen on Russian soil a stallion of that size, with hindquarters strong enough to take off like a rocket into high air? "

Dosha felt the stallion tense up under her. His ears pricked forward. Some sound had touched his senses –, a deep, menacing, rumbling sound. Drums were starting up a low roll. Rus and the two smaller grays started piaffing in place, their tails and polls held high, their powerful necks arched like swans. The chestnuts and their riders stood alert but motionless, as the loudspeakers from all sides thundered out the opening strains of "Finlandia."

The Finns, as if an invisible hand had reached into their bellies to pull out their guts, snapped to attention. After all it was their very own music the Red intruders had chosen as bait: Sibelius' famous rendering of Finnish fate and soul, an echo in reverse of the cries and anguish and last-ditch hopes of all those who had fallen for the sake of freedom, freedom at last.

The sun, like a blood orange in the sky, drew glowing mist from the heat-drenched soil. Dosha raised her hand. At once the herd of chestnuts started to walk powerfully in place. The stallion lunged forward and, in perfect control, reared up with her, balancing himself on his powerful hindquarters. Dosha could feel every muscle in his body stretch to the limit: he held himself like a bow straining to be released. Gently, she leaned into his neck, careful not to tip his balance. Through his fine skin she could feel his blood rush and throb, could feel him whinny, as with mane and tail flowing, he started to move forward, raking the fiery light with his front legs, playfully assuming the fighting position of the conquering stallion.

The pagan power of his beauty and innocence as he plunged toward the audience broke down barriers older than borders, reaching down into the deepest recesses of memory.

In the land between East and West, where alliances had shifted like drifts of snow in a storm, many of the spectators were the sons of fathers whom war had pitted against each other, as well as alongside each other. For at first, the great Russian Revolution—gathering strength under the slogan 'Workers of the World Unite" —' had spilled across their common border and the fight had been along the lines of Red and White, before it had turned territorial again. Workers and revolutionaries from both sides had worn red together, gotten massacred together, had stood huddled and freezing in the dark together, sharing drags from conquered cigarettes. When the two governments agreed on a new Finnish-Russian border, it separated those who had briefly been united under a new ideology of equality for all, leaving those Reds on the Finnish side who did not cross the border into Russia, feeling isolated and betrayed on the other side of the new divide.

Coming down on all fours, smoothly and still under full control, Dosha with downcast eyes atop that magnificent war booty of yet another war, started to perform with flawless perfection the dance of war and survival. No one knew better than she that, although this magnificent horse was of the finest German breeding with merely a Soviet brand, it was the horse people among the Soviets, whose love of the horse even Communism had failed to kill, who had taught him and these other magnificent beasts to dance as if they were moving freely. The fluidity with which they edged sideways, forming pairs or trios in troika formation, returning to single file, face to tail, as they barely touched ground at a Spanish trot. The horses crossed the roped-in arena with three-time, two-time, one-time changes of directions. In undulating lines, they separated into parallel rows, sideways to zigzag and inter-link, turned on their haunches to reverse direction; they performed side by side circles, narrowing down to canter pirouettes.

They lined up to face the audience, just as they had been ordered, and waited. Sporadic applause erupted, like random firecrackers. Dosha was to count to ten, and then all the riders were to pull off their white Cossack fur caps. Krematov had wanted Dosha to keep her hair loose throughout the performance, for extra effect but who could concentrate with hair flying over one's face? Besides, she was a rider, not some frivolous female posing on a stallion in his prime. So instead of falling loose, her heavy reddish-blond hair fell like a horse's braided tail halfway down her back, giving her the untouched look of a noble *boyar* bride.

The music started up again, softly, as in the form of a freestyle grand prix test, Dosha and her stallion started their solo, twirling, pirouetting, extending, and collecting. Dosha melted into her horse. The world around her receded, as together, in perfect harmony, horse and rider danced Sibelius' "Valse Triste." They were airborne.

The Finns swallowed the bait, hook, line and sinker. Politics were forgotten for just one brief moment. Hands clapped, wildly. Voices shouted, "Bravo! Bravo!"

Dosha raised her eyes for the break of a moment. There stood Vasili, at the center of a group of Kirov dancers on the other side of the yellow rope, adoration in those eyes that from the start had seemed so familiar.

She pulled her attention back to her horse as applause enveloped her like a welcoming hug. She and the stallion bowed in three directions in the manner of a circus horse, before pirouetting the stallion a full turn and racing after the other horses that had left ahead of her.

Seconds after Dosha left the roped-in arena, two Kaale *rom* stepped into her path, drawing her attention to a scattered line of Kaale Gypsies. Pretending the horse had been spooked, she spurred the stallion to bolt past the departing Kaale. The women in their colorful skirts marked her path like lanterns a road at night; pointing toward caravans lined up in the distance. There, Dosha assumed the switch of horses was to occur. On the far side of the last caravan, Khantchi stood waiting for her. He held the replacement horse, fully saddled, by its reins in one hand. The horse was somewhat smaller, but of a similar color gray.

She jumped off the stallion and threw the reins to Khantchi.

"Get the Tartar to pick you up in a car tomorrow," he said.

"Then look for me at the railway station, right after the motorcade has passed through. That's important," he emphasized. "It has to be around the time that Khrushchev's motorcade leaves for the embassy compound."

"What about my stallion?" Dosha asked, jumping onto the replacement horse.

"He will be on a ship to Sweden and safety by then. Now go!"

Khantchi slapped the horse on the rump with the flat of his hand, sending his granddaughter at a gallop back onto the field to rejoin the others.

She raced to catch up with the rest of the riders. Some of her team members turned to watch her approach, but made no comment. The timing of the exchange of the horses had been flawless. Khantchi must have shod the replacement horse with higher shoes, for although it felt smaller, it was still bigger than the other team horses riding ahead of her.

When they approached the barracks, Osap stood awaiting the return of the team. When she took off her saddle and threw the stallion's fly sheet across the exchange horse's back, for the split of a second she noticed surprise flare up in Osap's eyes. Dosha like the other riders started to hand-walk the horse, as if to cool it down. By the time she led it past a group of riders and into the stallion's stall, the expression on Osap's face was deadpan. At the onset of the few hours of muted light between sun-down and sun-up, the exchange horse looked believable.

# 35

# Under Siege

That brief moment of magic under the midnight sun, when Dosha's flawless ride to Sibelius' "Valse triste" had touched the hearts of Finns and Russians alike, by next morning had turned into a memory with the disembodied texture of a dream.

It was the day of Nikita Khrushchev's arrival in Helsinki, planned months ahead with the precision of a rocket launch. Soviet and Finnish foreign service officials had scheduled and co-ordinated every event, every move down to the minutest detail. Yet, upon Dosha's arrival at the embassy that morning, soldiers, waiters and guards, as if in the grip of some last minute stage fever, were hurrying in and out of the embassy building, crossing the fenced-in courtyard carrying chairs, tables and table cloths with the expressions of actors who have forgotten their lines.

Trapped in uniforms too heavy for the unexpected heat, they looked sweaty and disheveled. Nobody had foreseen the record-breaking heat wave in Europe's high north so early in June.

It was the first time Dosha got a chance to see which others, both riders and grooms, had obviously been hand-picked to spy out in the streets that day but even before all of them had climbed out of the four limousines that had brought them there, Krematov pulled Dosha aside and said, "Our Military Attaché, General Raskov, was much impressed by your performance last night. Today you have a special assignment." He swung around and ordered, "come along!"

Dosha wore a sleeveless summer dress, but despite the heat she felt a sudden chill. She followed Krematov past the main entrance doors to a side door she had never noticed before. The door was flush to the wall and painted the same gray as the walls of the embassy, so that the fine outline of the narrow door was only visible from close up. When Dosha was almost in front of it,

Krematov leaned forward and pressed a button under a tiny peep-hole placed at eyelevel. At once the door opened.

"You are about to reach a new level in your career," Krematov said, motioning Dosha to enter ahead of him toward an armed guard who stood at attention inside. After Krematov entered, the guard stepped in back of them and closed the door to the bright outside, casting the square landing they stood on and the narrow stairwell ahead of them into shadowy darkness.

"Go ahead," Krematov ordered. Dosha had no choice but to descend ahead of Krematov into deepening darkness and silence. The faint fall of their steps was cushioned by padded rubber covering the stone of the stairs. Down below, the air was dank and stagnant. Dosha thought of how, back in Leningrad, she had heard of hidden underground prisons right in the center of town, and of people who had disappeared from there without a trace.

Krematov had not uttered another sound, until they stopped in front of a heavy metal door along a dimly lit corridor. There, his hand on a doorknob, he informed her, "Your contributions as a street agent have been sub-standard so far. You now have another chance to prove yourself. The riding of a horse hardly qualifies as a sufficient contribution, not in times like these. You are here to help General Raskov study and translate headlines from Finnish newspapers into Russian. That, and whatever else he may request," his eyes fixed on hers, as if trying to hypnotize her into submission. "It would be unwise to fail rising to acceptable standards this time."

She knew at once that the threat that had shadowed her since the day she had left her people was about to catch up with her and never had she been more vulnerable than right at that moment; a girl alone, not only without her stallion and the other riders, but without the protection of the once powerful Galina. Most importantly she was a Gypsy girl deprived of the protection of the *rom* of her tribe.

Krematov opened the door. The old man was sitting in a bare office behind a metal military desk with a newspaper spread out in front of him. He glanced up as she and Krematov entered.

"Thank you, Comrade Krematov," the old man said lowering his eyes, "You may go."

It was an order. The KGB official clicked his heels and saluted, his thin lips were tightly pressed together. With one quick side-glance at the girl from the threshold of the door, he turned and closed the door behind him. Dosha was on her own.

"Come here!" The general beckoned her over with a wave of

his hand. He kept his eyes lowered to the newspaper in front of him. Dosha hesitated. What were her options?

"Here," the General said, finally looking up. There was a hint of impatience in his voice. "I need to know," he spread his pudgy hands across the paper in front of him, "what those Finns are openly feeding their masses, and what they're saying in between the lines? And since," he paused, "Finnish, so I am told, is your mother tongue ..." his eyes were now fully on her body as she started to move from the door toward the desk.

"Your mother, I'm sure, told you about the many Karelian Finns, who I was in charge of resettling. Did she?" His sly eyes, sunk in fleshly lids, screwed up to her face. So he counted on her knowing what had happened to thousands of Karelian Finns. Who, once their place of birth had been annexed by the Soviets, rather than being resettled as promised, had been simply dumped in the middle of nowhere and left there to die.

"I was able," he continued as if he were talking to a frightened child, "to personally save some. Some of," he coughed, "the young ones, the pretty..."

Every muscle in Dosha's body contracted. Why was he telling her this, was it because he guessed that her being part Finn was a lie? Was he the first one to observe that her Finnish in reality was barely good enough to read a headline, which she did slowly, without understanding most of it, since her spoken Finnish consisted mostly of matters of daily life?

When she stopped across the desk from him, he ordered, "This side, here my side of the desk." Where the old man grabbed a hold of her hand and pulled her close. He proceeded to stab the front page of the newspaper with the other hand. "And," he said," naturally these young things always ended up doing what was expected of them in the end. You want to know why?"

Frozen in place, she watched the barely perceptible movements of his slobbering fleshy lips, as he whispered, "It was because that was the only opportunity they had to survive!" His hand twitched as he started to squeeze the flesh of her arm. So far his touch remained tentative, gentle. But she could feel his rising agitation. When, suddenly, as if he had made the decision of wasting no more time, his hand grabbed her hip.

She gasped. Her eyes shot up to the ceiling, looking for surveillance cameras, on top of the door, in the corners of the room. Nothing blinked. Krematov had made a deal. For a moment she wondered what he was getting in return.

The old man's hand slid directly to her belly, at first still stroking her, before …. His hand dug in, triumphantly, hardening his
grip like a boy catching then trapping a bird in his hands. All
the while he kept on talking, like in a monotone, "there is nothing to fear … nothing at all," as if he were trying to soothe a
child through a traumatic event. "Has that little treasure cove
of yours…." He had closed his eyes, enraptured, as if savoring a
memory surging up from the deepest recesses of his past.

Flashbacks of Djemo suddenly bombarded Dosha's frozen
state of mind. Her father pulling her away from charred peasant
homes, "Close your ears," pulling her close, "they're hurting the
women in there," but the cries of women, of children, dogs yelping as if kicked never left her. They kept creeping into her sleep at
nights, when nightmares haunted her, and always Dzumila came
to her aid, pointing to a little metal flask she had given her somewhere along their trek to Russia's High North. "Should any bastard touch you in any funny way," her rough-edged Gypsy voice
now swirled through Dosha's mind. "Do nothing over haste, you
must wait, wait for when the moment is right, just when he thinks
he's got you. Do not cry, do not fear, but smile, the gentle smile
of an innocent. It will catch him by surprise. You choose that
moment to bring your knee up high and swiftly kick him in the
groins, while at the same time you pop the stopper to the metal
flask with your thumb and then you spray the acid in his eyes, his
face. That's the moment that you must run, that you must keep on
running…."

Dosha snapped to her senses. Her eyes sped around the subterranean interrogation room, for an interrogation room it was, of
that she was sure, searching the unadorned space for a weapon,
any instrument of assault. There was only a pencil, on the far side
of the newspaper, across the desk from where she stood.

Heat was rising from his hand; she felt its nervous twitch
through the fine material of her dress. She looked down on his
neck, as wide as his head, he was old but he had the bulk of a bull.
She narrowed her focus to envisioning him standing across from
her, ready to rape, her. She could see herself smile at him, unexpectedly, bring her right knee up to his groin, grab the pencil
and start stabbing his eyes. He was of massive built, but she was
counting on being taller and in top athletic shape.

For a moment nothing happened. She tried to step back, only
to have him pull her to him tighter and all this time his eyes
remained hooked to the same spot of the newspaper, his hand

blindly inching closer to her sex. Breathing hard, panting, his face was turning purple, as his hand traveled on, touching her.

That's when he pushed himself away from the desk. But instead of getting up, as she thought he would, he spread his legs, wide, exposing a grotesquely huge and flaccid mass, partially resting on the edge of his chair. His eyes, wide open now, lifted to her face, as if pleading. When she pulled back, trying to avert his eyes, his expression turned to fury. He grabbed her arm. With the violent force of a much younger man he pulled her down by the hand toward his lap, while his other arm shot up toward her neck.

She lost all fear. In the grip of a killer fury, she jumped forward and dove for the pencil on the farther side of the desk. The pencil was firmly in her hand, when he caught the back of her neck. Images of faces blown up by bombs, by hand grenades, blood gushing from every orifice of faces welled up in her. When suddenly red flashes flared up above the door and caught her eyes.

"Look," her voice rang out.

Surveillance lights had started to blink, blinking rapidly. His hand flew off her neck. There was a knock on the door. Raskov pulled up the zipper of his pants, moved the chair back close to the desk. A second knock, the door opened and a woman walked in.

"Natalia Yemekov," the woman introduced herself, "envoy of the First Chief Directorate of the KGB for Baltic Affairs." Her bespectacled face went from Raskov, to Dosha and back to Raskov again. She was dressed in the blue uniform of the KGB, the female version, with a straight calf-length skirt.

"I knocked, there was no answer." The lapel of her jacket was decorated with three medals.

Clearly Raskov had not been expecting her, but somebody loyal to him must have turned surveillance back on to warn him.

Dosha, still behind the desk next to Raskov, dropped her arms along her sides. Still holding the pencil in one hand, she let it slide to her feet. The woman struck up a conversation, there was much back and forth about the motorcade, security, the progression of the day.

Through it all the woman's eyes kept scrutinizing Dosha, who, trying to suppress the trembling of her hands, kept her eyes lowered. Until, on impulse, she started to translate the headlines of the paper.

At once, the envoy's conversation turned to questions about Dosha's papers, her files, her origins. When Rastov stated that the girl was a Finn, the woman inquired whether she was truly a Finn?

This silenced Dosha but to keep her body from trembling, she pretended to keep her own focus on the headlines of Helsinki's major newspaper, her supposed task. She even pulled it closer to her side of the desk. Until Raskov ordered, "Go on reading, translate."

She continued to read the Finnish one word at a time, before translating it into Russian, all the while praying—*please o'del, please let this gadji at least lead me out of here.*

That's when, almost like in answer to her prayer, the woman intoned, "I'll need her dossier tonight!" Dosha looked up. The intelligence officer's eyes were directed like a search light fully on her face.

"Follow me!" Comrade Yemekov ordered, nodding at Raskov and waving at Dosha. "There is no more time to lose." She opened the door and motioned Dosha to exit for her last day as a street agent.

Dosha forced her breathing to return to normal, but her mind kept racing. Somehow this unlikely woman had saved her, and she gratefully watched the Intelligence Officer resolutely close the padded door. But once back out in the corridor and all the way through the maze of subterranean corridors, Dosha realized that, far from being saved, she had merely been flushed out of a cove and out into the open. For all during their walk toward the exit the woman's mind kept hunting hers for hidden secrets and just as the exit to freedom came into sight, when Dosha was ready to breathe a sigh of relief the woman turned, and the barrage of questions began—Was she a dancer?—No, a rider—You're the rider of the stallion Rus? You're that girl? And where did this stallion come from? Some unregulated collective in the North, wasn't it? Didn't she read about it?—But it was only after "And where is the stallion at this moment?" that Dosha realized a trap had been set and she was about to step into it.

"Out in the country," she lied without a moment's hesitation, "in military barracks near the Finnish Olympic stadium," knowing full well that to Natalia Yemekov's thinking, who was smiling triumphantly, that meant the embassy was holding the stallion hostage. Which in turn meant it was keeping her, Dosha, on a leash tight enough to trust her not to escape once out in the streets of Helsinki that day.

Yet Officer Yemekov hesitated. It was too late for the KGB

woman to check out the true whereabouts of the stallion Rus. "Go on then," she waved at last for Dosha to walk out into the street.

Dosha stepped out into the light. The iron-forged gate of the Soviet Embassy was open to the street. She noticed a group of dancers and Finnish students, right by that open gate. They were jostling about and laughing. Amidst them she saw the dancer. He looked up just then. He tried to catch her eyes. That's when it fully hit her. She felt dark and polluted. *Mahrime;* never more than at that moment, when the brilliance of his eyes seemed to highlight the darkness she was trying to leave behind. She realized how close she had come to being defiled forever. Without a backward glance, she hurried out into the street and walked away.

It was only after Dosha had reached the blockaded South Harbor, gazing out onto the Gulf of Finland that stretched blue and empty toward the far horizon, that she paused. Closing her eyes, she prayed for the safety of her stallion and collected her thoughts. Piecing together the events that had shattered her mind, it sunk in that, Comrade Jemekov had come closer than anybody else to uncovering not only the horse-swap but Dosha's true identity as a Gypsy and in this round-up of Russia's last remnants of freedom, she would have never set foot on the Romany trail again.

Trembling again from head to toe, Dosha looked at her watch. It was 11 a.m. Nobody would catch her alive. She had only one hour, two at most to disappear and it had to happen during the short span of time from when Comrade Khrushchev stepped off his train to when his motorcade entered the Embassy compound. The time when all eyes would remain glued on the newly ascended Soviet leader and the possible dangers surrounding him.

*Till then,* she decided, *I better blend into the web of agents they've spread across the different routes of the motorcade.* She turned away from the quay and faced the coastal road, where a red banner 'Workers of the World Unite' had been stretched across the second floor of two buildings but on that Thursday morning, all the way from the empty harbor to across the deserted marketplace and to the road, there was nobody left to unite. No people, no booths, only an occasional car passed along the empty coastal road.

One man, short and dark, ill at ease in a gray crumpled suit hurried out of a side street to her left, walked right up to her, and asked, "Mannerheiminkatu? How do I get to the Mannerheiminkatu?"

Dosha pointed her hand toward the Northern end of the coastal road. "Take the Esplanadinkatu to the left," she said, "It will take you straight to the Mannerheiminkatu. Are you by chance looking for the railway station?"

The man ignored the question. "Have there been sirens?" he asked.

"No sirens," she said. *No call to rush to bomb shelters,* she thought, *thankfully not yet.*

Without a further word, the man hurried off down the emptied main road. As she passed the side street he had just come out of, Dosha noticed that cars, trucks and buses were parked on both sides of the street. In fact, as she followed in the steps of the man, she found all the side streets packed with parked vehicles, many of them covered with dust, as if they had come from far away.

She turned, following the departing figure. The man half walked half ran ahead of her. *Must be late for an appointment,* she thought. They were the only two pedestrians on what looked and felt like a path of evacuation. She was walking openly down the center of the empty street. By the time she reached the Southern Esplanade, the man had disappeared among a light crowd of pedestrians that lined both sides of the split avenues.

Somebody blew a whistle. It was a Finnish cop, who shouted from a short distance away, "You cannot walk in the middle of the street." That's when Dosha noticed that the twin avenues were clear of anything with wheels. Nowhere could she see a trolley, car, or truck, not as much as a bicycle, only pedestrians, neatly stacked like rows of shoes. Stone-faced Finns were lining their wide avenues—men, women and children, thin rows of them, but as far as her eyes could reach.

"You have to step onto the sidewalk," the cop emphasized, approaching her. "Like everybody else."

*There are so few of them,* she thought, as she stepped onto the sidewalk. She continued on, walking quietly in back of the people who stood facing the avenues. She was struck at how many of them kept glancing up at the impressive buildings in back of them that pointed like fingers into the glaring sky.

*Are they expecting planes?* She wondered. The heat pouring down into the street was so intense, it felt flammable. Yet there they stood, patiently waiting along their massive avenues, trying to look more numerous than they were.

She remembered the stories the Finns had told her back in her father's encampment. Of how, in wars past, they had gotten used to odds of one to fifty when it came to holding their own against their powerful enemy, the Russian bear.

*They have their bags of tricks,* she thought, *but most of all they have nerves of steel.* During the last war, twelve years earlier, when Russian attacks had come from the sky, her father had told her that the cunning Finns had created an array of shadow armies—cardboard figures with a couple of living persons moving here and there, to deceive the Soviet air force as it was trying to ascertain their strength from the air. Today, once again the pedestrians were doing their best to swell their small numbers by strategic placements. Every man, woman, and child seemed to be participating.

*Although,* she thought, *today their enemy is supposed to be arriving by ground, and not,* she lifted her face into the empty sky, *o'del help us,* by air.

*They are brave though,* she thought with admiration. *No Gypsy ever was that brave, patiently waiting for destiny to strike.* She thought of the students she had listened to in the student house. Who, so Jean-Marie, the son of the French ambassador had told her, were willing to make a stand of brotherhood for people hundreds of miles away, just because they shared, just as all the tribes of Roma do, the same linguistic roots?

Dosha only partially understood the history, but after her conversations with Jean-Marie, she had pieced together that the Hungarian rebellion of the year before had been sparked by Khruchshev's initial promises of liberalization. It seemed to her that Hungary and the Western world had mistaken propaganda for reality. Aware of the general jubilation of a change of regime and a promise of increased freedom back in the Russian motherland, Hungarians felt the time was ripe to demand their own freedom and independence from the Soviet Union. They soon found themselves abandoned by the rest of the world and mown down by a Soviet military more ruthless than even the Marxist-Leninist Jean-Marie had thought likely, and those Finns, out in those boiling streets today, knew exactly what that felt like. Hadn't they themselves lived through other Soviet invasions under flags of truce, when alleged Russian 'bread baskets,' dropped ostensibly to feed their starving population during aerial visits of the war of forty-four, had exploded upon hitting ground?

For now the Finns pretended they were staking their own fate on the promise that this was indeed no more than a state visit, and Finland's precarious peace-agreement with the Soviet

Union would continue as before. As every Soviet agent was aware, no effort had been spared to safeguard the visit, starting with a motorcade that was to take the new Soviet leader in an open car from the Central Railways Station to the Soviet Embassy and to insure a safe and unimpeded passage, Finnish cops and soldiers were positioned like fence posts every ten to twenty meters along the curbs of both sides of the highly orchestrated avenues. Dosha could not imagine that any Finn in his sane mind would jeopardize this nation's hard won peace by an impulsive act of defiance, such as jumping out from the crowds to shoot the bastard down but there were not just Finns to consider in this remote and underpopulated country.

Having crossed the *Gadje* world since childhood, Dosha was accustomed to seeing the usual mixture of majority and minority groups, bonded by common interests like everywhere else but now, scanning the silently waiting crowds for Khantchi, who could be anywhere, Dosha found that on this day these various groups had separated back into clumps of ethnic origin like sauce from too much heat.

Most striking next to the majority of dark and slight descendants of the original Finns, stood groups who at first sight looked exactly like Swedes, remnants of earlier invasions from the West, but looking more carefully at their faces, instead of the sculptured Nordic features of Swedish invaders, after years of intermarriage these Swedish or coastal Finns had the high cheekbones, slanted eyes and short noses of the Asiatic ancestry they shared with their countrymen, the Finnish Finns. In a show of support, many of the latter had come from various inland parts of the country for the day and stood spread out like solid foundation growth along curbs and sidewalks of the central avenues of their capital.

But those who stood out as truly different and therefore most suspect on this day of national threat, were Finland's true minorities, and none more so than their Gypsies, the dark-skinned Kaale. Only the men were present and these, in contrast to the patiently waiting Finns, didn't seem to be able to stand still. They shuffled their feet, pacing back and forth. Their fingers were busy lighting cigarettes, their own or each others, flicking ashes, pinching the fold of their hats. They appeared as edgy as animals in a zoo. These Kaale, who had crossed this land for centuries, today looked ominously dark and unpredictable under their wide-brimmed black felt hats and exotic attire, especially since they had left their colorful wives and rowdy children behind for

331

the occasion. *There's more here,* Dosha concluded, *than meets the eye. What's going on? The Kaale are sensing danger.*

Khantchi was not among the conspicuous Gypsies. Dosha guessed that if he were hiding anywhere, he would probably be hiding among another visible minority group, the semi-nomadic Samis or Lapps, who had also arrived to show their support and who, even more than their fellow Finns, remained in place like rocks on a shore. She ran her eyes over the largest group of Lapps, who were standing at a street corner across from the railway station and the square where Finnish welcoming committees were assembled on a wooden welcoming platform. A military band stood assembled to both sides of the station entrance. Just then Khantchi, dressed in the colorful national costume of his Sami friends and allies, stepped outside the group of Sami, caught her eye and carefully stubbed out a burning cigarette with his foot. He stared at her for a brief intense moment, then retreated back into the group. *So that's where I'm to pick him up,* she thought, *right at that corner across from the arrival point.*

Dosha caught her breath. If anyone knew about a live spark anywhere in this political mine field, one that could blow them all to pieces, she believed it was Khantchi, and he for the moment stood quietly lined up with the rest of them, like pawns on a board waiting for the next move in this latest round of cold war chess. At stake once again was Finland's freedom, to keep or to lose.

When 12 o'clock, the official time of arrival posted in all major newspapers, came and went, and there was no sign of the Soviet Union's rising new Red Czar, Dosha sensed the onslaught of an attack of national paranoia. More and more heads lifted nervously toward the sky. Children pulled at their mother's dresses to get attention. The Finns could no longer suppress their well founded fear that, coming from their neighbour, a super power whose primary crop had been bombs and by now more refined weapons of mass destruction, the unexpected could easily turn into a chain reaction of horror without end. The Reds next door might imperiously decide at the last minute to forego the visit altogether and drop off their surplus of bombs instead. Forget about this foreplay of cultural events. Or send another grim comrade in Khrushchev's stead, for after all the rise and fall of Soviet power was as arbitrary as the abuse thereof.

Dosha knew all this, yet there she stood, trapped amidst a waiting crowd of *Gadje*—*waiting for the bombs to drop*—amidst these Finns with their nerves of steel and the man-made cages they called their homes. What she had once observed from the safety of a forest when she was a child, German planes flying to kill Russians helplessly trapped in Leningrad during the war, was a destiny she was now forced to share with these Finns. Like these *Gadje* she started to throw anxious glances at the sky, helplessly waiting for whatever this latest abuser of power saw fit to drop. She cursed the day her people had fought alongside these very Russians in the name of freedom, only to have them abuse that hard fought freedom against those weaker than themselves.

Her only hope remained Khantchi, whom she saw standing calmly in the midst of his Sami allies. After her own brief experience as a Soviet street agent, there was no doubt left in her mind, that Khantchi had been and still was a double agent *but* his loyalty, she knew, was and always would be only to his own people. He would never leave her standing in what could turn into a battleground. He had information only few others could obtain.

By one o'clock Dosha could stand the uncertainty no longer. She was about to leave her post and by walking toward Khantchi initiate the risky escape. Suddenly an obvious commotion occurred behind the closed doors to the railway station. A Finn in uniform briefly stepped out onto the station square conveying some sort of signal to the welcoming committee positioned in front of the station.

"The Russian delegation has arrived," announced another Finn, who was dressed in a dark suit and top hat. He then proceeded to walk from the station entrance onto the platform and to the fore of the welcoming committee, from where he added, through a loudspeaker, "Along with Comrades Khrushchev and Bulganin."

Right after, the Russian delegation, consisting of thirty persons, stepped through the doors of the railway station onto the square. They had arrived, exactly one hour late, at Helsinki's Central Railway Station in a special Soviet train made up of three sleeping cars and two antique coaches converted into lounge cars. From one of the latter, Comrades Khrushchev and Bulganin were the last to exit. They were the only ones to step onto the welcoming platform. Both, so it was noted, wore the same lightcolored overcoats they had worn the year before on their State visit to England. By contrast, Finnish officials, including Mr. Sukselainen, Finland's new prime minister, like the announcer, wore formal clothes with a top hat.

On the platform a Finnish guard of honor in helmets formed

a straight line. A band played the two national anthems. A welcoming speech by President Sukselainen emphasized the "prized friendship" between the two countries, followed by a similar speech by Comrade Khrushchev, translated into Finnish through an interpreter from his delegation. After inspecting the Finnish guard, Mr. Khrushchev was the first to step down onto the red carpet, just rolled out by four soldiers from the platform to the waiting limousines, and walked, smiling and waving, past the small crowd of Finns. These civilians formed the informal welcoming committee, waving Finnish and Soviet paper flags of uniform sizes and shapes. The rest of the Soviet and Finnish dignitaries followed, and in measured steps walked to the open cars waiting along the street ahead.

Motorcycles revved up their engines and slowly took the lead, while a smiling Khrushchev stood in an open car that proceeded down the avenue at walking speed. His head moved from side to side and his hand waved as if he were a puppet on a string. Comrade Bulganin, a gray-looking bureaucrat and premier of the USSR, was securely seated in the back seat and appeared to be holding the fat smiling Butcher of the Ukraine by a pair of mental reins. As the motorcade passed, silent Finns continued to stand planted in the square, lined along their wide avenues, keeping an eye on the sky, as if there remained the possibility of bombers arriving overhead.

Red fender flags barely moved in the still air. The flash of cameras flared here and there, especially those belonging to the small number of Western photographers who stood like singly potted plants among the waiting crowd. It became clear, that despite the wining and dining, the dancing and singing and the horse extravaganza thrown in for an encore, this was no victory ride through cheering crowds for the newly ascended top comrade of the USSR. An eerie silence enveloped those streets and avenues shimmering in the heat, and although international newspapers would describe the reception as 'correct but unenthusiastic,' in reality the silence was broken only by the purring of limousines, and the roaring of the motorcycles that speared the way toward the Russian Embassy.

# 36
# Defection

As soon as the gates of the Soviet Embassy closed behind the motorcade, the staged crowds on the sidewalks spilled out into the streets like water through a broken dam. The rush started at the railway station where people dashed to catch their respective trains delayed by the reception. Some people started to line up at the various stops waiting for trolleys and buses to reappear, others walked to their cars parked out of sight on side streets. Finnish police who had been placed along the route of the motorcade like dotted lines disappeared as if sucked up by a suddenly opened drain.

Just as the scene came unstuck, Dosha spotted the dancer Vasili Kutunoff right across the street from her. Like many of the students spread through the crowds, he had donned the white cap of Helsinki University. He looked smaller than on stage. But what struck Dosha most was the change in his demeanor, the absence of the exuberance that characterized his walk on stage. For the first time she noticed the kind of lethargy often visible on the faces of those defeated by the System. However as soon as he saw her in the thinning crowd across the street from him, his face broke out in a spontaneous outpouring of joy and warmth. His eyes shone with the brightness that had kept entering her dreams and thoughts. He was about to cross the street.

*Not now!* She tried to stop him by lifting a hand just high enough to tell him to stay right there. An unauthorized meeting with Vasili at this point, a dancer by now famous back in the U.S.S.R., applauded in this country, was sure to attract the attention of any near-by Soviet street agent and could possibly barricade Khantchi's exit strategy. She turned away from the dancer and with calm measured steps started to walk closer to the

Railway Station where, at the corner of a nearby street, Osap had been told to wait for her in a car with its motor running.

Vasili, not to be deterred, as if the sight of her had restored his former boldness, had already caught up with her. He touched her elbow.

"Please let go," she whispered but he stuck close, as she wound her way through the rushing crowds. Although he had withdrawn his hand from her elbow, she sensed his intense blue eyes stick to her, not letting go. At last she spotted one of those unmarked Soviet Embassy car she had learned to recognize. This one was standing at the corner of the next street ahead with its motor running.

*Osap!* Dosha slowed her walk and looked around. For one dizzying moment she had the feeling of standing still, while everything around her began to move. It was the car that was moving beside her at walking speed. Its interior was blocked off from view by tinted glass. The windows were fully closed. She heard a faint click. The back door on her side unlatched and was pushed open from within. Dosha ducked inside, but not before Vasili had taken hold of the still open passenger door.

"What do you think you're doing?" She cried, panicking. "Go away. You must keep on walking! Please!"

Instead he jumped into the moving vehicle right after her, just as it started to pick up speed. Osap, who was driving the car, for the split of a second turned toward them, horrified, like someone who had stumbled across an unexploded bomb.

"What now?" he asked.

"Drive on," Dosha replied, "slowly, just as planned toward that group of Sami over there."

The Sami, still some distance away, upon spotting the car converged into a small crowd in the middle of the street and blocked traffic. Osap joined other enraged motorist and honked his horn. The Sami scattered into all directions as the car headed directly toward them, allowing Khantchi, who was holding a large satchel in one hand, to slide in next to Osap like a feather sucked out of flight.

Khantchi, old but supple, once in the car immediately turned to the backseat and noticed the dancer Vasili Kutunoff.

"Who is he?" he demanded in Lovaritz. "And what is he doing here?"

Dosha was about to tell her grandfather that the young *Gadje* had forced his way into the already moving car, but this was Gypsy to Gypsy, where a lie was a sign of disrespect. Khantchi knew as well as Dosha herself, that if she had truly been opposed to Vasili joining them, she would have fought him off. Gypsy girls were taught early on in life how to fend off aggressors.

"His freedom was on the line," she answered in Russian and wondered whether Vasili had acted out of impulse, or whether he had been searching for a way to defect all along. Maybe he had sensed way back in the halls of the Kirov that flight had always been uppermost in her mind. As the son of enemies of the people, he must have known he would forever remain suspect, and maybe he had looked upon her as an ally all along.

Vasili was openly taking a closer look at Khantchi. There was no mistaking Khantchi with his sharp features and restless eyes for anything but a Gypsy, especially when he exchanged his Sami cap for a wide-brimmed dark felt hat.

"You are defecting," Vasili said, turning to Dosha. "I knew it. I hoped that was on your mind all along."

"Nobody invited you to come along," Khantchi said. His Russian was perfect. *Exactly like one of them,* Dosha thought amazed.

"They were tightening the noose around my neck," Vasili said, leaning forward toward Khantchi. "In fact there was some last minute hold-up with my papers even before we left Leningrad, and I thought that's it, I'm done for. But now," he said, "if I'm right in thinking what you're up to, this all seems suddenly strangely unreal. I may never see my country again. I am the only survivor of my line."

"You can still return," Khantchi said, appeased somewhat, "We drop you off, you walk right back to the embassy and probably nobody will question you in all this upheaval."

"It's not an option," Vasili said. "I've been dancing far too long on a tightrope without a safety net of any kind. It was only a matter of time all along till they'd arrest me. If not for my parents' alleged crimes against the state, then for the seditious thoughts I am suspected to hide."

"That man is a dancer," Osap injected himself into the conversation, "a famous dancer." The Tartar looked more and more like a monkey clinging to his driving wheel in fear. "Driving a dancer of his fame, a defecting Soviet dancer is like transporting explosives."

"And drawing attention to it is like adding a fuse," Khantchi calmly replied. They had reached the three-way junction at the harbor road. Osap came to a full stop.

"If all went without incident, which it did, I was supposed to take the girl back to the stadium, to start packing. We're probably being observed this very minute."

"Drive in the direction of the stadium then," Khantchi said, relaxing into his seat.

In traffic as unregulated as in a city coming back to life after a bomb attack, they wound their way to the Mannerheimkatu, the normal route back to the Stadium. More and more Osap acted like a cocked gun ready to go off but whenever he stepped on the gas, Khantchi slowed him down with a gesture of his hand.

"They catch us," he said, "for whatever reason they'll throw us back across the border like fish too small to fry. We have an hour, maybe two before they'll start missing any of you. They've been on the look-out for defectors from the moment you set foot on Finnish soil. This visit so far is not going as planned. The silence out in those streets! Hardly the expected enthusiastic reception of a new regime, more like a funeral procession than a state visit, that's what I think. Bad for world press. They'll be scrambling for damage control and for us that's a lucky break. It will keep them busy elsewhere, but not for long. So now," he addressed Osap, "stay in the left lane, not too fast, not too slow. Turn left — now!"

As soon as they had left the Mannerheiminkatu Khantchi directed Osap through many side streets, turning right and turning left, all however at the same slow even speed, not ever passing any other car.

"Just stay in the flow of traffic," Khantchi insisted, but the suppression of speed increased the tension in the small passenger car to a breaking point. Instead of rushing out of what all of them considered the area of possible capture, Khantchi enforced a slowness that seemed unbearable, until they had driven beyond city limits. Even here traffic was much lighter than usual.

"But this is the road to Porkalla!" Dosha protested, which she knew had turned into an armed Soviet camp the moment the equestrian team had left.

"This will also take us to Turku," her grandfather informed her in Lovaritz, "where your horse, God willing, left by boat early this morning for Sweden, and where, again God willing, we will meet up with him by tomorrow night. The Finns will hold up their end of the deal, as long as we don't stick out in any way."

"What about the mare?"

"There was no way to spring the mare. She'll be fine, they'll breed her. Besides, she was your father's, no?"

"Still," Dosha whispered. She had promised to herself, she would not forsake the mare.

"You're speaking Gypsy, aren't you?" Vasili leaned toward Dosha, "I know the sounds of it."

"How do you know it?" she asked, turning to him.

"There were plenty of Gypsies back in Siberia, and that's where my mother and I were in exile. It was Gypsies who first taught me how to dance, there in the middle of nowhere where we were all starving together. Although I have to admit the Gypsies were better at survival, certainly than my mother. She didn't last long. I got lucky, Larkin pulled me out of there." he whispered.

Dosha wondered whether her grandfather had caught the name, and whether he knew Larkin, Patrina's friend, but by then Khantchi's eyes were entirely on the road ahead. They had passed the exit to Porkkala and were traveling on a southerly two-lane country road. Traffic had dwindled to the occasional car. They had traveled for close to two hours, when Khantchi suddenly leaned forward. "Turn left!" He pointed to where a horse-drawn Gypsy wagon stood in a field in sight from the main road. Osap took a sharp left.

A *rom* sitting on the driving bench up front waved at them as they passed his caravan. Khantchi with an impatient hand signaled Osap to drive on. "We're too close to the main road," he explained. "We don't want to draw any attention."

They now found themselves on a narrow dirt lane with fields and pastures on either side. There had been no rain for days, and the lane was deeply rutted with dried mud tracks. As they came to a four corner crossing Khantchi said, "Stop the car!"

With the agility of a much younger man Khantchi jumped out of the car, walked into the crossing where he bent down and, with his eyes and the tip of his shoe, he traced the different types and directions of the criss-crossing vehicle tracks. He stood back up, observed the sky before walking into each of the four corners of the intersecting lanes and up to a field with grazing cows that was fenced in with barbed wire. There, a few feet from the crossing, a few sprigs of flowers tied with grass were attached to the fence at eye level. Leaving the *patrin* in its place, he ran back to the driver's side of the car. He opened the driver's side, waved Osap to move over, and jumped behind the wheel.

Tires screeched as Khantchi took off taking the right hand road of the four corners. Guiding the driving wheel expertly with one hand, he kept his head stuck out of the open window. He drove in short spurts of stop-and-go looking for more roadside messages, shreds of materials from old dresses or sprigs from the bottoms of unfinished baskets, and there were plenty of *patrins*. Dosha, who had opened the window on her side of the car, also read the signs indicating the direction that would take them to fellow Roma, when suddenly she picked up the rolling sound of an approaching helicopter, a distance away still, but sounding close to the ground.

"I bet you, that's one of those Soviet helicopters," she leaned over to Khantchi. "They landed in Porkkala as soon as we left. You've got to race for cover. They've got men with dogs as well. They'll drop them off, and they'll pick up our scent in no time at all."

Khantchi stepped on the gas. With both hands on the wheel, he raced toward a pine forest at the edge of the fields and onto a narrow bridle-path just barely wide enough for one car. Almost immediately a cut birch sapling dropped into their path. Without a moment's hesitation Khantchi swerved the car sharply off to the left where it wedged between two trees. Everyone in the car flew forward as the car came to an abrupt stop.

In the momentary panic and to keep Dosha from flying forward, Vasili gripped her hand. Her upper body had fallen forward and whip lashed back. The dancer placed his arm protectively across her chest. Khantchi turned off the motor. All of them looked up. Through gaps in the tall dark tree crowns they saw an unmarked helicopter fly low and right overhead. The aircraft drew a wide reconnoitering circle, two more, before flying away.

"Luck," Dosha whispered with a deep exhale. "So far it is on our side." Only then did she become aware that, although Vasili had withdrawn his arm from across her chest, his hand still held hers. Afraid her grandfather would notice, she tried to pull her hand away from Vasili's, but paused for a brief moment, savoring the feeling of their first touch. A wave of tenderness for him welled up in her and looking into his eyes, she felt all differences between them melt away. They were, both of them, survivors of the same evil regime, the son of a famous poet and the still teenage Gypsy girl.

A sharp whistle broke the spell. It came from the other side of the bridle path where three Gypsies, sitting hunched forward and bareback on three painted ponies, stood watching them. Each was holding one extra pony by a rope halter and reins.

"Nobody was expecting you of course," Khantchi pointed at the number of extra ponies before turning to Vasili.

Since the door on the driver's side was partially blocked by a tree, Khantchi had to squeeze his way out from behind the wheel. He grabbed the satchel he had brought from the floor and now handed it to his granddaughter.

"Everybody out, except for you," his voice snapped like fingers. Then leaning toward Dosha, whose window had remained rolled down from before, he added a few words for her ears alone. "The bundle contains clothes proper for a Gypsy woman." He was ordering her to step back into Gypsy life.

"And these *Gadje* clothes?" she asked.

"Put them in the satchel," he said in Lovaritz, "shoes and all. You never know. They could come in handy on the other side of the water."

By the time they had all squeezed out of the car, the Gypsies had jumped off their ponies. They stood talking to Khantchi in a dialect of *Romani* that Dosha could barely understand. Then, with sturdy bush knives, they chopped off branches from the trees around them, with which they hurriedly covered the car. From the easy interchange between Khantchi and these Kaale, Dosha guessed they were friends of long standing.

"Is this where the old man will drop me?" Vasili asked Dosha in a terrified whisper. "After all, they only do have six ponies, and ...."

"The old man is my grandfather," Dosha said, smiling up at him. "And no, he will not drop you here. Your very presence in this car tells him you are no stranger to me. But can you ride bareback and with a rope instead of a bridle?"

Everybody had listened to their conversation, and now all eyes went to the light-skinned *Gadje*.

"I don't know how to ride at all," Vasili said, looking back at them.

"You and the dancer double up on one horse then," Khantchi turned to Osap.

With a nod Osap interlinked his hands and gave the dancer a leg up before jumping on behind him. The Gypsies, including Khantchi and Dosha, jumped up from the ground. Osap slid his arms under the dancer's armpits and picked up the rope reins. In unison all kneed their horses into a gallop and thundered off along the bridle path deep into the forest. The Gypsies lay low on their horses' necks, their faces right in the flying manes of the ponies to avoid being hit by low reaching branches. Turning back, Dosha saw Osap start lagging behind, his pony slowed by the added weight.

After a lengthy gallop the forest opened onto more fields and meadows. The five Gypsies galloped up an incline into a clump of deciduous trees and low growing shrubs, sheltering a cluster of twelve wagons lined up along a quietly flowing brook. Unlike the ornate caravans and fancy horses of the Lovara, these Kaale traveled in light, bow-topped wagons perched on four high wheels. The bow tops were covered with tattered canvas. These Gypsies were poor.

It was also an encampment on high alert. As the riders jumped off, Dosha noticed at once that instead of wildly blazing campfires, their cooking tripods were placed above small fires surrounded by heaps of dirt and buckets of water, ready to extinguish the fires instantly in case a quick departure became necessary. Large piles of *dunhas,* covered with fading brightly colored materials were already heaped in the wagons. Extra horses, small common looking ponies, were tied to the rear of the wagons ready for a quick escape.

Men, women and children came rushing toward them, talking and gesticulating. They pointed with lifted arms past them to where Osap and Vasili were slowly approaching. The dancer looked white as a sheet. Before the two latecomers had a chance to jump off, snarling Gypsy dogs, small children, some of them naked, and older women swirled around the Tartar and the *Gadje.*

Immediately a very dark stout old man, clearly the *rom baro,* picked up a pebble, skipped it towards the dogs and commanded the children and women to back off. With a nod toward Khantchi, the chief of the Kaale was welcoming Osap and Vasili into their *kumpania* as guests.

A group of young men and women were next to advance toward the riders and took their ponies, while the elders and married men gathered around one of the small camp fires in a decision-making circle. Some crouched on their heels, some settled cross-legged on bare earth. They motioned Osap and Vasili to join them, but only the *rom baro* and Khantchi were handed crates, turned upside down, as seats of honor. Dosha watched with apprehension. She knew the discussions that were about to begin would decide the fate of Vasili, an unforeseen addition to their flight.

She wished she could speak on the dancer's behalf, but a woman of her age would be excluded from the decision circle. Not so the *phuri dai*, the tribal mother of the Kaale as well as other elder women of importance, who she was sure had the right to participate in the decision-making for their tribe. To her surprise, she found the women settling in a circle apart. The *phuri dai* of the Kaale, an old woman with grey, disheveled hair held back under a loosely tied head scarf, was not as ancient as Patrina, but her face already was a map of the harshness of Gypsy life.

The *phuri dai* waved at Dosha to approach, then stared at her as if she were seeing a ghost, a *mulo*.

"*Patchiv tumenge*, honor to you," Dosha self-consciously walked into their circle. The old woman's eyes remained narrowed with fear and apprehension.

"Dosha of the Khantchisti," the old woman greeted her at last, "I've known your grandfather since I was a young woman when he traveled with his young family." She spoke in a mixture of Romani dialect and Finnish, aware that Dosha would not understand her otherwise.

*Sanija*, Dosha thought. It was clear these Gypsies also avoided mentioning the names of the dead but like Khantchi the tribal mother of the Kaale also saw the image of her grandmother when she looked at her. The old woman grabbed a small stick from the ground and lit a pipe with work-hardened hands. Dosha noticed the absence of gold on the women. Only their leader, the *rom baro*, sitting in the circle across from the women, wore a heavy gold watch on a chain that stretched across his chest under his black vest.

"I regret," Dosha said, trying to speak in the same mixture of ancient Romani and Finnish, "to have added danger to your people by bringing along this unannounced *Gadje*." She pointed to Vasili who stood outside the circle of *rom*, alone and lost. "Like us, he is persecuted. Like us he wants to defect."

"Gypsy life is laced with the unforeseen." The *phuri dai* stared straight into Dosha's eyes. "You must have had your reasons," she said, puffing on her pipe. She leaned toward the fire and started to tell Dosha in measured words about Gypsy life on this Finnish side of the Russian border.

The old woman had psychic powers, of that Dosha was

convinced. Most female Gypsy leaders did and right then, this *phuri dai*'s unrelenting stare was ripping off the protective defenses Dosha had used like blinders while crossing the world of the *Gadje*. Now back among Roma, who do not question the invisible, that which can be felt but rarely seen, Dosha felt a strange stillness wrap itself around her mind and body. She knew the feeling; it gripped her before the onslaught of some great upheaval or death, a burden she had carried since childhood, the sign of the true *shovani or* sorceress. Unlike the telling of good fortunes to entertain *Gadje*, this was true psychic power. It instilled both fear and respect in fellow Gypsies.

Dosha unlocked her eyes from the old woman's piercing stare and looked at the brook instead. Death was in the air. Her eyes followed the flowing water down to where young men and women had taken the horses. She watched them splashing the bodies of the animals with water, then washing their heads by lifting water with their hands. The river served as the ritual cleanser of Gypsy life, every type of cleansing had its special place along the riverbed, assigned by ancient Romani law.

Dosha's mind drifted off, mesmerized by the gurgling and splashing sounds of water. It ran clean and transparent across rocks of all sizes and colors. It was that peacefully flowing sound, as much a part of Gypsy life as the road they traveled, that she had missed above all. She grasped more than ever before, that, just like water, Gypsy life must flow.

# 37
# God's Chapel

A storm was brewing. Thunder was chasing its own rumbling echo across a churning sky. Khantchi and the elders of the Kaale decided that in order not to endanger the Kaale *kumpania* in case of a raid, Dosha and the light skinned *Gadje* would proceed alone to where the speed-boat would pick them up on the beach the next morning. During the night Khantchi and the Kaale leaders would decide on the best escape route for Vasili Kutunoff: either on the same boat with Khantchi and Dosha, or by land with two Kaale *rom* and Osap. Either route would take the defecting Soviet dancer to Sweden, where he could apply for asylum. Khantchi had bargained for Osap to travel and stay with the Kaale.

At the approach of night two painted Gypsy ponies, carrying Dosha and Vasili Kutunoff, picked their way through rocks and stones as they walked through the low waters of the brook that meandered from the Gypsy encampment to a tall pine forest in the distance. The ponies' hoofs were padded with straw and bound with strips of cloth, so as not to leave any visible tracks while riding on land. Dosha rode slightly ahead, leading Vasili's pony by its rope halter. When the terrain started to slope downward, the ponies walked in and out of the shallow bed of the brook.

The air felt oppressive and charged with the looming thunder storm. From beyond the pine forest reflections of lightning flared up, then faded like the after-glow of a gigantic torch in the glowing evening sky. Swishing their tails across their short summer coats, the ponies fought off the swarms of insects that Vasili and Dosha could only swat at helplessly. Suddenly the little paint mare who was carrying Vasili flattened her ears to her skull, lowered her head and spun around. The dancer, feeling he was about to be dumped, called out "Ana!"

"Unclamp your feet," Dosha shouted, wheeling her own pony around. "Sit loose! Let go of your legs!" Instead the dancer sat even more upright and rigid, trying to control the little Gypsy mare with iron legs.

"This is not ballet," Dosha cursed through clenched teeth. "Tightening your body is telling her there's something to fear and all she can think of is escape."

"It's the lightning," Vasili protested, not liking being scolded by a girl. *Only this one looks savage,* he thought, noting the deep furrow between Dosha's dark angry eyes. She had wrapped a big, red flowered head-scarf around her hair and lower face. The fringed headscarf was tied at the back of her head, and its corners trailed like loose hair down her back. A long-sleeved, red blouse covered her upper body, falling right to her hands, but the ankle length flowery Gypsy skirt had ridden up above her knees, baring her lower legs and feet. She looked wild and untamed to him. She had turned into a stranger he did not recognize.

"Aren't they supposed to sense a storm way before we do?" the dancer persisted, but nevertheless released his legs. Instantly the horse relaxed.

"Yes, like that," she said approvingly. "You must ride with balance. It's just another kind of dance. Use your balance, " she suggested, "not your grip."

"It's not that they're afraid of the storm?" he asked again.

"Gypsy horses live out in the open. They're used to storms and lightning. The good thing about this lightning," she added, scanning the sky, "is that it will keep the helicopters at bay, don't you think?" *And hopefully,* she thought, *grounded all the way back in Porkkala.*

What worried her, and what she did not divulge to the dancer, were the soldiers with their army dogs that had taken over the compound in Porkkala. Back at the Kaale encampment she had kept hearing, the faint roaring and whirring of helicopters crisscrossing the distant sky. There had also been intermittent periods when all flying noises had ceased, and these were almost as frightening as the thrumming of the chopper blades, for she knew they could be landing in random spots to drop off soldiers with search dogs. Like most Soviet soldiers, often pulled off their mothers' apron strings and trained to kill under the banner of war, so too these dogs were chosen while they were still innocent puppies and taught to go for the kill.

Her stallion's soulful eyes rose to her mind. Where was he out

346

there on wide open waters without her? He was the one being in her past that had sensed her sadness and had comforted her, and now she felt he was calling out to her. She closed her eyes and wove a shield of protection and reassurance around her rose-gray companion, the horse many Lovara thought of as *azukeral*, a symbol of hope. She swore that once back in freedom she would never be separated from him again.

The first drops of rain fell warm and heavy and just as Dosha and Vasili stepped into the forest-line, the long-awaited rain broke forth in one heavy downpour. Safe and dry under cover of a dense fir, they turned their ponies. Together they stared at the solid sheet of rain that drew a curtain between them and the rest of the world. For the first time they were alone, free of outside interference. Something close to intimacy sprang up between them, as if they had actual knowledge of each other.

*Except,* Dosha rebelled at her own longings, *all of this is based on fantasy, on dream. It has no place in reality.* One wrong word and the illusion of a shared love would shatter like glass. Memories flickered through her mind of twelve- and thirteen-year old Gypsy brides. They fell in love with their parents' descriptions of their grooms-to-be and suddenly, after the wedding festivities were over, found themselves in a wedding tent away from the tribe, alone with a total stranger. Of course Dosha of the Khantchisti was no virgin bride. She had eloped with Jano, and then had been forced to leave behind the *rom* she had come to love.

Vasili noticed the sudden sadness soften her features. Gone was the dark angry frown, her soulful eyes fastened on the rain. *Like a child in pain,* he thought. He jumped off his pony and took her left hand in his.

"Don't worry," he whispered. "All will be fine. The worst is over. Look," he waved to the isolation around them, "we are free."

Dosha, withdrawing her hand, jumped off her pony and gathered the reins of both horses. Silently, she led them deeper into the woods. At a short distance from where they had entered the forest the brook they had been following was veering sharply to the left. Right after the bend, the brook spread out as if turning into a pond, but instead almost immediately had its waters filter and sink into marshland. At that juncture, where the water stood still and dark, yellow iris grew in clumps.

"Look," the dancer shouted, and with a backward smile started to skip across the slushy terrain toward the bright yellow flowers.

By the time she cried "no," he had already bent down and picked one, two, a tiny bunch of the bright yellow woodland iris.

"Why no?" he asked smiling, slowly walking back to her. She threw the lead ropes across the ponies' necks. "Yellow to us is the color of mourning," she whispered and looked into his bright expectant face. "You cannot possibly know, but to most people I know cut flowers are a symbol of life cut short."

"Only these," he answered, "are meant for beauty, like yours," he whispered with gleaming eyes.

*Of course,* she thought, *a Gadje like him cannot possibly understand how deeply superstitions and dark forebodings inhabit the freedom of our lives.* She bravely took the flowers from his outstretched hand, not wanting to trust those ancient beliefs, the customs she'd been taught before.

His hands clasped hers that held the flowers. "We can leave these differences behind," he said in a voice full of hope. He squeezed her fingers tight.

His face moved close to hers, their eyes lowered to each other's lips. His breath touched her, then his lips, barely, gently. For a brief moment, she relaxed, lured into his close and human warmth but she quickly withdrew, back into reality. She stepped away from him. "We must make it to the beach," she whispered with downcast eyes.

The rain was letting up. Taking the two lead ropes in one hand and leading the dancer by the other, Dosha pressed farther into the trackless forest of tall, dark pine. Rays of light filtered through gaps in the high tree crowns and fell in lacy patterns onto the forest floor. Like waves the white noise of birds and insects surged and fell. The dancer blond and highly visible in his short-sleeved white shirt, open at the neck, was busy trying to keep his face clear of insects.

"How can you find your way in this?" he asked.

How could she explain to this *Gadje,* that a Lovara can read a forest like a *Gadje* a map; forest and war was the backdrop of her childhood. Besides, this was quite obviously the path the Kaale took to the sea, there were the little *patrins* at eye-level marking the way. The ponies never shied, never yanked at the ropes: they, too, knew this way. The tribal mother of the Kaale had told Dosha that the beach they were headed for belonged to a rich *raya,* a wealthy *Gadje* whom the Kaale worked for. They painted his buildings, helped with the harvest of his fields. He made sure the land along the ocean was left untouched, like a piece of holy land.

"The place we're headed for? The tribal mother of the Kaale assured me, and they know it well, is where we can safely wait for the arrival of the speedboat to Sweden. During the night my grandfather and the Kaale will decide on the safest route for you to get out. You'll also go to Sweden. Either by boat with me, or else you will cross the border higher up North with the Kaale and their friends the Sami, the Finnish Lapps."

"They will drop me as soon as you are out of sight," Vasili's voice was somber.

"They will not," Dosha assured him once again. "These are nomadic Gypsies, poor but honorable. They have given Khantchi and me their word. They will keep their word. Only Gypsies living among *Gadje* sometimes forget about our code of honor."

The land had started to slope downward. The ponies perked up as the fragrant smell of wet pine mingled with the salty air from the sea. Suddenly and abruptly the dense forest thinned out and stopped. Below a white sandy beach stretched in a wide flat curve to their right for as far as the eye could see. To their left a row of smooth granite boulders connected the beach to a giant glistening rock that rose high and alter-like above the sea.

"The Kaale call this place Kapelli, the Chapel," Dosha turned to the dancer.

Vasili sucked in his breath. He gazed upon a seascape seemingly untouched by human hand. The rain had stopped a while back and the sky had turned a dark shade of red at the approach of midnight. The burning light ignited the beach to frenzied heights of life. Swallows were swooping out of the sky like small fighter planes diving to within inches above the water and lifting back up again like clouds of stirred up dust. Seagulls dove off the promontory and sailed out across the sea, carrying reflections of the fire light on their soaring wings.

"It's a place of magic," he breathed, turning back toward Dosha.

Dosha tethered the ponies to trees at the edge of the forest where they could graze among the undergrowth.

"At sunrise the Kaale will pick them up," she said. Sunrise was only a few hours away, but so much could happen in a few hours. "If all goes well," she added, "that's when the speed boat will pick us up, and we can truly flee."

"Come," Vasili boldly took her by one hand and pulled her

down the sandy slope onto the beach. Their feet sank deep into sand that, despite the recent rain, was still warm from that day's heat. Hand in hand they ran down to where the water was lapping the foot of the promontory. There Vasili stopped and faced her. His eyes, a deep purple in the dying light, were searching hers. He picked up her other hand and slowly buried his face in both her hands. With soft nuzzling lips and a deep intake of breath, he drew the scent and the taste of her from the palms of her hands. An intense inner flame rose from his body to his lips and to her. Her hands rose to touch his face. Her gleaming eyes followed her fingertips as they softly explored his face. She caressed his brows, his lips and cheeks. She lowered his lids across his burning, glistening eyes. Blindly he opened his lips. Closing her own eyes, she listened to his breathing grow shallow. There was no escaping the heat, melting all resistance.

"You...," She whispered, weakly pleading to escape. He trapped her sigh with his lips, their racing blood effacing all sense of self. He slid down into the sand, his hands and face along her body, before he pulled her down to lie beside him. Trembling with desire they sought out each other's eyes while awkwardly pulling off their clothes, leaving them, at last, skin to burning skin.

Edged into her memory would remain the cry of a bird piercing the orgiastic sounds of nature as he entered her. Her body dissolved around his hardness in a melting embrace, until their bodies exploded, spawning wave after wave of ecstasy, a feverish pitch, receding ever so slowly.

"This is what forever feels like," Vasili whispered, nestling his head against her breast. For a moment he listened to her still racing heart. Lifting his face to hers, their lips touched. He watched her eyes close in rapture as again and again they fused to recapture what they never wanted to lose.

Their passion subsided slowly, along with the flames in the Northern sky. They lay, intertwined like the necks of loving swans, clinging to each other's mind and body as if the moment had to last them a lifetime. With the water lapping at their feet, they silently watched the smoldering remains of the light as the sky darkened at last. The harshness of reality returned to Dosha's mind. *Once again,* she thought, *the Fates are casting the dice.*

"You know, this does not have to end," Vasili whispered, one finger tracing her lips. "You and I can have a future, together. Russian dancers are in high demand in the West."

"I know," she whispered, placing his hand back onto her

breast. Larkin had told her, long before this, that a number of Russian dancers had defected to perform in capitals in Europe and elsewhere, where many had found both fame and fortune.

"And even," Vasili whispered into her skin, "even if we take different routes of escape this morning, we can re-unite in Sweden—or Paris. Or wherever else you tell me to meet you in the West. We can make a life together," he said, "I with my dance, you with your horse."

How could she explain to him, a *Gadje*, that Gypsies are tied to a way of life. "You must know by now," she said, "that I am Lovara, a tzigani."

"To me this does not matter."

He could not know that, although a Lovara of her standing had the right of choice, choosing a *Gadje* as her *rom* meant she would be ostracized by her people; to a *romni* a punishment worse than death and in the end Gypsies always return to their own, or try to. He would not understand. In silence she clung to him, waiting for the pain brought on by sudden but vague premonitions to subside.

The day broke barely two hours later with a spreading glow. Fog came rolling in from the sea. A couple of water birds, flapping their wings, rose into the air and crossed from the grey mist of the sea into the spreading mauve light of the deserted beach. Exposed to the rebirth of the light, Dosha felt shy about their nudity. Their skin was clammy and cool to the touch. She gently disentangled herself from his sleeping embrace and rose to her feet. She picked up the clothes they had dropped nearby, and hurriedly dressed. The dancer woke and followed suit. She kept her back turned to him in the way of Lovari women with their men.

Once dressed, they linked hands and he followed her as they climbed the rock jutting above the sea. Seagulls that had covered the flat plateau in sleep, rose, flapped their wings and flew away.

"Look," the dancer pointed to a sleek boat with a spear-headed bow. The boat was painted a grayish blue. They could barely hear its motor as it slowly chugged toward them in the empty stillness of the morning. A short distance from the promontory, next to another rock jutting out of the sea, the motor stopped. An anchor caught the light as it was thrown from the cabin overboard. Water flew up like a spray of glistening crystal into the misty air. Dosha and Vasili, his arm tightly around her waist, stared into the direction of what they hoped would be their future.

A man dressed in white and wearing a white cap now lowered

a small dinghy. It was of the same deep blue that almost matched the color of the sea. The man climbed a rope ladder down into the boat. He adjusted the oars and began to row through the mist to the right of the promontory toward the rounded tip of the beach.

"That has to be the one," Dosha whispered, "He has to be the man to fetch Khantchi and us." Her eyes traced the line of his direction from the shore up the gentle incline of the dunes where she noticed a band of Gypsies. She believed there were close to a dozen of them, leading ponies out of the forest by their halters. They had fully emerged from the pine forest. Once out in the open, they jumped onto the backs of their ponies, but remained on the edge of the cliff where the land dropped off to the shore.

"We'll soon know," she whispered, "who'll go with whom." After that, everything seemed to proceed in slow motion in the mesmerizing tranquility of the breaking day. The man in the white cap was holding his dinghy by a rope. His body turned from the Kaale up on the cliff, to Dosha and Vasili standing on the rock. That's when Dosha caught the sound. It was a sound that had lurked in the back of her mind ever since she had left the military base in Porkkala—the excited yelping of dogs on a scent. She raised her head and turned fully to the sound. It was coming from the left of the rock where woods had reclaimed almost half the strip of the beach. She reached for Vasili's hand, when a single shot cracked the silence. She felt the dancer whip around as if someone had slapped him hard on his back.

"Vasili!" His eyes were filled with disbelief.

The quiet of the instant before exploded into motion. From the top and sides of the boulders birds flew up in wave after wave, their frantic fluttering and flapping whipped the air alive. More explosions followed in rapid succession, gunfire followed by what sounded like hand grenades. A single yelp, *a death yelp*, she thought. So Khantchi and the Kaale had come armed. It was the last conscious thought that crossed her mind before she flew off the promontory pulled along by Vasili's desperate hold on her hand. Air-born, unbelieving, they floated amidst the screaming flapping birds, before they hit the surface of the water with flat bodies and, still hand in hand, started a cushioned descent into darkness where conscious thought turned to confusion, a quickly fading sense of awareness as she floated in a space void of time or direction.

A quiet overtook her, smooth and gentle. Vasili's hand was gliding out of her own, like a caress in reverse, leaving her afloat

352

in a state of well being, of peace so profound, she had never known before. It was a place she did not want to leave behind.

From a far dark distance a pinpoint of light appeared. It widened, she watched it grow until it filled the dark stillness with blinding brilliance. A dark figure, like a growing shadow, stepped in front of whatever was this source of the light. Silhouetted against the brilliance, Dosha saw a mirror image of herself. The image shifted and turned until, with delayed awareness, she realized it was her grandmother Sanija who was floating in front of her. She was dressed in her long Lovari skirt, her loose hair was blowing wildly as if she were standing in a windstorm. Her face bore the fierce look of a Lovari leader on the move, her lips were moving, but the sounds were muffled and distorted by the masses of still waters, echoing—"it's a traaaap!"

The stillness within Dosha's mind turned turbulent. Anxiety flooded her. Sanija's face grew indistinct. She was moving away, her voice kept undulating through the water, "You must get up! You must find your way back to the road." *The horse!* Dosha's mind cried out. Mounting anguish forced her body upwards, her legs kicked out beneath her. Her feet felt sand. She kicked again, her face surfaced above water. Hands were pulling her back toward the rock. She started to cough up water, retching. She was pulled out, dragged further toward the beach. Each of her arms was grabbed by a man. One of them was Khantchi, the other she did not know or remember. Face down they dragged her body across the wavy sand of the beach, on and on. It seemed forever, until they pulled her up to her feet and by her hips lifted her onto a horse. It must have stood waiting right there by the shore.

"Vasili Kutunoff!" she cried. "The dancer!" She pointed to the sea.

More Kaale on their ponies came chasing down the dunes into the shallow water, among them was Osap. He alone jumped off. He flung himself into the water. Dosha tried to gather enough strength to jump off the horse to rush back. Instead she felt Khantchi jump onto the pony in back of her. "It's been decided we travel by water," he whispered in her ear. "They'll take the costal trail, and we all meet up in Sweden, if all goes well." Her last view was of Osap swimming out, as Khantchi slid his arms along her body and grabbed the reins. She flew back against his chest, as he kneed the pony and they started racing toward the dinghy still waiting in the mist.

# Epilogue

After a short fierce thunder storm the night before, the unusual heat once again gripped the southern shore of Finland. It was June 7, 1957, a Friday. Early that morning, a special train marked by a Red star on a white background, pulled out of Helsinki's Central Railway Station. Without fanfare, Nikita Sergeeivch Khrushchev, the man who had barred forever the ancient treks of Russia's last nomadic Roma, rushed home to find his own future under attack.

That same morning Khantchi, the evasive leader of thousands of targeted families of traveling Lovara, and his granddaughter Dosha, the one whom the *Gadje* knew as Ana Dalova, sat on board a sleek blue boat that was speeding through the pristine archipelago as if it were cutting glass. The old man placed his arm around the silent girl's shoulders. Her dark eyes were points of bleeding pain.

"Do you remember," he shouted above the thundering motor, "the legend of when we Roma still had wings? When those forced to live on the ground envied the Roma people their beautiful wings, with which we were able to soar high above the misery below? That was the way of our life until the day the Roma were lured out of the sky by an open courtyard glittering with gold and precious stones. From the moment they landed, blinded by greed for the glistening treasures, dark ravens robbed the Roma of their magical wings. From then on we were forced to cross the land of the *Gadje* like everyone else on the ground."

Dosha's grandfather continued talking to her in a soothing voice, as if she were a child that had been lost but found again. She relaxed and leaned against his shoulder and closed her eyes. A gentle breeze brushed her face, touching her like the tips of wispy wings.